PRAISE FOR THE LADY DARBY MYSTERIES

"For readers, like myself, who consider Kiera and Gage to be dear friends, the high stakes in this immaculately paced mystery will have them biting their nails and firmly on the edge of their seats."
—Rachel McMillan, author of *Murder in the City of Liberty*

"[A] history mystery in fine Victorian style!"
—*New York Times* bestselling author Julia Spencer-Fleming

"Riveting. . . . Huber deftly weaves together an original premise, an enigmatic heroine, and a compelling Highland setting."
—*New York Times* bestselling author Deanna Raybourn

"[A] fascinating heroine. . . . A thoroughly enjoyable read!"
—National bestselling author Victoria Thompson

"Reads like a cross between a gothic novel and a mystery with a decidedly unusual heroine."
—*Kirkus Reviews*

"Includes all the ingredients of a romantic suspense novel, starting with a proud and independent heroine. . . . Strong and lively characters as well as believable family dynamics, however, elevate this above stock genre fare."
—*Publishers Weekly*

"A clever heroine with a shocking past and a talent for detection."
—National bestselling author Carol K. Carr

"[Huber] designs her heroine as a woman who straddles the line between eighteenth-century behavior and twenty-first-century independence."
—New York Journal of Books

"A must read. . . . One of those rare books that will both shock and please readers."
—Fresh Fiction

"Fascinates with its compelling heroine who forges her own way in a society that frowns upon female independence."
—RT Book Reviews

"One of the best historical mysteries that I have read this year."
—Cozy Mystery Book Reviews

An Artless
Demise

ANNA LEE HUBER

BERKLEY PRIME CRIME
New York

BERKLEY PRIME CRIME
Published by Berkley
An imprint of Penguin Random House LLC
1745 Broadway, New York, NY 10019

Copyright © 2019 by Anna Aycock

Library of Congress Cataloging-in-Publication Data

Names: Huber, Anna Lee, author.
Title: An artless demise / Anna Lee Huber.
Description: First Edition. | New York, NY: Berkley Prime Crime, 2019.
Identifiers: LCCN 2018045169| ISBN 9780451491367 | ISBN 9780451491374
Classification: LCC PS3608.U238 A89 2019 | DDC 813/.6—dc23
LC record available at https://lccn.loc.gov/2018045169

First Edition: April 2019

Printed in the United States of America
1 3 5 7 9 10 8 6 4 2

Cover art by Larry Rostant

For my older brother, Adam.

My first and best playmate. The original big-fish tale spinner.

He taught me to field aggressively, to explode from the hip, and to never take my eyes off the ball, and it has served me well in softball and in life.

I'm so proud of him and grateful he's my big brother.

ACKNOWLEDGMENTS

This particular book has been about eight years in the making, and these are just a few of the people I wish to thank. The rest remain named in my heart.

My sincere gratitude goes to . . .

My agent, Kevan Lyon, for believing in me and Lady Darby from the start, and shepherding us through book number seven.

Michelle Vega, my editor extraordinaire, for her keen eye and boundless enthusiasm for Lady Darby. It's an absolute joy to work with her.

Jen Monroe, Tara O'Connor, Jessica Mangicaro, Larry Rostant, and the entire team of talented editors, publicists, artists, marketers, and more at Berkley. Their tireless excellence never ceases to amaze me.

My readers, as well as librarians and booksellers. Their ardor and eagerness for more Lady Darby novels feeds my own passion and makes every restless night wrangling over a story line worth it.

My friends and family. Their love and support mean the world to me.

My mother. Words will never express how grateful I am for all that she does for me and for caring for my girls while I write. She is amazing.

My daughters. Every smile, every laugh, every exuberant dance, every slobbery kiss, every silly story is a treasure to me. I love them never-endingly.

And most importantly, my husband. He is my heart and part of everything that is good and wonderful in my life. Thank you for sharing this journey with me.

CHAPTER ONE

So full of artless jealousy is guilt,
it spills itself in fearing to be spilt.

—WILLIAM SHAKESPEARE

NOVEMBER 5, 1831
LONDON, ENGLAND

I didn't know whether to laugh or feel sorry for the poor fellow. For all his tailored clothing and the jaunty angle of his hat, which refused to stay on his head properly, he was in a ragged state. A scraggly tuft of hair flopped over one eye and his arms dangled limply at his sides, hindering rather than assisting the pair of footmen who struggled between them to guide him into his place.

With one last grunt of effort from the servants, he was hoisted into position to stare down at us with unseeing eyes. A crooked grin stretched across his face. I wasn't sure I wouldn't rather his expression have been more fierce. Gnashing teeth or a disapproving scowl would surely be more appropriate.

"I say, now, he looks *much* too jolly to torch," my brother Trevor remarked beside me, echoing my sentiments.

One of the footmen ascended a small stepladder before being

handed a bottle of brandy from the butler. He reached up over the lip of the raised serving bowl to douse the enormous oval of dried plum pudding at its center and then proceeded to pour a liberal amount of the liquor down the wooden stake stabbed into the dessert's middle, on which the smiling effigy had been mounted. The caramel liquid trickled down over the entire concoction to form a lake in the bottom of the crystal dish, perfuming the dining room with its pungent aroma.

"Ten quid it sets the flowers on fire," Alfred, the newly minted Lord Tavistock, muttered under his breath just beyond my shoulder.

The lush floral arrangements on either side of the display did appear a trifle too close for comfort. As was the greenery draped from the glittering chandelier overhead. The Guy was not so tall as to become tangled in them, but considering the copious amount of brandy the footman had used to drench the pudding, who knew how high the flames would leap.

Trevor scoffed. "Twenty, it sets the entire table alight."

At this dire prediction about the demise of the Countess of Redditch's lavish spread of food, my stomach rumbled, as it did so often of late.

My husband's gaze dropped to mine from where he stood at my other side, his lips quirking in amusement.

I lifted a hand to my abdomen self-consciously. "I can't help it," I whispered. "Not when there are tartlets being dangled before my eyes."

"Well, you are eating for two."

"True."

"I just wish they would get on with it," Lorna, Lady Tavistock, huffed.

I glanced over my shoulder at her heavily lashed green eyes.

Her pretty pink mouth twisted into a moue of displeasure. "This is torturous for a woman in my state."

I couldn't withhold a laugh.

"What?" Her lips creased into a coy smile. "I'm sure you know what I mean, Kiera, being in the same predicament."

Before I could reply, a murmur of excitement swept through the room. I turned back to see that the Earl of Redditch had stepped forward, brandishing a long spill of wood. He lit the tip in one of the candles positioned down the center of the large table and then paused for dramatic effect, grinning at the assembly before him, much like the effigy looming over his silver head.

"What say you? Shall I burn the Guy?"

Several of the men replied with hearty approval, while others began to clap. We soon all joined in, applauding as he lowered the spill toward the pool of brandy at the base of the pudding. Many of us gasped as a burst of flame flared upward, igniting the dessert and the base of the effigy's clothing. I pressed a hand to my chest, giggling at my reaction as the fire settled into a steadier blaze. Albeit, one more intense than would be to my liking were the spectacle taking place in *my* dining room.

I was not unfamiliar with the traditions of Guy Fawkes Night celebrations, which commemorated the foiled Gun Powder Plot of 1605, when Guy Fawkes and his collaborators schemed to blow up the Houses of Parliament. But my past experiences had been limited to the country. There we attended a church service in the morning for the reading of the Observance Act and then gathered with a small party of local nobility and gentry, sometimes walking out to see the bonfires lit in the nearest village after nightfall. These bonfires inevitably featured their own effigy of Guy, but this was the first time I'd seen one burned inside someone's home, and an earl's palatial residence, at that.

The celebrations among the nobility in London were generally quite tame. However, due to the King's coronation in September, a larger number than usual of the aristocracy had remained in town for autumn and all the fetes following the royal event. So the Countess of Redditch had decided to host a Bonfire Night Ball, complete with a makeshift bonfire on her dining room table.

"I do hope they anchored that effigy in more than that mound of pudding." Gage's brow furrowed as he studied the burning spectacle.

"Well, let's not stand around waiting to see. You and Tavistock fetch us some food before the whole thing goes up in flames," I declared as I swiveled to thread my arm through Lorna's.

"Yes, do," she enthused.

Gage's face split into a grin, but it was his cousin, Alfred, who prodded him forward.

"Far be it for me to disobey such an order. If I've learned anything in the last three months, it's never to stand between a woman who is increasing and her food." His eyes twinkled at us devilishly as he danced out of the way, narrowly missing his wife's playful swat with her fan.

Trevor escorted us, as well as his own dinner companion, Miss Ellen Newbury, through a maze of puffed sleeves, some so voluminous as to double the width of the wearer's shoulders. I wasn't sure I would ever reconcile myself to this ridiculous style, much preferring the narrower shoulders of my parma violet gown with à la Reine sleeves of blond net. Then again, I had never cared much for what was fashionable. Only recently had I made an effort, so as not to embarrass my new husband.

Sebastian Gage was one of the most dashing and attractive gentlemen in all of Britain. That he had wed me, a scandalous outcast, had shocked more than a few members of the ton, and infuriated the mothers of debutantes who each thought their own daughter would be a better match.

After settling us at a table, Trevor went off to do his duty filling Miss Newbury's plate. Unfortunately, I realized too late that we were situated much too close to where Lady Felicity Spencer held sway. Our gazes locked for a moment across the short distance before I looked away, not wishing to incite her antagonism. Though she had in no way confronted me directly—in fact, I believed I'd only exchanged greetings with her twice—I was well aware of her scorn and not-so-silent ridicule. No, a woman like Lady Felicity would never be so overt with her contempt. Instead, she let her veiled comments to others and reminders about my past do the trick.

As such, I had navigated the past ten weeks since our arrival in London by avoiding her and her like. I'd discovered that not all members of society held me in disdain, and so I gravitated toward those who were more welcoming. Lorna herself was somewhat of a persona non grata, being the illegitimate daughter of a nobleman, though in time her status as Viscountess Tavistock would render that fact obsolete. However, the Newburys were among those of sterling reputation who viewed me with kindness, and so I found I could converse easily with Miss Newbury.

The sweet-natured girl had just finished describing to me the bonnet she had purchased earlier that day when my friend, the Dowager Lady Stratford, appeared at my elbow.

"Are these seats claimed?" She dimpled at me, her cheeks flushed with happiness. The proscribed mourning period for her rotten blackguard of a husband had only recently ended, and I was pleased to see her attired in a stunning azure evening gown which highlighted her golden beauty.

"By you, of course," I replied, pleased to see my cousin Rye was once again her dinner companion. I strongly suspected he had something to do with my friend's radiance of late.

"In all the excitement over the effigy, I suspect you missed it," Charlotte exclaimed in a hushed voice as Rye moved off to fill her plate with choice tidbits. "But several of the gentlemen nearly came to blows in the front hall."

"You're jesting," Lorna gasped.

She shook her head, her eyes wide. "For a moment, I thought

Rye was going to have to step in to stop them." She leaned closer. "And one of them was Lord Melbourne."

"The home secretary?" I glanced over my shoulder toward the doors, though my view was blocked by those milling about the room.

"Fortunately, cooler heads prevailed. And Lord Gage was able to help resolve the situation."

This did not surprise me. Gage's father was a gentleman inquiry agent of some renown, with a number of highly placed friends, including the former prime minister and war hero—the Duke of Wellington—and even King William himself. That he might also number Lord Melbourne among his associates was more than probable, despite Melbourne being a Whig when many of Lord Gage's other allies were Tories. I'd long realized Lord Gage did not ascribe to one political position but adapted his words and views to move among them all.

"What were they fighting about?" I asked.

Charlotte grimaced. "What else? The Reform Bill."

Much of London continued to be unsettled by the agitation caused by the House of Lords' latest rejection of a second attempt at passing a Reform Bill some weeks earlier. The proposed law would have redistributed representation in the House of Commons, doing away with the so-called rotten boroughs—which consisted of a very small number of constituents controlled by a wealthy patron from the House of Lords—and increased the franchise to give the vote to more male citizens. It was popular among the middle and lower classes, a number of whom had reacted angrily at the upper class's refusal to grant them this concession. Several small altercations had occurred in London, while other cities, such as Bristol, had seen widespread rioting. The populace was seething with resentment, and the aristocracy could no longer continue to ignore it. Not with memories of the French Revolution, and the way their peasantry had overthrown the government and guillotined countless numbers of the royalty and nobility, still fresh in many minds.

I sighed. "In truth, I've been braced for news of violence. In many ways, Guy Fawkes Night seems tailor-made for such displays of public defiance, even if we *are* celebrating the *foiling* of a past plot of rebellion. But I never expected it to erupt between two gentlemen."

"Hadn't expected what to erupt?" Gage asked as he set a glass of claret and a plate laden with food in front of me.

"Apparently Melbourne almost came to blows with some chap in the entry hall over the Reform Bill," I explained briefly. "But your father is managing the situation."

A pucker formed between his eyes as he turned to gaze out over the assembled guests. "All the same, I suppose I should speak with him to be sure my assistance isn't needed."

"After you eat." I pressed a hand to his arm. "The matter is resolved for the moment, so there's no sense in hurrying off. Besides, you were correct. That effigy looks in danger of tumbling over into the food at any moment." The Guy slumped to the side, consumed by flame, and a hazard to any who dared pass around that side of the table.

"They're removing him," he replied. "Just as soon as the footmen return with a large tub of water to dunk him in."

"Thank heavens."

"Yes." His lips were tight with disapproval. "I gather our host did not think the matter through."

"I imagine not." I watched as a piece of smoldering cloth dropped into the serving bowl. "I doubt anyone will be enjoying that plum pudding."

Alfred snorted. "Not unless they're partial to burned yarn and wool."

The men went to fill their own plates with the splendid fare before returning to join us in our enjoyment of the feast. The earl and countess had spared no expense for the evening. Roast fowls and lamb, ragout of veal, lobster, galantine, and for dessert sweet custards, meringues, and even luscious *gâteau mille-feuile*. I ate my fill and lingered over another glass of claret, enjoying a pleasant hour of conversation. Not even the sharp glint I spied in Lady Felicity's eye when I happened to catch a glimpse of her could sour my delight.

Gage and I followed the others back toward the ballroom, where the notes of a waltz could already be heard spilling forth. Ladies in opulent gowns twirled in the arms of the men in their dark evening attire beneath the glittering chandeliers. The spectacular plasterwork ceiling and white paneled walls were gilded with rococo flourishes, and the floor gleamed to a high polish. Clusters of amaryllis and hyacinths were hung between each set of wall sconces, adding a welcome dash of color, as well as their pleasant scents, to the miasma of perfumes and body odor.

This was definitely an improvement over the stench of charred ash and fabric dueling with the aromas of food and spirits in the dining room, but only just. I'd discovered being with child made my already strong sense of smell even more acute, so we lingered for a moment at the edge of the ballroom, where fresh air swept up the stairs from the entry hall below.

"Lady Darby!"

I swiveled to see our hostess, the Countess of Redditch, bustling toward me.

"My dearest lady," she exclaimed gaily. "I was hoping to have a word with you."

"But, of course," I replied with a smile.

Some weeks after my return to London, I'd realized there was little point in continuing to ask those who were not close acquaintances to address me as Mrs. Gage rather than by the title accorded to me from my first marriage. For one, it was tedious, especially when the request was all but ignored. So amid society, I remained Lady Darby by courtesy, though not by right, since my late husband, Sir Anthony, outranked my second.

Judging from the bright sheen of Lady Redditch's eyes, I suspected she'd already drunk more than a few glasses of the madeira that scented her breath, but her carriage remained erect, her speech clear. Her soft brown hair, liberally threaded with gray, had been swept up onto her head in one of the most current styles and accented with ostrich feathers.

"I must compliment you on a lovely soiree," I told her. "It's an absolute crush."

"Thank you, my dear. What with recent events, it seemed we could all do with a bit of amusement."

What exactly she was referring to, I wasn't certain. But given the fact her husband was an outspoken opponent of the Reform Bill, I could only speculate it had something to do with the attacks that had been made on some of the members of the aristocracy, both in the press and via shouts and recriminations—and sometimes produce—hurled at their passing carriages. The warmth of my smile slipped a notch.

Positioned as we were before the doorway, we had a clear view out into the hall. So when a young man hurried up to where Lord Melbourne stood conferring with a handful of men, including Lord Gage and my brother-in-law, Philip, the Earl of Cromarty, I couldn't help but notice. Particularly when the messenger seemed anxious as he passed the home secretary a message. The letter must convey something of urgency if it was being delivered to Melbourne during the middle of the countess's ball.

"The Guy was certainly a festive touch," Gage told our hostess with every sign of having enjoyed it, even though I knew he had disapproved.

She laughed. "Yes, that was Lord Redditch's idea. And I thought it would be quite a treat."

Whatever the missive Melbourne had been handed contained, it must be concerning, for his brow was etched with deep furrows. He passed the letter to Lord Gage at his side, who read the note swiftly, before flicking a troubled glance toward where we stood.

Gage removed his arm from where it was laced with mine, squeezing my elbow as he withdrew. "If you'll excuse me. I believe my father wishes a word with me."

Lady Redditch waved him away with a flick of her wrist. "Lady Darby, am I correct? Are you still painting portraits? I believe Lady Morley informed me you had accepted a commission to paint her."

I was surprised by the eagerness of her words, but I recovered quickly. "Why, yes. I'm composing Lady Morley's portrait now actually."

"Excellent! We would be so honored if you would consider painting our son George's portrait. He recently reached his majority, you know, and I do find that is an excellent time to capture their likeness. Before the depravities of age can befall them," she jested with a trill of laughter.

Distracted as I was by the conference happening between Gage and his father in the hall, I could still sense the anxiety which belied her lighthearted tone. There was something she wasn't saying, something which distressed her.

"I would be honored," I replied, puzzled by her uneasiness. "Though I believe I've yet to make Mr. Penrose's acquaintance. He is your second-born, is he not?"

"I shall introduce you," she declared. "He's likely doing his duty, dancing with all the pretty girls in attendance." She turned to tap her eldest son, who had suddenly materialized at her side, on the shoulder with her fan. "As you should be."

Lord Feckenham smirked. "Yes, I'm certain he's putting on a good show. But I've no need to."

Lady Redditch frowned. "Have you been introduced to my eldest son?"

"Yes, I've had that pleasure," I answered, though I felt any-

thing but. From the spark of derisive amusement in Lord Feckenham's dark eyes, it was evident he realized what I truly thought
about him. He was a crude boar with ramshackle manners who
delighted in making others uncomfortable, including young
debutantes. Humble in appearance and address, as far as I could
tell the only thing to recommend him was his status as the heir
to an old and venerable earldom, and that consideration didn't
rank high in my book.

Out of the corner of my eye, I caught the worried look Gage
cast my way as he pulled Philip aside. Curious why the matter
would cause him concern for me, I opened my mouth to make
my excuses so that I might join them when Lord Feckenham
spoke.

"I've no desire to take a skittish innocent for a spin about the
floor, but I should be delighted to dance with you, my lady." His
eyebrows arched, daring me to accept as he held out his hand.

He had mistaken me if he thought I would be goaded into
such an undertaking by his challenge. Especially when I suspected he'd intended to insult me. The countess appeared to
think so, for her mouth had pinched into a tight moue.

"How kind," I replied in as bland a tone as I could manage.
"But my slippers are pinching my toes, and I must slip away to see
if the problem can be remedied. I'm sure her ladyship understands,"
I added, applying to her.

Being the mother of four children, her eyes lit with comprehension. "Oh, yes. Yes, my dear." At least, in this delicate rebuttal
I had not offended her. "Up the stairs and to the left."

"Thank you," I replied, gliding away as if to escape to the
lady's retiring room. I felt Lord Feckenham's narrowed gaze following me but paid it little heed. Let him wonder for a time if
he'd been the one slighted.

Once outside the ballroom, I glanced about me, trying to
discover where Gage and Philip had gone. They were no longer
in the hall or on the stairs, and I was fairly certain they hadn't

slipped past me. I turned to find my father-in-law's disapproving stare directed my way. Though it was not as hostile as in the past—since he wanted to at least appear amicable to his son's choice in his bride, even though he'd attempted to thwart us before our vows were spoken—I could sense the renewed animosity simmering beneath his hooded gaze.

I had hoped we'd moved beyond this, if not into friendliness—which I doubted we should ever feel—then at least into mutual regard. But something had happened in the space of the past few minutes to change that, and I suspected it was that letter.

As if to confirm this, Lord Melbourne's eyes lifted to meet mine. At first he didn't react as he continued to speak to the man at his elbow, but then something occurred to him that made his eyes crease at the corners. My chest constricted with uncertainty. What had that missive said to make them react this way?

I considered approaching Lord Gage to find out where his son had gone but then decided against it. Much as it pinched to realize, I knew my father-in-law was capable of great cruelty, and if he should snub me that would mean dire things for Gage's reputation, not just my own.

So instead I climbed the grand marble staircase toward the lady's retiring room, hoping to intercept someone who could tell me where I might find my husband. Rounding the corner, I nearly collided with my brother-in-law, Philip. His hands reached out to steady me.

"Kiera! Just who I was looking for," he gasped in relief.

Seeing the concern in his soft brown eyes, I pressed a hand to his upper arm. "What is it? I saw you and Gage conferring . . ."

Before I could say anything more, he cut me off—an action completely unlike him. "It's Alana. She's suddenly feeling quite ill."

I stiffened, alarm for my older sister sweeping through me. "Where is she?"

"Gage is with her. I'm having the carriage brought around."

His gaze flickered for a moment. "I wonder if you might be willing to accompany her home." He must have sensed my hesitation, for he rushed on to say, "I would attend to her myself, but regrettably there's a matter of business I must see to first."

I stared up into his strained visage. Calm, steady Philip was not acting like his usual self, and I could tell why. He was lying. The question was, why?

Undoubtedly, he and Gage—for I didn't for one moment believe my husband didn't have a hand in this—were trying to remove me from the ball without creating a scene. I felt my hackles begin to rise at this bit of high-handedness. Evidently, they were worried I would argue, which indeed, I wanted to do. Then Philip's gaze transformed to one of gentle pleading, and I realized he genuinely was concerned. But not for Alana, for *me*.

A trickle of unease ran down my spine. Given some of the events in my scandalous past, troubling scenarios began to form in my mind, but I shook them aside. "Of course. Take me to her."

The expression on Gage's face when we appeared in the entry hall, while restrained, did nothing to reassure me. I could read all too well the apprehension crinkling the fine lines at the corners of his eyes.

It was just as well that Alana had supposedly come down with some sort of complaint, for she could not hide her distress either as she reached out to clasp my hands. I gathered her close, falling in with their ruse, and allowed Gage to settle my furlined mantle around my shoulders. I pretended not to notice when he and Philip were also handed their hats and greatcoats.

However, once we were ensconced in the Cromarty carriage, hot bricks placed at our feet and blankets draped over our laps, and the door was shut behind us, I could no longer remain silent.

"You are doing it much too brown," I proclaimed, crossing my arms over my chest. "Alana is not ill." I glared at Philip and then Gage. "And you gentlemen obviously didn't have business to attend to. So why did you hurry me out of there?"

CHAPTER TWO

"And do not for a moment think to fob me off," I told the men as they shared a look of misgiving. "I saw the way Lord Gage and Lord Melbourne looked at me. What has happened?"

Gage hesitated a moment longer and then reached over to take my hand. "The New Police have arrested a group of bodysnatchers on suspicion of murder."

I blinked, the horrifying implications already trickling through me.

"They stand accused of burking the victim," he finished, making the matter plain.

Just three years earlier, the country had been shocked by the discovery that Burke and Hare, two morbidly enterprising men in Edinburgh, had smothered people from the streets near Grassmarket in order to turn a profit by selling their bodies to the local anatomy schools. They had killed sixteen people before being caught. Since then, murders of the same type had been called "burkings," after the man who had hanged for the crime when his partner turned King's evidence against him.

Panic had swept through the country when Burke and Hare's murderous activities were uncovered. The populace feared that other such criminals were at work—killing those who were least likely to be missed, and earning a few quid from the sale of their bodies. An act which, in time, would destroy the evidence of their foul deed.

And now the country's fears appeared justified, as another group of men stood accused of the same crime. This time in London.

A chill gripped me.

"They're certain?" I couldn't help but ask.

Not that certainty mattered in a case like this. When news of the arrests spread, the suspicions would largely be taken as fact.

Gage's grip on my hand tightened. "They'll be examining the corpse tomorrow. But . . . it seems fairly damning."

I closed my eyes, resting my head back against the squabs. The others did not speak as I struggled with this revelation. Shame flooded me, bitter and astringent.

"And so it begins again," I murmured. "The old accusations. The frightened glances and furious snubs." I gritted my teeth against a surge of anger. "Will the past never leave me be?"

"Perhaps it will not be so bad as that," Alana protested faintly. "Perhaps no one will remember."

I opened my eyes to glare at her. "They never forgot."

When my father had arranged my marriage to my first husband, the great anatomist Sir Anthony Darby, the man had not revealed the reason for his interest in me. Only when it was too late did I discover he had wed me for my artistic abilities, forcing me to sketch the dissections he conducted in his private medical theater for a comprehensive anatomical textbook he was writing.

Being a pompous and closefisted individual, he'd had no wish to share the glory or profit with another man. I'd suffered three years of his bullying and mistreatment, compelled to assist him.

Sir Anthony being my husband, I had no choice but to obey him. To speak out against his cruel conduct would have done me no good. No court would have taken my part over his, and the resulting scandal would have only infuriated him so intensely as to make my life an even greater misery. So I had endured as best I could until the day he died of an apoplexy.

I thought then that the nightmare would be over. And it would have been, had it not been for Sir Anthony's odious friend, Dr. Mayer, a man after my late husband's own ilk. Mayer had been bequeathed the completed portions of Sir Anthony's anatomical manuscript and tasked with finishing it so that it could be published. However, Mayer had recognized at once that the sketches contained within were far too skilled to have been completed by Sir Anthony himself, who was an infamously poor artist. It had not taken any great leap of logic to realize I had served as my husband's illustrator, and Mayer wasted no time in threatening me and then accusing me of desecrating a corpse and unnatural tendencies before the Bow Street Magistrates. Mayer had also been certain to mention Sir Anthony's presumed involvement with the resurrectionists in order to procure bodies for his dissections, slyly implying I had also done business with them.

The tumult and scandal that erupted after the reading of these charges had played into the fears of a public still reeling from the Burke and Hare trial, and I had been vilified and massacred in the press. I had been labeled the Butcher's Wife, the Sawbone's Siren, and accused of unspeakable acts. Fortunately, Trevor and Philip—whose status as an earl had lent his word considerable weight—had convinced the magistrates to dismiss the charges. But the damage was done.

As for the aristocracy, the discovery that a gentlewoman had assisted in a human dissection, in any capacity, was too shocking to be borne. I had been ostracized and shunned, relegated to the annals of lurid tales no one was to speak of, but everyone shared in aghast whispers.

That is until I had assisted Sebastian Gage in solving one terrible murder, and then another. Though shocking in its own right, my turn as an inquiry agent had begun to restore my reputation. As had my astonishing marriage to my investigative partner, whose taste was known to be unimpeachable. When one of our most recent inquiries had been undertaken as a favor to the Duke of Wellington, my return to favor among society was all but assured.

Until now.

I wanted to rail at the injustice, the unfairness, but I'd learned long ago how useless that was. Among society, it was not so much the truth of the matter, but the appearance of it. And my participation in Sir Anthony's dissections and everything they involved, forced though it might have been, would always be a black mark against me.

"Thank you for whisking me away to tell me," I said, grateful for their discretion. Had word of the bodysnatchers' arrest spread through the ball, it could have led to a shocking scene. One I might not have been prepared for. I searched their faces. In addition to my brother, they were the people I most loved in the world. "What is to be done now? Should . . . should I go into hiding?"

I had hesitated to ask it, my entire being rebelling against the notion of suffering such an ignominious fate yet again. I had run away two and a half years earlier when the scandal over my involvement with Sir Anthony's work had first broke, too beaten and scared to fight. But I was stronger now, more resilient than I'd ever been. And I was no coward.

Nevertheless, I had more people to think of than just myself. My family had all been hurt by my earlier disgrace, though I knew none of them blamed me for it. Or at least, most of them.

I couldn't speak for all my aunts, uncles, and cousins on my father's side of the family. But that was not of the moment.

"I think that's the worst thing you could do," Gage replied.

Philip nodded in agreement. "It would only make you look guilty, like you have some reason to feel ashamed. Which you do not," he added sternly.

I warmed at his show of support. As my brother-in-law, he had every right to resent the discredit I'd brought to his wife's family, and to him by association, but he had never made me feel less than a cherished sister.

"We shall not pay the least bit of attention to what any of society's vicious gossips might say," Alana declared, having always been my staunchest defender. Her eyes narrowed to slits. "Including Lady Felicity Spencer."

Gage stiffened.

She shook her finger at me. "Don't think I haven't noticed she's been stirring up all sorts of trouble behind your back. I've seen the daggers she sends your way, veiled though they may be by those coquettish glances of hers. She can't abide to see you looking radiant and happy." She arched her chin proudly. "Your expectant state becomes you. Especially now that you're beginning to show a bit of welcome rounding to your figure. And that's a relief, for we all know it never suited me so well."

Given the fact that her last two confinements had been difficult and the deliveries fraught with danger, none of us would refute that statement.

Her gaze slid toward where Gage sat with a furrowed brow. "There's no use in expecting you to have realized what your father's chosen paragon has been doing. Gentlemen never notice such things."

I was torn between astonishment and amusement at this declaration. I should have known better than to think Alana wasn't aware of all of Lord Gage's machinations, try as I had to keep them from her.

"Be stouthearted, Kiera, and let's wait and see how matters unfold," Philip counseled. "Perhaps the newspapers will not make much of these burkers."

All of our expressions, including Philip's, showed none of us had much hope of that.

"Do you have any social engagements planned for tomorrow?" he asked.

"Morning service," Gage replied, as it would be a Sunday. "But nothing further." He glanced at me in question. "And nothing Monday either, I believe."

"Nothing but my portrait session with Lady Morley that morning."

Philip nodded. "Then let us see what the next few days bring."

I suspected I already knew, but I bowed to his wisdom. After all, there was no use borrowing trouble when it might not occur.

But when Gage joined me in our bedchamber a short time later, he found my spirits already sunken low. Though unfashionable among the wealthy, we had followed the happy example of Alana and Philip's marriage and shared a single bedroom since the day we wed. Pale blue and soft gray diamond printed wallpaper covered the walls, a pleasing background to the lovely satinwood Sheraton furniture and damask drapes. I sat propped against the pillows on our bed, glaring at the cornflower blue counterpane while I rubbed a hand absently over the gentle swell of my abdomen. My expectant condition had only just begun to show.

A fact Lord Gage had not failed to allude to a week before. Given the fact I'd allowed him to believe I was already heavy with his son's child when we wed in April, I'd been expecting just such a terse comment. Since he'd been the one to assume such an uncomplimentary thing about my character, and I'd merely been using his prejudice to my husband's advantage, I felt not one iota of guilt at misleading him. Even if my cheeks *had* burned at his obliquely referring to it.

Regardless, I probably should have withheld my flippant response. The consequence being, I had already rekindled his rancor toward me. And now he had this new sin to lay at my door.

I sighed. As if he needed another excuse to object to his son's choice in a bride.

"Is the baby well?"

I shrugged. "I suppose. I can't feel her, or him, yet."

When Gage didn't respond, I looked up to see worry etching his brow.

"There's no cause for concern," I assured him. "I'm healthy, and Alana tells me it will be a few weeks longer before I feel the wee one move."

He nodded, wearing the expression all men, particularly those inexperienced with fatherhood, seemed to exhibit when confronted with the mysteries of gestation.

I smiled and held out my hand to beckon him closer.

He rounded the bed to sit beside me. "Is that a new wrapper? And nightdress?" he added, allowing his eyes to trail over the lace-trimmed neckline revealed beneath my indigo dressing gown. "It's quite fetching."

I brushed my hand over the silken fabric. "Yes, well, I decided it was time to purchase some new nightclothes." My lips quirked. "Before I outgrow the others."

Gage's pale blue eyes glowed with gentle humor. "Now that doesn't truly bother you, does it?"

"No," I admitted. "Though I daresay it will feel strange. Alana always looked dashed uncomfortable when she was increasing." I tilted my head in thought. "Granted, that might have been more the fault of her continual queasiness. Thank heavens I haven't been plagued with that."

"Well, all in all, I must say I heartily agree with your sister."

I glanced up as his fingers touched my face.

"Being with child does become you."

I flushed under his regard, pleased by his words. But I couldn't stop a pang of my ever-present anxiety from fluttering in the pit of my stomach. I supposed all new mothers must have doubts, but I had been wrestling with mine perhaps more than others.

I feared what sort of mother I would make—dashing off to murderous inquiries, becoming absorbed in my artwork to the exclusion of all else, often struggling in social situations with things that seemed so natural to others. I hardly seemed the ideal candidate for such a role, and I wondered how I would manage it all. We would undoubtedly hire a nanny to help with the day-to-day matters, but I would be the child's mother. What if I wasn't a very good one?

And now, as if I hadn't enough misgivings, there was a new potential threat to my reputation.

Missing nothing, Gage's gaze softened with sympathy. "You're thinking of those arrested resurrectionists."

"How can I not? I hate that I've embroiled my family, and you . . ." I pressed a hand to the merlot red fabric of his dressing gown where it draped over his chest ". . . in this mess yet again."

He clasped my fingers, holding my hand over his heart. "First of all, there is no mess. Not yet. Remember, you promised not to put the cart before the horse. And second, we are all well aware that any unsavory remembrances of the scandal that might be dredged through the gossip mill again are not your fault. You haven't embroiled us in anything."

Much as I appreciated his fervent effort to reassure me, his arguments were refutable. Perhaps no imbroglio had yet erupted, but we had been forced to contemplate it. And as much as he might deny my fault in any of it, the fact that I was linked to it, and that *they* were linked to me, entangled them in my trouble.

But I let the matter pass, offering him a tight smile. "What are the facts of the matter? Do you know?"

He hesitated to speak, though I could tell he knew something.

"Is it distasteful?" I guessed.

"No. But . . ." He raked a hand back through his golden hair as he heaved a sigh. "I was about to say the investigation doesn't concern us. But I suppose it does." One corner of his lip curled upward in chagrin.

He leaned his head back against the headboard, frowning at the bed curtain. "From what I could glean from my father, the men arrested were attempting to sell the body at King's College when either the dissecting-room porter or the demonstrator . . ." He looked to me in question.

"A demonstrator is a lecturer for the anatomy school, and he, well, demonstrates for the students." I didn't think I needed to be any more specific than that. "He would be a junior colleague to the professor of anatomy at the head of the school."

"Well, one of them recognized that the body appeared suspiciously fresh, and the other concurred. So they contrived to keep the resurrectionists waiting for payment while they sent for the police, who took them and the body into custody."

I tapped my lip. "That would be the Covent Garden branch, wouldn't it?"

He nodded. "I've dealt with the branch's superintendent a few times since the Metro Police were formed, and before when he was but a parish constable, and I have to say while he's capable enough in his own way, I have serious doubts about his competency in matters of murder. Especially one as thorny as this may prove to be." He stretched his long legs out toward the end of the bed, crossing one over the other. "But then again, any intensive investigating that needs to be done will likely be undertaken by the Bow Street Runners."

I couldn't tell by his tone of voice whether he held much faith in their abilities either.

The Metropolitan Police Act had passed Parliament and taken effect only two years prior. Spearheaded by Sir Robert Peel, it had formed a single unified police force for London. Before that, the city had been patrolled by a higgledy-piggledy mixture of parish constables, day and night patrols, horse patrols, the river police, the Bow Street Runners, and the elderly and much-mocked watchmen called Charleys. A new manner of policing the capital had been needed, despite popular opposition to placing the central British government in control instead of the individual parishes. Many Londoners were hostile to what they claimed to be state surveillance.

As such, a bargain had been struck, excluding The City—the "square mile" administrative enclave at the center, which comprised the Bank of England, St. Paul's Cathedral, Fleet Street, and the Barbican—from the Metropolitan Police Act. This created another kind of confusion, as criminals would dash back and forth across the City border to escape apprehension. Or, if the rumors were true, were driven across at the instigation of City aldermen for the New Police to contend with.

However, the New Police were not meant to be an investigative force. Their task was to prevent crime from happening. Any mysteries were still to be solved by the Bow Street Runners, a small plainclothes force which had been at work in London for more than eighty years. This was not an ideal arrangement, for while the Runners received a retaining fee, they relied on the rewards earned for solving crimes to net most of their income. This had led to some notable cases of corruption and cooperation with the very criminals they were supposed to be apprehending.

The entire system—the New Police, the City constables, and the Bow Street Runners—relied heavily on informants, some of whom were paid before testifying, while others were compensated after for a successful prosecution. Analysis and detection had little to do with it. So it was no wonder that the upper class chose to hire gentlemen inquiry agents, like Gage and his father, to solve any crimes perpetrated in their homes or upon their person, rather than call the police or Runners.

I sank deeper into the bed, resting my head on his shoulder. "Do you think they'll ask your father to assist?" Such a crime seemed far outside of Lord Gage's normal purview of stolen gems and blackmail. Gage was usually tasked with the more unsavory cases of misconduct, though even those didn't often involve the murder of a member of the lower classes.

He draped his arm around me. "It depends. It was natural that Melbourne should have been informed of the matter so urgently by the commissioners. He is home secretary, after all, and the New Police falls under his aegis." He shook his head. "But he's not like his predecessor. He has no great interest in the lower classes or criminality. Under normal circumstances, he would monitor the matter from a distance, if at all."

His chest rose and fell on a deep breath. "But given the general unrest over the House of Lords throwing out that second attempt at a Reform Bill, and the troubling similarity of this crime to those committed by Burke and Hare, Melbourne would be a fool not to recognize how critical the matter is. And though I've often found him to be apathetic and indecisive, he is not a fool." His voice was grim. "The city is sitting on a potential powder keg."

"I hope that wasn't meant to be an abominable pun given tonight's history," I remarked, lifting my head to gaze at him in chiding.

It took a moment for him to make the connection, and when he did, his face lit with humor. "Guy Fawkes? No. But I suppose I have gunpowder, plot, and treason on the brain." His eyes searched my face. "Speaking of which, has Lady Felicity truly been giving you trouble?"

I gave a shout of laughter. "How on earth does that relate to gunpowder, plot, and treason?"

Gage's eyes danced with mischief. "If you'd seen the way she plots her way through an evening at Almack's, you wouldn't wonder."

I collapsed back against my pillow, shaking with mirth.

He rolled over to smile down at me, pleased to have caused me such amusement. "In all seriousness, she is the most calculating female I've known. And that's saying something," he muttered drolly. "So when your sister says she's slyly stirring up gossip about you, I believe her." He scowled. "I'm only angry I didn't notice it myself."

I pressed a hand to his jaw, the evening's growth of his facial hair rasping against my fingertips. "Darling, she's been very careful. As you said, she's sly. If she's too overt, then she risks being seen as envious and bitter, and disproving the 'official' story that *she* rejected *you*, not the other way around." I brushed my thumb over his bottom lip. "Besides, what could you have done? Confronting her would only compound the problem. As would speaking to her father." I shrugged a single shoulder. "Best to ignore it, to ignore her."

"Yes, you're probably right." His brow furrowed. "But I still wish I hadn't been such a dolt. I could have at least been more attentive to you."

I arched a single eyebrow. "If you'd been any more attentive, I would have locked you in a closet for a few hours so I could escape it."

His gaze softened, just as I'd intended. "Smothering you, am I?"

"No. But you've been quite solicitous." I glanced down at his mouth as I pressed my thumb against his bottom lip again. "Although, I could use some of your thorough attention now."

His eyes darkened. "Could you?"

"Mmm."

"Thorough, you say?"

"Yes."

A wicked smile crooked his lips as he inched closer. "Exhaustive?"

My breathing hitched. "But, of course."

"Well, I certainly wouldn't wish to disappoint," he murmured before his lips captured mine.

And he most certainly didn't.

CHAPTER THREE

Gray clouds had plagued London for almost a week, so the following morning when we emerged from the South Audley Street Chapel to find the sun shining, I elected to put the light to good use. After our wedding, Gage had sent our ever-efficient butler, Jeffers, ahead of us to London and ordered him to oversee the conversion of the small conservatory at the back of his Chapel Street townhouse into an art studio. So that when we arrived in the city in late August following our honeymoon—and the numerous delays imposed upon us by a pair of inquiries we had felt compelled to undertake—he could surprise me with the result.

I was thrilled with it. Not only did the conservatory's three glass walls and ceiling provide ample natural light, but it also faced the sunny south. Plus, the townhouse's deep garden, and those of our neighbors—a rare thing in fashionable Mayfair—meant there were no obstructions to that light. It was also sheltered from the wind, making it possible for me to paint in just a long-sleeved dress and apron even on this chilly November day.

Though I'd only been using the studio for a little over two months, I'd already adapted the space to my needs. Jars of pigments and bottles of linseed oil, turpentine, and gesso lined the custom shelves Gage had constructed for me, and rolls of canvas and stacks of wooden frames stood in one corner. Several easels dotted the space, each displaying one of my portraits in various stages of completion.

Other finished works were draped carefully in a shadowy corner, protecting them from the sunlight. Two of the dozen or so paintings were commissioned portraits, while the others were intended for the ambitious *Faces of Ireland* exhibit I'd embarked upon since we returned from our trip to Ireland in July and the fraught inquiry we conducted there. We had both been greatly affected by the plight of the Irish and set out to do what we could to help the situation.

Lifting my brush from the canvas, I arched my back, already feeling strain on my body from standing in such a position—but a taste of the further changes that would need to come, no doubt. I'd already been forced to teach my lady's maid, Bree, how to prepare my paints. The pigments which had to be ground and mixed with linseed oil to create the colors I desired were sometimes toxic, and although I had always taken precautions for my own health, I'd decided it would be safer not to risk harming the baby. This task fell outside Bree's normal realm of duties, but she was the only one I trusted to do it.

In any case, our relationship had never followed protocol. I was far more familiar with her than most ladies were with their maids, as evidenced by my calling her by her first name. She also often assisted Gage and me with our investigations alongside my husband's valet, Anderley.

Happily, Bree seemed to take an interest in my artwork, and so I had given her a few rudimentary drawing lessons. Her sketches showed little promise of artistic achievement, but if she enjoyed it, I was not going to discourage her.

So when Jeffers entered the studio late in the afternoon, just as the sun was beginning to sink behind the mews at the back of the garden, he found me at one of my easels and Bree seated in the corner, her pencil rasping across the paper as she shaded some image. I flicked a glance at him as he gave a short bow.

"My lady, Mr. Gage wished me to inform you that Lord Gage has arrived, and that they await your attendance in the drawing room."

I couldn't stop myself from frowning in displeasure. A most improper reaction, but I knew Jeffers would understand. He held almost as little liking for the man as I did. It was one of the reasons Gage had poached him from another lord, though truth be told, Jeffers had intended to leave the baron's service anyway.

I sighed and nodded. "Thank you, Jeffers."

He bowed and turned to leave as Bree bustled over and untied the strings of my apron.

"I'll tidy up here, m'lady," she told me as her eyes scoured my appearance.

I dipped a rag in linseed oil and scrubbed at the paint stuck to my hands while she adjusted a few of the pins in my chestnut hair and fluffed the curls at the side of my face.

Her gaze dropped to my plain lavender kerseymere gown. "Did ye wish to change?"

I considered the matter for a moment and then shook my head. "Lord Gage's sartorial taste will undoubtedly be offended, but he shall have to overlook it." At least I wasn't wearing the drab brown or muddy puce dresses I also used when painting.

On my way to the drawing room, I paused to wash my hands and then inspect my reflection in one of the entry hall mirrors to be certain there were no flecks of paint on my face before joining the gentlemen.

As a bachelor, Gage had done little entertaining. So when we had arrived in London, he had urged me to redecorate the house as I saw fit, saying he trusted I would not make it overly feminine or ostentatious. I had little experience or interest in such things, but I did know what I liked in other people's homes and sought to emulate it, with Alana's wise counsel to assist me.

I had the walls in the drawing room painted a lovely sea green color, and the woodwork and moldings a shade darker for contrast. The fireplace brick was whitewashed to soften its appearance, and I chose pearl gray drapes for the windows. Much of the furniture was not to my taste, being too large and bulky, but I was careful to replace them with sofas and chairs that would not be too dainty for a man of Gage's height to sit comfortably. A few of my own portraits graced the walls—the ones I could not part with. My painting of Gage held pride of place over the mantel. However, I had not covered all the walls, leaving space for some of the artwork I had inherited from Gage's late grandfather when we collected them from his home on Dartmoor.

Overall, I was quite pleased with the results, and I knew only the most finicky of individuals could find fault with it. Which, unfortunately, described Gage's father.

I found both men standing before the hearth. Lord Gage glowered at the pale brick as he listened to his son. What they were discussing, I didn't know, for he broke off as I entered the room. Bracing myself for whatever criticism my father-in-law would offer, I crossed the room toward them, holding my head high despite the derisive sweep of his gaze over my person.

Just like his son after him, Lord Gage was rumored to have been one of the handsomest men of his generation. Truth be told, he was still quite attractive, even at the ripe age of fifty-eight. His golden hair had turned gray, and his face was weathered and perpetually bronzed due to his decades at sea as a captain in the Royal Navy, but his jaw was still firm, his physique trim, and his charm legendary. I had witnessed its effect on others, even if he'd never seen fit to turn it on me.

"My apologies," I told them. "But I expect Jeffers informed

you I was in my studio. How do you do, sir?" I offered Lord Gage my hand, which he clasped while dipping only the barest inch of his head. "Shall you be joining us for dinner?" Not that I wished him to, but it was polite to ask.

His nose wrinkled, smelling the oil and turpentine clinging to my gown, no doubt. "Is that what you intend to dine in?"

"Of course not." I arched a single eyebrow in chastisement. "But I supposed you would be cross if I kept you waiting any longer. If you intend to dine with us, I shall go change immediately."

I knew better than to expect him to be the least contrite. "I'll be dining at my club."

"Very well. Tea, then?" I offered, leading them toward the pair of cream upholstered Hepplewhite sofas with mahogany cabriole legs which faced each other before the fireplace.

He waved this offer aside impatiently as he sat across from Gage and me. "I suspect my son has informed you of the resurrectionists arrested at King's College on suspicion of murder." His voice was clipped, precise, and cold, as it always was when alone in our company.

"I have. Has the parish surgeon examined the corpse?" Gage asked, taking hold of my hand where it rested on my knee.

His father nodded. "Along with Herbert Mayo and Richard Partridge." The professor of anatomy and demonstrator at King's College, respectively. I had made both of their acquaintances when wed to Sir Anthony.

"Partridge is the man who sent for the police?"

"Yes." His expression turned grave. "And it appears he was right to do so."

"Murder, then?"

"Without a doubt."

None of us spoke for a moment, each contemplating the ramifications of such a certainty while the clock ticked away on the mantel.

Lord Gage roused himself to further explain. "They estimate the boy was about fourteen years of age and in fair health. He'd only been dead about three days, and never buried, though his chest and thighs were smeared with earth and clay to try to obscure that fact. The three surgeons had differing opinions on how exactly death had occurred. But they all agreed his blood-shot, bulging eyes; caved-in chest; and the evidence of coagulated blood and hemorrhages below the scalp, as well as the fact his damaged jaw was still dripping blood, indicated murder most foul."

I bit my lip to withhold the improvident words gathering on my tongue, but Lord Gage's eagle eyes missed nothing.

Those eyes narrowed. "Do you have something to add?"

I glanced at Gage, hesitant to speak, but in the name of truth I felt I had to. "By your mention of a damaged jaw, do you mean to say his teeth had been removed?"

If possible, Lord Gage's cold stare turned even more frigid. "I do."

"Well, then, it's probable the bodysnatchers removed them to sell separately to a dentist. At least . . . that's what I was led to believe was their standard procedure." Of the numerous corpses Sir Anthony had forced me to sketch, only one had retained any teeth, and they were so damaged as to be worthless.

"One of the accused had an injured hand and tried to claim he'd done it while removing the teeth from the body with a bradawl. And that he had, indeed, sold them to a dentist," he admitted. "Though that in no way clears him of the murder."

"Of course. But . . . I feel I should also mention that there are some surgeons who disagree with the widely held belief that blood never coagulates after death. They suggest that it could also do so in a still-warm corpse. I heard one such anatomist argue with Sir Anthony about it often enough," I added by way of explanation.

"Well, I suggest we trust the findings of the noted surgeons on this matter."

My cheeks flushed at this sharply worded reminder that I was not.

"She's only trying to help, Father," Gage said in my defense.

"The last thing this investigation needs is her airing her theories and clouding the issue. The situation is serious, and growing more worrisome by the hour."

I would have taken him to task for thinking I would share my thoughts willy-nilly to just anyone, but for the evidence he was troubled. Some of his calm assurance had been stripped away. He almost seemed unable to sit still.

"What else has happened?" Gage asked in a low voice.

"As of yet, we don't know the boy's identity. But multiple parents have come forward after reading the description of the boy in the police handbills and notices posted about the parish. They are all reporting missing sons of the same age and asking to view the body." He paused, seeming to gather himself. "There are others stepping forward as well, to share their stories of missing children, both male and female, of varying ages."

My hand tightened around Gage's where he still clasped it, my stomach hollow with dread.

"You grasp the implications," he murmured. "How many more missing children are there? How many more missing people? And do they have anything to do with the resurrectionists?"

Gage muttered a horrified curse.

His father nodded. "Alarm is building, and it is going to take a great deal of discretion to stave off a full-blown panic." His gaze shifted toward me where I sat staring at the floor, my other hand draped protectively around the small swell of my abdomen. "What of you?" he demanded.

I blinked in confusion.

"Are you saying you knew nothing of this?"

My head reared back. "Of the missing children?" I asked in astonishment. "Of course not! You . . . you honestly think that had I known about them, had I even contemplated the possibility that they were being taken and sold . . ." I broke off, unable to voice the words. "What kind of monster do you think I am?!"

"Then what of the resurrectionists' business? What do you know of it?"

"Father, that is enough," Gage barked.

"Nothing! I know nothing," I snapped back. "All I concerned myself with was the appearance of Sir Anthony's subjects once they rested on his dissection table, nothing before or after."

"You never wondered where his supply of fresh corpses came from?" he asked incredulously.

Hot shame stained my cheeks. "Of course I did! But I knew better than to ask. He made certain of that." I broke off, turning to gaze into the fireplace, wishing the flames could burn the memories from my mind. I inhaled a shaky breath. "I didn't want to know. I couldn't handle it. Not if . . ." I shook my head, halting the thought, and turned back to face Lord Gage. "If you wish to know more about bodysnatchers and their . . . their methods, I am not the person to ask."

Lord Gage's face showed not the least amount of sympathy, but his stony expression had softened. I could see the speculation behind his eyes. I had said too much. Gage might know about my first husband's cruel and sometimes violent mistreatment of me, but I had never spoken of it to his father, and I knew Gage better than to wonder if he had. He would never disclose such a thing without my permission.

When Lord Gage spoke next, it was with more care. "I've been given to understand it is not uncommon for the bodies of children to be dissected. Did Sir Anthony Darby ever do so in front of you?"

I shook my head vehemently, though for the sake of honesty, I added, "That's not to say he didn't plan to, for I was not privy to his designs for his anatomy textbook. I merely sketched what I was told to. But I never witnessed such a thing."

He accepted this with a single nod.

"If you're done interrogating my *wife*," Gage bit out in a hard voice, "can you tell me what any of this has to do with *you*? Has Lord Melbourne asked you to investigate?"

He sank back into the sofa, crossing one leg over the other. "Not officially. But he has asked me to keep informed on the matter, and ordered the authorities involved to grant me access."

"And I suppose this is your way of keeping us abreast of the matter in turn," Gage muttered, obviously suspecting the same thing I did. If Lord Gage had been asked to assist, then he would be dragging Gage and me into the inquiry along with him.

However, the nature of the murder and its intersection with my past complicated matters.

"Yes." His gaze shifted to me. "Though I shall wish for any part you might play to remain behind the scenes, for obvious reasons." He reached down to pick an invisible piece of lint from his coat sleeve. "I told you your imprudent bride's past would come back to haunt you."

"Through no fault of her own," Gage fired back, growing angry at this far too familiar refrain.

I pressed a hand to his arm. It was pointless to argue the matter with his father. He did not care to listen, as evidenced by his careless shrug, which communicated quite clearly that he believed the exact opposite. I would forever be the villain of this piece in his mind.

In any case, I'd long ago recognized the truth of the uneasy truce that had developed between us since my return to London. He'd simply been watching me, biding his time, waiting for me to make a mistake. What I hadn't known was whether he intended to pounce on it or smooth over my misstep. Whatever the case, I knew it would come with a price. I only had to wait for him to name it.

For now, he glossed over the matter. "The newspapers are calling the murdered child the Italian Boy."

Gage startled, but when I glanced at him, he swiftly masked his shock.

"They're seizing on the connection to the number of Italians who stepped forward to view the body, claiming one such boy had gone missing. Several of them thought it was him." Lord Gage glowered. "But none of them could tell us his name."

He pushed to his feet but added one last parting comment. "I do not know how people will react tomorrow when the story appears in all the newspapers, but you should be prepared." With that ominous warning, he took his leave.

As the door shut behind him, I turned to face my husband, but before I could speak, he began apologizing for his father.

I pressed a hand to his lips to forestall him. "No, Gage. Please stop. How many times must I tell you? You are not responsible for your father."

He sighed, lowering my hand to clutch it with the other in his lap. "I know. But when he says such things . . ."

"Yes, I know." I leaned forward, trying to catch his eye. "He makes both of us want to commit violence."

This surprised a smile out of him, and I lifted one of his hands to my lips, kissing the knuckles.

"Let's forget him for the moment." I gazed down at the callus along the side of one of his fingers. "Instead, tell me why his mention of the Italian Boy so unsettled you."

"It's nothing," he replied, shrugging the matter off. "Only, one hates to think of such a terrible fate befalling one of those lads."

"They usually are quite arresting, aren't they?"

With their dark hair, imploring eyes, and sweetly melancholy dispositions, they were easily some of London's most sentimental street figures. Some of them acted as image boys, carrying trays of plaster busts and figures of the great and good upon their heads throughout the city for their artist masters and hawking them to passersby. Still others were entertainers, performing music or pathos, or exhibiting animals, be it white mice in a cage hung around their neck, a tortoise, or a dancing monkey.

The economies of the Italian states had been devastated by the Napoleonic Wars, so it was no wonder why so many of those countrymen had migrated to England. For the most part they were welcomed, particularly for their renowned craftsmanship with optical devices, musical instruments, and waxworks. However, I did not know why so many of the Italian boys seemed reduced to near vagrancy. And I'd never contemplated the matter until now.

"It somehow makes this crime all the more horrifying," Gage replied, his brow puckered as if trying to understand why that was so.

I sobered. "Yes."

But despite his convincing response, I could tell there was something else he wasn't saying. It was betrayed by the tautness of his shoulders, the manner in which he continued to avoid my gaze. My first thought was that perhaps it involved one of his past inquiries. Perhaps one that had not ended satisfactorily. But then why the evasion?

Before I could press him, he forced a smile. "Well, if you'll excuse me, I must speak with Anderley about something before dinner."

"Of course."

I watched him go before rising more slowly to follow.

It was only later, as Bree was buttoning up the back of my dinner gown, that I realized how strange his parting words were.

After all, as his valet, Anderley would already be helping him to dress for dinner. So why did he need to speak with him particularly?

Was it something to do with the Italian Boy investigation, some point of fact he wished clarified? Or was it a personal matter? Something related to his reaction over the body's identity?

CHAPTER FOUR

As it happened, there were two major domestic stories featured in the newspapers the following morning. Apparently, a group linked to pro-Reform measures had been pressured
into canceling their meeting out of fear that the rally would turn
into a violent mob. But the most salacious article by far was that
of the poor Italian Boy, and the attendant discovery that a possible Burke and Hare–style gang of resurrectionists had been at
work in the city.

I perused several of the articles and then set them aside,
along with my breakfast. Such news—and the realization that
all of polite society would soon be aware of it—had soured my
appetite. Still, I was determined not to hide. I'd done enough of
that after the initial allegations were made following Sir Anthony's death. So I inhaled a deep breath past the quavering in my
stomach, gathered up my supplies, and set out for my scheduled
appointment with Lady Morley.

Though the Morleys' townhouse was only as far as Mount
Street, and I was tempted to walk given the fair autumn morning,

I elected instead to take the carriage. After all, there was a difference between bravery and stupidity. Had I the misfortune to encounter one of society's more sanctimonious matrons and endure her snub, I might have lost my courage. Or said something I would later regret. My emotions were such a jumble; I wasn't certain which would emerge victorious when I was first tried.

The Morleys' butler did not bat an eyelash upon admitting me to the house, though I was certain he must be aware of the inquest into the Italian Boy and my unhappy past. Butlers always knew. He announced me into the back parlor, where Lady Morley stood behind a chair positioned before a set of French doors. She was attired in the white organza silk gown she'd chosen to be captured in, her hair dressed in a style I thought too young for her but was not about to criticize. I might gently steer a subject to choose a gown of a different color or style—using art terms to explain why it would not suit the canvas rather than tell them that shade of pink made them look anemic—but there were certain things I never broached, and hair was one of them. It was something ladies and gentlemen, even those who had little, felt particularly attached to.

Nevertheless, while Lady Morley was prepared for our session physically, it was clear she was not contented with it. Her hands fluttered about her as I swept into the room, having decided to maintain my usual efficient demeanor. Even when I realized Lord Morley stood before the hearth, though he usually absented himself from his wife's sittings.

I greeted them both as my footman, Samuel, set my bag of art supplies on the table provided. "If you'll give me but a few minutes to prepare my palette, your ladyship, then we'll begin." I spoke distractedly, removing the necessary items from the valise while Samuel removed the sheet draped over the unfinished portrait on the easel and then departed. But not for a minute was I unaware of Lord Morley's continued presence and evident agitation. He seemed hesitant to speak while I was otherwise engaged, but I preferred him to say whatever he wished to before I hadn't the means to conceal my own uneasiness.

"Are you here to observe?" I asked him as casually as I could.

He cleared his throat. "Hmm . . . well . . . in a manner of speaking." He dithered for a moment longer before coming to the point. "I wonder if you've seen the *Times* this morning."

I shook out my folded apron with a snap. "My husband has any number of newspapers delivered to our breakfast parlor."

"Yes, humph, of course." His feet shifted. "But did he happen to mention the article on the front page to you?"

I glanced up at him as I tied my apron strings, some devil inside me urging me to deliberately misunderstand. "That 'Monster Meeting' in the East End? Yes. Lucky the rally organizers canceled it before anyone was harmed."

His face reddened. "Er, no, the other one." I thought his flush was caused by embarrassment and not anger, but one couldn't always be certain. Some men could go on speaking quite cordially even while their blood was boiling.

Either way, I decided I'd demurred enough. "That Italian Boy?" I shook my head sadly as I began opening jars of prepared paint and adding dabs to my palette. "The poor lad. Such a horrid tale."

"Yes. Indeed." Out of the corner of my eye, I watched as he rocked back on his heels before sending his wife an uncertain look. "We were both troubled by it."

I nodded. "As I should think any rational, God-fearing person would be. But I trust the New Police shall get to the heart of the matter."

But Lord Morley wasn't prepared yet to let it go. "So you had no knowledge of such things?" he began haltingly.

My hands stilled, irritation bubbling up inside of me, warring with remembered shame. That anyone should ask such a thing of me, even if half the ton was thinking it, was insulting. I turned my head sideways to glare at him.

"It's only, one can't help but recall your late husband. That you . . ." He seemed incapable of speaking the words, and I didn't need him to.

"Yes. It's one of the reasons you wished me to paint your wife, isn't it?" I charged, as weary of the fickleness of society as I was baffled by it. Too scandalous to be tolerated one moment, and then desirably infamous the next, at least for my artistic ability. "'The Notorious Lady Darby.' My portraits have become all the rage." At least, for the moment. Perhaps I was about to be relegated an artistic, as well as, social pariah.

"Yes, well, that was before . . ."

I lifted my hand, forestalling him, furious that I should have to defend myself in such a way yet again. "I shall only answer this once, so you may repeat it to all of your friends. I had *nothing* to do with Sir Anthony Darby's procurement of bodies. I did only what was demanded of me by my husband. As a . . ." I faltered over the word ". . . dutiful wife, I had no other choice. But I had no part in obtaining subjects. That was all my late husband's doing."

This conversation was distasteful in the extreme, to me and to the Morleys, but his lordship was the one to have forced it upon us. If I could have slapped the disgusted sneer from his lips, I would have.

"Thank you for answering me," he said. His gaze dipped to the palette gripped in my white-knuckled hands and then toward his wife. "I shall retire to my study and leave you to your session."

This had been stated for the benefit of his wife, whose wide eyes communicated how distressed she was. What she believed I would do to her, I didn't know, but I took a few moments to settle my specially weighted brushes to my liking so I could compose myself.

Once I felt certain I would not snap at her, I offered her a small smile. "Shall we begin?"

She nodded jerkily and settled into her chair.

I counted it a fortunate thing I was not focusing on the details of her countenance that day, for her expression remained rigid and distraught. It took all of my own hard-earned self-possession not to throw my paintbrush down in a fury and end the session. But I knew such a display of temper would not help my case. News of such a volatile display would reach the ears of every member of the ton before nightfall.

However, I decided ending the session half an hour earlier than planned would do no harm, and in fact, it might do some good. Especially when phrased as a diplomatic kindness.

"Lady Morley, I know sitting in such a confined position for so much time is quite a strain. Perhaps I scheduled today's sitting for too lengthy a time. Indeed, my hands are even cramping. Shall we adjourn until tomorrow?"

"Oh, yes. Please," she stammered.

I dipped my head and turned to clean my brushes. She did not waste a moment in beating a hasty retreat, leaving me with a bitter premonition. If I didn't receive a letter the following morning canceling the commission, I would eat my hat.

When just such a message awaited me at breakfast the following day, I choked back a harsh laugh. But once I lifted it to find another letter beneath it, any humor I might have been able to summon about the situation quickly fled.

I sliced open the seal on the missive from Lord Morley first, and a draft on his bank fell to the table. The sting of the implied insult washed over me. I was compensated for my portraits, but as a lady, a gentlewoman, this was not something I sullied my hands by managing. Such matters were referred to my solicitor to arrange.

Setting it aside, I read the short note. Contrary to the bank draft, it was unexpectedly polite. He claimed his wife was not in her best health, and so they'd decided to cancel the portrait commission until a more propitious time. This when he could have simply told the truth—they wanted no scandal attached to their name—or declined to give any explanation at all. I didn't know what to make of the man.

Breaking open the second letter, I glanced at the signature at the bottom, discovering it had been sent by the lady whose portrait I was to begin in a fortnight. With a sinking feeling in my stomach, I perused its contents to learn she was withdrawing her commission as well.

I slowly set the missive down on the table next to my customary cup of warm chocolate. Jeffers had delivered it moments before while I was reading. Fortunately, he'd already withdrawn, so I didn't have to face the awkwardness of meeting his gaze.

Thunder rumbled in the distance, presaging a rainy, gloomy day. I stared out the window past the floral chintz drapes at the damp garden beyond, suspecting this wet weather would usher in even cooler temperatures than before. Autumn was beginning to give way to winter.

I felt at odds with myself, not knowing which emotion to grant reign. Though I'd expected just such a thing would happen, that didn't stop me from feeling anger and frustration, or quiet the part of me that feared this was only the beginning. However, venting my rage or dissolving in despair would solve nothing.

Gage strode through the door looking as attractive as ever in a Spanish blue coat, slate gray waistcoat, and sorrel fitted trousers. "Be certain you take the carriage today. I don't want you walking in this weather." He paused in taking his seat, arrested by my expression.

What was stamped there, I could only guess.

"What is it?" he asked, lifting the tails of his coat to settle across from me. His sharp gaze took in the sight of the missives arranged before me.

Rather than speak, I passed them across the round, gleaming

wood table. He scowled at the sight of the bank draft but said nothing until he'd read both letters. As he set them aside, I could see he was struggling with some strong emotion, and perhaps it was this answering well of fury that quieted my own.

"Well, we said there would be some repercussions, didn't we?" I reached up to finger the amethyst pendant dangling from my neck—a gift from my mother before she died. "Society does love a good scandal, so long as it does not touch them."

"You're remarkably calm about this." His voice sounded almost accusatory, but I knew his aggravation was not directed at me but the Morleys and their like.

"Oh, I'm not," I replied with a huff of dry amusement. "But there's no use in yelling now. Not when the people I wish could hear me aren't present."

Some of the vehemence drained from his pale blue eyes, leaving behind a look of concern and uncertainty. "I wish there was something I could do." His hands clenched where they rested on the table. "I wish I could make people see reason."

"I know, darling. Don't we all?" I sighed. "But sadly, I suspect this is only the beginning." I released my grip on the pendant and raised my cup of warm chocolate to my lips but hesitated before drinking. "Should we consider bowing out of our invitation to attend the theater with Trevor and my cousins tonight?"

Gage lifted his gaze from where it was boring a hole in the wooden table. "I should think that would be the worst thing we could do. Philip was right. If you hide, that only makes you appear guilty." He inhaled a deep breath, clearly trying to release the rest of his anger, and forced a smile to his lips. "Besides, I believe your brother was counting on you to act as chaperone."

I returned his smile over the rim of my cup. "Yes. Can you imagine a less appropriate duenna than myself?"

Gage's gaze warmed. "That's not what I was implying."

"Maybe not. But I see you can appreciate the irony of my

playing chaperone for Miss Newbury when Lord Morley doesn't even trust me to paint his wife." I arched a single eyebrow before taking another sip of my chocolate and returning the cup to its saucer. "So tell me, what are your plans for the day?"

He sliced into the sausage on his plate. "I thought I might stop by Tattersall's to see what gallopers they've currently got up for bid. And then, of course, the coroner's hearing for the Italian Boy begins today. I thought I might visit the Unicorn pub, where it's being held, to get a sense of these fellows who are suspected of burking."

It said much about how our relationship had grown—both privately and as investigative partners—that he didn't attempt to hide this last part from me. In the past, he would have glossed over the matter, hoping I wouldn't notice. But for once, he had no need to fear I would try to persuade him to take me along. I had absolutely no desire to set foot near the maelstrom of this case. The reporters would undoubtedly spot me the moment I walked through the door, and no end of outrageous speculation would begin. As it was, they were certain to recognize Gage, but his presence could be explained by his and his father's reputations as gentlemen inquiry agents. My involvement with their favorite hobbyhorse was too recent, and my scandalous past too tempting to overlook.

"Well, take care," I said, uncertain what manner of men would be attracted to such a hearing. "Perhaps you should take Anderley with you."

"I planned to," he assured me. "What of you? What will you do with your day now that you find yourself a lady of leisure?"

It was a searching question, and well I knew it. I smiled. "I'm not going to come after you, if that's what you're thinking." Some of my good humor abandoned me as my gaze skimmed over the missives still resting on the table and then up to the Paul Sandby painting of the English countryside hanging above the mahogany sideboard. "I suppose I shall still paint. There are the Irish portraits, after all." I frowned. "Though with my re-newed infamy I'm not certain how much good they will do."

I did not attempt to hide my dissatisfaction and restlessness from him. I'd enjoyed the challenge my portrait commissions had given me over the past few months, the press for my time, the chance to stretch my abilities. And I would be lying if there wasn't also an element of pride, even if I knew part of my allure was the notoriety of my name. I hoped all of that wasn't about to change.

Gage offered me a gentle smile. "Don't fret. Something will turn up."

"I trust you're right," I replied, forcing a brave face. No use dwelling on such a dismal thought.

If only he'd chosen his words with more care.

CHAPTER FIVE

Despite the stormy weather, the boxes of the Theatre Royal, Covent Garden, were packed with spectators, and I doubted it was the rather indifferent performance of *Fra Diavolo* which had drawn them. Particularly when I could feel what seemed to be half the opera glasses in the theater trained on our box for much of the evening. I ignored them as best I could. Just as I ignored the hushed whispers that had begun in our wake when we arrived at the theater. Thus far, only the haughty society matron Lady Willoughby de Eresby had dared to snub me, but she had never liked me and was pleased to have any excuse to cut me dead.

That being said, I was touched and gratified by the number of people who visited our box during the intervals, almost in defiance of the ton. The subject was never broached, but their determined presence and kind smiles made it clear why they were there. Some were ladies and gentlemen Gage and I had assisted in the past, or the relatives of those people, while others were acquaintances formed since our return to London or old friends of Gage. Even Lord Gage dropped by, though I suspected that was more to do with the matter he discussed with his son at the back of our box than a show of support for me. Whatever the case, I was relieved to discover that not all of polite society had abandoned me.

On the carriage ride home, I'd intended to speak with Gage about what his father had to say, but after such an emotionally harrowing day, I had struggled to keep my eyes open. The warmth of Gage's body, the drumming of the rain, and the rocking of the conveyance as we waited in the London theater traffic all contrived to put me to sleep. Normally I found it impossible to slumber sitting up, even leaning against my husband's shoulder as I was. I supposed this weariness was yet another consequence of being heavy with child.

Upon our return to Chapel Street, Gage had to practically carry me inside, and in fact, would have, if I'd not objected. As it was, I'd forgotten all about his father until the following morning, when he asked me to join him in the morning room.

The sky was overcast, shedding a pall over the brilliant autumn garden beyond the French doors, but the morning room was still the cheeriest space in the house. I'd had the walls painted in a shade of primrose yellow with white drapes. The cozy furniture was upholstered in varying patterns of apple green, fawn, and white, with the same primrose used sparsely as accents. All of it revolved around the painting *Le jeune dessinatrice* by Louise-Adéone Drölling, whom I greatly admired.

Gage stood staring up at this painting, his arm draped over the mantel beneath, when I entered the room.

"Is this about your father?" I guessed. "I intended to ask you about your exchange last night, but, well . . ." I smiled sheepishly as he swiveled to face me ". . . apparently my body had different ideas."

His gaze softened. "Understandable, what with all those people intent on speaking to you."

It had been no more than two dozen, but that was still more friendly acquaintances than I could have claimed a year prior.

"Yes, I was heartened by it," I admitted.

He draped his arm around my waist. "And surprised. I could tell. You're very humble in your expectations of others."

"Can you blame me?"

"No. But I think you underestimate your own charm. And I'm not speaking of magnetism or attractiveness," he added, forestalling my protest. "Though you know I find you maddeningly irresistible."

A soft rap on the door prevented him from kissing me as I knew he intended to.

Anderley's dark head poked itself through the door. "You sent for me, sir?"

"Yes," he replied, releasing me. "Is Miss McEvoy with you?"

"Samuel is searching for her."

"Good. Have a seat. Let's not stand on ceremony."

This was not the first time we had met with our personal servants to discuss an inquiry, so I had no trouble in deducing the reason Gage had requested Anderley and Bree both attend us here. As such, I sank into the apple green upholstered chair near the hearth, where a merry fire crackled away. Anderley took the chair opposite me, near the Queen Anne walnut escritoire where I penned most of my letters.

His normally handsome countenance appeared somewhat haggard and worn, making him less the dark foil to Gage's golden good looks I was accustomed to. Even his bronzed complexion was looking a bit sallow. Seeing him in such a state, the mischievous twinkle missing from his eyes, I couldn't help but comment on it.

"Anderley, are you feeling well?" I murmured softly, sliding forward on my chair to be nearer to him.

His eyes lifted, and I could see the surprise in their brown depths. Perhaps a normal gentlewoman would have referred such a concern to her husband instead of addressing his valet directly, but given our past inquiries, Anderley and I were more familiar than that. I wasn't about to ignore his evident unhappiness.

"If you should need a few days off, you need only say the word."

"No," he replied, finally driven into speech. "I thank you, my lady. I am well."

Gage stared over his valet's shoulder at his profile, though he did not speak, and I sensed he saw, or knew, more than either of them was saying. It was not my place to force an unwanted confidence, so I merely nodded.

"Well, if you should need anything, I hope you know you only need to ask. I'll do everything in my power to help."

"I do, my lady. Thank you."

I wasn't certain I would ever know the true depths of my husband and his valet's relationship. I knew they had traveled the continent, taken part in the Greek War for Independence, and undertaken countless inquiries together, some quite dangerous. Anyone who had seen them stand shoulder-to-shoulder as they threatened or interrogated a suspect recognized their bond was a deeply forged one. I sometimes wondered whether Gage trusted me or Anderley more, but then I understood trust could take many forms, just as love could.

Bree entered the room then, pushing a stray strawberry blond curl behind her ear as she dipped a curtsy. "Ye wished to see me?"

Gage ushered her inside, where she perched on the edge of the settee next to Anderley's chair, her hands tucked in her lap. Her eyes met his briefly before turning back to my husband, who was addressing her.

"Have you been kept informed of the current police inquiry occurring in Covent Garden?"

"About that poor Italian Boy?" she replied in her Scottish

brogue. "Aye. I've read the newspapers doon in the servants' hall."

"Sometimes before they reach the breakfast parlor," Anderley muttered under his breath, though some of his usual devilry sparkled in his eyes.

Bree wrinkled her nose pertly at him.

Gage ignored this, sitting down on the other end of the settee to form a square between us all. "The New Police are, of course, handling the matter. However, Lord Melbourne has requested that Lord Gage monitor the situation. And he has asked for our assistance."

His eyes met mine briefly before sliding toward Anderley to gauge his reaction. Why he should be so intent on doing so, I didn't know, but I observed the pair of them with interest.

"What does he wish us to do?" I asked, not altogether surprised by Lord Gage's request given the intensity of their conversation at the theater, but somewhat puzzled by what he wanted from us.

"To listen. To the members of society, and the servants belowstairs." He dipped his head to Bree. "To the shopkeepers and tradesmen, and passersby on the street. He wants to know what the general mood of the metropolis is. Is there resentment, fear, signs of malcontent?"

"They're trying to prevent a riot," I realized with some alarm.

Gage nodded guardedly. "That is one of their concerns. Apparently, two of the defendants, Bishop and May, are well known to traffic in anatomical subjects. If that's the case, then who knows how often they might have resorted to burking to turn a profit, though they both swear the body was dead when they took possession of it. May claims the body was stuffed in a trunk in Bishop's washhouse in Bethnal Green the first time he laid eyes on it."

"But I thought the coroners said the body had never been buried?" Anderley asked in some confusion.

"Yes, but I've been speaking with some men, and apparently exhumation isn't the only way bodysnatchers procure bodies. They also pose as the family members of unclaimed paupers or steal corpses from the bone house and undertaker's premises. That's why the freshness of the body didn't at first raise any suspicions, but the fact that they'd tried to make it appear as if it *had* been buried when it *obviously* had not raised doubts."

I tapped my fingers against the arm of my chair trying to decide if the names *Bishop* or *May* were familiar to me in any way. Just because I had avoided learning about Sir Anthony's interactions with resurrectionists didn't mean I might not have overheard him mention their names. "What of the other two men? Are they not associated with the bodysnatching trade?"

"Williams is the son-in-law of Bishop, and new to the profession, if I'm interpreting matters correctly. Whatever happened, he's in it as deep as Bishop, no matter how innocent he appears." He crossed his arms over his chest. "They all have prior arrests. They've all spent time in one prison or another. But the fourth man, Shields, is undoubtedly innocent of murder, at least. He's a frightened old man who makes his living by carrying heavy loads. His only crime is that he allowed himself to get roped in with the resurrectionists, hiring himself out to carry the bodies. He didn't even enter the story until the morning of the fifth, long after the surgeons agree the boy was killed."

"Then why don't the magistrates release him?"

"They're hopeful that the other men will let something slip and he'll turn King's evidence."

"He'd be a fool not to," Bree surmised.

Gage's expression was grim. "Yes, well, as of now it sounds like the police have precious little proof the defendants actually killed the boy. There seems little doubt the lad was, in fact, murdered. But as they've yet to establish identity, it's difficult to definitively assign blame. That's something else we may be able to help with."

He swiveled to face Anderley directly. "The coroner's inquest continues today, and I'd like you to attend. Try to blend in with the general crowd. Listen to what they have to say. Maybe question a few of the witnesses who came forward with information about a missing Italian Boy."

Anderley nodded eagerly and departed.

"Miss McEvoy, I suppose you know your part?" Gage remarked with a small smile.

"Aye. Listen and sympathize. Tenderhearted, I am," she added, clutching her chest. Then she flashed us an impish grin. "Perhaps you've a few errands ye wish me to run?" she prodded me.

"Of course," I replied without hesitation. "Maybe a new ribbon to match my cornflower silk gown. And I'm sure you'll find the clasp on my pearl bracelet is loose."

Her lips twitched. "If I may, your jar o' rose hips ointment is also low, so I'll visit the apothecary."

This, at least, was true.

"Then I won't expect to see you until I need to dress for dinner."

She curtseyed and hurried off to undertake her commissions. I shook my head at her departing figure. She was deriving too much delight from such subterfuge.

I turned back to my husband and arched my chin. "And what, pray tell, do you wish of me?" When he didn't reply, the amused curl of my mouth flattened. "Unless you think I should stay away from this one?"

The faint lines at the corners of his eyes creased in chagrin. "Actually, I was just thinking that for once I wished Sir Anthony had shared more with you."

"About his involvement with bodysnatchers?"

He nodded, rubbing a hand along the back of his neck. "How irrational is that?"

I moved over to the settee to sit beside him. "You wish to understand them better?"

"Among other things."

I bit my lip, hesitant to speak. "I am acquainted with several surgeons, and most of them have used resurrectionists at one time or another." I brushed a hand over the lace insets of my Pomona green skirt. "Not all of them are hostile toward me. If I selected carefully, I'm sure I could convince one of them to speak with you."

Rather than answer me, he asked a question of his own. "How many of them are like Sir Anthony? Ruthless in their pursuit of knowledge and renown," he clarified.

I blanched. "I can't possibly answer that. But . . ." I pressed a hand to my abdomen. "I could tell you stories about some of them that would shock you. Perhaps even make your stomach turn."

I did not want to recount these stories. Even thinking of them now made my insides quaver. And I didn't see how they would help with the investigation. But I would tell him, if he wished me to.

Comprehending the distress this caused me, he brushed it aside for now. "Let's wait to consult another surgeon for the moment. It may not be necessary."

I breathed a sigh of relief. I had no desire to reinsert myself into London's medical community. Edinburgh had been different. Most of the surgeons and physicians there had had nothing to do with Sir Anthony or the charges brought against me. But London's close-minded ranks—centered on the Royal College of Surgeons—were a different story, even if journals like the *Lancet* and anatomists like the late Edmund Grainger were attempting to challenge that. It was why we'd already made plans to return north before my confinement. I preferred to give birth in Edinburgh or with the eminently qualified midwife in Elwick, Northumberland—my childhood home.

There was a rap on the morning room door, and Jeffers entered in response to our summons. "My lady, Lady Stratford and

Lady Tavistock are here to see you. They insisted they need not wait on ceremony."

At this, he was practically pushed aside as Charlotte and Lorna brushed past him into the room in a flurry of lavender-scented silk and satin.

"Oh, Kiera, we just heard the news last night," Charlotte exclaimed. "Of all the utter nonsense!"

CHAPTER SIX

"How can they possibly be so stupid as to draw a connection between you and that poor Italian Boy?" Lorna sneered, flopping down into one of the chairs.

"And that insipid Lady Morley has been telling anyone who will listen how she's canceled her portrait commission with you." Charlotte settled her skirts with a furious flourish. "I told her she was an absolute fool."

"Charlotte, you didn't?" I gasped, having difficulty imagining the perfectly proper Dowager Countess of Stratford uttering such words.

Someone had once said I would have a terrible influence on her. It appeared they were right.

When we'd first met, she'd been renowned for her icy reserve, though that had been more the fault of her circumstances than her natural disposition. Regardless, she had stringently disapproved of me. That is, until I saved her from death and false imprisonment. Since then we'd discovered we were more alike than we'd realized, and our friendship had blossomed.

"Of course I did." She scoffed. "As if it's a blessing for anyone to paint her beak of a nose." She dismissed her with a wave of her hand. "Good riddance, I say."

Gage's mouth creased into a smile. "I believe that's my cue to take my leave. I know I can rely on you two ladies to bolster my wife." He dropped a kiss on my cheek before bowing to each of my friends and striding from the room.

Jeffers still hovered near the door, and I nodded to him. "Tea, please."

"Of course, my lady."

The door shut behind him, and I sank deeper into the sofa with a scowl. "Unfortunately, Lady Morley is not the only canceled commission."

"Fustian!" Charlotte declared, tossing her reticule down on the tea table. Her soft gray eyes flashed with fire. "They cannot be so foolish as to think you had any part in this Italian Boy's death."

"No, but I'm learning that society does not like to be reminded of anything unpleasant," Lorna replied, twirling a rose silk ribbon on her dress around her finger. From the distracted look in her eyes, I could tell she wasn't thinking only of my reputation but also her illegitimacy. Her father might be a lord, and he might have been in love with her mother until the day she died, but they had not been wed. Lorna's marriage to a viscount smoothed over some of those improprieties, though it was fortunate the scandalous details surrounding that wedding were not widely known.

In truth, I was heartened by how well she seemed to be adjusting to her new life. She had maintained an independent existence, one riddled by rumors of witchcraft, herbalism, and unnatural behavior—rumors that were not so very different from those that swirled around me. However, unlike me, the gossip about her had largely been isolated to Devon, so most of London had never been privy to those choice bits of tittle-tattle.

"She's right," I said. "So long as one's . . . indiscretion is not recent or thrust in their faces, there are many who are content to ignore it."

"I'll take that as a hint that perhaps I should be delivered of this child in Devon rather than London, if there is any hope of convincing polite society he or she has been born prematurely," she muttered wryly, rubbing her hand over the swell of her stomach, which showed she was further along than the three months she had been wed.

Charlotte's mouth tightened briefly in what I thought might have been jealousy, and my heart went out to her. Here Lorna and I sat, growing round with child, when Charlotte wished more than anything for such a blessing. It was a cruel twist of fate that she could not conceive.

So I hastened to change the subject. "This inquest on the Italian Boy, and the manner in which he is suspected of being killed, has only served to remind everyone of my shocking past. And for many, that is unforgivable."

"But it's not your fault," Lorna protested, sitting forward.

"Yes, but if you haven't noticed, society has no problem blaming wives, or daughters . . ." Charlotte dipped her head to Lorna ". . . for the sins of their husbands and fathers. We're guilty by association, no matter how little power we had in the situation." She spoke calmly, but I knew she was thinking of her vile deceased husband.

I wasn't certain Lorna was aware of Charlotte's past, having only arrived in London a little over a fortnight ago, but it appeared she'd heard something of the matter, for her face creased with sympathy. "Are you thinking of what that odious woman with the double chins said? Because someone should have taken her out to the depths of Dartmoor and left her there long ago."

I looked to Charlotte, who grimaced. "Lady Westlock informed me recently that if I'd only seen fit to produce an heir for

Lord Stratford, nothing that had followed would have ever happened."

My hands tightened into fists at the mention of the woman who had poured no small amount of scorn over my head during my and Gage's first inquiry. "That woman is a harridan! I hope you paid her no heed."

"Not the least," she replied, fluffing the fashionably puffed sleeves of her jonquil gown. I could tell by the tight lines between her eyes she was lying.

I turned to gaze out through the French doors at the dreary garden beyond, breathing deeply to settle my temper. Once I felt I could speak evenly, I turned back to examine my two dearest friends other than my sister. Both were beauties, though Charlotte outshone us with her pale blond hair and porcelain skin. She had been the Incomparable the year of her debut. However, Lorna's green eyes flashed with a brilliance and intelligence I wasn't certain either of us could match.

Both should have been adored and eagerly courted members of society, not only for their beauty and wit but their warmth and graciousness. But both had been wounded, threatened, and snubbed. That was how they'd found their way into my life. While I would not have traded their friendship for anything, I did wish the world was a little more kind. Or rather, the people in it.

I reached up to rub my forehead, fighting off the beginnings of a headache. "I've stopped trying to understand the fickleness and foolishness of society. But regrettably, one has to live among it. At least for the sake of one's loved ones."

Not so long ago, I'd considered turning my back on it once and for all. I did not regret my decision to relinquish that notion and wed Gage. But I could not deny that, at times, I felt I'd chosen the infinitely harder path, despite its ample compensations.

Jeffers entered with the tea tray laden with a mountain of the cook's scrumptious little cakes. I stifled a giggle. Apparently, my staff believed two women in the family way could consume the same amount of food as a horse.

I poured the tea, and as we each sat back with our cups, Charlotte picked up the strands of the conversation.

"Well, from where I sit, the first thing to be done is to find you another portrait commission. One for a lady whose reputation is either so impeccable or status so unassailable that no one would dare naysay her."

"Don't you already have scores of people waiting for you to paint them?" Lorna asked after licking a dollop of frosting from her lip. "Why, just the other evening, Lady Fleming approached you."

"Yes, as did Lady Redditch." I frowned into my tea. "But I hesitate to contact the people further down my list and risk each of them refusing."

Charlotte's eyes narrowed, considering the matter. "No, that won't do. And much as I like Lady Fleming and Lady Redditch, neither is unassailable." She tilted her head in thought. "Are you acquainted with any duchesses?"

"My cousin's wife," I admitted. "The wife of my father's mother's nephew."

In fact, it was through the Dukes of Chatton that my grandmother had been given the dowry property that had later become my father's holding and my childhood home—Blakelaw House.

I sighed and shook my head. "But the Duchess of Chatton barely acknowledges me. I can't imagine her condescending to have me paint her portrait."

Charlotte's mouth pursed, evidently familiar with how tedious and high in the instep the duchess was. "No, she won't do at all."

"What about the Duchess of Bowmont?" Lorna suggested before popping a morsel of cake into her mouth.

We both turned to stare at her, and her eyes widened in question.

"You're acquainted with the Duchess of Bowmont?" Charlotte asked as Lorna swallowed.

"Yes. She's my godmother."

I blinked, wondering how exactly this had come to be, and whether I was silly to be so surprised. "How . . ." I began to ask, but didn't know how to continue without it sounding insulting.

Lorna smiled. "My father was one of her young swains, once upon a time, and later they remained friends, even after my father had met my mother and fallen in love."

She seemed to think this was explanation enough, but Charlotte and I shared a look of mild disbelief. That the Duchess of Bowmont had claimed Lord Sherracombe as an admirer, and possibly a lover, despite his being approximately a decade younger than her, was not a wonder. But Lorna's ability to speak so sanguinely about the matter, and the infamous duchess's willingness to play godmother, was.

I had never met the Duchess of Bowmont, but I was well aware of her reputation. Everyone was. For she and the duke took no great pains to stifle the rumors surrounding them. The duchess had given birth to six children, but it was widely accepted that the younger four had been fathered by different men than her husband, even though the duke had claimed them as his own. Although, far from playing the part of the cuckold, the duke himself had a number of side-slips birthed by a string of mistresses.

From all appearances, the duke and duchess seemed to find it an amicable arrangement. There was little to no tension displayed between them when they appeared in public together or exchanged greetings at a soiree. They were either very good actors or they truly didn't care.

Regardless, the duchess's reputation was far from impeccable. In fact, she was about as notorious as one could be.

"I'm sure the duchess is lovely," I hedged. "But I'm *not* sure how my painting her portrait is going to bolster my standing. Far be it for me to cast any aspersion, but her own reputation is not exactly unimpeachable."

Charlotte tapped her lips with her finger. "Yes, but her status *is* unassailable."

I couldn't deny that. Scandalous she might be, but a duchess was a duchess. And this one happened to be related to half the royalty of Europe, including our own. She and the duke might have done nothing to squash the rumors surrounding them, but they were also careful to never do anything beyond the pale. Publicly, they behaved with perfect propriety. Of course, they flirted and cajoled, but anything disreputable was done behind closed doors. As such, they were neither snubbed nor shunned, even if they were gossiped about voraciously and criticized behind their backs.

Charlotte's eyes gleamed with speculation as she appeared to warm to the idea of my painting the Duchess of Bowmont more with each passing second, a shocking thing in and of itself. "Do you think she would be interested in Kiera painting her?" she asked Lorna.

"I'm sure she would leap at the chance. Particularly when I explain a bit of the circumstances."

Charlotte nodded decisively. "Then I think Kiera should do it."

"I think you've been spending too much time with your great-aunt," I couldn't help but tease. Much as I enjoyed Lady Bearsden and her lively chatter, I couldn't deny she was an incorrigible rattle and nearly impossible to shock.

"Oh, fiddlesticks!" she retorted, making me laugh out loud, for Lady Bearsden exclaimed this in exactly the same manner.

She smiled, waiting for my humor to subside before pressing me. "Say you'll do it. Let Lorna speak to her godmother on your behalf."

"Yes, do," Lorna said. "I think it's a capital plan, and I know the duchess will approve."

Met with two such eager faces, I could hardly say no. In truth, the thought of painting the Duchess of Bowmont appealed to me. She was a beauty, but an aged one, and so lively that I knew it would take all of my considerable skill to capture her on canvas.

"If you could arrange a meeting for me, I would be much obliged," I told Lorna.

She beamed. "I shall call upon her today."

"Now that that's arranged, my great-aunt, whom I believe you meant to unpardonably disparage earlier . . ." Charlotte bantered, knowing full well my affection for Lady Bearsden ". . . is demanding you and Mr. Gage be her guests of honor at a small dinner party she's hosting tomorrow evening. Just a few of her particular friends."

This could mean a party of ten or eight dozen. Lady Bearsden had a lot of "particular friends." But I was pleased to accept, touched beyond words that the good lady wished to do such a thing for me.

I had just finished attempting to express my gratitude, when the door opened and Jeffers ushered my sister inside. Upon finding me pleasantly ensconced with Lorna and Charlotte, Alana hesitated on the threshold for but a moment before striding forward.

Her concerned expression warmed. "Well, I'm glad to see I'm not the only one fed up with such nonsense."

I nodded to Jeffers, who I knew would bring more tea, and then rose to embrace my sister. If she hugged me a trifle tighter and longer than usual, that was to be expected. After all, she'd seen me at my lowest and most beaten-down after my appearance before the Bow Street Magistrates, when I thought the mob outside would tear Philip's carriage apart to get to me.

She said nothing, but I watched as she blinked away a

suspicious brightness. She sat beside me on the sofa, still clutching my hand. "Now, I trust you ladies have already formed a plan to deal with this folderol."

"We have," Charlotte replied.

She nodded. "Good. Now, tell me."

I should have known better than to doubt Charlotte. Despite her assurances, I had been nervous about attending her greataunt's dinner party the following night. Any number of things could have gone wrong, and yet they hadn't.

Three dozen guests had graced Lady Bearsden's table, and none of them had glared or cut me. There had been a moment or two of awkwardness when the conversation had inevitably turned to current events, but no one had been rude. Or perhaps, more accurately, no one had dared to be rude to me in Lady Bearsden's presence. For all her impish, good-natured demeanor, everyone knew the baroness could be feral when she was crossed.

I had enjoyed myself exceedingly. If only all of society's events could be like that one, I would not mind taking part.

Gage and I would have remained longer, but Lady Bearsden's home had become stifling thanks to two crackling fireplaces and the heat of so many bodies. In my current condition, I was prone to overheat, and consequently grow nauseous. So I had begged Gage to walk home, despite the cold evening, knowing the fresh air would set me to rights.

The chill of the evening air blew blessedly cool against my flushed cheeks as Gage and I set off down Park Street. A light mist had begun to gather, along with all the peculiar scents that seemed to accompany a London fog—coal smoke, a salty scent like the sea, and a pungent undernote of ale or some other bitter draft. It being Mayfair, the streets were tidy and quiet but for the leaves gathering in the gutters and the rumble of a passing carriage. From time to time, a burst of laughter could be heard coming from inside one of the elegant Georgian townhouses lining the street, and we passed one other couple strolling like ourselves, but other than that, we were alone.

"You must feel gratified," my husband said, tucking me closer to his side, as if he feared I'd already grown cold.

I tilted my head to consider his words. "I would more describe myself as relieved. But, yes, I suppose I'm glad, too." I looked up into his sparkling blue eyes as we passed under a gas-lit streetlamp. "It was a lovely evening. And I was very pleased to see Charlotte and Rye looking so cozy together."

He chuckled. "Playing matchmaker, are we?"

"Not in the least. They seem to have gravitated toward each other without the need for my interference." I allowed Gage to guide me around a suspicious puddle on the pavement. "Nothing could be more ideal. They're both the finest of people. Quiet in their pursuits. And Rye is a widower in need of a mother for his young children, and Charlotte a widow desirous of children she can never have herself."

Already being aware of this, he was not shocked to hear me say so. "Yes, if the course of love and companionship were to run that direction, it would be ideal."

What he didn't say was that sometimes things were not so smooth or simple. Something I well knew.

We passed an estate agent's office and then the narrow shop-front of a bookseller, both shuttered for the night. I could see copies of Sir Walter Scott's *Tales of a Grandfather* and Benjamin Disraeli's *The Young Duke* displayed prominently in the window next to Eugène François Vidocq's memoirs—a criminal turned informer, who later became Napoleon's head of police in Paris. Beside these sat stacks of the most recent editions of the *Police Gazette*, and then newspapers and cheap broadsheets, all embla-zoned with headlines about the inquest into the Italian Boy, each more sensational than the last. It seemed everywhere one went there were reminders of the city's current turmoil.

"Do you think the coroner's jury has finally reached a

verdict?" I asked, recalling Gage's earlier comment that he didn't think the hearing could possibly last for another day.

"I suppose we shall find out from Anderley when we return home." His nose crinkled. "I certainly hope so. The matter has gone on long enough. They're almost certain to be brought up on charges of 'willful murder against some person or persons unknown,' so they should simply get on with it and pass it on to the magistrates to sort out."

I could sense the frustration behind his sharp words. He was as anxious as I was to see the matter resolved. That the facts were already to receive two more airings—assuming the Bow Street Magistrates remanded the men to Newgate for trial at the Old Bailey—would only serve to keep the crimes fresh in Londoners' minds.

I squeezed his arm where it linked with mine, briefly resting my head against the shoulder of his caped greatcoat. "Well, for now, let's think on happier things."

He exhaled a long breath. "Agreed."

Bracing my arm, he helped me step down to cross Upper Brook Street. The pavement was slick with damp and wet leaves, and the peel of an orange lay discarded in the gutter. To the west, there was the distant clatter of a passing carriage driving past Hyde Park, its noise muffled by the fog. I turned to ask him what he'd decided regarding the beautiful stepper he'd been waxing eloquent about since his visit to Tattersall's near the park's Rotten Row two days prior, when my words were arrested by a shout.

Both of our heads swiveled toward the sound, which seemed to have come from the east in the direction of Grosvenor Square. At first we could see nothing through the eddying mist despite the thumps and sounds of shuffling feet, which communicated there was a scuffle of some sort occurring. Then the fog parted to reveal the outline of two figures locked together at the edge of the glow of one of the streetlamps.

"Stay here," Gage ordered me as we reached the corner.

I huddled inside my amethyst mantle as he moved forward to intercede. The two men twisted back and forth in conflict, and then one of the men dropped to his knees before pitching forward to strike the pavement with a loud crack. The second man backed away, his face obscured by shadow and mist. By his stance, I could tell he clutched something in his hand. His head jerked upward at the sound of Gage's rapidly approaching footsteps, and then he turned and fled.

Gage called out after him to stop. He hesitated for a moment next to the crumpled figure, throwing a glance back at me over his shoulder before resuming his pursuit of the other man.

Though he hadn't spoken to me, his intentions had been clear. I hastened forward, kneeling next to the man in dark evening clothes. "Sir," I said calmly. "Sir, can you hear me?" I reached over to roll his face toward the light, my hand catching on some cloth. But when I tried to brush it away from his cheek, it remained fast. Turning his face with the article still attached, I was astonished to discover not only that it was a sticking plaster normally used to treat wounds but that I knew him.

It was Lord Feckenham, the Earl of Redditch's disagreeable son. Except he would no longer be making himself disagreeable to anyone. He was dead.

CHAPTER SEVEN

L ord Feckenham's eyes stared vacantly up at me, their malicious light extinguished. The sticking plaster that had snagged
on my glove dangled limply from his face, adhered to one cheek.
Confounded, I draped it forward to find that if applied correctly
it would cover both his nose and mouth.

My blood ran cold at the implication. The iconic woodcut
images of Burke and Hare showed them using such devices as
sticking plasters to smother their victims, and the more lurid
broadsheets had already implicated their use in the images of the
London burkers. But Feckenham could not have been smothered to death. The timing wasn't right. We had watched him
struggle. Perhaps he'd fainted, but the sticking plaster had been
dislodged from his mouth by the fall, which would have allowed
him to breathe again.

The sight of his wide eyes gazing up at me from above the
cloth unnerved me, so I brushed the plaster aside and swiped a
hand over his eyes to close them. A splash of red on the pavement next to where he lay compelled me to turn his head to

examine it. Above and behind his left ear, his hair was matted with blood. This, then, must have been what killed him. When he'd fallen, whether he'd been unconscious or not, he'd struck his head.

I was about to rise to my feet again when I remembered how the other man had been holding something. It had been difficult to see in the fog, but I could have sworn it was a knife of some sort. Sparing a moment to pray that Gage had recognized the weapon as well, I spread aside Feckenham's greatcoat and began to carefully run my hands over his torso, the likeliest place he'd been stabbed.

It didn't take me long to find the wound. On his right side, midway down the chest, I found a gash. From all appearances, the knife had not bit deep, perhaps striking a rib and being deflected. It had undoubtedly been painful, but had he not hit his head, I suspected he would have survived.

I glanced up at the crunch of footsteps approaching, peering warily into the dark mist.

"It's me," Gage gasped between breaths, emerging out of the gloom. Finding me alone, he tucked the pistol I'd grown accustomed to him always carrying back into the pocket of his greatcoat. "The blackguard darted down one of the mews and then an alley." He shook his head. "I lost him after that." He nodded to the figure at my feet. "Is he dead?"

"I'm afraid so."

"Who is it, then?" He moved a step closer, his eyes widening as he recognized his face. He lifted his head to look up and down the street. "Doesn't the earl live on this street?"

"Yes," I replied, taking the hand he offered me to rise to my feet. "Two houses that way."

Gage followed my finger before glancing down at Feckenham again, his brow tight with unspoken words. "I can't say I liked the man, but no one deserves to be murdered."

His gaze then caught on the blood staining the fingertips of one of my long white evening gloves as I rolled it down my arm, wrapping the offending stains inside as I removed it. I destroyed an alarming amount of gloves this way.

"Did the knife wound kill him?" he asked, taking the glove from me and stuffing it into his pocket.

"No, it's not deep enough." I described my findings and suppositions, and he nodded in agreement.

"You're undoubtedly right. Unless the victim suffers a stab to the heart, the wound usually takes at least several minutes if not hours to bleed out. But a hard enough blow to the head could kill instantly."

"What do you make of the sticking plaster?"

His gaze met mine, dark with foreboding. "I suspect I'm thinking the same thing you are. But let's save that discussion for later. We need to alert Redditch's household." He took a step in the direction of the earl's townhouse and then swiveled back to say, "Remove the sticking plaster and put it in your reticule."

I immediately complied, not allowing myself a moment to reconsider.

By the time Gage returned with the earl's butler and two footmen—all of whom appeared to have been summoned from their beds—I stood a foot away from Feckenham, doing my best to appear meek and compliant. I knew horrified and alarmed— the emotions any respectable young lady should feel upon such a discovery—were beyond me. In any case, my reputation was well set. No one would believe it if I suddenly began to shriek with hysterics and threaten to faint.

With Gage's assistance, the body was carried into Lord Redditch's townhouse and deposited into Feckenham's bedchamber. A groom had been dispatched to inform the earl and countess, who were attending the theater. In the meantime, Gage and I were ushered into the drawing room to wait for them.

The butler tugged at his hastily donned attire as his gaze dipped to my single white glove. "If you'll excuse me, I'll request a pot of tea be made ready."

In his absence, I removed the other glove, deciding it would be more peculiar to continue to wear one glove than none. Gage helped himself to a fortifying glass of the earl's whiskey from the sideboard while I struggled not to worry about the repercussions of this evening's crimes. Given the state of my mind, I was tempted to partake of a wee dram myself, even though I'd never been a great devotee of whiskey. However, I'd consumed a glass of madeira at Lady Bearsden's soiree, and while its dulcifying effect had been ruthlessly nullified by the murder of Feckenham, I felt it better not to drink any more spirits.

It was difficult to believe only five days prior I'd waltzed through the ballroom upstairs and watched an effigy of Guy Fawkes burn on the dining room table. Then my most pressing concerns had been avoiding Lady Felicity's flinty gaze and one baron's particularly fetid breath. How fast things changed. As they were about to for Lord and Lady Redditch, their eldest son and heir having been killed, practically on their doorstep.

I offered the stalwart butler a smile of gratitude when he returned with the tea tray.

"I trust the groom will be able to locate his lordship and her ladyship swiftly," he assured me, displaying a grandfatherly urge to offer comfort. I noted in his absence, his clothing had also been set to rights.

"Hotchkins, isn't it?" Gage asked, rejoining me.

"Yes, sir."

"I imagine you've been with the family for many years." It was phrased with compassion rather than as a query, but the butler answered the implied question anyway.

"I've been fortunate to serve his lordship for thirty-two years, sir."

"So you've known Lord Feckenham all his life, then. My condolences."

It might have been a trick of the light, but the slight flicker in the old retainer's eyes appeared to me to be a wince. "Thank you, sir."

Gage's brow furrowed with concern. "As I'm sure you noticed, his lordship was attacked on the street but a few dozen feet from the house. Did you happen to notice anything out of the ordinary this evening? Any odd noises or suspicious fellows hanging about?"

"I wish I had, sir. But everything seemed as usual. Only the Lawsons in the house adjacent leaving at about ten o'clock."

I glanced at the clock to see that it was half past eleven. Which meant the Lawsons had departed too early for them to have noticed anything unusual either.

The sound of a carriage being pulled up to the door propelled Hotchkins toward the entry. "If you'll excuse me. That must be the earl and countess."

Gage and I rose to our feet, waiting for Lord and Lady Redditch to join us. My skin felt tight across my bones, and dread swirled in my stomach. How much had the groom told them? Did they already know the worst, or would we have to reveal it to them?

My question was soon answered by the countess's flustered voice. "What is this, Hotchkins? Billy intercepted us leaving the theater, insisting we return home. Some nonsense about Feckenham. Well, where is he?"

"I believe I'll allow Mr. Gage and Lady Darby to explain that, my lady. They're waiting for you in the drawing room."

The silence that followed this pronouncement reverberated with a horror so palpable I wanted to speak just to fill it with something else. Then there was a flurry of footsteps rushing toward the room.

"What is it?" Lady Redditch gasped, our reputations preceding us. "What's happened to my son?"

"It grieves me to inform you that . . ." Gage began, but before he could finish the statement, Lady Redditch swooned, latching on to her husband's arm. Between the earl and the butler, they maneuvered her over to a sofa before she collapsed, moaning her son's name.

"Find her ladyship's maid," Hotchkins ordered the footman standing in the doorway. "And tell her to bring her ladyship's smelling salts."

The earl sank down beside his wife, chafing her hands as she stirred fitfully. His gaze lifted to Gage. "He's dead?"

"I'm afraid so, my lord."

This seemed to stupefy him for a moment, for his ministrations to his wife ceased.

"My lord, shall I send for the physician for her ladyship?" Hotchkins asked softly.

"I . . ." He seemed to mentally shake himself and then nodded. "Yes, yes, do."

Gage and I returned to our seats, feeling odd standing over Lord and Lady Redditch as the butler departed.

It took several moments longer for the earl to speak again, his eyes wild. "When? How?"

"Just a short time ago. In the street outside. He was attacked."

In deference to the countess's anguish, Gage's explanation was brief and concise, but she still keened like a wounded animal.

"Attacked?" the earl exclaimed, his round face growing red. "By whom?" His eyes flared wide. "You don't mean . . ."

Before he could say the words, the door opened to admit an older woman wearing a phlegmatic expression.

The earl stepped aside as she bustled forward. "She's had a great shock, Hettie."

"So I've heard. Come with me now, my lady," she coaxed,

managing between herself and Hotchkins to usher the weeping Lady Redditch from the room.

Once the door had shut behind them, the earl whirled back around to face us, apparently having relocated his self-possession. "Now, what's this? Don't tell me these bodysnatchers are trying to burk the nobility now."

I studied the earl's face, wondering how natural it was that he'd almost immediately suspected the burkers. It was true the current inquest was featured in all of the newspapers and broadsheets, and so must be on everyone's minds, but none of the criminals had been seen in Mayfair.

The guarded look in Gage's eyes told me he was contemplating the same thing. "Such a scenario makes little sense. For one, I'm sorry to say, your son was stabbed. Though it was the blow he suffered to his head when he collapsed to the pavement that killed him."

"But why wouldn't that make any sense? Stabbing a fellow seems a simpler way of killing him than some of the more contrived methods I've seen mentioned in the papers."

Gage's leg muscles tightened next to mine, telling me he was gathering his patience. "Because a stab wound would immediately alert the medical school or surgeon who purchased the body to the fact there had been foul play."

At first, it appeared the earl might argue further, but then comprehension dawned in his eyes. "Ah, yes. I see." He frowned down at the medallion-patterned Axminster carpet under his feet, his narrow shoulders slumped. "Then what about a footpad? They prowl the streets of Mayfair as well as the East End."

"It's possible," Gage conceded with a frown. "But I searched his pockets. Nothing was taken, and he had quite a healthy bankroll on him."

I glanced at him in surprise, realizing he must have done so after they'd taken the body upstairs.

The earl growled. "Gambling."

"That was my assumption. Did he do so often?"

"Nearly every night. Had the devil's own luck." He shook his head in begrudged wonder. "Never knew a man who had such good fortune with the cards."

My husband's gaze slid sideways to meet mine, and I could tell he was thinking the same thing I was. Perhaps Lord Feckenham was helping that luck along. Perhaps someone found out.

"Wait." Redditch glanced between us in startlement. "You think someone deliberately murdered my heir?"

"The evidence does seem to point in that direction," Gage said.

Redditch sank back into the sofa as if he'd had the wind knocked out of him.

"Does that surprise you?"

He lifted a hand to rub his forehead. "Actually . . . no."

I straightened, surprised by his frank answer.

"Why do you say that?" Gage pressed.

But before the earl could reply, the sound of raised voices in the entry reached us.

"What's happened? Is it Father?"

The earl pushed himself upright as a younger man burst into the room. The sight of the earl seemed to dumbfound him momentarily, for he stood blinking at him. Then his breath left him in a rush and he charged forward.

"Thank heavens! You are well, sir?"

"Yes, my boy," the earl replied, seeming discomforted by his son's concern.

This must be the younger son Lady Redditch had spoken to me about at her ball. The one she'd been eager for me to paint a portrait of. Whether or not he was given over to dissipation, as his mother had jested, I didn't know, but he certainly didn't look it. His build might have been average, but his face and form were more than handsome.

"Then why did Hotchkins send for me so urgently?"

"It's your brother."

His face flushed, and his hands fisted at his sides. "What has he—"

"He's dead," his father stated bluntly, cutting off whatever he was about to say.

A range of emotions swept across the young man's face— shock, alarm, pain—but the one that most interested me, though it had only registered for a brief moment, was relief.

I looked at Gage, curious whether he'd noticed the same thing I had, but he was intent on watching the interplay between the father and son.

"How can that be?" the son was demanding to know. "Has there been an accident?"

"I'll explain in a moment," the earl retorted, silencing him. "First, let me see Mr. Gage and Lady Darby on their way."

With this firm directive, we were forced to follow him out into the hall, where Hotchkins stood waiting to assist us. While Gage helped me into my mantle, the earl pressed a hand to his forehead again, suddenly appearing overwhelmed. His ruddy face had drained of much of its color, and dark circles shadowed his eyes.

"What is to be done now?" he murmured, clearly out of his depths.

Gage accepted his greatcoat before replying in a deceptively indifferent voice. "I can send a servant to Bow Street, if you wish. I am on good terms with a number of the Runners and could recommend one to you."

"A Bow Street Runner?" he contemplated in bewilderment, and then shook his head. "Oh, no, no, no. That will never do." He glanced up at us, his gaze suddenly hopeful. "But you could look into this matter for me, couldn't you? You could figure out who killed my son?"

Gage paused in buttoning his coat. It had been evident, at least to me, from the first that this had been the outcome my husband wished. The earl could not have fallen in with his plans more neatly. However, before accepting, he turned to me, allowing me the chance to object.

After all, we already had an inquiry we were assisting his father with, though as of yet I'd been able to contribute very little. The reactions to our questions would undoubtedly prove awkward once the location of the murder and the inevitable specter of the burking bodysnatchers was raised. But the sticking plaster stashed at the bottom of my reticule also made it impossible for me to say no.

So I nodded my assent.

"We'll call on you tomorrow," Gage told the earl.

CHAPTER EIGHT

Hotchkins, being the exemplary butler he appeared to be, had ordered that the Redditch carriage wait for us after it returned from the theater with the earl and countess. So rather than having to walk the remaining three blocks home, we were able to ride inside the warm town coach. A fact I was grateful for, as the cold night air that had felt so good on my cheeks such a short time ago now sent shivers through my frame.

Seeing this, Gage tucked the lap rug about me before wrapping a strong arm around my shoulders to secure me to his side. "Better?"

"Yes. Thank you."

He gathered my bare hands in his other hand, chafing them lightly while I stared out the window at the passing buildings. "Are you reconciled to us conducting this inquiry? Because if you're not, I can always tell the earl we've changed our minds."

I looked up into his concerned face.

"I'm sure murder, particularly the way this one was presented, was the last thing you wished to see." He sighed. "Especially after such a pleasant evening."

My gaze dropped to where our hands were joined, his tanner in hue and larger than mine. "Actually, I was thinking how glad I was that you and I found him and not someone else," I replied somewhat in chagrin.

"Because someone else would have leaped to the conclusion the killer hoped," he supplied.

"Yes. Even the earl did so, and we never mentioned the sticking plaster."

Gage nodded grimly. "Well, I suppose that tells us one thing about the murder. It was a crime of opportunity. Not so much in the execution, but in the fact that the recent inquest into the burking of that Italian Boy gave the killer a scapegoat. A ready bogeyman to conceal their crime."

"The resurrectionists."

"A friend of mine with the New Police informed me they've already received several reports of attempted burkings, and the number is certain to increase."

Just as it had in the months following the arrest of Burke and Hare in Edinburgh. How many of these complaints would be legitimate and not imagined from a street robbery or other assault, no one could say. But the fear of the populace was real, even here in Mayfair.

Contemplation of Burke and Hare also led me to another thought. "We also know that the killer must be getting his information about burkings from the newspapers and broadsheets. They all depict bodysnatchers holding sticking plasters over people's faces. But during Burke's trial, Hare revealed that they'd plied their victims with drink until they lost consciousness, and then held shut their nose and mouth to make it look like a natural death."

"Yes, but for most people those images in the broadsheets are what stick most in their minds, not the facts of a three-year-old trial," he pointed out.

"True. But doesn't that also mark him an amateur? He plainly never contemplated the technique involved with smothering someone."

"As does his failed attempt to stab Feckenham. Anyone with experience would know to thrust below the rib cage, especially in a heated scuffle. The weapon is much more likely to strike true."

I'd had the same thought when examining the wound. "Did you catch a better glimpse of the killer than I did while you were pursuing him?"

He shook his head. "Much of him was in shadow, and the fog didn't help. All I could tell was that his clothing was dark and well made. Whether it was the cut of a gentleman or something below that, I can't say, but it wasn't the type of garments you'd find at the Rag Fair," he said, referring to the area near the Tower of London where secondhand clothing was sold.

"Yet another indication he wasn't a resurrectionist."

Bodysnatching was a trade for the lowliest figures of society, not those who could afford tailored clothing.

"Whoever he was, either he knew the area or he got dashed lucky and found a good hiding place." Gage flicked aside the curtain drawn over the window as the carriage turned. "I would have kept searching for him, but I didn't want to leave you alone for long on the street with an injured—or dead—man."

"Yes, what if someone else had come along? I can only imagine how that would have improved my reputation," I muttered wryly.

He glanced down at me, his gaze troubled. "I was thinking more of your safety and sensibility, but . . . yes."

I turned into his shoulder, both relieved and touched that he still saw me as someone who needed shelter when so many others thought I hadn't a heart or normal human feelings to be considered.

The carriage slowed to a stop, and while the servants scrambled to let down the step, I asked one more question. "What will your father say about us taking on another inquiry?"

He stiffened. "I suppose we shall find out when I write to him in the morning. But in truth, it's none of his concern."

Before I could respond, he was climbing from the conveyance, and I was forced to bite back my words. For Lord Gage made everything his concern, whether it was or not. And I'd yet to encounter an instance where his interference had been beneficial.

When we returned to Upper Brook Street late the following morning, the earl's door already sported a mourning wreath. Its ribbons dripped with rain, splattering the black and white tiles of the entry hall as the door was opened.

Hotchkins ushered us inside wearing a black armband. "His lordship is just finishing his breakfast, but he asked that you be shown into his study when you arrived."

Considering her agitated state the night before, I expected to find Lady Redditch prostrate with grief, confined to her bedchamber. But the sound of her well-modulated voice carried through the door of what I assumed to be the breakfast parlor across the hall from the study. Most curiously, it did not sound the least bit distressed. Maybe a trifle flat, but nothing approaching the despair we'd witnessed ten hours earlier.

"Her ladyship seems to have recovered rather quickly," I couldn't help but remark as Hotchkins left us to notify the earl.

"Yes," Gage replied, his eyes narrowed in consideration of something unpleasant. "Either she's made of sterner stuff than I'd suspected, or she's not grieving half so much as she wishes us to believe." Clasping his hands behind his back, he turned to peruse the books covering the dark shelves along one wall. "That makes anything she chooses to tell us questionable."

I allowed my gaze to travel over the contents of the room, from the gleaming wooden desk whose surface was clear but for one neat stack of papers, to the ornamental fireplace. A second door stood shut next to the only painting of any interest hanging above a cabinet. All the while, I considered what I knew about the countess, but regrettably it wasn't much. I'd met her a handful of times, and always at balls and soirees where one was least inclined to be genuine.

"Is your father acquainted with the earl?" I asked, leaning closer to examine the brushstrokes of the Cotswolds landscape.

He pulled a book from the shelves to examine it. "I'm sure they're acquainted. But how well, I couldn't say. The earl is a rather prominent Tory, and my father's political beliefs lean more in that direction than any other."

He was returning the book to its place when the earl strode through the door. "So you *are* here. I was half-afraid you'd change your mind." He exhaled as if in relief, but his eyes said otherwise. I began to wonder if he regretted asking us to investigate.

He gestured for us to be seated in the two mahogany caned bergère chairs set before his desk, before settling into the chair behind it. "Now, how do you intend to proceed?"

Gage couched his words in his most diplomatic tone. "First, we'll need to speak with you and your family about Lord Feckenham's activities, particularly in the past few days. And we'll also need to question your staff to discover if anyone might have seen or heard anything that could point us to the killer. Those things will tell us what to do next."

The earl reached out a finger to fiddle with the edge of the blotter on his desk, and then, as if conscious of my eyes scrutinizing him, hastily clasped them in his lap. "Then I suppose you have further questions for me."

"We do."

He nodded. "Go on."

"Do you know what your son's plans were for yesterday evening?"

He sank deeper into his chair. "I'm afraid not. I didn't pay much mind to either of my sons' comings and goings."

"But he was living here, correct? All of your family is?"

Why this question should make him twitch, I didn't know, but he shifted restlessly. "Yes. Both my sons are . . . *were* in residence. My daughters are currently at Silvercrest with their governess."

Gage rested his ankle over his other knee. "Do you have any suspicion what his intentions for yesterday evening were? Any notion to his usual haunts?"

"I believe you're referring to my mention of his gambling. I know he frequented several dens." Redditch's eyes flicked briefly toward me. "As well as other disreputable establishments. But his friends could tell you better than I which those were."

Gage dipped his head once, accepting this answer, though the look in his eyes communicated he didn't believe the earl was quite so ignorant of his heir's movements. In response, the earl's already ruddy complexion reddened further, but he held his gaze.

"Last night, you said you weren't surprised that someone would murder your son," Gage reminded him. "Why?"

At this, the earl's gaze fell to the blotter he no longer resisted touching. "Don't get me wrong, I cared for my son." His gaze lifted. "But that doesn't mean I was blind to his faults. And he had many. He was skilled at driving people into a blinding rage." He sighed heavily. "Including me." His brow furrowed in discontentment. "I'm certain he ruined more than one man at the tables. And he trifled with a few young ladies when he knew better."

At this, Gage's expression turned forbidding. A gentleman did not sully an unwed lady in such a manner.

Redditch scowled in return. "Yes, I know. Fortunately, between the ladies' families and ours, we were able to stifle any rumors before they could begin. Otherwise I would have *forced* Feckenham to offer for them. I would have done so the first time it happened, had I not thought the girl better off escaping such a lot."

Of all the surprising things he'd revealed, this might have been the most astounding of all. Regardless of the gentleman involved, young ladies were almost always considered better off marrying him whether she'd encouraged his attentions or not. That the earl should take her well-being into consideration was not only open-minded, but indicative of his low opinion of his heir.

"Did these young ladies' families agree with you? Might they have desired retribution?" Gage asked.

"I can't say." His jaw hardened. "And neither will I share their names."

My husband began to argue, but Redditch would not be swayed. "I promised them I would never reveal their identities or the scandalous details of the incidents, and nothing shall make me break my word. I owe them that." His chin arched defiantly. "Despite what you may think, I do have my honor, even if my heir had none."

Gage studied the other man across the desk. "I can't fault you for that. And in fact, if it should prove that was the motive for Feckenham's murder, I'm not sure I wouldn't rather it *remain* unknown. I suppose we shall confront that possibility if we come to it."

The two men shared a look of mutual understanding, and I couldn't help but wonder if the earl had broached this subject as a distraction. After all, if he wished to divert suspicion from his family, what better way than to mention the people his son had wronged while also refusing to name names. Anyone who knew a smidgen of Gage's character would realize how outraged he would be on behalf of these young ladies. It was one of the reasons I loved him. But it was also an area in which he might fail to exercise proper restraint and judgment.

A soft rapping broke the silence, though it hadn't come from the door through which we'd entered, but the second door I'd noticed across the room.

"Come in," the earl called.

"My lord, I noticed the numbers . . ." The walnut brown–haired man who entered glanced up from the paperwork he was studying and stumbled to a stop at the sight of us. "My apologies, my lord. I thought you were alone."

"It's no matter, Poole," the earl replied impatiently. "I'll be with you in a moment."

The man bowed and retreated through the door he'd entered. I decided he must be a secretary or steward of some kind.

Redditch tapped the arms of his chair, eager to be finished. "Is there anything else you wished to ask me?"

"That's all for now," Gage replied. "Do you know where we might find her ladyship?"

"Hotchkins will know. And he'll be able to assist you with the staff."

"Of course."

Gage and I rose to our feet, though I noticed as we departed the study that the earl made no move to summon his secretary. Instead, he sat staring out the window behind his desk, his brow puckered and his mouth tight.

Hotchkins directed us to the countess's parlor—a small room wallpapered in silk patterned with pink twining roses. The creamy furniture was dainty and soft, and the fireplace tiled in white marble. Everything was decorated in the height of elegance, except for the half-dozen needlepoint pillows scattered about the furniture. That they'd been embroidered by her daughters, I had no doubt, for the efforts were not altogether successful. But the very fact she kept them displayed so prominently rather than tucked away made me soften toward her. I could well imagine my sister doing much the same thing once my nieces, Philipa and Greer, were old enough to wield a needle.

Pressing a surreptitious hand to the tiny swell of my abdomen, I wondered if this child was a girl who would one day also follow suit.

We were admitted by the same phlegmatic maid who had assisted her mistress the night before. She scrutinized us with a swift glance from head to toe before stepping aside. Much as I'd expected, the countess lounged across a fainting couch, her morning dress covered by a stylish capucine dressing gown. The dark orange color was not one I would have chosen for the countess, but it was actually quite flattering.

At the sight of us, she pushed upright, gesturing for us to take a seat. "My husband told me you would likely wish to speak to me. I *do* apologize for my hysterics last night," she leaned forward to say. "It was such a great shock. I thought I wouldn't be able to bear it." She sighed. "But, of course, one must. For the sake of the family."

Her gaze dipped to the claw-and-ball feet of the tea table, her thoughts dwelling on something specific. Something that tugged the corners of her mouth downward in disapproval. Then she seemed to gather herself, offering us a weary smile. "Tea?" She glanced at her maid, who lingered by the door. "Hettie?"

"Oh, no, thank you," I said.

Gage also declined, and Lady Redditch dismissed her maid with a wave of her hand.

"Now, what can I tell you? I'll answer anything I can. I do so want this villain who killed my son to be found and punished." Her hands tightened into fists as if to choke the life from the person herself.

"We're trying to establish Lord Feckenham's movements during the days and hours before he was killed, to discover what, if anything, might have happened to precipitate his demise."

"Oh, I wouldn't know anything about that," she demurred. "My son wasn't in the habit of confiding in me."

Gage seemed momentarily nonplussed by this swift denial after she'd just assured us she would assist us to find her son's murderer. "So you don't know what his plans were last night?"

She shook her head. "Off to one of his clubs. Or out to dine with some friends. I really can't say."

"When was the last time you spoke with him?" I interjected. Surely she could tell us that.

She tapped her chin. "Let's see. He dined at home three nights past. And then . . . oh! I spoke with him briefly yesterday afternoon."

"About?"

"He was protesting his brother's desire to move to a set of rooms at The Albany. Thought it was silly for him to take up residence elsewhere when the townhouse was large enough for all of us. Personally, I agreed. But my husband wasn't opposed to the move. Said George was merely showing proper feeling for the fact his brother would one day inherit this house while he would not."

I didn't know what to make of this speech. From what I'd observed of Lord Feckenham, he hardly seemed the type of man who cared where his brother lived. In truth, I found it easier to believe he wished his brother to leave than stay. Unless he thought that would place his mother's undivided attention on him. But from all appearances, Feckenham did precisely whatever he wished, regardless of parental feelings.

"Did Mr. Penrose begrudge him that fact?" Gage asked.

"Oh, no! Of course not. He's known, since birth, what is coming to him. And his settlement as a second son is not ungenerous. More generous than most, I should say. He has no cause to complain, and he would be the first to tell you so."

Yes, but a generous settlement is quite different from a venerable earldom and all the wealth and property that goes with it. All of which, with his brother's death, he would now inherit.

As if this same thought had just struck her, her head rocked backward. "My goodness. George shall now inherit. Oh, but that's . . ." She broke off, as if suddenly mindful to whom she was speaking. "Well, I'm not sure he will like that, but he shall simply have to adjust."

I wanted to glance at Gage to see what he thought of this statement, but I couldn't do so without revealing to the countess my interest in it.

"George is such a good boy," she ruminated softly. "Came rushing straight home from White's the moment he learned. He's such a comfort to me."

"I suppose we should speak to Mr. Penrose next, then," Gage informed her.

"Oh," she gasped. "I do apologize. But he's not here."

At this pronouncement, I couldn't help but look at Gage.

"I sent him to Silvercrest to inform his sisters. I thought they should hear of their brother's death from family, not by letter or through some hateful gossip."

I couldn't argue this point. It would be cruel not to inform them in person. But that didn't mean that George Penrose's absence wasn't also suspicious. After all, he was the person who gained the most from his brother's death. Of course, that didn't make him guilty either.

"How soon do you suspect he'll return?" Gage asked.

"A few days. He'll wish to be here for the funeral."

Then we would merely have to accept this delay. And in the meantime, perhaps a stronger suspect would emerge.

CHAPTER NINE

Hotchkins was waiting for us when we emerged from the countess's chamber to inform us the morning room had been set aside for our use in interviewing the servants. And indeed, I was pleased to find it truly had been made ready for us. A tray of refreshments sat on the tea table next to a stack of foolscap and pencils. Gage and I rarely took handwritten notes, at least not before witnesses, but I was grateful for the butler's thoroughness. It was a relief to discover we appeared to have at least one ally in this business.

Now, if his testimony only proved as obliging.

Hotchkins perched at the edge of one of the Gillows fruit-wood armchairs before the hearth, his hands clasped before him as Gage asked his first question.

"Perhaps you can be the person to answer this. Do you know where Lord Feckenham went last night? What his plans were?"

"In general, his lordship did not inform me of his intentions. But as it so happens, he did tell me he was feeling lucky yesterday evening. I took that to mean he meant to visit a gambling establishment of some kind. But, of course, I may be wrong. There are any number of ways one might test one's 'luck.'" He paused. "And sadly, that feeling proved rather quickly to be wrong."

At first, his statement baffled me, but then I realized I had been contemplating the chain of events in error.

"When did Lord Feckenham leave the townhouse last night?" I asked.

"About a quarter of an hour before Mr. Gage came to the door."

So he had just departed for the night, intent on trying his luck, when he was attacked. But then what had waylaid him for ten minutes? The time between when Gage and I happened upon the altercation and Gage knocked on the earl's door had been about five minutes.

Had he and his attacker argued in the street? Somehow that didn't seem right. Few gentlemen carried knives on their person, and the use of the sticking plaster seemed to signal the act was premeditated. Perhaps Feckenham had been returning to the house for some reason. Maybe he'd forgotten something.

"I take it he set out on foot?" Gage asked for clarification.

"Yes, sir."

"Did he intend to hail a hackney?"

"He did not say."

Gage frowned, clearly wondering, as I was, whether his intended destination had been close enough to walk to. "Was there anyone else in the street when he departed?"

The butler's brow furrowed. "I've been considering that very thing, wondering if there might have been someone standing in the shadows. Someone I failed to notice. But at the time, I didn't give the matter much thought. I saw his lordship off and then prepared to retire for the evening. Normally, I would have already retired before he departed, but there were a few matters belowstairs which required my attention. A footman was posted by the door to assist the family when they each returned."

He seemed troubled that he could not recall any further details, but no reasonable person could have expected him to. He couldn't have known Feckenham would be attacked.

"You mention the footman—we'll wish to speak with him next—but what of the rest of the staff? Was anyone else awake at that hour, or would most of them have retired?" Gage asked.

"Lord Feckenham's valet. And the earl and countess's personal servants would have been waiting for their return. In fact, I recall them being seated in the servants' hall when I passed through. But beyond that, the rest of the staff should have been retired." He appeared to ruminate on the matter further. "His lordship's personal secretary, Mr. Poole, was here for some length during the evening. One of the maids took him a cup of tea at about nine o'clock. I'm not certain what time he eventually departed, but the antechamber where he works next to the study was dark when I made my rounds before seeing Lord Feckenham out the door. Perhaps Mr. Poole saw someone lurking nearby when he left the house."

This bit of information made Gage straighten. "Was it unusual for Mr. Poole to be here so late?"

"Not particularly. I don't claim to know the earl's business, but I understand he has many properties to manage, as well as Parliamentary matters to oversee. As such, upon occasion Mr. Poole has remained late in order to finish some task or another for the earl."

"We shall need to speak with him as well, then." Gage studied the butler with a measured gaze that, while not intimidating, let him know he wanted a direct answer. "I'm sure you realize this matter is delicate. That anyone with any motive to see Feckenham dead must be considered, no matter how one might shrink from the possibility."

"You are speaking of the family," the butler replied, his resolve never wavering.

"Yes. I comprehend you must feel some loyalty to them, but the fact of the matter is Feckenham is dead, and someone killed him. That someone could conceivably have been a family member."

At this, Hotchkins seemed to balk, his mouth tightening in disfavor. "The *fact* of the matter is that Feckenham was a brute and a blackguard, of the highest order. I am not surprised he was killed. Someone should have done so long ago." Seeming to recall himself, he straightened his jacket. "But as for it being a family member, I don't believe it. Not in the manner it was done. It would have been far easier to do so quietly and without fuss. No need for such a messy charade."

He did have a point. But what if something had happened to force the killer's hand? What if they had needed him dead *now*, leaving little time for careful planning? So they had seized upon the distraction the London burkers had caused.

Letting him go, Gage turned to me with a frustrated grunt. "Well, it's clear we'll be getting no information from him on the family. And you can be certain he'll instruct the rest of the staff not to share gossip as well."

"Yes, well, there's more than one way to inveigle information from a servant."

His lips quirked. "Bree?"

I leaned forward to pour myself some tea. "My maid is remarkably good at convincing people to confide in her." As evidenced from the number of people she'd gotten to talk to her about their anger and distress over the London burkers. "And perhaps if Anderley can be spared from the other inquiry, he can work his charm on some of the maids." I glanced up to see that Gage's brow had clouded again. "Or perhaps not."

His gaze shifted to meet mine, but he did not speak. He didn't have time to before the footman who had been on duty after Hotchkins retired was shown in to the morning room.

He was young, perhaps no older than twenty, and struggled to sit still in the chair indicated to him. Tall and pleasing to the eye, as all footmen were desired to be—especially in the best households—he at least showed enough poise not to stammer his responses to the questions Gage put to him. Though he did sneak glances at me from time to time, whether out of curiosity that a lady should be present, or because my reputation preceded me.

"Yes, sir. I've been a footman here for two years."

"Do you often mind the door in the evening?" Gage inquired casually, attempting to put him at ease.

"Yes, sir."

His eyes twinkled with humor. "Given the fact there are two young gentlemen in this household, I imagine you've witnessed your fair share of amusing sights. I suspect my footmen have tales to tell about my salad days."

The footman's mouth cracked a smile, but he did not rise to Gage's bait. "Yes, sir."

My husband cleared his throat. "Last night, then. Either before or after Lord Feckenham departed, did you happen to see anyone, or hear anything out of the ordinary?"

When he squeezed his hands together in nervousness, it became apparent he had. "After I took over for Mr. Hotchkins, I peered through the window to see if all was quiet," he began hesitantly.

"And was it?" Gage prodded.

"Yes. Except . . . I saw Lord Feckenham cross the road to speak to someone."

I sat a little taller.

"Did you recognize who it was?"

He shook his head, but his gaze dropped to Gage's chest. "They were too far away. And the fog. No, I didn't recognize him."

Gage didn't say anything for a moment, contemplating the same thing I was, no doubt. That the footman's mouth said he hadn't recognized the man, but his eyes seemed to communicate that he had.

"How long did they stand talking?"

"I don't know. I never peered out the window again. Not until you knocked, sir."

"So you didn't hear Lord Feckenham shout?"

His eyes widened. "No, sir."

Given the dampening effect of fog, if the footman had positioned himself even a short distance from the door, this was possible. The shout had not been overloud. Which also meant that if *he* hadn't heard it, then it was doubtful *anyone* in this house had. But what of the townhouses nearer to the altercation? Had their servants witnessed anything?

The earl's and Feckenham's valets and the countess's maid couldn't tell us anything helpful, or perhaps more accurately, *wouldn't* tell us. It was true enough they hadn't seen or heard anything of the attack on Feckenham, but they were not telling all. Of that I was certain. Whatever secrets this family held, they were not going to be given up lightly, and that made me all the more anxious what they might be.

Jonathan Poole, the earl's secretary, was slightly more forthcoming.

Though rather unremarkable in appearance, he still had a pleasing countenance nonetheless, and a quiet, prepossessing demeanor. Which I supposed was an asset for a man of his position. While educated and of gentle address, he could not call himself a gentleman, because he worked for his living. Yet I suspected he came from a nobler family, perhaps a branch fallen from wealth and distinction. I gauged him to be approximately thirty years of age, older than Feckenham, but younger than my husband. However, fine lines radiated from the corners of his eyes and scored his forehead from squinting over his work by candlelight for so many years.

I had grown accustomed to men of his station during my time wed to Sir Anthony. Most of his colleagues, and the anatomy students he mentored from time to time, were of this ilk, including the dresser and apprentice he employed for a short duration. Though not all of them spoke as genteelly as Mr. Poole.

"How long have you served as secretary to Lord Redditch?" Gage asked him, beginning in much the same manner as he had with the others, garnering their background and familiarity with the family.

Mr. Poole glanced upward, giving this some consideration. "Just over two years. Prior to that I was employed by the elder Lord Vickers before he passed away."

"The social reformer?" I asked in interest.

"Yes, Lord Vickers was greatly concerned with the welfare of the lower classes, and enfranchising more of the population to vote. He was a great advocate for reform."

That was putting it mildly. Some had even accused him of being a revolutionist, eager to follow in France's footsteps.

Mr. Poole's eyes glinted with subtle humor. "You are perhaps wondering how someone who worked for a lord of such liberal views could then work for a staunch anti-Reformist like Lord Redditch."

I smiled, for that was exactly what I was wondering.

"Well, Lord Redditch had shown some inclinations that he was not unwilling to change. He voted for the Catholic Relief Act, after all." He smiled in self-deprecation. "And I suppose I thought I might help continue to persuade him to another way of thinking."

"Does he know this?" Gage asked, as curious as I about this strange working relationship.

"Oh, yes. His lordship might be a determined Tory, but he's not so close-minded that he's averse to hearing well-reasoned arguments for the opposition."

I couldn't help but wonder if he was genuinely as sangfroid about this as he professed. Little as Gage or I was involved in politics, I'd heard Philip's discussions with lords of the opposing faction grow heated often enough to recognize it was not so easy to set such beliefs aside. Or did Mr. Poole place professional advancement above principle and simply did not wish to appear so mercenary?

"Hotchkins told us it's not uncommon for you to work here late into the evening, as you were last night," Gage remarked before taking a sip of tea.

"Yes. Depending on the demands of his lordship's estates or Parliament's schedule, I'm often forced to remain late to finish the draft of something, as I was last night. His lordship prefers to work from home, rather than his offices at Parliament. And I also find working here more comfortable."

"I've heard the Parliamentary offices can be quite drafty."

"Frigid, sir. It cramps the hands during the winter. But my small antechamber here is always warm and I don't have to search far for sustenance." He grinned. "So I don't mind the bit of inconvenience and awkwardness I sometimes must contend with."

"Awkwardness?" I repeated.

"Well, yes. Being in his lordship's house nearly every day, one hears things one might rather not."

"What about yesterday?" Gage gestured nonchalantly. "Did you hear anything awkward then?"

Mr. Poole shook his head. "I'm afraid not. I left the house at about a quarter 'til eleven through the mews, so I never even approached the front of the house."

"Can anyone verify that?" Gage asked calmly. The servants had all been able to vouch for one another, and the earl and countess had shared a box at the theater with four other people, whom we expected would confirm their alibis. Lady Redditch had also volunteered the information, unasked for, that her second son, Mr. Penrose, had been at his club. However, no one had seen Mr. Poole leave.

"I suppose not," Mr. Poole replied, steadily lifting his cup to his lips and then pausing. "Except . . . one of the grooms from the neighboring house tipped his hat to me. He should remember me."

As alibis went, this wasn't very solid. After all, he could have easily circled around to Upper Brook Street and intercepted Feckenham. But the fact that he didn't appear in the least perturbed by the question, or any that we'd set to him thus far, spoke in his favor.

I watched Mr. Poole drink his tea, recognizing he was in a unique position. He was not part of the family, nor was he a longtime servant or under the thumb of Hotchkins. Yet he walked among them, nearly every day, as he'd said. He might be able, and willing, to tell us the information we sought. As long as we didn't press him too hard.

I glanced at Gage, wondering how I might communicate this to him, but I could tell by the manner in which he was scrutinizing the other man, and the way he phrased his next question, that he'd already thought of it.

"Did you have much interaction with Lord Feckenham? What sort of fellow was he?"

The secretary studied the contents of his cup. "I take it you were not well acquainted with his lordship."

"Not in the least."

"Well, then, you should count yourself lucky." His eyes lifted. "Though that's not telling you anything any number of gentlemen wouldn't happily inform you of." He tilted his head. "I suspect Lord Redditch has told you of his gambling and past . . . indiscretions." At this word, his jaw tightened in disapproval, the first ill-disposed display of emotion we'd seen from him.

"He has," Gage admitted, unable to keep his own censure from tainting his voice.

The two men regarded each other, and whatever Mr. Poole saw in my husband's eyes—be it his mutual aversion to scoundrels or another of his noble qualities—seemed to settle him in our favor.

"I can tell you he tried Lord Redditch's patience sorely," he confided as he leaned forward to set his cup on the tea table. "But the British inheritance laws being what they are, there was little he could do. He could threaten to cut him off, but then Lord Feckenham didn't need his money. And . . ." He hesitated, seeming uneasy about what he must say next. "I think Lord Redditch was afraid of what his son might do if he was not looking over his shoulder."

Gage's expression registered the same startlement I felt. For if Feckenham would go so far as to compromise young ladies for sport while under the earl's watchful gaze, then what did Lord Redditch worry his son would do if he was not monitoring him?

"Has the earl . . ." Gage began, but Mr. Poole cut him off before he could finish.

"It's merely an impression." He watched us guardedly, as if worried he'd said too much. "The earl has never said anything to that effect, but I've watched them together. I've seen the way he looks at his heir, particularly when Lord Feckenham isn't paying attention."

I appreciated his insight, and I was inclined to respect his judgment. As far as I could tell, he had no reason to lie about such a thing.

He rubbed his hands on the legs of his trousers, a nervous gesture I suspected he wasn't even aware he was making. "I can tell you Lord Redditch didn't trust his heir. But I will not tell you why I know that. I cannot," he stated firmly. "So you will have to decide for yourself whether to believe it."

Gage nodded, realizing he was referring to some legal issue, one we would have to uncover the truth of in another way. "What of his second son? Does Lord Redditch trust him?"

Mr. Poole sat tall and searched Gage's eyes, as if he was trying to figure out what he was thinking. "They have their differences, as all fathers and sons do. But yes, he trusts him."

"And how did Lord Feckenham treat his brother?"

He frowned. "Abominably. But if you're asking what I think you are, then I will tell you unequivocally, no." He shook his head. "Mr. Penrose did not kill his brother. It's true they had no great love for each other, but he did not covet his title. If you knew him, even slightly, you would realize he is incapable of such a thing."

I was somewhat taken aback by his defense of George Penrose, but given the brother he was being compared to, it would be a wonder if Mr. Poole did not prefer the second son to the first. I also pondered whether Mr. Penrose's political leanings were not more aligned with Mr. Poole's. Lord Feckenham's certainly weren't.

"Then I shall have to remedy that situation. As soon as he returns to town," Gage added with a trace of sarcasm.

Mr. Poole comprehended his meaning immediately. "I told Lord Redditch he should not send his son to Silvercrest without first allowing him to speak to you. That it was bound to arouse misgivings. But he would not naysay Lady Redditch, who was most anxious for their daughters."

Gage's head sank back, considering his words. "I cannot fault her concern for her daughters, but you are right. It does arouse suspicions. He is now his father's heir, after all. But I am assured he will return in a few days' time, and then hopefully he will be able to convince me to put those doubts aside."

Mr. Poole responded affably to this reasonableness. "I will send a note around to you the moment I become aware of his return. But if I am familiar enough with his character, I suspect he will already have done so himself."

"Let us hope."

For despite his assurances to the contrary, George Penrose was still our best suspect.

CHAPTER TEN

As Mr. Poole left us, Hotchkins entered the room, his face rigid with disapproval. "Sir, there are newspapermen gathered at our front door."

This did not seem to surprise Gage. "Well, it was only a matter of time before they got wind of the crime. It *is* the murder of an earl's son, after all. And on the streets of Mayfair, no less." He reached into the inside pocket of his hazelnut frock coat. "I suggest you ignore them as best you can. And tell the staff to say nothing to them unless they wish to have their words twisted in the papers." He rose to his feet, passing one of his calling cards to the butler. "Have a footman go around the house through the mews and pass this to a fellow with thick red facial hair. He'll likely be wearing a flashy waistcoat, and goes by the name of Phineas Day."

"With the *Observer*?"

"Yes. And Hotchkins," he called after the butler as he turned to leave. "I shouldn't worry they'll be out there long." He glanced at the window, where rain streamed down the glass in rivulets. "Not in this weather."

He nodded and departed.

"Why are you giving Mr. Day your card?" I asked.

"Because it has occurred to me that speaking to a reporter could be quite useful."

I turned to face Gage more fully. "How do you mean?"

"For one, I have no desire to knock on all the doors in this street and ask to question their staff. But in exchange for a few details about the inquiry, I'm sure Mr. Day will be happy to place a request in his paper for anyone who saw or heard any-thing suspicious in the vicinity of Upper Brook Street on the night of November tenth, to notify us. I could send some of the lads I've employed in the past to uncover this information, but I have another task in mind for them."

"Then why do you not address them all?"

He reached for my hand. "Because that would create a spec-tacle. And that is something we do not want." His eyes dipped to where his thumb traced a pattern on my skin. "Not to men-tion the fact that I've noticed newspapermen feel absolutely no qualms about asking the most impertinent questions when they are vying with each other for answers. But one-on-one, they are almost always respectful."

I grasped what he was implying. He was afraid they would ask brazen questions about me, about any connection I might have to the London burkers. But that was not all I'd perceived. "You've done this before."

His lips curled into the semblance of a smile. "From time to time. The chaps are most persistent here in London, but as I said, they have their uses."

"Aren't you worried they'll twist your words as well?"

"They wouldn't dare," Gage replied blithely. "For they know I'll correct them in the other newspapers and never choose to inform them first about an inquiry again. You see, I don't always use Mr. Day. I choose between a half dozen or so who have impressed me with their integrity." He pushed to his feet, crossing to the window to look out over the garden. "It's quite effective really. The newspaper I've chosen gets to publish the information I share before all the others, who will then include the information in their next editions. All without the fuss of my speaking to a mob of insolent hacks."

I had to admit, it was rather a good arrangement. Of course, it meant the spread of our request for information would be slower than we might wish, but sometimes that could not be helped. If the other newspapers did not post the full story until Sunday or Monday, we would have to be satisfied that was soon enough.

I glanced toward where Gage stood watching the rain. "Are we going to wait here until they leave?"

"No. I don't see any men lurking near the garden gate, so I'm going to have the carriage brought around to the mews." He looked back at me. "Unless you wished to stay?"

I shook my head, weary from the day's questionings but trying to conceal it.

In short order, he bustled me down the garden path, holding an umbrella over our heads, and out the gate to the carriage waiting beyond. If there were any newspapermen loitering nearby to intercept us, we couldn't hear them through the drumming of the rain. The umbrella was passed to the footman, the carriage door secured, and we were on our way, no worse for wear save for a few water spots on my woolen skirts and a bit of mud on my half boots.

I stifled a yawn, blinking my eyes to stay alert as we turned out of the mews and gathered speed. "I've been thinking. Would it be worthwhile to discover who has purchased sticking plasters from apothecaries recently?"

"I had the same thought. Though it's just as likely our killer took them from the supplies in their home, or someone else's."

He frowned. "We'll have to find a way to ask Redditch's house-keeper without arousing suspicions. But for the sake of thor-oughness, I'm going to send those lads I mentioned I've employed in the past to ask around."

"What of the knife?" I asked, suppressing another yawn. "From what I could see, it appeared rather narrow."

He turned to look at me, his eyes trailing over my features. "Yes. Some sort of Scottish dirk perhaps, though I did not get a good enough look at it to say for certain."

"Do you suppose our killer could be Scottish, then?"

"Maybe. But I've known plenty of Englishmen who possess such blades as well. So I don't think we can conclusively say."

I nodded and covered my mouth with my hand as a wide yawn popped my jaw.

His gaze turned tender. "Darling, why don't you rest your head on my shoulder and close your eyes?"

"It's merely a yawn."

"Your fifth one. Sixth." His own mouth cracked open. "And now you have *me* doing it. So for heaven's sakes, listen to your husband," he teased, draping an arm around my back to pull me to his side.

"Very well," I huffed, allowing my head to loll against him. "But we're almost home."

"Where you're promptly going up to our bedchamber to rest for an hour."

"I will do no such thing," I retorted, lifting my head to glare at him. I wasn't entirely certain why I was arguing with him when such a suggestion sounded delightful, but I resented his imperiousness.

He pressed my head back to his chest. "You will if I have to carry you there myself. In any case, I would rather not have you about when Mr. Day arrives. It would be best if I speak with him alone."

I conceded this was probably wise, lest the newspaperman's

inquisitiveness be stretched too far. But that didn't mean I liked being ordered about. "I'm not made of porcelain. You need not treat me with kid leather gloves."

"No, but perhaps I wish to do so. You are my wife, after all. And you are carrying my child." At this, he lifted his hand to gently press it to the swell of my belly. "It's my privilege to see to your comfort."

It was difficult to object when he phrased it like that, and with such affection. All I could do was sigh in acquiescence.

His mouth lowered to my temple. "Once Mr. Day leaves, I'll join you."

His warm breath feathering over my ear sent a frisson of awareness through me, just as he knew it would. However, I was a quick study, and the six months of our marriage had taught me much about how to tease my husband in return.

Feeling the carriage slowing to a stop, I arched my chin to look up at him, tossing him a saucy look through my lashes. "Then you'd better finish his interview quickly, or else I might lose interest."

I sat upright, turning toward the door, but Gage pulled me back to him. I laughed.

"Lose interest, will you?" he murmured against my lips. "Then I'll simply have to make sure that doesn't happen."

His mouth captured mine, driving out all other thoughts. When the footman opened the door, he released me, a spark in his eyes that promised much more. I entered the house in a haze of anticipation, acutely aware of my husband watching me as I removed my outer garments.

"Has a Mr. Day called to see me?" he asked Jeffers.

"No, sir."

"Well, he shall be in short order. Show him into my study."

"Very good, sir. This arrived for you a short while ago."

Gage finally tore his eyes away from me to accept the missive. His brow furrowed as he examined the seal and the handwriting.

I moved closer as he broke it open to scan the pages. Looking over his shoulder, I could tell from the permanship that it was from his father, and felt a pulse of annoyance. His correspondence always signaled inconvenience or trouble for us, and I was sure this would prove no different.

"We're being summoned," he bit out mockingly.

And I was certain that was exactly what he meant. Lord Gage never requested. He commanded.

"He wants us to report to his townhouse as soon as possible." He folded the missive, offering it to me.

I shook my head. I felt no desire to read his caustic words. "Then shall we go?" I sighed, feeling the weariness that had melted away under my husband's attentions return tenfold.

His jaw firmed. "No. He can wait. I have matters to discuss with Mr. Day, and you need to rest. An hour's delay will not make much difference, despite what my father might think."

I smiled at him in approval, and the hard look in his eyes softened.

"Do you wish me to send Bree to you?"

"No."

He pressed a kiss to my temple. "Then go on. I'll wake you in an hour or so."

I hadn't missed the fact he'd said *he* would wake me, and let him see that knowledge in my eyes as I gazed at him over my shoulder while striding toward the staircase.

It was rather more like two hours later that Gage and I finally presented ourselves at Lord Gage's home in Hill Street. My husband had been right. A short rest and his inspired attentions had revived me and relieved Gage of some of the tension which always beset him when forced to confront his father. As such, we were both in equitable spirits when we were ushered into Lord Gage's drawing room.

But a short distance from Berkeley Square, Hill Street was a more fashionable address and boasted larger homes than Chapel Street. Our little townhouse stood only a few blocks away, still situated in Mayfair, but the difference was striking. Lord Gage's interest in his abode lay in status and pretention, while Gage preferred privacy and comfort. Of course, one day the Hill Street house would be his, as would his father's title, and perhaps by then we would welcome the extra space. For now, I was quite satisfied with our dwelling and couldn't care less if most of our neighbors were gentry and wealthy tradesmen rather than nobility.

Lord Gage's drawing room was an airy chamber painted in a shade of soft rose gray. However, this delicate color was where my enjoyment of the room ended. The moldings, woodwork, and drapes were all white, as was much of the furniture, and every-where there was gilt. Gilt mirrors and platters. Gilt sconces and trim. Gilt spindles and brackets. I had seen enough London draw-ing rooms to understand this was purported to be the height of elegance, but I found it cold and gaudy.

Worst of all was the artwork, which was the type that had been chosen solely because it matched the room's aesthetic, rather than for the particular skill of the artist, or the emotion it stirred, or the personal connection the owner felt to the subject. It made me want to curl my lip in disgust every time I was forced to look upon it. I'd tried to broach the subject with my father-in-law once but had soon realized he cared as little for art as I did for becoming a successful political hostess. It seemed we were hope-lessly mismatched in our desires for the other.

My steps faltered at the sight of Lord Melbourne rising from his chair before the hearth. His thick dark hair had largely gone to gray, as had the large swaths of facial hair down the sides of his face. However, it was his hooked nose and bushy eyebrows, which moved up and down expressively, that were his most prominent features. At fifty-two, he was still a striking man, even standing in the shade of Lord Gage's charms.

I didn't know quite what to expect from Melbourne's presence, but at least I could count on Lord Gage being civil. Abhorring deleterious gossip, he always treated me with faultless politeness in public now that my union to his son was sealed. It was only in private that he turned his cold hauteur on me.

Once greetings were exchanged and we were settled before the fire, Lord Gage moved straight to the point of our summons.

"I don't know how much leisure you've had to read the newspapers, given how busy you are . . ." Though his tone was genial, his sharp gaze made it clear he had noted the late hour of our arrival. "But there has been a grave development in the Italian Boy inquiry."

"I heard the coroner's jury finally returned their verdict at half past ten last night," Gage replied evenly, refusing to be baited. "'Willful murder against some person or persons unknown,' just as expected. Is there more? Has the boy finally been identified?"

"Not yet." Melbourne braced his elbows on the arms of his chair, clasping his hands together in front of him as he examined us both in turn. "And to be sure, his unknown identity is troubling, but that is not the grave development we speak of." His gaze locked with Gage. "You are perhaps familiar with James Corder, the Covent Garden vestry clerk?"

"Yes. I've made the man's acquaintance."

"Well, given the obvious similarities to the Burke and Hare murders, I asked him to report to me directly any pertinent discoveries once the verdict came in. I received a hand-delivered letter from him last night at eleven o'clock."

The matter must have been urgent for him to have felt the need to apprise him of it at such a late hour.

His formidable eyebrows rose. "Apparently, in the course of the inquiry, it was disclosed that several boys of similar age to the deceased have, in fact, gone missing. But more than that, there seems to be grounds for assuming that they have, with the Italian

Boy, been the victims of the resurrectionists who supply the medical schools."

Gage and I shared an apprehensive look. We and Lord Gage had come to this uneasy suspicion several days past, but to have it seemingly confirmed was horrifying.

"Then the Italian Boy is likely not the first victim of such an appalling crime—whether or not they were committed specifically by the men who are accused of killing him or by other resurrectionists—and he may not be the last," Gage surmised.

The home secretary leaned forward in agitation. "Worse still, this has all now been made public knowledge, aired before all at the hearing."

"The newspapers have already seized upon it," Lord Gage added in forbidding tones. "They will stir the populace into a frenzy."

Melbourne nodded dully, his eyes staring unseeing at the floor. "First the unrest over the failure to pass the Reform Bill, and now this. London is a simmering pot waiting to boil over. If this matter is not handled with utmost care, we could have a full-fledged rebellion on our hands."

"You *must* consider passing emergency legislation against sedition," Lord Gage coaxed, clearly picking up the thread of an earlier argument.

Melbourne seemed to consider his words for a moment but then shook his head. "No. Stifling the press would only increase the public's ire. I will trust in the normal rule of law and our New Police to keep the peace."

I agreed with him, and I could tell Gage did as well, for his shoulders relaxed from the position they'd taken up around his ears after his father had made the suggestion.

Melbourne's eyes were deeply troubled. "But measures must be taken. I told Corder to find out how it's possible that so many young people could go missing without anyone noticing."

I glanced between the two older men, wondering if they were

truly as clueless as their expressions implied. "Surely you're aware that, despite the Vagrancy Act, there are hundreds of children still sleeping on the street," I ventured to say, having taken interest in several charities which aimed to help them. "Orphaned and destitute, or afraid to return home because of the rough treatment they receive. Some of them are sent out to beg for money and told not to return unless they have it." Covent Garden, in particular, was notorious for the number of children who slept beneath the market stalls or among the fruit and vegetable baskets, trying to escape the cold.

Melbourne sighed, crossing one leg over the other as he turned his gaze toward the fire. "Yes, I've been apprised of the issue. I'm informed many of the constables are prone to take pity on them, and so do not round them up as they are supposed to. That many of them have already run away from the parish workhouse several times." He glanced up, his face drawn. "But some of these boys reported missing are not among the destitute. They're sons of respectable tradesmen. Indeed, one of these fathers wept openly in court. If even they can disappear, what chance do the street children have?"

Instinctively, my arm lifted to cradle my stomach, as if I could somehow shield myself and my unborn child from such realities. The thought of someone harming him or her, of killing him in order to sell his body to a medical school for profit, sent a quiver down my spine and a chill through my body.

I glanced up to find Lord Gage watching me. He had seen my protective gesture. But rather than sneer at me, as I'd half expected, his gaze seemed almost gentle. Given the fact he'd never looked at me with such kindness, I could be excused my astonishment. This reaction must have registered on my face, for his lips curled into a smile of mild chagrin as he turned away.

"What of the medical schools?" Gage asked. "Can't they be called to give an account of the bodies they've procured from resurrectionists in, say, the past three months? Wouldn't that tell you whether an inordinate amount of children have been sold to the interests of science?"

"Yes, and many of them have already done so," Melbourne confirmed. "But you must grasp that the situation is an embarrassing one, for the medical profession and the legal one."

This was an understatement if ever I'd heard one. There were laws against the illegal exhumation of a corpse, but the crime was only a misdemeanor. The theft of the property of a corpse carried a far stiffer penalty than the actual theft of the body. Still, I would wager there were a fair number of resurrectionists who had served short prison sentences for bodysnatching, but few, if any, medical professionals who had served time for providing impetus for the crime. The courts knew what was happening, and yet this covert official connivance went largely unchecked and unchallenged. Until Burke and Hare. And now this new case of Bishop, Williams, and May.

"So we may never know the truth," Gage summarized, sinking deeper into the settee on which we perched. His furrowed brow communicated his frustration.

Personally, I thought it improbable even a moderate amount of children had been trafficked to the anatomists without someone noticing the irregularity and raising an outcry. There were only so many places to sell corpses. London had four hospital medical schools and about a dozen and a half private anatomy schools, in addition to a handful of anatomists who required corpses for their own research, like Sir Anthony. Most of these men were not monsters. They were simply trapped in an impossible situation. They needed bodies in order to teach their surgical students, and the legal supply of them from executed criminals was not even remotely enough to meet the need.

No, if burkers were at work in the city, they would be after adults, particularly men. Their corpses would draw little attention, so long as they appeared to have died by natural causes. But I also knew that the truth didn't really matter. The terrified populace of London would assume any missing children had been burked, regardless of how illogical such an assumption was.

However, I didn't say any of this aloud. No need to draw any more attention to my past than necessary. Especially with Lord Melbourne seated among us.

The statesman dipped his head in acknowledgment. "Just so. So from this point forward we must focus our efforts on keeping it from happening again." He inhaled a deep breath, shifting his shoulders so that he faced us more squarely. "But that is a matter for the Home Office and the New Police to handle. Lord Gage called you here because I wish to know about this murder of Redditch's heir. Word has reached my ears that you are investigating the matter."

Gage confirmed this. "We actually witnessed the attack on Lord Feckenham, and if not for the fog I might have apprehended the culprit."

His eyebrows lifted in surprise. "You're the ones who found him?"

"Yes."

"Then you can tell us if the whispers we've been hearing in some quarters are true."

I glanced at Gage in apprehension.

"What whispers?" he murmured.

Melbourne leaned forward. "That Feckenham's death was the work of a burker. That they're now haunting the streets of Mayfair."

CHAPTER ELEVEN

My stomach dropped at this pronouncement. We had antic-ipated such rumors sprouting up, though we'd never ex-pected they would be entertained by the people who would whisper them into the ear of the home secretary.

Gage held my gaze, silently sharing my disquiet.

When neither of us spoke for some seconds, Lord Gage was shocked into speech. "It's true, then?"

"No. It wasn't a burking. We're certain of that." Gage scowled. "The culprit only wanted it to appear like it was, to conceal his real motive. And he might have succeeded, or at least raised doubts, if the act wasn't so poorly executed." He explained the crime and the manner in which we'd found the body. "But most telling of all . . ." our eyes met again ". . . was the sticking plaster partially covering the face. The murderer was obviously emulating the images he'd seen in the broadsheets, without suc-cess. It was the blow to the head that killed Feckenham, not suffocation."

Melbourne and Lord Gage both appeared deeply displeased by this information.

"Then the rumor is certain to circulate through the papers." Melbourne stifled a curse.

"Not for long," Gage replied in a leading tone of voice that made both men sit up and take notice. "We disposed of the sticking plaster before fetching assistance, so no one outside of this room, save the killer, knows of it."

Lord Gage looked upon us with reluctant approval, but the home secretary had no trouble voicing his approbation.

"Good man! Your father said you were quick on your feet."

"I also relayed a few strategic bits of information to Mr. Day with the *Observer* this afternoon. By Monday all of Mayfair will believe that Feckenham was the victim of a thief with a knife."

"By Jove! Well, that is good to hear." He sat forward, smacking his leg. "And now I am assured I can leave this matter safely in your hands. Any suspects?"

"Nothing conclusive yet. But the family is not being entirely forthcoming."

A rap on the door, followed by the entry of Lord Gage's butler, stopped Gage from saying anything more.

"Excuse me, my lord." The butler bowed. "But this was just delivered for Lord Melbourne."

Melbourne nodded, taking the letter from the proffered silver salver. "Understandable given Feckenham's reputation," he replied as he broke open the seal, swiveling in his chair to better catch the light of the fire. "You'll likely find he ruined the wrong man at the tables."

We sat quietly as he perused the missive. While we'd been chatting, the afternoon light had all but faded to night. The butler moved about the room, turning up several lamps to combat the gloom of the day, and then departed. Meanwhile, I couldn't help but notice the growing concern deepening the brackets at the corners of Melbourne's mouth.

When the door had closed behind the butler, Melbourne lowered the note. "Bishop's and Williams's wives have been arrested. Little surprise there. Given the small size of the home, the police are convinced they must have known about the killing. But apparently they were found at the Fortune of War pub with a petition they intended to use to apply for support from the various surgeons Bishop was known to supply."

Gage glowered in affront, but Lord Gage only shook his head. "Why am I not surprised such people would resort to blackmail?"

"It's a common practice. One most of the surgeons and anatomists do not scruple at," I retorted before I could bite my tongue. My father-in-law's derisive response had made my temper bristle, for I could not help but feel some empathy for these ladies. The police accused them of, at the very least, willingly concealing their husbands' actions, but the truth was they'd probably been bullied and beaten, and threatened with much worse if they did not obey their husband's orders. I knew all too well what that was like.

I lowered my chin, shrinking into myself in the face of Lord Gage's and Melbourne's stares. However, Gage's hand stole into mine where it lay clenched in my lap, calming my inner turmoil. "After all, it's not the surgeons who face prison if their suppliers are arrested in the process of procuring what they need for their work," I continued more sedately. "So in order to keep them loyal and content, most medical men are happy to exert their influence to try to get the charges dropped, or provide funds for bail, attorney's fees, jail comforts, or support for the resurrectionist's family if they are not. Though, in such circumstances, the resurrectionists in question are usually accused of illegally disinterring a corpse, not murder," I acknowledged.

"And you know this *because* . . . ?" Lord Gage bit out. The vein throbbing in his temple indicated that he thought I'd lied to him about my knowledge of bodysnatchers.

"I stumbled across one such letter when it had been slipped under the door of our home for Sir Anthony." I hadn't expected an explanation when I later gave it to him, but my confusion must have been evident and his mood jovial enough that he'd condescended to give me one.

Melbourne considered this information and then nodded. "That makes sense. I've been told these resurrectionists can be vindictive fellows when their demands aren't met. Leaving body parts or even entire disfigured corpses strewn about an enemy's home." He wrinkled his nose. "It's a nasty business."

None of us responded to this. There was no need to.

He pushed to his feet. "Well, I must be off. Keep me apprised of these goings-on in Mayfair through your father," he instructed Gage before dipping a shallow bow to me.

Lord Gage escorted him to the door of the drawing room, murmuring to him in a low voice. My husband took the opportunity to lower his head closer to mine. "Are you well?"

"Yes," I replied, comforted by his concern. I traced the pattern of the brocade cushion between us with my eyes. "It's funny the things that come back to you. I hadn't thought of that letter in years." Or Sir Anthony's peculiarly merry reaction to it. I never could predict what sort of temper he would be in. When I'd thought he would be furious, he instead responded with laughter, and when I thought him calm and complacent, he would suddenly erupt in violence. It was all part of the terror of living with him, and why I'd tried to avoid him. As naturally as possible. If my evasion of his person became too obvious, he would take savage delight in it, which was always a dangerous state to find him in.

I glanced up to find Gage studying me, his jaw taut, as if he'd read my thoughts. Stuffing the memories back down inside me, I forced a smile, trying to reassure him. But that only seemed to trouble him more.

"How do you propose to proceed with this Feckenham

investigation?" Lord Gage inquired as he lifted the tails of his coat and settled back into his chair. "Anything I can assist with?"

Gage sat straighter again, releasing my hand. "We need to speak with the younger son, but he's been sent to their country estate to inform his sisters of their elder brother's death."

Lord Gage's eyebrows arched at this, and Gage's lip curled in sardonic agreement.

"We've been assured he'll return in a few days. Beyond that, we need to speak with a few of Feckenham's friends, find out which gaming hells he was known to haunt, and which characters might have wished him to the devil."

His brow lowered. "The earl didn't know?"

"He said not," Gage replied, though his tone conveyed his doubt.

"Why would he deny knowing such a thing?" I ruminated, having stewed over this same question myself. "Surely he must realize we'll discover the answer from other quarters."

"Perhaps it's out of some delayed fatherly devotion. Maybe he feared he'd been too harshly critical of his son."

I blinked in surprise as Lord Gage spoke these words, his eyes trained on the ceiling in thought. Could this insight have come from his own personal reflections, or was he merely speculating? Whatever the truth, I could tell from the wide-eyed uncertainty in my husband's eyes that he'd been just as taken aback.

"Maybe . . ." I conceded, studying the two men. "Except in the next breath he informed us of how his son had trifled with multiple young ladies."

Lord Gage did not seem surprised by this. "I'd heard whispers of something to that effect, but only about Paddington's niece. Miss Holt was her name, I believe. Though now she's Lady Wilmot."

We'd been informed of Miss Holt's engagement to the notorious scoundrel Lord Wilmot a year before, though there had been no mention of Miss Holt having been compromised. And by a different gentleman. But I supposed the matter hadn't been generally known.

Lord Gage sneered. "I suppose it comes as no surprise, given Lord Feckenham was known to run with Lord Wilmot's set. The two likely cooked up the matter together. Otherwise Paddington, as Miss Holt's guardian, would never have agreed to a match with Wilmot, the fortune-hunting bounder."

This mention of Lord Wilmot's set did not come as welcome news, for I knew of someone else who had once been counted among them, and I did not relish asking him for information about the men he once called friends. It was certain to cause us both a great deal of embarrassment.

Wrapped up in my own concerns, I failed to notice the tension caused by another part of this pronouncement until Gage spoke. "I don't suppose you're still on easy enough terms with Lord Paddington to ask him about the matter?"

His father cast him a withering glare. "And all but accuse the man, or one of his relatives, of having something to do with Feckenham's murder? Paddington is no idiot. He'll grasp rather quickly why I would dare to broach such a delicate subject with him." He shook his head. "No. You're on your own there. And I strongly advise against questioning him unless you have some solid evidence for doing so. Your rejection of his daughter, no matter how pretty a tale they wove about the matter, is rather a sore subject with him."

"I never rejected Lady Felicity," Gage snapped, nearly leaping to his feet in his fury. "A few dances and a handful of drives in the park does not an offer make. Especially when she was doing the same with any number of other eligible gentlemen. *You* and Paddington were the ones who decided upon the attachment."

"Which was as good as done when you suddenly balked and rode off to Scotland."

Where he'd met me.

The black look Lord Gage flicked at me clearly communicated this. *I* had foiled his plans. Gage's feelings didn't matter, nor did his insistence that he'd had no intention of marrying Lady Felicity whether he'd fallen in love with me or not.

The corner of Gage's jaw leaped as he choked back the words that had already been spoken too many times to no avail. "None of this is of the moment," he finally managed to say. "I shall heed your council and avoid questioning Paddington unless necessary. Heaven knows I don't want to speak to the pompous prig either."

Ire flashed in Lord Gage's eyes, and it appeared he was about to rise to the defense of his old friend. But then he slumped deeper into his chair, as if growing as weary of this tedious argument as we were. He actually unbent so much as to tip his head, propping it up with his fingers. "What of your valet? Has he had any luck with these Italians who claimed they recognized the murdered boy?"

I glanced at Gage in curiosity.

He sighed. "Not yet. But you know I will send word as soon as I have anything to report."

I was still pondering this matter when we returned to our carriage a short time later, the rain drumming sharply against the roof. "I didn't know you'd tasked Anderley to look further into discovering the Italian Boy's identity beyond the inquest."

"Yes. He's familiar with the area of London where they live," he muttered, digging his fingers into his temples.

I pushed his hand away and arched upward so I could clasp his forehead between my hands, rubbing my fingers in circles to relieve his discomfort.

He sank his head back against the plush morocco leather squabs with a tiny groan. "Thank you." His hands lifted to loosely clasp my waist to steady me as the carriage jostled over something in the road. "I suppose I shall have to seek out Lord Wilmot to find out more about Feckenham's reprehensible habits." He grimaced, either from the pain of his headache or the task before him. "Though I am loath to do so."

"I've been told Lord Wilmot is a scoundrel."

"Yes. But there are scoundrels, and then there are Scoundrels."

I slowed my ministrations, and he cracked open his eyes to see my confusion.

"Let me put it this way. Our dubious friend, the Marquess of Marsdale, has proved himself to be a rascal and a rake and would no doubt seek to seduce you if he had you alone . . ."

I scoffed. "He might try."

His lips creased into a smile. "But I do not quail at your being in his company. For I've learned that while his comments are often quite outrageous, and his manner irreverent, he is not without scruple or honor. Nor would he force himself on you or allow you to come to harm." His face darkened. "However, Lord Wilmot, as far as I can tell, hasn't the least amount of integrity or principle. He does what he wishes, and be damned to everyone else."

I was astonished to hear him speak in such a harsh manner. Gage was not one to bandy such words lightly. "Then why hasn't he been blackballed by most of the ton?"

"Because he's a sly one. Knows who to cozen and manipulate when necessary. And his marriage to Paddington's ward has gotten him back into some people's good graces."

I contemplated this for a moment before hesitantly offering a solution. "Perhaps we don't need to go to him for information. I know someone else who might be able to give it to us."

Gage slanted a gaze up at me again. "Who?"

"My brother."

His pale blue eyes opened wide. "By gad! I'd forgotten St. Mawr fell in with their lot for a short time. Though it's been over a year since I've heard his name in connection with them." He scrutinized me. "How did you know about that? Did Philip tell you?"

"No, my brother told me himself. He was rather ashamed of it." My chest pinched as I recalled that painful conversation. "I gather he punched someone in Almack's for insulting me after my scandal and caused some other trouble, which got him shunned from much of polite society for a time. He was angry and resentful, and fell in with the wrong lot. But fortunately he came to his senses before he lost more than he could mend." A sudden thought struck me, and my ministrations faltered. "Goodness! I wonder if Trevor lost money to Feckenham."

"I should say it's likely, but I imagine he paid him his debt long ago."

"Yes, I'm sure."

Still, I wasn't certain I liked my brother having any such connection to the odious man. Not with this investigation hanging over us.

I shook myself, resuming the kneading motion of my fingers. "In any case, he probably knows things about Feckenham that others don't."

"It's worth asking him." He gritted his teeth. "Especially if it means avoiding Wilmot."

"Stop that." I brushed a hand over his jaw, trying to smooth the tension away. "You're only making it worse."

"It's this blasted weather." The corners of his eyes crinkled at my skeptical look. "And my father."

"Well, stop thinking about him, or anyone else for that matter. We're going to enjoy a nice quiet evening at home, *not* discussing suspects, or murder, or resurrectionists." I feathered my fingers through his hair behind his ears, enjoying the warmth that leaped into his eyes. "I've had quite enough of that for one day."

"Is that an order?" he teased.

"Most certainly. And should your legendary charm suddenly desert you . . ." I leaned closer ". . . I'm sure I can divert you to some suitable topics."

His hands tightened where they gripped my waist, pulling me even closer as his eyes trailed over my features, leaving little licks of heat. "Oh, I already find you most diverting."

"Do you?"

"Yes. But as far as suitable topics, I'm afraid I shall have to object." A roguish glint entered his eyes. "I would much rather discuss unsuitable ones."

I smiled coyly. "Like the shape of the mole on Lady Perkins's face?"

He threw his head back and laughed. "No, you minx. Like the delightful shade of pink you flush when I . . ."

"Sebastian," I chided breathlessly.

This time when he laughed, he did so against my mouth, before applying himself to make me do just that.

CHAPTER TWELVE

"Good morning," I remarked cheerfully as I entered the breakfast parlor the next day to find Gage already enjoying his meal. He made to rise, but I pushed him back down, brushing a kiss to his cheek as I rounded the table to my seat.

"Lovely weather today," I remarked to Jeffers as he pushed in my chair for me. Sunshine streamed through the windows, drying the rain-kissed garden and sodden walkways strewn with damp leaves and burning away the chill of the night.

"Yes, my lady. Mrs. Alcott believes it shall last through the weekend."

"Does she? Then it undoubtedly will." Our cook seemed to be a fount of weather predictions, and most of them proved to be true. "Perhaps a stroll or a ride in the park would be just the thing before we attend to other matters," I suggested to Gage as Jeffers went to fetch my normal morning repast.

He nodded, taking a sip of his coffee. "Best to enjoy the weather while we can. There won't be many more days like it until spring."

The newspaper at his elbow caught my eye. "Is that the *Observer*?"

"Yes. Would you like to see it?"

"Please. Did Mr. Day include your request for information?"

"He did. I asked that anyone who saw or heard anything suspicious in the vicinity of Upper Brook Street on Thursday night apply to Jeffers here." Gage glanced at our butler as he set my eggs, toast, jam, and a cup of warm chocolate before me. "I hope you don't mind."

"Not at all, sir. I presume you wish me to separate the wheat from the chaff, so to speak?"

"Precisely. Thank you, Jeffers."

This was not the first time we'd asked Jeffers to undertake such a task, but it never ceased to amuse me how much enjoyment our fastidious butler seemed to derive from it. Apparently, he had a hidden yearning for adventure. One that might better explain his eagerness to accept a position in the household of a pair of inquiry agents known to have faced more than their fair share of disruption and danger. He practically became giddy when he uncovered any information that might be of importance.

I hid my grin behind the newspaper as I perused Mr. Day's article about Feckenham's murder. It focused on the details Gage had shared and did, indeed, include our request for further information. But Mr. Day also couldn't resist inserting a mention of bodysnatchers and their possible, if unlikely, connection to the murder. I shook my head good-humoredly. The sensational sold newspapers. I knew this well. At least the man hadn't descended into rampant speculation.

"What of the other papers? How did they report the crime?" I asked, folding the *Observer* and setting it aside.

"They're fairly sparse. Not much of interest."

However, the bland tone of his voice was too determined, and his proclamation that the stories held little of interest patently false. I glanced up to find him absorbed in his breakfast, the newspaper at the top of his stack turned to some financial page. If Gage paid any attention to matters of economics, it was not at the breakfast table.

"That's doing it much too brown, darling." I held out my hand, demanding he give me the papers.

He hesitated for a moment, the solemn look in his eyes making my nerves tighten, but he relented. No doubt realizing it was better for me to discover what was being bandied about in print here in my own home rather than somewhere more public.

What good cheer I had greeted the morning with dissipated as I caught sight of some of the headlines: *Possible Burking in Mayfair. Dark Deeds in the West End. Earl's Heir Targeted by Burkers.*

Picking up one to peruse its contents, I was frustrated to find it filled with few details and a great deal of conjecture. It didn't help that the articles surrounding it were tales of attempted burkings on the streets of London after dark. Though we'd known through Gage's contact at the police that such reports were on the rise, this was the first evidence of their sheer volume, and the first time they'd been listed in print for public consumption. Some were obviously products of the public's paranoia—a robbery or attempted assault transformed into a bungled attempt at burking. Others were not so clear. Either way, they had the potential to incite panic. Which meant that, regardless of the facts of the matter, the word *burking* would continue to haunt our inquiry into Feckenham's murder until proven otherwise.

I slapped the last paper down, scowling at it. "Perhaps you should have risked addressing all the newspapermen. Maybe then they wouldn't have resorted to this . . ." I gestured at the print ". . . this fabrication."

Gage set down his coffee cup. "It may seem that way, but no. They still would have printed what they wished. And they might have added some sly reminder of your past experience with such matters." His brow furrowed. "We can be thankful at least they didn't do that."

"Thankful" was not the response I had in mind, but I grasped what he meant. Either way, things were growing ever more complicated.

As if the fates were determined to oblige this thought, Jeffers returned to the room carrying a silver salver. "This missive was delivered for you, my lady."

I plucked the smudged paper from the gleaming tray, curious who would have sent me such a soiled missive. Perhaps the footman or errand boy who delivered it had dropped it. I did not recognize the handwriting, and flipping it over, I discovered the seal was unstamped. Baffled, I slit it open with my butter knife and unfolded the single page.

I frowned at the poor penmanship and spelling as I began to read. All too swiftly my confusion turned to dismay and then outright horror. Suddenly I felt like I couldn't draw breath. My chest constricted as if I'd been punched in the abdomen. And whether it was the child protesting this treatment or my own stomach rejecting the little food I'd eaten, my insides cramped with fear.

"Kiera, you've gone pale. What is it?" I heard my husband ask, his voice tight with concern. But I could not respond, only stare at the words before me, blinking rapidly as if that would change them or clear them from my sight.

"Kiera?"

I made some attempt at speech, which emerged as more of a mewl, and then Gage snatched the paper from my hand. I did not resist. But neither could I sit and watch him read it.

Air rushed back into my lungs as I pushed back from the table, the chair scraping against the floor and nearly toppling over in my haste. I whirled toward the windows, my hands shaking as I gripped the sill. I couldn't see Gage, and he made no sound, but I could imagine the shock radiating through him as it had through me moments earlier.

My lady,

*You may not no us, but we no you. Just like we new Sir Anthony
Darby. He called us his paticular Friends. Asked us to call on
him in Henrietta Street at the creeper covered blue Door with
certain Subjects he rekwested. Such paticulars as we hold we
thinks woud be of Interest to the Papers. Specially them that
pertain to you. And we thinks they will not care whether these
Paticulars can be prooved.*

*If you do not want these Secrets printed in the Papers to
besmirch you and your husband's name, we woud be obliged to
foreget them if you saw fit to reward us in Sir Anthony's usual
manner.*

By the time Gage joined me at the window, I'd at least re-
gained some measure of self-possession, if not all my faculties.
He didn't attempt to touch me, perhaps realizing that if he had
I would have retreated from him.

"I take it the creeper-covered blue door is familiar to you," he
murmured, staring out at the soft white candytuft blooms bordering the terrace.

It took me a few moments to gather my words. "Yes. The . . .
the door at the back of Sir Anthony's house. It led to the cellar."

"Where he . . . conducted his research?"

Had the discussion not been so fraught, I might have laughed
at this polite bit of understatement. "Yes."

He nodded, pausing before he ventured his next question.
"What is it that you think they know?"

I glanced sideways at him into his steady gaze. His calm,
matter-of-fact manner of speaking loosened the alarm gripping
my chest.

"I don't know," I said. "Not . . . not for certain."

"But you have a guess? A fear?"

My eyes dropped, unable to hold his sympathetic gaze. "Yes." I swallowed, trying to force down the lump of dread blocking my throat. "The . . . the number of bodies he purchased. The manner in which they were procured. The instructions he gave to acquire what he sought. The reason . . ." But at this, I shook my head, balking at speaking my next thought, my greatest fear. "Frankly, it doesn't matter. With enough details in their possession, they could lie and say whatever they wish. About Sir Anthony. About me. And most of London would believe them," I finished in a low voice.

His eyes flashed, allowing some of his tightly restrained emotion to slip through. "I don't give a fig about Sir Anthony. But for them to wrongfully implicate you . . ." His hands tightened into fists at his side. "That's a problem."

I didn't need Gage to point that out. My heart already raced with the panic I'd felt so many times during the weeks after the scandal over my involvement with Sir Anthony's work erupted. I'd thought to never feel that again, but the lurching sensation of my pulse flooded me with memories. The anxiety I'd thought I'd learned to control made my skin prickle and my stomach turn.

"Do you know who these blackmailers are? Could they be these men on trial—Bishop, Williams, and May?" Gage asked.

"I don't know. I told you, I never met the resurrectionists Sir Anthony purchased from! I don't know their names. I don't even know what they look like."

He took hold of my arms. "I know, Kiera. I'm sorry. I'm merely trying to make sense of this."

"Well, I am, too!"

He gathered me close, even as I stood rigidly in his embrace, staring over his shoulder. "I know this is a shock for you. I'm not accusing you of lying or withholding anything. I'm merely trying to garner information so we can decide what to do next." He pulled back far enough to see my face, though he did not remove his arms from around me. "You're my wife. I'm not going to abandon you to face this alone."

I knew he said this to reassure me, but the swirling in my stomach only worsened at this reminder that my life and reputation were no longer all that was at risk. If I was ostracized or worse, he would be also. And so would our innocent child.

But even worse than society's disfavor, if the London mob were to somehow seize hold of us . . .

I shuddered at the thought.

In response to my shiver, his hands rubbed up and down my arms and his lips curled into an encouraging smile. But he hadn't been in London when my scandal broke. He hadn't seen the way society crossed the street to avoid me, or read the words printed about me in the newspapers. He hadn't witnessed the snarling, angry mob outside the Bow Street Magistrates' Office. And now the terrified populace hovered on a knife's edge because of the Italian Boy's murder, waiting to take their enmity out on any likely suspect. One which I fit quite handily.

"I suppose we could pay the criminals what they wish," he proposed. "But I dislike that course of action for a number of reasons. The first and foremost being, I despise the idea of blackmail. The second, that they might decide they can extort us for more money in the future. It sets a dangerous precedent." His head tilted in thought. "Do you have any idea what they meant when they referred to rewarding them in Sir Anthony's usual manner?"

I shook my head. "I never really gave the matter much thought. I guess I always assumed Sir Anthony or his butler paid them directly when they delivered a subject."

"Then we couldn't pay their demands even if we decided to."

"Unless they expect us to ask Stilton." I paused to consider. "If he's even still employed by Sir Anthony's heir. From what I could tell, he didn't approve of his nephew, and the feeling was mutual."

Gage looked up as the door opened behind me. "Jeffers, who delivered this missive for my wife?" he asked, moving forward to lift it from the table where he'd dropped it. "Was it an errand boy, or did it come by post?"

His expression didn't reveal even a flicker of surprise at such an unorthodox question. "I shall have to inquire, sir. One of the footmen accepted the delivery."

"Please do."

He bowed and departed as Gage turned back to me.

"Maybe there's a way we can trace the letter back to whoever sent it."

This seemed like a genuine possibility. Although the men hadn't signed their names to the missive for obvious reasons, it was doubtful they'd gone to great lengths to keep their identities secret. And if they *had* paid a messenger not to snitch, his allegiance could probably be swayed by a few coins.

Gage coaxed me back to the table, where my food and cup of chocolate had grown cold. I pushed aside the stack of newspapers with their morbid headlines glaring up at me, feeling I somehow should have foreseen this blackmail letter coming.

After all, the public's awareness was now heightened. For the moment, bodysnatchers would find their usual method of plying their trade seriously hindered. Those who typically turned a blind eye to such a thing would now be vigilant and unwilling to dismiss them so easily. In the meantime, they had a living to make, and as few of them had legitimate employment, extortion seemed the likeliest option. The only shock should have been that someone had not tried to do so to me before. But then I hadn't returned to London until three months prior, and there hadn't been the inquest into the Italian Boy providing extra inducement to comply with their demands.

A few moments later, Jeffers returned with our footman, Samuel. "He says an errand boy delivered the message. I thought you might wish to question him about the lad."

"Yes, very good, Jeffers," Gage replied before addressing the footman. "Did you get a good look at the boy?"

Samuel clasped his hands behind him, rocking back on his heels. "I would say so, sir. Though I can't say there was anything unique about him. He looked much like all the others. About twelve years old. Short. Dark hair under a cap. Though now that I think of it, this one appeared a bit neater than some of the others I've seen."

"Did he look like one of the Italian Boys?" Gage remarked, voicing the same question that had formed in my mind.

"Yes, sir. Very like."

Gage's gaze swiveled to meet mine before he addressed Samuel and Jeffers again. "If either of you or the staff should happen to see the lad again, detain him. But do not do so harshly. We have some questions we need to put to him, and it would be best if he was in a cooperative frame of mind."

"It could be a coincidence," I ventured after the servants had departed.

"It could," Gage conceded, and then grimaced. "But I doubt it. It seems far more probable they wished to scare you."

I stirred the chocolate in my cup listlessly. "Or implicate me by having an Italian Boy seen near our home." I refused to flinch from the truth.

His expression turned blacker, perhaps recalling, as I already had, what Lord Melbourne had said about how spiteful the resurrectionists could be. In the course of our previous inquiries, we had become associates of a sort with the head of one of the largest criminal gangs in Edinburgh, all in the pursuit of the greater good. But we would be fools to delude ourselves into thinking these bodysnatchers were in any way the same. We could not make the mistake of believing they had the least amount of honor, or that they would hesitate to inflict harm.

"Perhaps Goddard, my friend with the Bow Street Runners, might know how to trace these fellows." His eyes narrowed at the letter where he'd laid it on the table before him. "Or at least have some idea who the plausible culprits are. I'll send a message to him at the Great Marlborough Street Police Office asking him to meet with us." He sat taller, seeming relieved to have a course of action to take.

"We should also inform Bree and Anderley. Maybe they have some insights we do not." I suggested.

He nodded. "Anderley has been spending enough time in the dredges of London on this Italian Boy inquiry. He might even recognize them if he happens to see them skulking about. Or if the errand boy returns again."

I studied his pensive countenance, wondering again at Anderley's connection to all of this. "You trust him greatly, don't you?"

Gage glanced up in distraction, but his attention swiftly focused, as if he sensed all the words behind that small query I hadn't said. I'd never asked about their history together. Never questioned why they worked so well together, why they seemed to fall into a familiar rhythm. But this investigation seemed different somehow, though I couldn't figure out exactly why.

"With my life," he replied seriously, and then amended it. "With *your* life." His gaze dipped to include that of the child I carried.

I lifted a hand to cover the precious mound of my stomach, opening my mouth to voice my next question, but he rose to his feet before I could do so.

"I'll pen that letter to Goddard now. The sooner he can meet with us, the better." He rounded the table to drop a kiss on my head before beating a hasty retreat.

He'd known I was going to ask further questions about Anderley. I was certain of it. What I wasn't certain of was why he was so determined to dodge them.

I knew next to nothing about Anderley's past. I'd never needed to. But I suddenly realized that, even with my keen artist's eye and sharp intuition, I'd deduced very little about him. Very little beyond what he allowed me to. He was somewhat of a chameleon, shifting guises as the situation called for, but almost always steady and contained.

He was darkly attractive, fiercely loyal, and possessed a mischievous sense of humor—one that did not quail at being made the figure of amusement. His valet skills were unmatchable, as evidenced by Gage's impeccable appearance and his ability to meet even the most absurd of his master's whims. But he could also ride, shoot, and engage in fisticuffs as well or better than any man I'd ever known. He had a decided affinity for the theatrical, and a pleasing tenor singing voice. If not for the fact he'd been with Gage for nearly fourteen years, since his days at Cambridge, I might have believed him an actor playing a part.

There was but one thing I'd been able to recognize in him that it was evident he'd not wished me to—his ability to blunt his emotions, to stifle and pack them away and refuse to give them sway. I recognized that capacity in him because I also possessed it. It was how I'd survived my marriage to Sir Anthony. Since meeting Gage, I'd been freed from such a necessity, but the ability never went away. It was still an impulse I had to suppress whenever the situation was fraught or I feared Gage's reaction.

Anderley had only recently begun to display more than polite regard for me, and I supposed I was the same with him. Our mutual mistrust had meant we hadn't taken to one another easily. Perhaps because we'd realized what that mistrust meant— that we were each hiding a deep pain.

Maybe that was why we were both so devoted to Gage. For he'd also sensed that in us, drawn us out, and attached himself to us anyway.

I turned to stare out the windows at the orange and gold leaves of the ash tree in the garden. Given this devotion, it would take much for Gage to break his valet's trust and reveal his past.

I could not ask that of him. Not unless it became necessary. For although I sensed it had some bearing on this inquiry into the Italian Boy, it was but a peripheral matter. Let him keep his secrets. As I would keep mine.

My gaze dropped to the grimy resurrectionists' letter where it still rested against the gleaming wood.

For the moment.

CHAPTER THIRTEEN

"Oh, hail, bright one," Trevor declared good-naturedly, glancing up from his perusal of the newspaper as I strolled into his library-cum-study.

I'd never stood on ceremony in what had been our family's London residence since before either of us was born. Our father had always welcomed us in this domain, so long as we were courteous and quiet, and as a consequence the space was cozy and well loved, the chairs upholstered in softened leather and bleached from the sun shining through the tall windows.

He grinned as I plopped into the chair across from his. "I was just longing for visitors, and here you are. But what brings you to my door?"

I cast my gloves onto the table at my side. "Perhaps I simply wished to see my brother."

His eyebrows arched skeptically as his gaze flicked from me to Gage, who'd trailed behind me at a more sedate pace. "Now I *know* you're here for a particular reason." He tipped his head toward the open windows, where outside the lovely weather continued. "Why aren't you strolling or riding in the park on this fair afternoon?"

"We strolled here."

"Quite an exertion."

As the walking distance from our townhouse to his on South Street was a matter of minutes, I did not fault him his droll rejoinder.

"We missed you at services this morning," Gage commented casually as he sank into the chair next to mine.

"Yes, I overslept." Trevor's brow puckered. "Please do not tell me you are here to castigate me for my failure to attend church."

"Of course not," I snapped. "Don't be such a clunch."

His bright blue eyes flashed. "Then why remark on it?"

"Just making conversation, old boy," Gage said, attempting to defuse our family squabble. "We'd intended to invite you to dinner."

But rather than ease Trevor's mind, this only increased his suspicion. He sat back in his chair, narrowing his eyes. "Then you're definitely here on some purpose." His eyes dipped to the newspaper draped in his lap. "I see that the story you told the *Observer* seems to be circulating through all the papers today."

"Yes, that was our hope."

His brow cleared, though his eyes became guarded. "Is this about Feckenham?"

I fought the urge to squirm. "I know you probably have no wish to speak of him or . . . or to claim the connection. But we need information, and it's come to our attention that Lord Feckenham was part of Lord Wilmot's set. And you mentioned . . ." I faltered upon seeing the deep shame in his eyes.

"I was once part of that set as well," he finished for me.

I nodded, hating to cause him embarrassment. Especially since part of it was my fault. If not for my scandal, he would not have needed to defend me, and consequently been shunned for his actions. I knew he didn't blame me, but it didn't lessen my guilt.

His jaw tightened as if he wished to speak of anything else, and then released. "What do you wish to know?"

"What do you know of him? Of his character?" Gage's expression was carefully neutral, displaying neither sympathy nor censure.

Trevor frowned. "I'm sure you haven't heard very complimentary things. And I daresay if much of what you've heard has come from his family, you should compound it by ten."

To hear my brother state it so succinctly chilled me, affecting me far greater than the recital of any number of unsavory details.

"That bad?" Gage replied.

Trevor's eyes dipped to the arabesque pattern of the rug. "I would not have believed any despicable or unscrupulous thing beyond his ken. He seemed incapable of empathy or fellow feeling. And he delighted in manipulating others into doing things they would never have otherwise considered doing."

My chest tightened in dread. "Did he . . . ?"

Trevor shook his head, knowing what I was about to ask. "No. But he tried. He . . ." His mouth twisted as he seemed to reconsider his words. "I gambled and lost quite a tidy sum to him. And he offered to forgive that debt . . ." His eyes lifted to meet Gage's. "If I introduced him to my sister."

There was no doubt which sister he meant. I was about to ask why a simple introduction would have been so distasteful, when his smoldering gaze flicked to mine.

"Turns out I balk at the idea of selling my sister."

My eyes widened, now understanding the implication. "But why would he want to . . . 'meet' me?"

"Because he is . . . he *was* a sick bastard, and you were an oddity. And a lovely oddity at that." He turned away. "Plus he knew it would inflict the maximum amount of harm to me to be forced to do such a thing, especially given the fact I'd fallen into their set because I'd been defending your honor a bit too fervently."

My conscience smarted again. "Well, thank you for not selling me."

Trevor looked up at this in shock and then shook his head as if I'd just said the most bewildering thing possible. "I would sooner slit my throat, you funny thing. I would hope you'd know that."

"Well, thank you for not doing that either."

He shook his head again, and then his mouth cracked a grin. "You can't help but confound people, can you?"

I shrugged, rising to go to him. "It's what I'm good at."

He gave a dry laugh at that, pushing to his feet to pull me tight to him. I pressed my face to his coat, breathing in the familiar scent of his starch and bay rum, grateful I was blessed with such an honorable brother. But what of those who were not?

As so often happened, Gage's thoughts followed the same path. "Had he made such a bargain with other men who lost to him at the tables?" he asked as Trevor and I pulled apart and returned to our seats.

"I can't tell you if he made that exact offer, but I do know a number of gentlemen owed him quite sizable debts." His expression turned forbidding. "Some of which appeared to be wiped away rather quickly when it had been well known their pockets were to let." He reached out a hand to square the position of a box on the table next to him. "He could be ruthless in getting what he wanted. Had I not paid him what I owed and left London when I did, I'm certain his first attempt to trap me under his thumb would not have been his last."

"His father mentioned that he'd trifled with more than one debutante and nearly brought them to ruin. Was that part of his ruthlessness? Did one of their relatives defy him?"

"Trifled?" he scoffed. "That makes it sound like he coaxed them into the garden for a kiss. From what I hear, he pestered them, more like. Backed them into a corner or forced himself on them. I can only hope they were interrupted before matters went too far."

I stared at him, horrified to learn that a "gentleman" and an earl's heir would behave in such a manner.

Gage's voice was hard, and the fury that rippled through his muscles made me suspect he would have done Feckenham bodily harm had the scoundrel not already been dead. "What of Miss Holt, Lord Wilmot's new wife?"

"I've been wondering the same thing," Trevor admitted. "But I can't tell you whether the matter was arranged by Feckenham and Wilmot, or if Wilmot merely took advantage of the situation his friend created." His brow furrowed. "I doubt Miss Holt's guardian, Lord Paddington, was so foolish as to find himself in debt to Feckenham. But his heir might have. Yaxley is a hothead."

"And prone to dip too deep. A terrible combination when one is determined to gamble," Gage added with a grimace. "Had I been foolish enough to offer for Lady Felicity, I would have forever been helping her brother out of scrapes."

"More luck to you, then, that you didn't," Trevor said. "For I also would have had to draw your cork for breaking my sister's heart."

Gage turned to me with a smile. "No risk of my doing that."

I smiled in return but refused to be drawn off the subject at hand. "What of Feckenham's card play?" I asked Trevor. "Did you ever find it suspicious?"

"As far as I could tell, or anyone could prove, he didn't cheat. Though his devil's own luck didn't stop people from speculating about it." He drummed his fingers intently against the arm of his chair. "For all his abominable behavior, Feckenham was no idiot. In fact, I often wondered if he might be one of the most intelligent chaps I'd ever known. He simply didn't have any scruples about how he used it."

"What of his brother?" Gage tilted his head in curiosity. "I'm not acquainted with George Penrose. Is he anything like Feckenham?"

Trevor shook his head. "Like chalk and cheese. They couldn't be more different."

"Were they on friendly terms?"

"I can't tell you that. But I do know that if there were difficulties, it was Feckenham's doing. Penrose is just about the most affable fellow you could meet. You'll find few who will speak ill of him." He dipped his head at me. "You should talk to Lord Damien Marlowe. He knows Penrose far better than I. They were up at university together and remained chums."

Lord Damien was my brother-in-law Philip's cousin and a more chivalrous, kindhearted young gentleman I'd yet to meet. I was extremely fond of him, despite his slight naiveté and inclination to correct the errors of those who were younger than him—both traits I suspected he would outgrow with time and maturity.

"Then we shall have to ask him to pay us a call," I remarked. "For if we visit Hollingsworth House, his mother, the Dowager Lady Hollingsworth, will insist on being included in the conversation, and we shall get nowhere." If she permitted my entrance at all. It was no secret Philip's aunt did not approve of me.

Gage's lips curled into a smile at my jest, but Trevor's thoughts were still on the previous matter.

"I know you must look to Penrose as a suspect. He is now heir to his father's earldom and all that entails, after all. But I must say, I think you're following the wrong scent. Penrose isn't the type to commit murder. Not for an earldom."

"But what if the earldom wasn't the motive?" Gage pointed

out. "What if he was protecting or defending something or someone else?"

Trevor considered the possibility and then nodded. "It's possible. But if that's the case, I can't say I blame him." His eyes blazed with righteous ferocity. "Feckenham was rotten through and through. And I doubt you'll find many who mourn him," he challenged.

We couldn't argue that. In fact, I wasn't sure anyone truly grieved his passing. Not even his family.

We returned to Chapel Street to find a lovely yellow barouche with a folded hood pulled up to our door. On the forward-facing seat sat Lorna and Charlotte, the latter of whom called to me as we approached.

"Mrs. Gage, there you are!" She waved me forward. "Isn't it a lovely day? We've come to take you for a ride with us in the park." She smiled at Gage. "That is, if your husband can spare you?"

He chuckled and executed a bow. "Ladies, I am quite pleased to commend my dearest wife to your care, so long as you mind she doesn't take cold." His eyes twinkled with teasing.

"Not in this sunshine," Lorna declared, though the rug thrown over her own lap belied these words. Warm it might be for November, but it was not July.

"We shall take the utmost care with her," Charlotte assured him.

"You do realize I'm not a child," I declared, interrupting this good-natured banter. I arched my chin in defiance. "I shall remove my bonnet and allow the wind to blow through my hair if I wish." Not that I would ever do something so outrageously improper in the middle of Hyde Park, and well they knew it.

"Of course, darling," Gage humored me by saying, but then leaned close to whisper in my ear as he assisted me up into the carriage. "But then my fingers will be jealous of the wind, and I can't be held accountable for what mischief they will get up to later in revenge."

I flushed at this suggestive comment. As such, my cheeks were decidedly rosy as I settled into the seat across from my friends. They grinned at me knowingly.

"You heard him. There is a bit of a nip in the air," I said by way of explanation as we drove on.

Lorna's mouth twisted impishly before she murmured under her breath, "I don't think that nip was the air."

I looked to Charlotte for reprieve, but she merely dimpled.

"I'm simply glad to see Mr. Gage is living up to his reputation."

Lorna laughed out loud at this, and my blush burned even brighter.

"Forget *my* influence," I said as soon as I could gather my words. "I blame your great-aunt. She's obviously had a detrimental effect on you."

Charlotte gave a gurgle of laughter. "I think she would be rather pleased to hear you say that."

"You're probably right."

All of fashionable London appeared to have turned out to enjoy the fine November weather. The rows and paths were choked with carriages and riders, meandering along beneath the trees still sporting a riot of colors. In another few days, they would be nothing but a memory, but for now they were enjoying their last hurrah. In any case, we were happy to be carried along at such a sedate pace, enjoying the scent of the leaves crushed beneath the barouche's wheels, the sun warming our skin, and the amiable company.

Without their saying so, I was well aware of my friends' intentions for this outing. They wanted me to be seen behaving as any normal lady, and to be observed chatting with respectable and high-status members of society, hoping to sway the insipient gossip stirred by the news of failed burkings and Feckenham's murder in my favor. Because of it, Charlotte had little need to beckon people over to our barouche. They practically flocked to it, rabid with curiosity.

My limited social skills were severely taxed by this. I'd become better at following cues and feigning interest over the past few months under Charlotte's and Gage's tutelage, but there were still times when I could tell I'd failed to respond properly. The more forgiving members of society accepted this as an amusing eccentricity. The rest shook their heads or turned their noses up at me, no doubt pitying Gage his choice in wife.

I did my best to ignore them, as I did those who did little to hide their disgust of me, and steer the conversation toward Feckenham himself. The reactions to his death seemed to vary from the politely reserved to almost outright pleasure at his demise. The latter came from men I'd decided must have been crossed by the scoundrel at some point, likely at the gaming tables. But they let nothing slip about him that might be helpful to our investigation.

The earl was another matter. At least two different ladies mentioned that Lord Redditch suffered from ill health, and the fact that he had such an obliging spare should be rejoiced at. For my part, I couldn't help but wonder just how grave the earl's illness had been, and just how obliging his second son had determined to be.

A cool wind picked up as we rounded a curve in the path, and I was about to suggest we cut our drive short, when a lady riding a magnificent bay mare with a white blaze came abreast of us. The cut of her merlot riding habit was exquisite, and the tall plumes adorning her hat quite dashing. So striking a picture did she make that it took me a moment to even notice the man riding beside her as the Earl of Wansford, a prominent man in politics who had been a leading arbiter of fashion in his younger days and still maintained a trim waist.

This must be the Duchess of Bowmont, I realized, for Lord Wansford was reported to be her most recent lover. When Lorna performed the introductions, this swept away all doubt.

We eyed each other with genuine interest. I was not surprised to discover how undeniably lovely the duchess was, even at the age of almost sixty. But given all the gossip about her hard living, I was amazed by how smooth her complexion appeared, and how lively her eyes. I decided then and there that most of the rumors I'd heard were exactly that, rumors. Although those about her irreverent manner swiftly proved to be true.

"So you are the notorious Lady Darby," she declared, having assessed me from head to toe as she rode alongside our carriage. "I saw you at the Covent Garden Theatre last week, from a distance, and I must say I've been impatient to meet you ever since." Her eyes sparkled with devilry. "Anyone capable of capturing the heart of that delicious Mr. Gage *and* creating a scandal even bigger than my own is certainly worth one's time."

"I daresay my appearance is not what you expected, Your Grace," I said, having long learned that my demure exterior often did not fit the image others had concocted of me. Had I known my friends intended to take me for a drive in the park, I might have chosen something more stylish than my reddish fawn redingote and rice straw bonnet.

"No, it's even better. How dull it would be to find you some long-lashed Aphrodite or sharp-eyed witch." She tilted her head. "Though I do understand now why they say your eyes are 'witch bright.' They are quite an envious shade of blue. Lapis lazuli, is it not?" Her lips curled into a puckish grin. "And I suspect I shall find them quite penetrating when you paint my portrait."

"I cannot promise the experience will be comfortable," I remarked dryly, recognizing that the duchess was the type with whom it was best to give back as good as one got.

She laughed. "No, I'm certain not." Her head dipped to Lorna. "But my goddaughter assures me it will be skillfully rendered and accurate." Her voice grew serious. "I trust you won't attempt to court my vanity like all the male artists who promised to capture my true essence and delivered nothing but conceit."

I wasn't certain if this was some sort of test—for the duchess seemed to have few flaws that a painter would wish to correct—but it wasn't in my nature to prevaricate. "If you are looking for vanity, I am not the artist for you. I'm afraid I find there is far more beauty in truth." I searched for the words to explain. "That the splendor and richness in a portrait lies not with the perfection of the subject's appearance, but in the spark of life captured by naught but such humble things as pigment and canvas."

Something I'd said must have intrigued her, for her coffee brown eyes sharpened with interest. I continued to meet her penetrating gaze, letting her know I was in perfect earnest. When finally she broke eye contact, it was to flick a glance at the man who rode beside her, who I'd just realized was also staring at me.

The duchess smiled. "I can see now what snared Mr. Gage's regard. For you've already captured Wansford's as well."

The earl grinned at her teasing.

"Will you come Wednesday?" she asked me. "I shall be ready to receive you then. And I know precisely what I shall wear."

"I would be pleased to," I replied.

After we arranged the time, they rode on, leaving me to face Lorna's self-satisfied smirk.

"I knew the duchess would be perfect. Once you've secured her endorsement, you shall have every lord and lady in Mayfair—from royal dukes to no-account baronets—begging you to paint their families."

"And Lady Morley will be forced to eat crow." Charlotte's eyes sparkled with vicious delight.

"Remind me never to cross you," Lorna told her, eyeing her with the same surprise I did.

"I also think we may be getting ahead of ourselves," I

murmured, my worries over the implications of the blackmail note and the inquiry into the Italian Boy never far from my thoughts. "We don't yet know what trouble might arise."

"Don't fret, Kiera." Charlotte leaned across the carriage to clasp my hand. "You're already past the worst of it. I just know it."

If only I'd realized how wrong she could be.

CHAPTER FOURTEEN

"My lady."

I turned from my contemplation of the rain-slicked street outside the drawing room window, my shawl draped around my shoulders against the cold that had settled overnight. The townhouse creaked as yet another blast of wind buffeted it.

"Mr. Gage has requested your presence in his study," Jeffers announced. "A Mr. Goddard is there with him."

"Thank you, Jeffers. I'll join them presently."

He nodded. "Very good, my lady." His gaze dipped to where I absently rubbed my stomach in circles. "If I may be so bold," he added, tentative at first, and then more assured. "I could send to the apothecary for something to relieve your discomfort."

I should have known Jeffers's eagle eyes had not missed my lack of appetite the past few days. I had left more food on my plate than I'd eaten. A fact Bree had already taken me to task for the evening before, insisting the bairn needed more nourishment than the pecking I'd been doing. But I was not ill, nor troubled by nausea from the baby. My nerves were simply too tangled, my anxiety too acute, to allow much food to pass my lips.

"No, thank you," I demurred with an encouraging smile. "I'm sure it shall pass."

He did not appear the least convinced by this, but he did not argue. "Of course, my lady."

"If Mr. Gage hasn't yet ordered tea, please have some brought to the study."

And if some of my favorite lemon cakes didn't appear on the tray, ordered up special by either Bree or Jeffers, then I would eat my hat.

He bowed and departed.

I soon followed in his wake, pausing before the mirror hanging over one of the console tables in the hall to check my appearance. Seeing that all was in order, I entered my husband's study to find him seated behind his burr elm kneehole desk. The man that was perched on the Windsor armchair swiveled to look at me before rising to his feet and bowing quite correctly.

"Kiera, this is Mr. Goddard, the Bow Street Runner I mentioned," Gage said. "Goddard, my wife."

"How do you do," I murmured, advancing into the room.

Having no experience with the Runners, I hadn't known what to expect. Goddard was a spry man of about thirty years of age, with a medium build and a head full of dark hair. His clothing was plain, but respectable, likely chosen for its ability to blend in to most settings, from the slums of the East End to the streets of Mayfair. In fact, there was very little that was remarkable about him except the dark shadow cast by his shaved facial hair over the lower portion of his face. That, and his keen eyes, which studied me with respectful interest. It was evident he was aware of my reputation. He might have even been present during my appearance at the Bow Street Magistrates Court two and a half years prior, waiting to bring another criminal to court.

I crossed the room to sit on the claret damask cushioned window seat to the left of Gage's desk, where I sometimes curled up to read while Gage handled business and estate matters at his desk.

"Mr. Goddard and I have been discussing the Italian Boy inquiry," Gage explained before turning back to our guest. "The Runners haven't yet been called in, have they?"

He shook his head. "No. But I suspect it's only a matter of time. Though it's like to be one of the veterans. Probably Taunton, seein' as he's particular friends with Minshull, the magistrate for the case." Though more polished than some, his accent still betrayed his origins as being from Southwark, south of the Thames.

"I'm sure you're correct. And the sooner Minshull calls him in, the better. Superintendent Thomas seems eager enough, but he has little experience in these matters"

"His first murder case, I believe," Goddard replied, choosing his words with care. He was savvy enough not to be caught directly criticizing a man who might be considered his superior, even if Thomas was with the New Police and not part of the Runners.

"Well, let us hope they don't bungle it." Gage sat forward, clasping his hands on his desk as he dismissed that matter and moved on to the real reason we'd asked him here. "I have a matter I'd like to hire you to look into. Something of great delicacy." He stared at the man in frank appraisal. "I know I can trust your discretion."

"Of course, sir," Goddard replied without hesitation.

Gage opened his desk drawer to remove the blackmail note and passed it across the desk to the Runner. "My wife received this the morning of the twelfth. It was delivered by a messenger, most likely an Italian Boy hired to run the errand."

Goddard's eyes sharpened at this information, but otherwise

he didn't react, not even while reading it. When he'd finished, he lifted it to his nose to sniff it and then flipped it over to examine it for stray marks, as Gage and I had already done. "And you want me to find out who's threatenin' her ladyship?" he guessed.

"Yes," Gage confirmed, nodding toward the letter. "Based on the information shared in the missive, we assume it's one or more of the resurrectionists her late husband procured subjects from. But there's always the possibility one or more of them talked, or that someone on the fringes of such work—like that man Shields, who the burkers employed to carry the body of the Italian Boy—is seeking to profit from such knowledge."

Goddard's eyes lifted to the ceiling as he considered this. "'Tis possible. These sort of men like to frequent the same haunts. Pubs and inns where the trade is known, and they can drink without sufferin' the scorn of other workin' folk. Anyone willin' to be associated with or hired out by such characters would know to go there. And if they were to blabber about it, who knows who heard."

"And you know which pubs and inns they meet at?"

He nodded and shrugged. "'Tisn't a secret. In the old days, they used to store the bodies under the benches and return for 'em later. Can't get away with such brass now." He folded the letter. "I'll pay a call to a few of these establishments and see what I can find out. Their porters and barmen should be in a more cooperative frame of mind given recent events." His eyes slid sideways to meet mine. "Unless her ladyship has a better idea where I should start."

I understood what he was trying to ask without giving offense. "I had nothing to do with Sir Anthony Darby's procurement of bodies. I suspected, of course, that he was using resurrectionists, but I never met such men nor took part in the process."

Goddard accepted this response without argument, though I could tell by the glint in his eyes that he wasn't completely convinced of my truthfulness.

"What of you?" Gage interjected. "Do you have any suspicions who the culprit might be?"

He sat back, rubbing his chin. "Well, nowadays, snatchin' has become a bit of a specialist's trade. Many of the best made their money and got out after the work became too dangerous when London graveyards started hirin' armed guards. Most of those that are left either work in gangs or undertake the occasional odd job, lured by the blunt." He waved the letter. "'Tis far more likely this is the work of one of the gangs than an outlier. I expect I'll find your blackmailer among them."

His sharp gaze shifted once again to meet mine. "What of Sir Anthony's servants? Were any of them involved?"

"To be certain. The butler, for sure. And perhaps one or two others." I felt no qualms accusing Sir Anthony's odious butler.

"Then I had best question them, discover what they might know."

"Best of luck with that," I remarked wryly. "I believe they are still employed by Sir Anthony's nephew at the same address. But a word of caution," I added when he would have turned away. "Do not mention my name or the letter. Most of the staff, particularly the butler, was loyal to their employer. You'll find they spare me little sympathy."

Out of the corner of my eye, I saw Gage's jaw clench with anger, but I was more concerned with Mr. Goddard's reaction. His eyebrows quivered, and I could almost see the questions piling up behind the tight line of his lips, but he showed remarkable restraint when he did not voice them. I wouldn't have blamed him if he had.

"I shall approach the matter with care," he assured me.

"Thank you."

Either he was unused to being thanked or the genuineness of my tone had startled him, for he shifted awkwardly in his chair before nodding in acknowledgment. "What do you wish me to do with the blackmailers when I find them?" he asked Gage.

My husband drummed his fingers against the desk, his eyes narrowed in contemplation. We certainly didn't want the men arrested and brought before a magistrate. That would mean having to publicly reveal the contents of their letter. "Nothing for the moment. Simply bring their names and possible whereabouts to me. Then we can decide what is to be done."

Goddard seemed to understand the complexities of the situation. "I've a fellow, used to be part of the Bow Street Foot Patrol, who I can set to watch the men until you resolve what to do."

"Yes. That would be suitable." Gage pushed to his feet, forcing Goddard to rise as well.

"The letter. May I keep it? I may be able to match the handwriting."

Gage turned to me, and I nodded. If he trusted this Runner, then so did I.

Goddard tucked the letter inside his waistcoat. "I'll report back to you in one week, or sooner if I have anything of importance to share."

Gage told him this was acceptable and then rang for Jeffers to show him out through the servants' entrance, as he'd entered.

"I expected you to ask him if he knew anything about Feckenham," I commented when Gage returned to the side of his desk.

"Goddard knows we're investigating the murder, and we are well enough acquainted for me to know that he would have shared anything he thought I should be aware of." He crossed the few steps to where I sat, taking hold of my hands. "For me to ask him without first offering him a commission in the inquiry would have been overstepping. He makes his living from such retainers, after all."

"Does he resent your taking some of his business?"

"With my and my father's inquiries?" He sank down onto the cushion next to me so that I wouldn't have to crane my neck to look up into his face. "No. Most of the Runners understand the clients who hire us would never have allowed them over their thresholds in the first place." He grinned crookedly. "Although those clients do not realize that Father and I often hire those same Runners to do a portion of the work for us. Though we pick and choose judiciously which ones we use."

I smiled, leaning my head against his shoulder.

"Whether that makes up for the loss of income from our 'interference'?" He shrugged. "I can't say. But they seem satisfied with the arrangement. Most of them would rather not have to contend with outraged lords and haughty butlers. And I don't blame them."

"Considering the amount of trouble some of those lords and butlers give us, I can only imagine how uncooperative they would be to those of a lower social class."

"Precisely."

We fell silent, sitting companionably side by side as we listened to the rain patter against the window behind us. It was a dreary day, and as much as there was still to do, I rather hoped we wouldn't need to go out in it.

Gage seemed to be of a similar bent, at least for the moment. He shifted to lean back against the pillow propped alongside the wall, lifting his leg around me and drawing me toward him so that my back was cradled to his chest. I sighed as his arms wrapped around me, content to sit snuggly in his embrace, the spicy scent of his cologne teasing at my nostrils. Closing my eyes, I let the rise and fall of Gage's breath and the soft tapping of the rain lull me.

"I heard from the lads I hired to find out who might have

purchased that sticking plaster," he murmured. "But they haven't had any luck. Then again, I didn't expect them to."

Being in agreement, and too contented to care, I didn't comment.

"I also sent a note to Lord Damien Marlowe, asking him to pay us a visit outside of normal calling hours so that we might speak to him alone."

"Excellent. So long as he doesn't arrive within the next hour," I mumbled. "Then I shall be very vexed with him."

Gage chuckled behind me, jostling me in his amusement.

"What's so funny?"

He shook his head, and then pressed his lips to my temple as he spread his hands over the slight swell of my abdomen. "I wonder if it's wrong that I long to see you round with my child."

His words were so tender that I felt a catch in my chest. I lifted my hands to cover his, spreading my fingers so they sank between his longer digits. "I suspect it's something to do with male prowess," I remarked lightly, and was rewarded with another chuckle. The pale bristles just beginning to show from his morning shave scraped against my cheek as he smiled.

"Probably." His lips shifted to graze my ear. "Though your reaction has never left me in any doubt as to my competence."

Tingles raced across my skin and my breath audibly caught as his mouth captured my earlobe between his teeth.

"Have you considered any names yet?"

I fumbled for words, trying to understand how he expected me to think when his mouth was now doing delicious things to my neck. "For the baby?"

"Yes."

"N-no. Not really."

"If it's a boy, how about Stephen?"

"Stephen? I . . ." Such was my distraction that it took a full five seconds for this name to penetrate through the haze of my desire. I pulled back. "After your father?"

Gage's eyes twinkled with mischief. "No?" He bent his head to my neck again. "Then maybe Meryasek."

"Mery-what?" Laughter tinged my voice as I leaned away.

"Meryasek. It's Cornish. One of my great-grandfathers got saddled with it."

I shook my head. "And you want to name our son this?"

"No."

"Then why suggest it?"

"To see you smile like that."

My heart turned over in my chest, and I lifted a hand to cradle his cheek. I knew now what he was doing. Since the moment I'd learned about the burking of that poor Italian Boy, the pain of my past had not been far from my thoughts. That he should wish to lift that from me, even if for but a moment, flooded me with joy and gratitude. It made the ever-present ache more bearable. And it made me want to give him anything he wished.

With the possible exception of naming our child Meryasek.

"I don't know about a boy. But if it's a girl, why don't we name her Emma."

A light flared in Gage's eyes. "After my mother?"

"Yes."

He didn't respond. At least, not with words.

And several agreeable minutes later, when he did speak, it was only to say, "If Lord Damien arrives within the next hour, I shall be very vexed with him as well."

As it happened, Lord Damien didn't call on us until the following day. Gage and I were emerging from our front door when he strolled up the pavement toward us. I almost didn't recognize him, for he'd grown out his dark facial hair into the popular chinstrap beard. He cast one glance at our carriage where it was waiting for us and hastened forward.

"My apologies. I was in the country until yesterday evening

and did not receive your note until I returned. Shall I call at a better time?"

Seeing he had walked, Gage made another suggestion. "Are you bound elsewhere, or would you like to ride with us? We're only traveling as far as Cromarty House. Then my carriage can take you wherever you like."

"Capital," he proclaimed with his easy grin.

We climbed inside, and he settled onto the squabs facing the rear, smoothing down his ivory waistcoat crisscrossed with gold trim. I hid my amusement at his sartorial pride. It seemed Lord Damien had belatedly determined to become a fop. Under this sumptuous waistcoat, he wore a black shirt and cravat, which he paired with a pair of pale trousers with stirrups at the feet and a velveteen emerald green morning coat. I'd seen just such an ensemble in a fashion plate from one of Alana's French magazines.

Such clothing might easily have cast a simpler dressed man in the shade, but not Gage. Even attired in a modest deep charcoal tailcoat, camel breeches, and Hessians, each tailored to perfection, he cut a dashing figure.

"I heard about Feckenham," Lord Damien said, the smile fading from his face. "Are you investigating his death?"

"Yes," I replied.

He nodded, his gaze straying toward the window and the Georgian façades of the homes we passed. "I suspected as much. Then you must have heard I was a particular friend of his brother, George."

"Trevor St. Mawr said you were up at school together," Gage said.

"Shared a room at Eton our first year."

"I suppose you had much in common," I remarked.

"Younger sons of noble families? True enough." His brow furrowed. "But my brother James was always dashed more kind to me than Feckenham ever was to his brother."

"How do you mean?" Gage asked.

Lord Damien eyed us both, seeming to consider his words. The good humor he generally exhibited had all but vanished, making him appear much older. I sometimes forgot he was only three years younger than me.

"Feckenham taunted him mercilessly. He was always making one mean-spirited crack or another."

"About?"

He huffed. "Whatever came to him. His appearance. His ability at sport. His manhood."

Gage frowned. "I'd heard George Penrose was an out-and-out rider."

"He is. One of the best. And he displays to advantage in the boxing ring." He sank back, shaking his head. "I don't know whether Penrose threw himself neck or nothing into becoming so good because of his brother's teasing, or if he was already prime, but the truth never mattered much to Feckenham." His face twisted in aversion. "By Jove! I guess Penrose *is* Lord Feckenham now." He sighed. "He won't like that, going by his brother's title. But I suppose he has no choice."

I could empathize.

"How did Penrose react to his brother's taunting?" Gage asked.

"Did his best to ignore him. Behaved like the gentleman his brother was not. Unless Feckenham turned his sharp tongue on one of his friends. Then he wasn't above giving it back to him." Lord Damien's eyes gleamed in approval, but then he shrugged. "Mostly I think he tried to avoid him."

"But they lived in the same house?" I pointed out in puzzlement. If he wished to evade him, he could hardly do so while sharing the same roof.

"He led me to believe that was temporary. If I'm not mistaken, he meant to leave for the continent soon."

Gage and I shared a look, wondering if Lord and Lady Redditch had been aware of this. They'd made no mention of it.

Perhaps they hadn't thought it had any bearing on Feckenham's death. But that begged the question, what else had they thought had no bearing on the matter?

"Why are you asking so many questions about Penrose?" Lord Damien asked mistrustfully. "You don't think he has anything to do with his brother's murder, do you? Because that's ridiculous."

"He *does* have the most to gain from his death," Gage reminded him. "We wouldn't be very good investigators if we didn't consider him a suspect."

"Maybe so, but I can tell you right now it's impossible. I could readily believe Feckenham capable of murder, but not Penrose." He shifted forward, gesturing in enthusiasm, as if he'd just remembered. "And he was with *me* when it happened. It was Thursday night, correct?"

Gage straightened. "You were at White's?"

"Until one o'clock in the morning." He crossed his arms in satisfaction.

"What time did you arrive?"

"Shortly before nine that evening. And Penrose was one of the first chaps I spoke to."

"Were you with him all evening, then? That is, until he was summoned home."

At this, Lord Damien faltered. "Well, no. But I did see him around half past ten. He was speaking to one of the porters." He frowned. "Seemed a bit agitated. But then I saw him again just after midnight."

Since Feckenham had been murdered at approximately a quarter after eleven, this was not an altogether sound alibi. It was possible Penrose had left White's, murdered his brother, and then returned. But that seemed doubtful.

"That does seem indicative he isn't the culprit," Gage admitted. "But it would be helpful to speak to a few other gentlemen who were present that night. Do you recall who else was there?"

Lord Damien rattled off a few names, and Gage thanked him just as the carriage pulled to a stop before Cromarty House.

Before the footman could open the door, Gage asked one last question. "Who do you think killed him?"

"From what I understand, his enemies were too numerous to name." Lord Damien's voice dripped with scorn. "Pick up a copy of *Debrett's* and choose a page. You'll undoubtedly find one of them on it."

CHAPTER FIFTEEN

"*Someone* must have cared for him?" I muttered as we strolled toward Alana and Philip's drawing room, no more standing on ceremony here than at my brother's home. "He can't have been all evil? Such people don't exist."

"They do," Gage replied dampeningly. "But you're right. It's rare."

"Maybe a mistress?" I speculated, trying to imagine who might feel more fondness for Feckenham than the fickle affection we'd witnessed from his mother.

Gage cast me a quelling look as we entered the room to find my sister and her family gathered en masse. Philip bounced a giggling Greer on his knee, her golden curls springing about her ears, while Philipa perched impatiently beside him, awaiting her turn. Eight-year-old Malcolm seemed as if he wanted to appear above this playfulness, standing tall before his mother and baby brother as he recited a poem learned from his tutor. He looked like he'd grown another three inches since I'd last seen him but a fortnight before.

Upon our entrance, Philipa's face split into a wide grin. "Aunt Kiera! Uncle Gage!" She raced to Gage's side, already smitten with him at just six years old. "Will you play hobbyhorse? Please, please!"

Philip panted a laugh, resting his legs. "Yes, I think that's an excellent idea." His eyes glinted with teasing. "After all, your uncle needs the practice."

Gage smiled and allowed Philipa to lead him toward the sofa, where she promptly clambered into his lap. "Where are we off to, then?"

Philipa chattered away while her little sister grunted in protest, forcing her father to join in the race.

I shook my head at their antics, squeezing Malcolm's shoulders as I passed him to move closer to the fire. With Gage joining in, Malcolm's reluctance seemed to have melted away, for he went to cheer on the men's efforts, giggling as loud as his sisters.

Alana passed me wee Jamie, who at eight months old was flush and chubby like a cherub. "If only the members of the House of Lords could see them now."

"Aren't you a sweet one," I crooned to Jamie as I sat in the chair across from my sister. I glanced up with a grin, returning her jest. "Their dignified reputations would be in tatters."

Our eyes slid to the side to watch them romp and play, and I suspected Alana's chest felt as full and happy as mine did. I pressed a kiss to Jamie's fuzzy head, realizing I would soon have a child of my own to love and cuddle, to watch Gage bounce so high on his knee that they screamed with laughter. The thought made my heart swell to almost bursting.

But then a cold lump settled in my stomach. A reminder of just how precarious my circumstances were. If the inquiry into the Italian Boy wasn't resolved to the public's satisfaction, if the blackmailers weren't stopped before they could spread their lies, if we didn't solve Feckenham's murder and lay to rest all the rumors about burkers in Mayfair, our little family could be facing a difficult road.

I turned to look at Alana, her bright lapis-lazuli eyes so like my own alive with laughter. She and her family would also suffer, just as they had before. And so would Trevor.

I couldn't let that happen. I wouldn't.

Jamie cooed and fumbled with the silver rattle he clutched in his pudgy little hands. I secured it for him, helping him keep hold of it as he perched on my knees.

"Were you aware that Lord Redditch has been ill recently?" I asked my sister.

"Yes," she replied absently. "Something with his heart, I believe."

"Is it serious?"

"I don't know." Her gaze returned to mine, her smile dimming slightly when she realized the import of such questions. "But I do know, for a time, there was some concern he wouldn't recover enough to return to politics." She flicked a glance at her husband across the room, where he tickled Greer. "Philip expressed some concern after Redditch returned to the Lords that perhaps he should have stayed away. That he wasn't certain his heart could bear the strain." She sighed. "But with the battle over the Reform Bill being waged so heatedly, he wasn't surprised Redditch was determined to be there to help defeat it."

"Are he and Redditch well acquainted?"

Her brow lowered. "Well enough we weren't omitted from the guest list for their Guy Fawkes Ball." I could sense there was more she wasn't saying. It hovered in the air at the end of her words.

"But . . . ?" I prodded.

Her mouth flattened. "But Lord Redditch called Philip a . . . a bloodthirsty Jacobin."

My eyebrows arched in surprise. "Simply because he supported the Reform Bill?"

"Yes."

I frowned, wondering why he would tar Philip in particular

with this offense. "He does realize that Jacobins and Jacobites are not the same thing?" One did not equate with the other. *Jacobin* was largely used to deride the supporters of the French Revolution, while *Jacobite* referred to those who had supported the deposed Stuart king and his heirs' rights to the British throne, and suffered for it during the subsequent failed uprisings in the late seventeenth and early eighteenth centuries. Many of the Jacobites had been Scottish, especially from the Highlands, as Philip was.

Alana's eyes glinted with wry humor. "No one has ever accused the Earl of Redditch of being of more than average intelligence, so it's possible."

I nodded, having already developed a similar impression of the man.

"Does Redditch's health have something to do with his son's murder?" she asked curiously.

"Possibly. For now, I'm purely trying to understand all the variables."

If Lord Redditch had a weak heart, that could explain why his younger son had anticipated his father was the reason he'd been summoned home on the night of Feckenham's murder. This assumption, coupled with his obvious concern, made it seem he'd had no idea his brother had been killed.

Unless it had all been a clever ruse. After all, what better way to throw off suspicion? We hadn't seen his face when he first arrived, only overheard him speaking to the butler, and the eyes were so much more telling than the voice. They often betrayed the emotions one was so desperate to hide. What would George Penrose's eyes have revealed? Apprehension? Fear? Or elation?

A s so often happened of late, I found my footsteps dragging and my eyelids drooping just when I needed to prepare myself for one evening soiree or another. That night we were to attend a ball hosted by one of Lady Bearsden's particular friends, and while I understood the reasons why it was important we put in an appearance now, more than ever, I would have rather stayed home. Preferably in bed with a book, a cup of tea, and Gage to warm my feet against.

Instead I plopped down on the bench before my dressing table and allowed Bree to begin dressing my hair. She brushed through my long chestnut tresses in such soothing strokes that I sighed.

Bree smiled at my reflection in the mirror. "Lady Cromarty's maid told me yer hair would become more lustrous than ever while ye were expectin'." She lifted my tangled ends, pulling the bristles through the snarls. "And then it'd fall oot in clumps after the bairn is born."

I arched my eyebrows. "Well, isn't that a comforting thought."

This bit of sarcasm either went over Bree's head, or she chose to ignore it.

"Jenny has been offering you advice, then?" I asked, referring to my sister's longtime maid, who had helped her through four confinements.

"Aye." Her brown eyes sparkled. "I think she was more excited by the news than even Mr. Gage."

Since Gage had reacted with an elation I'd rarely seen him display—one that had eclipsed any hope of our briefly withholding such a development from our family and closest friends—I found this assertion difficult to believe.

"How did Anderley react?" I asked in genuine curiosity. Given the fact his acceptance of me had been guarded and slow, I could only imagine how he felt about adding a baby to his master's household.

"Stoic and reserved, as usual," Bree replied. "But I could tell how pleased he was for Mr. Gage. And you, o' course."

"Have you become good at reading him, then?"

She shrugged one shoulder as she began parting my hair into

sections. "Fair. He's no' really so difficult to follow once yer used to his ways."

I reached out a hand to toy with the bottles on the dressing table before me. "And how has he been recently?"

"Quiet. Sullen. Like he's bitten into somethin' rancid and wants to spit it oot, but can't." Bree's gaze lifted to meet mine in the mirror. "But I suspect you ken that already."

"It has to do with this inquest over the Italian Boy."

She nodded. "I think so, too."

"Do you know why?"

"Nay. I ken he spent some time in London afore he was in Mr. Gage's employ, but I dinna think he was born here." She tilted her head. "Actually, I heard him speakin' in some foreign language once to a fellow that came up from the mews. I dinna recognize it."

I contemplated this. "German maybe?" I knew he could sing in that language, for Gage had ordered him to do so once. Upon the occasion we became engaged.

"Nay," Bree replied in a drawn-out voice, as if searching her memory. "I dinna think so. That sounds all harsh and guttural. Like Gaelic. This was more soft and rollin'. Spanish, maybe. Or Italian."

I straightened, almost making her lose her grip on my hair. Our gazes met, both of us coming to the same thought.

"Italian, you said?"

"Aye."

Was that what so disturbed Anderley about the inquest? Was he Italian? He did have the same dark hair and eyes, the same bronzed complexion that many of them shared. But I'd never heard even a trace of an accent in his voice. Perhaps he was only partly Italian. Maybe a parent, or grandparent, had given him that language and heritage, but he'd been raised in England.

There were some who sought to hide their foreign origins

because of the prejudice they encountered. It was one thing to have a French lady's maid or chef, or an Irish stable master—such nationalities were renowned for their skills in those areas, right or wrong. But many among the aristocracy preferred the rest of their servants to be of British stock.

I hoped Anderley realized I was not so narrow-minded, but I could also understand his desire for privacy. It was none of my business what the ancestry of my husband's valet was. So long as Gage was content with them, then so should I be.

I didn't say anything more about the matter, and neither did Bree, perhaps sensing, as I did, that we were treading on a sensitive subject. But rather than returning to her cheerful chatter about the baby, her brow darkened. Evidently, the subject occupying her thoughts was even less pleasant than Anderley's secrets.

"Have you had an opportunity to speak with any of the staff from the Earl of Redditch's household?" I asked, wondering if perhaps her shift in mood could be related to the investigation.

"Aye, m'lady. I contrived a way to speak to two o' the maids and a footman. They was all right talkative, despite protestin' their butler had cautioned 'em to hold their tongues."

If only the newspapermen realized the best way to get information was to send a pretty, sympathetic maid to listen to the lower staff's tales of woe. No nobleman or woman's secrets would be safe.

"What did they have to say?"

Her lips pursed with displeasure as she began inserting hairpins into my coils of hair. "Well, I can tell ye none o' 'em were sorry the earl's heir died. The maids were terrified o' him. Seems they tried to do everythin' in the house in pairs. And the footmen delivered his tea and answered his summons."

"Then Hotchkins and the housekeeper knew. Otherwise they never would have assigned a maid's task to a footman."

"Aye. The footman I spoke to said they even had a covert

signal to alert everyone in the servants' hall when Lord Fecken-ham returned. Said protocol changed when he was at home."

"Good heavens!" It was difficult to imagine living in a house where one person had such a profound and detrimental effect on everything else. They all must have been bracing themselves for the moment when Redditch died and Feckenham became mas-ter. "I'm guessing the staff must have turned over frequently."

"Oh, aye. 'Twas difficult to keep maids, let alone footmen. But the upper servants never begrudged them a good reference, they said."

I frowned, the idea that had been forming in my mind dis-solving. "So they wouldn't have had any difficulty finding other work after they departed. Particularly with a reference from an earl's butler or housekeeper."

"Aye."

But there was something in her voice, some note of disquiet that made me stare at her reflection in the mirror, waiting for her to speak again. She slid the last hairpin into place and then stood back to examine her handiwork. She crossed her arms in front of her, clutching the opposite elbow in each of her hands as if to ward off some troubling thought, and I didn't think it had any-thing to do with my appearance.

I swiveled to face her, gazing up at her in encouragement.

"There was one more thing one o' the maids told me, and it's been gnawin' at me ever since." She eyed me warily, her mouth twisting before she relented and spoke the words. "She said Lord Feckenham had to be kept away from his sisters."

My head reared back in shock.

"Said that's why the oldest girl hadna come oot yet, even though she's o' age. That the earl and countess kept 'em at their country estate just so Feckenham wasna near 'em."

The sickening darkness that lurked under those words threat-ened to turn my stomach. "Did she seem to be in a position to know?" I murmured in a low voice, matching her tone.

"I dinna ken, m'lady. It could be vicious rumors stirred up by the staff. But if the rest is true . . ."

"And it seems to be," I agreed, given the actions of the upper servants.

Her eyes were wide in her pale face. "Then I dinna find it so hard to believe this is true, too."

I sank back, overwhelmed by all the implications. If Feckenham had been kept away from his sisters, then there was a reason. Something had happened in the past. Something I didn't even want to entertain was possible. And yet there it was. It couldn't be turned away from.

If Feckenham truly had been culpable of all he'd been charged with, then it was a wonder he hadn't been murdered long ago. Despite my strong compulsion to discover the truth, I found it increasingly difficult to care whether his killer was ever caught. I knew Gage would argue that no one should be allowed to take the rule of the law into their own hands, but I was less convinced of this. Not when doing so would cause the victim irreparable harm, or the crime committed could not be punished by the courts.

However, the fact that the culprit had attempted to mask the murder as a burking changed things. We could not ignore that fact. And until we knew who had done it and why, we could not turn away from the truth. No matter how troubling.

CHAPTER SIXTEEN

The Duke of Bowmont possessed an opulent mansion on Grosvenor Square. One I was surprised to discover he still shared with his duchess. The tales of their notorious infidelity had led me to believe they would live separately, regardless of how amicable their relationship appeared to be.

Not that they would have ever needed to see one another living in such an immense house. The duchess could inhabit one floor, and the duke another, and they never need cross paths, or, indeed, hear one another's footsteps.

After removing my snow-dusted coat, the formidable butler led me through a series of rooms and hallways, each one more luxurious than the last. We sped past gilded trim, rich fabrics, priceless ornaments, and over sumptuous carpets, much of which I barely noticed, for my eyes were riveted to the artwork. David, Caravaggio, Titian, Turner. I was completely agog at the remarkable paintings hung on what seemed to be every wall, trying to take them all in as the butler hurried me past. By the time we reached the parlor where the duchess was seated on a blue velvet settee with a tiny white dog perched on her lap, I must have looked thunderstruck. I certainly felt it.

"Boodles, you've winded Lady Darby," the duchess admonished her butler, confirming my suspicions. "She's in the family way, you know. You can't go bustling her about like she's one of my young roués. What would her husband say should he learn of such treatment?"

"My apologies, Your Grace," he intoned in such a manner that made it difficult to believe he felt any regret.

The duchess shook her head, though her twinkling eyes belied any real disapproval. "Tea, Boodles. And something of sustenance for her ladyship."

"Oh, I am not hungry," I demurred.

She eyed me up and down in skepticism. "Really? Lucky for you. I was incessantly famished when I was increasing. But I shall eat, even if you do not." She waved Boodles away with a flick of her wrist. "Good butlers are always quite impervious to censure," she turned to inform me with a little sigh. "But tell me, shall this gown do, or should I choose something else?"

Contrary to the current popularity of white dresses in portraits, the duchess had chosen a dress of rich midnight blue with silver braid. Her decision not to wear an extravagant necklace struck me as odd, but then I realized this accentuated how creamy and smooth her neck and shoulders were. Her white hair was swept into curls, and a silver diadem with a floret emblem rested on her forehead.

She waited as I gave all of this careful consideration and then nodded. "Yes. Very well." My fingers already itched to hold a paintbrush. Then my gaze fell to the dog, who studied me with equal interest. "Did you wish me to include your dog?"

It was not that I disliked animals, but they were the very devil to capture on canvas. They often refused to sit still or cooperate, despite their owners' assurances that they were the sweetest creatures in all of Christendom.

As if the duchess sensed this, she gave a little gurgle of laughter. "No, I shall pass her off to my maid." This she promptly did before crossing the room toward a window looking out on the soft flurry of snow. A crimson drape had been pulled across the aperture at an angle, and a mahogany long stool with sable-colored velvet was positioned before it.

I opened my bag on the table provided for me and pulled out my charcoal and sketchbook while she twitched the swathed fabric slightly to the right. Then I stood to assess the alignment of the setting, shifting left and right, forward and back, until I found the most attractive angle.

"Is there a chair I might use?" I asked.

The duchess nodded to her maid, who moved a walnut side chair so that it sat just behind me.

"I always begin my portraits with a number of sketches," I explained as I settled into the chair. "To become familiar with your features and those of the room, to find the pose most flattering and comfortable for you, and to adjust any details I find displeasing. How do you wish to be positioned? We shall begin with that."

She sank regally onto the bench, and her maid hurried forward to adjust her skirts.

"The draping doesn't have to be exact," I informed them as the servant continued to tuck and smooth. "Just on the day I intend to paint the details of the folds in the skirt."

The maid glanced up in surprise. I presumed the artists who had painted the duchess in the past had not informed her of this. They had probably paid her efforts little attention.

She stepped aside, and I began to draw in broad strokes, periodically rising to my feet to verify the positioning, as I would be standing when I painted. The duchess accepted a cup of tea, aware she needn't sit perfectly still, though she limited her movements. I nodded my thanks to the maid, who set a cup beside my elbow, along with a plate filled with tempting little sandwiches.

"The first snow of the season is quite lovely, is it not?" the duchess remarked, her head turned toward the window, which looked out on the garden. "No matter where you are. Though I find I infinitely prefer such weather in the country. London turns it to muck too quickly. But there's much to be said for a snowy winter scene outside one's window when one is tucked up cozily inside." She smiled. "It's no wonder four of my children were born in the autumn."

I blinked at my sketchbook, trying not to react to this reference to the boudoir that some ladies wouldn't even broach with their friends, let alone a slim acquaintance. But then again, this *was* the Duchess of Bowmont.

"But summer in the country is lovely as well." She cast me an arch look. "Especially when one is newly wed."

"Yes, I find I generally prefer the country to London," I replied, refusing to rise to this bait.

"Oh, pooh. You won't share any details about your delightful husband?"

"I prefer to keep his delightfulness to myself."

She smiled. "Fair enough. But don't imagine I'm discouraged. I'm a terrible influence, you know. Absolutely incorrigible."

That she felt no remorse for this fact was quite evident. My lips curled upward at the corners of their own volition, unable to resist her charm, but I remained stubbornly absorbed in my sketching.

Far from frustrated by my silence, she set her teacup aside and turned the conversation to another matter. "What of this murder of Redditch's heir, then? You and your husband are investigating, are you not?"

"We are."

"Well, who do you think did it? Was it really a gang of burkers?"

I lifted my gaze to glare at her. Just because she was doing her goddaughter a favor by commissioning me to paint her did not mean I was going to allow her to malign me. But I saw only avid interest stamped across her features, nothing to indicate her question had been a subtle taunt. In any case, I doubted the duchess's insults were anything but direct. Given her status, she had no need to veil them.

"It wasn't a burking," I stated decisively, returning to my drawing. "As for the rest, I'm afraid I can't share the details of an ongoing investigation."

"Of course you can," she replied with amazing aplomb. "I know how to keep my own counsel. Perhaps not as well as you. But I'm no tale-teller. You'd be surprised the secrets I've never breathed to a soul. Men have a terrible propensity to chatter after intimate moments, you know. I find nothing loosens their tongue more. And the more secrets a man has to keep, the looser his lips."

I was vexed to feel myself once again coloring at her blithe reference to matters of the bedchamber. Had it not been for the airy, carefree nature of her comments, I would have suspected she was deliberately trying to make me uncomfortable, but it seemed, in fact, she was right. She was absolutely incorrigible.

It made me wonder briefly what it would be like to be so incautious with my words and demeanor. But, of course, I wasn't a duchess. And my scandal was of a far more horrifying nature than merely taking a lover. Or ten.

"I assume the family are all suspects," she remarked, determinedly sticking to this topic. "But, of course, Lord and Lady Redditch were at the theater. Several people have told me so. So I suppose that rules them out." She tapped her chin. "Unless they hired someone else to do it. That's the way the earl would go about it. He never was one to get his hands dirty."

At some point during this litany of speculation, my charcoal had come to a stop as I stared across at the duchess. When she noticed this, she arched her eyebrows in expectation.

"We're considering all possibilities," I told her, lowering charcoal to paper once again.

A pucker formed between her brows. "Then you must also be considering the second son, given the fact he now stands to inherit an earldom." Her eyes strayed toward the wintry scene outside, their crystalline quality shadowed.

Much as I had not wished to be drawn into such a conversation, I could tell she knew something. Each second she remained silent only confirmed that.

"Are you acquainted with Mr. Penrose?"

"Hmm . . . vaguely."

I waited, knowing there must be more.

She looked up. "But I've heard things about him. From my third son."

That this should mean something to me was evident, but I had no idea why.

"I'm afraid I've never had the pleasure of meeting your third son." I frowned, wondering if my memory was faulty. "That I can recall. Just your firstborn and youngest."

Her head tilted to the side. "I forget you have only recently returned to London." She brushed a hand down her skirt to remove some lint or dog hair. "And such rumors as would surround him would undoubtedly be thought inappropriate for a young lady's ears."

My brow furrowed in confusion, wondering why this, of all things, she did not speak plainly about.

She shook her head. "I will say no more about my son or Mr. Penrose. Their secrets are their own to tell. Except to say, I'm quite certain Mr. Penrose hadn't the least desire to inherit his father's earldom. In fact, I would wager he's quite distressed by it."

I opened my mouth to ask her how she could possibly know that, but she had already turned away. Sensing she spoke the truth—I would get no more from her on that subject—I resumed my sketching.

But I was still contemplating it two hours later when I returned to our townhouse. I'd decided I would ask Gage if he knew what the duchess had meant, and so inquired of Jeffers where I could find him.

"He's not home at present, my lady," he replied. "But the Dowager Lady Stratford is awaiting you in the drawing room."

"Oh, how wonderful." I hastened forward, thinking she might be able to explain the matter to me.

However, one look at her harried expression as she paced before the hearth told me this was not to be a happy visit. She glanced up as I entered, and the way her eyes flared wide made me hesitate in taking my next step. For Charlotte to be so unnerved must mean something was very wrong indeed.

"Charlotte, whatever is the matter?" I demanded, moving to stand beside her before the warm fire. I wriggled my fingers, which were numb with cold and hours of wielding charcoal. The snow had ceased, but the air was still damp and biting, and I was grateful for the heat.

"Kiera, I learned something today. Something I thought you should know immediately." She halted abruptly before saying more and cast a glance at the sofa nearest the hearth. "Perhaps you should sit."

I stared at her in astonishment. "Charlotte, you're scaring me."

"I . . . I didn't intend to. But what I have to say I know will be rather . . . alarming."

All I could think of was the blackmail letter I'd received. Had the senders already followed through on their threat?

No, that didn't make sense. The point of blackmail was to force the recipient to do your bidding. If you revealed their secrets before they did so, then you no longer held any leverage. Besides, it had been but four days. Surely they would not take action so quickly.

"I assure you, I'm not so fragile," I replied, not wanting to relinquish my place before the warm hearth. "Tell me."

She swallowed. "Are you acquainted with a Dr. Mayer?"

"Yes," I said warily.

"There are reports—verifiable ones—that he intends to publish your first husband's journals."

I blinked at her several times, unable to comprehend this. "His journals?"

She nodded.

"His medical journals?"

"I . . . I don't know precisely what is included in them. But they are rumored to be his private journals, his diaries."

I stumbled back a step, and Charlotte clasped my elbow, leading me over to the sofa, where I sank down heavily. "I . . . I didn't know he'd kept a journal," I murmured somewhat inanely, struggling to accept their existence.

I knew Sir Anthony had kept detailed notes for the anatomy textbook he was writing, for these had been passed along to Dr. Mayer along with the completed portions of the manuscript, including my beautifully rendered anatomical illustrations. Sir Anthony's will had specified that his friend and colleague was to finish his work and have his book published for him posthumously. If I'd had any inkling what was to come later, I would have hidden those drawings or burned them, even if it smarted to destroy something I'd labored over so keenly and suffered so much to complete. But the opportunity to do anything had passed. His nephew, the executor of his will, had arrived within hours after Sir Anthony's death and taken them into his possession, along with all his other papers.

Which, if the rumors proved true, must also have included his private journals. I wanted to deny the possibility, but I knew Charlotte. She would not be so alarmed if she did not believe them to be true, nor would she have relayed the gossip to me in such a manner.

Still, I couldn't help but question her halfheartedly. "You're certain?"

She clutched my hands in hers, chafing them. "As certain as I can be, though I wish it wasn't so."

I forced a deep breath into my lungs. "What of the anatomy textbook? Is Dr. Mayer publishing that, too?"

She shook her head. "I don't know. All I heard of was the journals."

That Dr. Mayer had chosen not to finish Sir Anthony's book or pursue publication was not a great surprise to me. I'd always sensed he was a jealous, bitter man. I was certain he was only too glad to use my role as the book's illustrator as an excuse not to execute the matter charged to him. So his sudden decision to publish Sir Anthony's private journals was justifiably upsetting and suspicious.

Charlotte interrupted the fraught silence that had descended. "You say you didn't know of their existence, but have you any idea what these journals might contain?"

I shrugged helplessly. "How can I know what he chose to record?" I pressed a hand to my temple, closing my eyes. "*But . . .* if Dr. Mayer is pursuing publication, I must suppose they include information far more interesting than the weather and his dietary intake. Notes on his clients, maybe. His interactions with bodysnatchers." I opened my eyes to stare at the crackling fire. "And I can only surmise I do not feature well in these writings, for the loathsome man never liked me."

"Ugh! Loathsome man indeed," Charlotte exclaimed in disgust. "Can he be stopped?"

"I don't know." I bit my lip in contemplation. "I shall have to speak to Gage."

My stomach dipped. Yet another way my past could harm him. I pressed a hand to my belly. Could harm our child.

Then another thought struck me. "How widespread are these reports?"

"Not far." Her brow puckered. "At least, not yet."

Which meant it would only be a matter of time before Lord

Gage, and the rest of the ton, learned of their existence. If he hadn't already.

"Thank you for telling me," I said. It would have been horrid to learn of it in a different way. Now, at least, I could be the one to tell Gage, not some smirking gossip.

"Of course. Is there anything I can do?"

"Just keep me apprised of any developments you hear."

"I will." She squeezed my hands, making me look up into her soft gray eyes. "You are not alone in this, Kiera. Even if the worst should happen, you have friends who will stand by you."

I felt tears bite at the back of my eyes. "Thank you."

It was a relief to know that unlike the last time I'd faced scandal, I would not be cut by all except my closest family. But how many would stand with us? How many would still come to Gage with the delicate matters they needed investigated? And if anyone did come to him, would the rest of society cooperate with our inquiry?

How many more challenges were to be thrown at us? How many more threats made to our status and well-being?

I had feared that Gage would come to regret his marriage to me, that my past would forever haunt us. But Gage had sworn he did not care about my reputation, about the troubles I brought with me. I very much feared that assertion was about to be sorely tested.

CHAPTER SEVENTEEN

I had several hours to contemplate the existence of the journals, so that by the time Gage had returned home at least my own shock had subsided and I was able to safely tuck away my more intense emotions. I'd decided to lay the facts out before him bare, with no histrionics. To this, he listened calmly without interruption. But at the end of my short recitation, he leaped to his feet to pace before the hearth in short, quick strides.

I watched him, awaiting his response as the sour taste of dread collected at the back of my mouth.

"He cannot be allowed to do this." His voice snapped like a whip. "It's unconscionable." When I didn't speak, his gaze darted to mine almost in accusation. "How can you be so sanguine about this?"

I reared back. "I . . . I'm not. But recall, I've had several hours to consider all this."

"And you've simply accepted it?" he asked incredulously.

"No!" I clenched my hands in my lap, stifling my frustration. "I have no more desire to see him publish whatever detestable things Sir Anthony wrote than you do. There must be a way we can stop him."

"Oh, I'll stop him." His eyes flashed with savage anger. "Even if I have to choke the life from his body."

I'd rarely seen Gage so furious, and it gave me pause. "That won't help. Not if you are hanged."

"You underestimate my intelligence. I would never be caught."

"Gage, be reasonable. You are not going to murder the man. At least . . . that should be a last resort."

This finally seemed to penetrate through the haze of his righteous anger. His frantic steps were arrested as he turned to stare at me in disbelief.

"I jest," I replied testily. "If you're allowed to speak of choking a man to death, I can make a quip about it being our final option."

He exhaled a long breath. "I suppose I am being a bit irrational."

I arched my eyebrows. "A bit?"

His expression softened as he offered me a tight smile. He sank down on the sofa beside me, staring into the fire. "What is to be done, then?" He scowled. "What do you suspect is written in those journals?"

"Well, knowing Sir Anthony, there is a great deal of unkind commentary accompanied by his pompous opinions."

His eyes narrowed. "About his medical patients?"

"I should say undoubtedly."

He sat taller. "Then there may be sensitive information about our royalty in there. After all, he was sergeant surgeon to George IV, was he not? I doubt the current monarch would be so pleased to discover such things about his brother were about to be put into print."

"I hadn't thought of that," I replied, relief flooding through me. "Could it be so simple?"

"I don't know. The publisher might just as easily refuse to bow to royal pressure, or insist he'll exclude such information.

Though there is also the matter of the journals including confidential information about other members of society who sought his medical expertise. I wonder if it's quite legal for him to reveal such things, even if the names are obscured. 'Lord F__ approached me to treat his syphilis.'"

Since I hadn't the foggiest, I did not comment.

This time, he didn't seem to require a reply. "I shall speak with a barrister friend of mine and then discover what publisher Dr. Mayer has approached. Perhaps they can be dissuaded or reasoned with." He swiveled to look at me. "Do not worry. I'll handle this."

I nodded, relieved he'd accepted the matter so equably after his initial burst of temper. That I wouldn't be required to face Dr. Mayer myself was also a relief. But the hollow in the pit of my stomach warned me this difficulty would not be cleared up so easily.

His hand reached for mine. "I told you I would protect you, and I shall."

"Sebastian . . ." I began to protest, fearful he placed too much of an emphasis on his ability to do just that. But a light rap on the door brought my words to a stop.

"Come in," he called.

Our butler stepped through the door, his shoulders back and his head held even higher than usual. "Sir, if I'm not interrupting, might I have a moment of your time?"

"Of course, what is it, Jeffers?"

He closed the door and crossed the room to stand before us. "I have just had a visit from a servant in one of the houses on Upper Brook Street."

A pulse of excitement went through me, for I knew our butler would not bring anything to us that was not of probable importance, and judging from his proud posture, this must be something important indeed.

"He did not see or hear the attack on Lord Feckenham. But

shortly after eleven, he did see him speaking with his brother, Mr. Penrose. He said the discussion did not appear to be an amicable one. At least, not on Mr. Penrose's part."

Gage and I exchanged a speaking glance. I could scarcely credit that such a piece of evidence had been dropped in our laps.

"Thank you, Jeffers. I trust you asked for the servant's name and direction should we need to speak with him again."

"Of course, sir."

"Well done. You are a topping fellow."

"Thank you, sir." He bowed very properly before exiting the room with, dare I say, a spring in his step.

It was almost enough to make me smile, but for the dreadful implications of the information he'd presented to us.

"Has Mr. Penrose returned from the country?" I asked Gage.

He shook his head. "And I employed a pair of lads to watch Redditch House so that the moment he does return, I'll be notified."

"You don't trust Mr. Poole to do so?" I remembered how the earl's secretary had promised to impel Mr. Penrose to write to us, or that he would do so himself.

"On the contrary, I believe the fellow will follow through. But what if Mr. Penrose should arrive when he is not there? Not to mention the fact that letters take time to write and send. No, it is much better this way." His brow darkened. "But if he does not return by the morning, I think another visit to Lord Redditch is in order."

"Lord Damien mentioned he had plans to move to the continent. Do you think the earl might have lied? Could Mr. Penrose already be beyond our reach?"

His fingers tapped an agitated tattoo against his knee. "We shall address that if we must."

This talk of Mr. Penrose reminded me of another matter I wished to discuss with him. "What do you know of the Duke of Bowmont's third son?"

He appeared confused by this shift in topic. "Not much. I'm familiar with Lord Edward, of course. He was a year ahead of me at Cambridge. But we've never exchanged more than polite remarks. Why do you ask?"

I shifted to face him more fully. "The duchess spoke of him during her portrait session this morning. She said something about how she'd heard things about Mr. Penrose from Lord Edward. I could tell that was supposed to insinuate something, but when I expressed ignorance as to what it was, she suggested the topic might be too delicate for a young lady's ears."

That this was true was evident in the change that came over Gage's demeanor. His shoulders stiffened, and his face drained of all expression.

"Curious," he remarked.

When he said no more, I scowled. "Do you think me bird-witted? I can tell you know something." I searched his eyes, looking for some sign of yielding. "Is it truly too shocking?"

"No, not really. But it isn't something a gentleman discusses with his wife."

"Which could be any number of things, given the crotchets you take into your head when it comes to sheltering my unworldly person."

He arched an eyebrow at my withering sarcasm. "All I will say is that Lord Edward has . . . interesting proclivities."

"That doesn't tell me anything!"

He glared back at me. "It wasn't meant to."

I huffed and turned away, struggling to retain control of my temper. "Then I suppose we should assume that Mr. Penrose possesses the same 'interesting proclivities.' Proclivities he may remark upon when we interview him. Do you wish for me to learn of them for the first time from him?"

His lips clamped into a thin line, and I knew I had him. He spoke carefully. "Because of their inclinations, Lord Edward and Mr. Penrose are unlikely to be interested in you." His gaze lifted to meet mine to see if I understood. "But they might be interested in each other."

I opened my mouth to speak and then stopped, suddenly grasping what he meant. "Oh," was all I could say as a blush burned its way into my cheeks.

Gage nodded once.

"I suppose that explains why the duchess said he wouldn't wish to inherit the earldom. He'll need an heir. And that means taking a wife. A . . . woman," I stammered.

"Well, he wouldn't be the first nobleman in such a predicament."

I glanced at him in surprise.

"But we are getting ahead of ourselves. We do not have proof that any of this is true. And there are some men who are not so particular."

I stared at the edge of the rug, feeling like I was receiving an education I hadn't been prepared for. I was vaguely aware that there were men who preferred the company of other men, but that had seemed an altogether foreign concept, not something I expected to encounter among society. Why society was so determined to keep what they deemed improper from young ladies' ears made little sense to me. Wouldn't it be better for us to be prepared for such a discovery than to feel like utter dolts?

"We shall see what he has to say when we speak to him," Gage hastened to say before pushing to his feet, clearly eager to abandon the topic. "Now, I must change my clothes." He wrinkled his nose. "I can still smell the stink of Smithfield clinging to them."

I hadn't noticed anything, and my sense of smell was stronger than ever, but Smithfield was notorious for its filth and disorder, mainly because of its live-meat market held in the heart of the city. I'd had little occasion to venture near there and no desire to do so.

"The Italian Boy inquest?"

"Yes. Trying to help Anderley run to ground a witness who

might be able to identify the boy." He exhaled a weary sigh. "The first hearing before the Bow Street Magistrates begins in two days, and they've yet to put a name to the lad."

"Will that hurt the inquiry?"

"It certainly won't help it. And it might introduce doubts in the minds of the magistrates or an eventual jury. Best to have a name."

"Yes, but will it be the right one?" I questioned as he moved toward the door.

He turned back with a troubled smile. "Aye, there's the rub."

Shortly after dinner a letter arrived for Gage. We were seated in the drawing room, when Jeffers entered holding the silver salver. I felt a moment's qualm that the blackmailers were contacting me again. But the missive proved to be addressed to my husband, and the handwriting was too neat and precise to be that of my extortionists.

"It's from Mr. Poole," Gage explained as he read. "He says Mr. Penrose returned to London this evening. That he did as requested and asked him to write to us, and Mr. Penrose entreated him to write to us on his behalf. He shall be pleased to receive us in the morning to answer our questions."

"Well, it appears your lads fell asleep on the job," I murmured, as he'd heard nothing from the boys he'd set to watch Redditch House. "But this is a good sign, is it not? At least, it seems Penrose wishes to cooperate."

His brow furrowed. "Yes, but does he have any other choice? If he refuses to speak with us or dodges our visits, that only makes him look guilty. Best to attempt to brazen his way through."

"True. But maybe now we can get some answers."

"Yes," he agreed, though his tone was distracted. His gaze shifted to study me. "I think it would be best if you take the lead when we question him."

My eyes widened. "Me?"

"Penrose is expecting me to charm him into giving up the truth. He won't be prepared for you or your forthrightness." His eyes softened. "Gentle though it may be. I have an inkling of the two of us, he'll find you the easiest to confide in."

"Because of my past," I stated baldly, unwilling to beat around the bush.

"Yes. Much of society knows me as a charming gallant and a reformed rake, who's never suffered a day of strife in his life." His pale eyes glinted with weary cynicism, and I reached out to take his hand. He had no one to blame but himself, for he'd cultivated such an image purposely, but since it was far from the truth, I knew that some days it was difficult to sustain. "He might see similarities in your experiences, and that might make him less guarded than he usually would be."

I nodded in comprehension. If even a quarter of the things said about Feckenham were true, then living with him could not have been easy. His rumored treatment of his brother in many ways echoed Sir Anthony's treatment of me, though the power of a brother over a brother could never surpass that of a husband over a wife. Not when all that she possessed, including her loyalty and her very self, in effect belonged to her husband.

Still, I could empathize in ways others could not, and Penrose was likely to sense this.

"I'll do my best," I told Gage.

He squeezed my hand. "You'll do well. You always do."

George Penrose was waiting for us the following day in the same morning room we had utilized during our previous visit. He stood at the window, his hands clasped behind his back, looking out over the garden. Much of the snow from the previous day had already melted in the bright sun. When he turned, I could see that his posture was stiff, his jaw tight, but he made an effort to appear pleased to see us when Hotchkins introduced us.

He bowed over my hand before turning to nod to Gage.

"Thank you for agreeing to see us so promptly upon your return, Lord Feckenham," Gage said.

Penrose blanched. "Please don't call me that."

Gage appeared contrite, but I strongly suspected he'd addressed him by his murdered brother's courtesy title on purpose. "Too soon?"

He nodded.

"My apologies. Mr. Penrose, then."

"Please."

He gestured toward the chairs, and we all sat while tea was offered and declined. When the door shut behind the butler, Penrose shifted forward abruptly in his seat, as if he could contain himself no longer.

"I told Mother that sending me to Silvercrest before speaking with you would only make me look guilty, but she would not be reasoned with. Said she would travel to Worcestershire herself to fetch my sisters if I wouldn't, and I couldn't let her do that. Not when she was evidently so overcome."

"Your sisters returned with you?" I asked.

"Yes." His eyes flicked back and forth between me and Gage, sensing our interest in this bit of news. "Father has decided to have my brother buried here in London rather than at Silvercrest, and Mother wanted her daughters close."

"Forgive me," I replied. "But then why didn't your sisters live here with you in London? I would have thought your eldest sister would already be out."

"My sisters have not always been in the best health, and the London air affects their lungs. They do much better in the country." This answer sounded as if it had been recited by rote, and I had every reason to believe it had been. It was the type of response a family agreed upon ahead of time to answer any questions about the sisters' continued absence.

"They must be bereft over the loss of their brother."

He coughed, as if choking on his answer. "Yes, of course."

I tilted my head, studying his gray eyes. "Are you?"

He was handsome, though not strikingly so, being possessed of an average build and soft brown hair. But he did claim a remarkably fine pair of eyes the shade of pewter, fringed with long dark lashes. These were clouded with a mixture of anxiety, defiance, and a weariness that seemed to pull down all the muscles of his face. I wondered which of these emotions would win out.

"If you are as good as the reputation that precedes you," he began, "then I suspect you already know the answer to that." He frowned at the rug, the fingers of his left hand restlessly tugging at the wooden arm of his chair. "I am not sorry my brother is dead. He was not a good man. And he loved to torment me." His gaze lifted to meet mine. "But I did not kill him."

I was inclined to believe him until he arched his chin in obstinacy.

"I couldn't have. I was at White's the entire evening until one of Father's footmen came to fetch me home. Any number of people saw me. You can ask them."

"You're right. You were seen by a number of members of that club," I admitted.

He sat back, satisfied he'd proven his point.

"But there seems to be a gap in all their remembrances. One that centers around the precise time your brother was murdered."

His shoulders ratcheted upward again.

"And a witness saw you arguing with your brother in the street outside this house minutes before he was killed."

His face drained of what color remained, and his knuckles turned white where he gripped the chair.

"Care to explain what you were discussing, and why you were so upset?"

CHAPTER EIGHTEEN

Penrose appeared to struggle to find his words, and when he did it was an appeal to his maker. Pitching forward, he braced his elbows on his knees and covered his face. "I swear to you, I did not kill my brother." His gaze lifted to plead with me. "I . . . I do not deny I wished him to the devil, but I did not send him there."

"Then what did you argue about?" Gage interjected.

Penrose inhaled a shaky breath, his hands trembling as he scraped them through his hair.

Guessing at what might be the cause for his hesitation, I sought to reassure him of one point. "You know we are only interested in one crime—who murdered Lord Feckenham and why." I glanced at Gage. "I know I can speak for my husband when I say that all other alleged offenses . . ." I frowned, not liking that word, but I had no better one to use ". . . are not our concern. Not unless they directly impact the outcome of the investigation."

If possible, this seemed to alarm him more. But after a few

agitated moments, my calm regard seemed to work some effect on him. His breathing began to slow, and a welcome tinge of color returned to his complexion. His eyes, which had been as wide as saucers, returned to their normal size and his hands dropped back into his lap.

When he finally spoke, his gaze dipped to the floor again. "I was upset because I'd discovered he had been harassing a . . . particular friend of mine." His gaze flicked up to meet mine briefly. "He'd threatened to expose my friend's associations if he didn't perform a foul task for him." His eyes blazed. "I'm not going to tell you what it is, for it involves a number of gentlemen who do not deserve to have their names besmirched."

"And your friend?" Gage asked.

"I would rather not reveal his name," he bit out. "But if you must know it, I will. Trusting in your discretion." He sank back in his chair. "The truth is, my brother liked secrets. He liked knowing them. He liked having people either beholden to him or in his debt because of them. And he was forever using what he knew to compel and manipulate others into doing things they would never otherwise contemplate simply for the pleasure he derived from it." His mouth twisted bitterly. "I should know. I was his favorite puppet. And I hated myself for it." His chin lifted. "Until one day I couldn't stand it anymore and I refused. I decided it would be better to face the consequences of his threats, to let him tell our family the truth about me, than to continue to submit to his ploys."

"And did he?" I said.

He huffed humorlessly. "Oh, yes. He never made idle threats. But . . . the family didn't react the way my brother thought they would." His brow furrowed as if he still found this difficult to believe. "They didn't shun me or cast me from the house. They were upset and worried, and they've each tried in their own way to . . . remedy what they see as my problem. Giving me books, or pushing young ladies in front of me, or taking me to visit . . ."

He broke off, flicking a glance at me as he cleared his throat. "But they haven't turned away from me."

"Which I imagine infuriated your brother," I ruminated, feeling a bit more kindly toward the earl and countess for not ostracizing their son, as many might have done.

"He tried threatening to make my secret public, but I knew he would never dare do so while Father was alive. Not when he couldn't be sure Father wouldn't refute such rumors and keep me close."

"But once your father died and he became earl, it would be different."

"As the head of the family, his word would be law. And society would see it as fact." He inhaled an uneven breath. "I want to believe he wouldn't actually have had me brought up on criminal charges, but I've learned to never underestimate his cruelty." And given the fact that sodomy was still one of about a dozen crimes punishable by death, this was no mean threat.

"So you've been making plans to go to Paris."

His gaze registered surprise that I knew this and then softened with wry humor. "Yes. Mother told me she made up some faradiddle about my removing to the Albany, that she thought Paris seemed too suspicious. I told her it was a stupid thing to say."

I studied the earnest young man's face. "You do realize you've only given yourself a stronger motive for murdering your brother." I couldn't decide whether he was culpable or not. My instincts were inclined to believe him innocent, but I had been fooled by sympathetic young men before.

"Except I was not going to Paris to stay. Not yet."

I glanced at Gage, who lowered the leg he'd crossed over his knee at this pronouncement. "What do you mean?"

His fingers tapped restlessly against the arm of the chair again. "I suppose I must tell you all."

"That would be best," I coaxed.

"I was going to Paris to set up a residence, and then I was to return to London until my Father died." He suddenly found something of great interest to study in the palm of his hand. "His heart is not good. The physicians say it's only a matter of time. And when he does die, my brother would take control of most of Father's property and assets. He can't break the entailment, after all. But he has been quietly selling what smaller properties he can, and placing the sum in an account in my name." His eyes rose to see how we had taken this news. "And he changed his will so that the guardianship over my mother and my sisters lies with me."

"That is rather extraordinary," Gage remarked.

"Well, he couldn't trust Feckenham with any of them." This seemed to pain him to admit. "I was to collect my mother and sisters the moment I learned of Father's death and set off for Paris."

"That's why you were so concerned for your father when you returned home the night of Feckenham's murder," I guessed.

He nodded. "I knew my duty. And I knew it was a matter of haste. That it must be carried off before my brother knew what I was about."

All this subterfuge, this urgency in keeping Feckenham away from his sisters, could only mean that the rumors were true, in one form or another. I felt sick in my soul, and somewhat tainted. The reality of such awfulness was like an itch in my brain that crawled down my spine.

"If we speak to the earl, to his solicitor, will he confirm what you've told us?" Gage asked, dealing with practicalities, though I could see what it cost him to control his outrage over what Penrose's revelation implied about Feckenham. It completely rubbed against everything he believed a gentleman should be, as well as heightened the sense of protectiveness he'd developed almost since birth. That a man should seek to exploit the privileges granted to him to harm the females under his protection rather than shield them must disgust him as almost nothing could.

"Yes. It is the sordid truth, and I am heartily sorry of it. That I should have such a brother . . ." He closed his eyes and shook his head, perhaps realizing it was impossible to voice all the shame and affront he must be feeling. When he opened his gray eyes again, they were sharp with challenge. "I trust you will keep this to yourselves."

"Of course," Gage snapped back. "I would not see a young lady come to harm for all the world."

Penrose nodded. "I know you to be honorable. I meant no offense. But I had to be certain."

"Just so," he conceded before glancing at me. "I believe that's all the questions we have for you at the moment. But I ask that you remain in town for the time being."

He agreed and then rose to leave, promising to send the earl to us.

"You do realize this doesn't clear him of suspicion," I said softly after the door shut. "Because I can't help but notice that killing his brother solves his problems even better than running off to Paris." I frowned. "For that matter, it solves all their problems."

"Yes, but I just can't see him doing so in such a dramatic manner," Gage replied, his eyes narrowed in contemplation as he settled onto the sofa beside me, taking hold of my hand. "Perhaps if it had been poison. That is a passive form of murder where one can distance themselves somewhat from what they've done. But stabbing someone, having their blood literally on your hands, is not so simple to brush aside."

I conceded his point, pulling my hand from his as I felt a twinge in my wrist.

"And why would he confront his brother in the street outside, where he must have realized anyone might happen across them, before attacking him?" he argued further. "Such an attack would seem to be spontaneous, when the attempted use of the sticking plaster tells us otherwise. No one carries such a thing on their person on the chance it might be needed."

"Unless he'd already planned what to do if his brother did not agree to stop his threats against his friend."

"I more readily believe the friend might have done it, to protect himself and Penrose."

I nodded, such a thought having already occurred to me, and continued to roll my wrist. "We should have insisted he give us his name."

"I already have a suspicion who it might be, and should be able to confirm it fairly easily." He reached for my hand. "Why do you keep moving your wrist like that? I noticed you doing so on the way here, though you managed to keep it in your lap during our interview with Penrose."

"Oh, it's nothing," I retorted as he examined it. "I wrenched my wrist this morning when I slipped coming down the stairs. I had to grab the banister to stop myself from falling."

Gage's eyes brightened with concern. "Does it still hurt?" he asked as he pressed a particularly tender spot.

I flinched. "A little. But only when I twist it at a certain angle. Or you press on it." I glared at him as he did so a second time.

He ceased his ministrations. "Perhaps Dr. Shaw should take a look at it."

"It's not as bad as that. But I will have Bree wrap it if it will make you feel better."

"You must take care," he cautioned me.

"I'm well aware," I replied, trying to keep my testiness out of my voice. "It's quite normal to be a bit clumsy during this stage. I'm still growing accustomed to the changes the baby has wrought to my body, and my balance isn't what it was."

"Perhaps I should begin carrying you up and down the stairs."

I cast him a withering glare. "Don't be ridiculous."

Far from chastened, he grinned. "You don't like the idea of being carted about like an empress?"

"I have two perfectly good legs, thank you."

I was saved from whatever quip had brought a roguish twinkle to his eyes by the arrival of the Earl of Redditch. Whatever I'd expected of the earl, it was not to see him looking even haler than he had a week ago. The dark circles under his eyes were gone, and his complexion exhibited a healthy flush. Evidently, he wasn't losing sleep over the loss of his heir.

"My son said you had a few questions for me about my will." A slight puckering of his brow was all that showed he was even concerned.

"Yes," Gage said, taking the reins of this conversation. "We have it on good authority you've been ill."

This appeared to disconcert him, for he sniffed and fidgeted with the front of his frock coat. "I'm not sure how that pertains to your investigation, but yes, I have." Evidently he didn't want word of the seriousness of his ailment spreading.

"And you recently changed your will because of it?"

He scowled. "I suppose George told you. The boy must have had no choice." He heaved an aggravated breath. "Yes, I changed it." His already ruddy face reddened further. "Do you need to know the specifics?"

"I'm afraid so. If you please."

In the midst of much harrumphing, he relayed most of the details Penrose had told us, though he remained stubbornly silent on why. We did not press the matter, but Gage did ask if he would write to his solicitor, asking him to speak with us about the will. To this request, the earl flatly refused. But he was willing to send his secretary, Mr. Poole, to us, as well as Hotchkins, who both served as witnesses. The butler would only share the bare basics, but Mr. Poole was more forthcoming.

"To be honest, I was surprised by the earl's ingenuity," he

confided to us, sitting tall and straight in the chair Mr. Penrose had vacated. "I doubt it will surprise you that I am privy to more than my fair share of the family's confidences, and it pains me to say I'd long despaired the earl would do anything to counter his heir before his own demise and the full weight and power of the earldom had descended to him. I was relieved to discover I was wrong, and quite happy to sign it."

"So you did not help with the arrangements?" Gage clarified.

"Of the will? No, sir. But I was parcel to the selling of the earl's smaller properties and investments, and the management of the account the proceeds were deposited into for Mr. Penrose."

"Feckenham was unaware what was happening?"

"It was imperative he not know."

"How were you able to do that? What if he'd chosen to visit one of these smaller properties?"

"Lord Feckenham rarely traveled outside of London, and most of these properties were far from the city. So long as his suspicions were not aroused, it seemed unlikely he would take such an initiative."

I turned to stare at the display of Meissen figures adorning the mantel above the fireplace, finding it difficult to accept what a scurrilous fellow Feckenham was that his own father—an earl, no less—had to tread so delicately around him. How much power had Feckenham wielded? And who else had suffered for it?

"It truly seems better for all that Feckenham is dead," Gage remarked with surprising candor.

Mr. Poole hesitated and then nodded, his expression strained. "It does."

We departed the earl's townhouse with a cloud hanging over us, both literally and figuratively. The sunny skies of earlier that morning had turned leaden, casting a wintry pall over the city.

It did not take much insight to understand what troubled Gage, for it was the same thing that troubled me.

"How do you continue to investigate the murder of a person

so abominable?" I posited, staring out the window of the carriage at the bustling midday streets of Mayfair, willing to broach the subject even if he couldn't. Girls carrying pails of milk skirted carefully around smartly dressed ladies and gentlemen. Near the corner, a smattering of people gathered around a hot potato seller, eager to warm their hands as much as consume the tasty fare.

"I admit I'm conflicted." He crossed his arms over his chest and appeared to scrutinize the Moroccan leather across from us as if it held the answers he sought. "If Feckenham was killed by someone who was angry because they'd gambled and lost to him, or because they were too weak to refuse whatever foul demands he made of them, then I do not believe they should escape punishment." His voice deepened. "But if it was a member of his family, someone seeking vengeance for the abominable things they've hinted he has done, or to prevent further outrages in the future, then I find it harder to condemn them."

"Maybe they saw no other way."

Gage turned to me in interest, and this time I met his gaze.

"They must have realized what a remorseless monster he was. Maybe they realized they couldn't let him inherit. Men with such lofty titles are too protected. They wield too much power. While the earl was alive, he held some sort of check over him, small though it might have been. After he died, there would be none." I allowed the ramifications of that to hover in the air between us, unspoken. "The only other way they might have stopped him was to bring him up on charges, if they could gather the proof. But that would mean a scandal of immense proportions, and would forever shame anyone connected with it, regardless of whether they were innocent victims." I plucked at the hazelnut wool of my redingote. "Maybe they felt they had no other choice."

"Kiera, are you suggesting the entire family was party to it?" Gage whispered in astonishment.

"No, they couldn't be," I protested, but then paused. "Could they?"

He didn't respond, and I could tell the same incredulous doubt had crept over him as it had me. Neither of us spoke again, not even when we returned to the townhouse. We were both too absorbed in our own unsettling contemplations. Contemplations we took along with us to our evening engagement and into our disturbed slumber.

When the knock on our bedchamber door came in the predawn hours, I was already awake, and had been so for some time. My dreams of late had been a vivid mixture of bizarre and arresting. This was not extraordinary for a woman in the family way. Alana had experienced much the same. But they were new to me.

Overall, I had to say I vastly preferred the more carnal dreams I'd experienced, even if I did wake tingling and disoriented. It made me appreciate all the more the advantages to sharing a bed with my husband.

But that night had not been filled with pleasant imaginings.

I'd dreamed of Sir Anthony—something I hadn't done in many months. One minute I'd been standing beside him, sketching the intricate muscle tissue laid open to me, and the next I was staring up at a man from a great height. I'd tried to push to my feet, but found I couldn't move. When the man lifted a shovel full of dirt to rain down on me, I understood why.

I'd woken with a start, sweat beading my brow. One glance at Gage had told me he was still asleep, his handsome face relaxed with slumber. So I'd lain still, tracing his features on the pillow beside me in the dark as my breathing slowed and my sweat dried in the cool night air.

There was no real wonder that I should have such a dream given the current stresses I was under. It had only been a matter of time before memories of my life with my first husband and the activities he undertook crept into my dreams. I could only feel grateful the worst of my nightmares had not returned, but I was braced for them anyway. They had always plagued me at the most inopportune times.

My stomach had begun to rumble, making its hunger known, and I had just been contemplating whether I should rise for the day or try to go to sleep again when the knock roused me. I knew the staff would not disturb us at such an hour unless it was a matter of urgency, so I prodded Gage on the shoulder.

"Sebastian," I murmured. "Wake up."

He groaned and blinked open one bleary eye before closing it. "Yes, darling." His arm draped around me, pulling me closer. "You know I'm always at your service."

I blushed lightly. "No, Sebastian. Someone's at the door."

Both eyes opened to slits to stare at me as if I'd said something absurd. But when a second knock sounded on the door, he released me and pushed up onto one elbow to gaze at the offending piece of wood. Then he scrambled from bed, pulling his dressing gown over his bare shoulders and knotting it loosely.

I could not see around the door when he opened it, but I heard him softly confer with someone. From the sound of the pleasing baritone, I realized it was Anderley. He passed Gage a paper of some kind, which Gage lost no time in opening, holding it up to read it in the light of the candle his valet held.

The change that came over him was immediate. His back stiffened and his shoulders hunched. It must have been but a few short lines, for he soon dropped it to his side and reached for Anderley's candle.

"Set out my clothes for the day, and order the carriage made ready." He started to turn away, but stopped to add one more request. "And send Miss McEvoy up to attend to her mistress."

"What is it?" I demanded, sitting bolt upright in bed as he strode over to the hearth.

Having stirred the banked embers to life, he rose to his feet to face me. "There's been a second stabbing in Mayfair."

Shock sent a tremor down my spine, but I retained enough

control of my senses to realize he hadn't said murder. "Is the victim alive?"

His expression was grim. "Barely."

I pressed a hand to my pounding chest. "Then we must hurry." I pushed the sheets and blankets off me, mindful of my wrist, and climbed out onto the rug. I moved toward the dresser where my undergarments were stored, but Gage stopped me with a gentle hand on my arm.

"Kiera."

I glanced up into his shadowed eyes, my alarm growing.

"The victim is David Newbury."

I gasped.

He nodded. "Miss Newbury's brother."

"Oh, poor Ellen. She's such a sweet girl." I wondered if I had time to dash a letter off to my brother. He would wish to know.

"And Kiera." The strain in his voice made my eyes snap back to his. "You should also know the letter mentioned a sticking plaster."

His words sank into the pit of my stomach like a lead weight. Had we been wrong? Had Feckenham's murder been at the hands of an amateur burker?

I inhaled a shaky breath. "Then I suppose we shall have to confront that like the rest."

CHAPTER NINETEEN

Though the drapes were still drawn at Lord Newbury's townhouse at such an early hour, light illuminated the curtains in several windows, and sought any gaps in the fabric to send tiny shards of light spilling out across the street. Much of Mount Street was populated by cabinetmakers, upholsterers, and sculptors, as well as a handful of taverns and coffeehouses, but desirable homes were interspersed among them, including Lord Newbury's. Situated in a block of houses between Berkley Square and St. George's Workhouse, the Newburys' position was respectable, although not as vaunted as the Earl of Redditch in Upper Brook Street.

We were ushered into the small drawing room, where Lord Newbury paced the floor while his wife and daughter perched fretfully at the edge of the furniture, still attired in their nightclothes, with warm wrappers pulled over them. Though a fire blazed brightly in the hearth, I was glad I'd insisted on keeping my woolen redingote to combat the night's chill permeating the room.

Lady Newbury was the first to approach, leaping to her feet at the sight of us. However, contrary to the warm, maternal figure I was accustomed to encountering, we faced a vengeful fury. "Is this because we allowed your brother to pay addresses to our Ellen?"

I stiffened as she pointed a finger in my face.

"Are you responsible for bringing these burkers down upon us, upon our dearest son?"

Gage stepped forward to intercede as she loomed over me. Whether she was actually intent on doing me harm, I didn't know, but her face was a twisted mask of anger, grief, and pain.

"Alma," Lord Newbury called out, moving forward to restrain his wife. "We do not know that Lady Darby is to blame." But I could tell from the glint in his eyes he was close to condemning me as well. "Let us hear what they have to say before we make any accusations."

She allowed him to coax her back to her seat on the sofa, though her wrathful eyes never left my face.

Faced with such naked animosity, I retreated inside myself, trying to numb the hollow ache that reverberated with the echoes of such a familiar refrain. I couldn't summon the anger I'd learned to use to guard against it, not when faced with Lady Newbury's evident pain. She had lashed out in worry and grief, and shouting back at her was not the answer, no matter how unfair her allegations.

So I allowed Gage to lead me over to a settee facing the Newburys, welcoming the support of his hand clasped in mine. However, I could not bring myself to meet Lady Newbury's gaze, though I felt it boring holes into my skin. Ellen sat beside her, pleating the trim of her pea green wrapper, her eyes rimmed with red. They dipped briefly to the wrist Bree had wrapped in a bandage, but she didn't speak.

"Now, tell us what happened," Gage stated calmly. "When was Mr. Newbury attacked? And where?"

"A constable on his rounds found him lying at the mouth of a stable yard which opens onto Mount Street just west of here. It was apparent he'd either been shot or stabbed, and an attempt had been made to suffocate him. A sticking plaster covered his face." Lord Newbury's eyes flicked to mine and then back. "Fortunately, it didn't hinder his breathing as much as the perpetrator hoped."

"How long ago did this occur?"

His eyes glanced at the clock. "The constable pounded on our door at about half past four. So perhaps an hour ago."

"I assume a physician has been called for?"

"He's examining him now."

Gage nodded. "I hate to be indelicate, but did the constable relay any further information about the state he'd found your son in? Did it appear as if he'd been bleeding long?" he clarified.

Lady Newbury gave a little gasp and turned aside.

Lord Newbury patted her hand where it gripped his shoulder. "Steady on, girl." His own face appeared pale. "The constable expressed concern at the blood he'd lost. Said he couldn't be roused."

Gage did not speculate on what this could mean, waiting to speak to the doctor first before he remarked on the possible timing of the attack. "Did he mention anything else?"

The baron shook his head, the dark hair he normally kept ruthlessly pomaded back from his face flopping side to side with the motion.

"Is the constable here?"

"No. But I'm sure Lockwood can provide you his name and direction." He dipped his head toward the door, obviously referring to the butler who had shown us in.

"Mr. Newbury resides here with you? He was returning home?"

"Yes. Plenty of room. No need for him to take quarters of his own." Lord Newbury's abrupt manner of speaking reminded me he had once been a younger son and an officer in the army, an *aide-de-camp* to Wellington during the latter part of the wars against France. He hadn't inherited the barony until a decade ago, when his older brother had died without male issue.

"Merely a point of clarification," Gage replied, attempting to soothe his evident affront. "Do you know where he was returning from?"

"Why the blazes does that matter? Seems dashed obvious to me what happened."

"I would like to discover whether he was followed, or if someone laid in wait for him. Was he specifically targeted, or was the attack random?" Gage explained.

Lord Newbury's face reddened with outrage. "Why should my son have been targeted? He's neither a scapegrace nor a hellhound."

Before Gage could reply, the door opened to admit a middle-aged gentleman possessed of a fiery crop of red hair and freckles.

"Dr. Woods," Lady Newbury gasped, rising to her feet. "How is he?"

Lord Newbury and Gage both stood out of politeness as the physician moved closer. "I've made him as comfortable as I can. Stanched the wound, and addressed the bruising along his collarbone." His brow furrowed. "But he's lost a significant amount of blood, and the wound continues to bleed. I could recommend a surgeon to stitch it, but the problem is internal. The knife likely severed a vein or pierced an organ. He hasn't regained consciousness." He gazed solemnly at the family. "I'm afraid you should prepare yourself for the worst."

Lady Newbury crumpled before our eyes, and it was her daughter who turned and gathered her weeping mother into her arms even as silent tears streaked her own cheeks. There couldn't have been a clearer distinction between the genuineness of Lady Newbury's outpouring of grief and the feigned one of Lady Redditch a week earlier.

His hands hanging by his side, Lord Newbury glanced listlessly between his spouse and child, and the doctor. "There's . . . no hope?"

"Very little, I'm afraid."

He nodded in acceptance, though I could tell he was far from feeling it.

Dr. Woods turned to us. "You are Mr. Gage, are you not? And Lady Darby?"

I couldn't tell by his expression whether he was pleased to make our acquaintance or not, but as always, I was wary of medical men who were unknown to me. They undoubtedly knew of my reputation and Sir Anthony, and many of them had harsh opinions of me.

"Yes," Gage replied.

"I assume you'll be investigating this matter." He scowled. "And I'm heartily glad of it, for there is a clear indication of foul play." His eyes shifted to the family, and he lowered his voice. "But perhaps we should discuss this elsewhere."

"No!" Lady Newbury protested, her voice trembling with tears. "No, I want to hear."

"Alma, it won't be pleasant," Lord Newbury shook himself from his stupor long enough to caution.

"I don't care. I don't want them discussing this behind our backs. I want to know the truth."

Dr. Woods shrugged. His eyes dipped to my waistline, noting my expectant state. "Shall we sit?" he told Gage.

Once everyone was settled, he leaned toward us. "Now, I'm sure you have questions for me, but first allow me to tell you my impressions. Mr. Newbury was stabbed in the right side with a blade. Something long and thin. Might have killed him within minutes, except it appears to have nicked a rib."

Gage and I shared a speaking look.

"As for the sticking plaster, I must tell you, I think someone is trying to stir up a hornets' nest with these burkers being on trial. There was no need for such a contrivance, not with the knife wound. Which would clearly denote the presence of foul play to any surgeon the culprit might attempt to sell the body to. But based on the bruising, it seems they knelt on his chest and applied it to his face anyway, before running away." He shook his head in disgust. "I blame it on these penny broadsheets and their lurid caricatures of the burkers. Never saw such nonsense in my life."

"He wasn't burked?" Lord Newbury asked in astonishment.

"No, my lord. But whoever did this wanted you to think he was."

Relief trickled through me at his words, pleased to hear the physician state the case so decisively. But I also couldn't halt a niggle of doubt from worming its way through my brain. His outrage seemed genuine, and the facts lined up with his opinion, but I wondered whether his motivation was more from a desire to salvage the medical community's reputation than an observation of actual fact. After all, it wasn't just the surgeons and anatomy schools who were facing criticism and closer scrutiny, but all of the medical establishment, if to a lesser degree.

"What you've described aligns almost exactly with the attack made on Lord Feckenham a week ago," Gage told the doctor. "Even the sticking plaster, though in his case it was found next to the body," he added smoothly, telling a small lie, lest they question our judgment. "That matter was not disclosed publicly to prevent panic, but now I'm glad of it for another reason. It tells us that the person or persons who killed Lord Feckenham also attacked Mr. Newbury."

"But why? Why would someone do such a thing?" Lord Newbury argued. "Feckenham, I can understand. He was rumored to be a scoundrel. But why would they wish to murder my son? Unless you think it was random?"

Gage narrowed his eyes in thought. "It's possible, but I cannot see that being the case. No, I think he must have been chosen specifically. As for why, I do not know."

"The only immediate thing I can see that they have in common is that they're both the heir apparent to a noble title," I murmured. "But maybe it's not a matter of something they are . . . or were," I added awkwardly. "But something they did or saw."

"My wife is right. It could be any number of things. But I think this is perhaps not the time to be racking our brains for such details." He cast a sympathetic glance at the Newburys. "Later, if you have the strength to do so, cast your minds back and try to recall anything Mr. Newbury might have done or said in the preceding weeks or months, any connections he might have had with Feckenham, no matter how innocent. Write them down, and send them to me."

Lord Newbury answered for them all. "We will."

"And should Mr. Newbury regain consciousness, write down everything he says. Perhaps he recognized his attacker, or something about him. Details matter." His gaze locked with Lord Newbury's. "Right now, I need to know where Mr. Newbury was coming from this morning. Did he share what his plans were when he left the house yesterday evening?"

I was surprised when it was Lady Newbury who answered. "He escorted Ellen and I to Lady Aldcott's Ball, and then went back out after returning us safely home for the night. I assume he was meeting friends." She hiccupped. "Lord Damien Marlowe might know."

I wasn't surprised to hear the two young men were friends. They were of an age and possessed similar temperaments. But that didn't mean I wasn't alarmed to discover he had a connection to both murder victims.

"We'll speak with him," I replied.

"Then we shall take our leave of you now," Gage said. "Send word . . . should there be any developments." He had chosen his words with care, but Lady Newbury still flinched, realizing this was a request to be informed if David succumbed to his wounds.

"I'm terribly sorry," I told Lady Newbury in earnest, and then glanced to Ellen. "I like David. I like him a great deal." I felt emotion burn the back of my eyes at the realization that the smiling young gentleman might soon no longer be with us. "I shall pray," I added before pushing to my feet to follow my husband from the house.

Before I could take more than a half-dozen steps, Lady Newbury halted me. Grabbing my arm, she whirled me around and pulled me to her. I'd struggled to adjust myself to the baroness's penchant for hugging ladies of even the briefest acquaintance, uncomfortable with such an embrace. But after the accusations she had flung at me earlier, this was the most awkward one of all. I patted her back as she sniffled against my shoulder.

"Please forgive me. I'm horrified by the things I said."

"Think no more of it," I replied. "We all say things we don't mean when we're in pain."

"Oh, you are so good." She released her hold on me, dabbing at her face with her handkerchief.

I smiled tightly. "No, just rational."

I hurried away, wishing I could believe what I'd said. That the words that arose from our pain were nonsense, and not the truth we were too polite or too afraid to speak.

While donning my hat and gloves, I listened idly as Gage asked the butler for the constable's direction, and then conferred with Dr. Woods on another point. Shaking the good doctor's hand after we descended the stairs to the pavement, we parted ways. But instead of assisting me into our conveyance, Gage signaled to the coachman to swing around and follow us down the street.

"Where are we going?" I questioned him, clinging to his side as my breath fogged in the cold morning air. The city was still cloaked in twilight, sunrise not beginning for another hour.

"To examine the place where young Newbury was attacked. It's too bad even the taverns are shuttered at this hour, or else we might have had multiple witnesses in such a location," he remarked as we passed by an eating house. When I didn't respond, he looked down at me. "I thought you would be eager to accompany me." His eyes scoured my features, undoubtedly noting my nose growing red. "Oh, I am bird-witted! It cannot be good for you to be out in such cold."

I smiled at his concern. "I am quite well, thank you. I can't say I enjoy promenading in the freezing cold darkness. And when I'm tottering around, as round as a barrel, I would be very cross at you for such a thing. But just now I'm not complaining." I arched my chin, staring straight ahead. "Besides, you need my sharp eye." At just that moment, the wind blew in our direction, and I lifted my hand to cover my face as I caught a whiff of something foul amid the comparatively milder stenches of horses and manure. "And nose."

Our steps slowed as we reached the mouth of the stable yard Lord Newbury mentioned. It was little more than a narrow alley which cut between two blocks of houses in the direction of Farm Street. There was a dark stain on the pavement where David Newbury must have lain, and I felt a pang at the evidence. Dr. Woods had good reason not to offer the Newburys false hope. If David survived, it would be a miracle.

The area around the stain was clear of debris, but I pointed deeper into the shadowy recesses of the yard. "There's a pool of vomit not far inside," I remarked, struggling to control my own gag reflex. Thank heavens I hadn't consumed anything in our haste to reach the Newburys' townhouse.

"I wonder if it's from David Newbury or the killer," Gage ruminated as he moved forward to confirm my assertions. "If Newbury was slightly boozy, then his casting up his accounts might have afforded the killer an opportunity."

I turned my body away from the wind, hoping to block the

scent from reaching my nostrils. "That suggests he'd been following David, waiting to strike. But the fact that he was murdered so close to home, just like Feckenham, makes me more inclined to believe he was lying here in wait."

"I agree."

He spoke much closer behind me than I'd expected, and I jumped.

He swept his hand toward the ground as he moved in front of me. "Notice, all the gravel and detritus has been swept away so there's nothing to crunch underfoot." He gestured over my shoulder. "That alley is pitch black for about fifty feet between these houses until it opens up into the area where the stables extend. It's the perfect place to hide in wait for someone." He frowned, propping his hands on his hips. "He certainly wasn't taking any chances this time."

"And yet his thrust was still flawed," I pointed out, reaching for Gage's arm to tug him toward our approaching carriage. The coachman slowed, pulling the horses to a stop before us as the footman leaped down to lower the step.

"Yes, but David Newbury is a rather tall chap, isn't he?"

"Over six foot, I should say."

Nothing more was said until we were both bundled into the coach and the door shut behind us.

Gage tucked the lap rug firmly around me. "His great height could account for it."

"Whatever the cause, the killer is most definitely an amateur." A shiver worked through me that had nothing to do with the cold. "Or rather, he was. And he hasn't a strong stomach for this sort of thing if he vomited either from nerves or after the deed was done. But with each murder, he's gaining experience. If there is another murder, I would wager his thrust will be true."

Neither of us spoke for several minutes, each contemplating the horrific possibility that we had some sort of a lunatic rampaging through Mayfair. Except these killings were more controlled than the raving rush of a fearsome Highlander. They were cold and calculated, and whatever his motive was, I was blind to it.

Jeffers was waiting for us when we returned, ready to receive our outer layers as if we'd just arrived from an afternoon call and not a predawn investigation.

"Have breakfast set in a quarter of an hour," Gage informed him. "And send Miss McEvoy and Anderley to the morning room."

"Very good, sir."

I half expected our personal servants to already be waiting for us; they'd become so attuned to our whims, especially during an investigation.

"Did we miss something?" I groused, dropping into one of the bergère chairs. "Should we have predicted this?" I rubbed my fingers over my temple and then slapped my leg in frustration. "We wasted an entire week thinking the motive had only to do with Feckenham. Who knows what we failed to detect?"

Gage reached over the back of the chair to rub my shoulders. "It is provoking, but let's not be too hasty to dismiss Feckenham as the cause. Maybe Newbury is a diversion meant to throw us off the killer's scent."

I glanced up at him in startlement, halting his ministrations. "Do you really think so?"

His eyes clouded. "No, not really." He began to knead again. "But we must keep our minds open to every possibility. At this point, we don't know what information is pertinent and what is not. Something we've already learned may prove to be useful, or even the key to it all."

My head lolled back with a sigh as his hands began to melt some of the tension tightening my frame. "You sound as if you're trying to convince yourself as much as me."

He gave a huff of laughter, lifting his hands from my shoulders. "Maybe I am."

There was a rap on the door, followed by the entry of our

personal servants. Gage moved to the chair across from me, quickly filling them in on the details of that morning before we addressed anything new.

"Anderley, I need you to be my eyes and ears at the hearing at Bow Street today." The faint lines at the corners of his eyes crinkled in displeasure. "I hate to miss it, but this Mayfair investigation must take precedence since the killer is still at large, and we're only assisting in the Italian Boy inquest." He passed him the sheet of paper Lord Newbury's butler had given to him. "I also need you to track down this constable and hear his version of events regarding when he stumbled across Mr. Newbury this morning. I'd particularly like to know whether he encountered anyone on his beat in the hour or so before he found Newbury."

He nodded, glancing at the ormolu clock above the mantel. His eyes were surrounded by dark circles, and his shoulders slumped with fatigue, but he didn't object or complain. "He should be ending his shift soon. I'll try to catch him before heading to Bow Street."

I watched Anderley as he hastened from the room, recognizing the signs of someone who was trying to outrun something. I knew because I had been a master at it. Except you never could outdistance your troubles. They always caught up with you in the end.

"I'll chat wi' the Newburys' servants. See what I can find oot," Bree offered.

"Yes, that would be helpful," Gage replied. "But I also have a specific task for you."

She perked up at this request.

"I want you to pay a visit to Mount Street, to the stable yard that runs between Numbers 110 and 111. Find out if the grooms have seen anyone suspicious lurking about, anyone who shouldn't be there. And speak with the gardeners at Number 108. Sir George Philips's home sits back from Mount Street a bit, and its gardens open onto that stable yard. Perhaps one of them saw something."

"Aye, I can do that. If I take some o' Mrs. Alcott's biscuits, I imagine I can get the younger lads to talk easily enough." She grinned. "And a wink and a smile should do the trick wi' the rest."

"At least someone is deriving some enjoyment from this investigation," I said, shaking my head as she capered from the room.

"Should I have sent her on such an errand alone?" Gage mused, his voice tight with concern.

"Don't fret over Bree. She may be cheerful and eager for adventure, but she's no fool. She'll be circumspect." I pushed myself upright. "Now, how do you propose we proceed?"

He rose to his feet, crossing toward me. "Well, first we are going to partake of the excellent breakfast that is no doubt being laid for us." He helped me from my chair to guide me toward the room across the hall. "And then I think we would both benefit from a short nap."

By this, I knew he was implying *I* would benefit, though he was savvy enough to couch it in more amenable terms. In any case, reluctant as I was to admit it, he was correct. I stifled a yawn. "Then what?"

"Then I believe we should pay another visit to the Earl of Redditch. Perhaps he or Penrose might know of some connection between Feckenham and David Newbury that Lord Newbury did not."

"We should also send a note around to Lord Damien asking him to call again." I tilted my head to the side in thought as Gage assisted me into my chair at the table. "Though it might be easiest to wait to speak to him at Aunt Cait's soiree tonight."

"I had the same notion." He settled into his seat across from me. "You might also suggest Bree attend tonight to assist your aunt's maids in the lady's retiring room."

"That's an excellent idea," I replied, much struck by it. "I'm certain Aunt Cait's staff would welcome the extra pair of hands. Ladies are prone to be somewhat indiscreet with their words while having their hem fixed or hair pinned."

"Is that so?"

I shrugged a single shoulder. "I shouldn't wonder if all of society's little mysteries could be solved by eavesdropping on such retiring rooms."

"Now, why do I not find that thought comforting?"

"It's no different than gentlemen with their port and their cigars. Scratch that. *Some* gentlemen with their port and their cigars." Gage had never given up his secrets easily.

"True. I suppose polite society, in general, is not known for their discretion when it comes to the latest on-dit."

Which meant *someone* should know of a connection between Feckenham and Newbury. We could only hope.

CHAPTER TWENTY

"Young Newbury has been murdered," Lord Redditch gasped in astonishment. He raked a hand through his silver hair, making it stand on end. This announcement seemed to have shocked him even more than the death of his own son and heir.

"I suspect it's only a matter of time before he succumbs to his injuries, my lord," Gage pronounced.

We'd arrived to find the earl closeted with his remaining son and secretary. At first, he'd seemed hostile to our making another visit so soon upon the heels of the last. His red face had suggested he was about to deliver us a setdown concerning our suspicions about Penrose and the rest of the family. But Gage's pronouncement had abruptly taken the wind out of his sails.

The two younger men had looked rather careworn, the events of the past week evidently having taken their toll, even on overworked Mr. Poole. But now Mr. Penrose appeared deathly pale. What little color had remained in his cheeks had drained from them.

"I can't believe it," he murmured. "I like David. He's a jolly good chap."

"You are acquainted with Mr. Newbury?" I asked, having already guessed he must be through his friendship with Lord Damien.

"Yes. Same year up at Eton, and all that."

"And you believe Newbury was attacked by the same fellow who killed my son?" the earl interjected. The earl waved Mr. Penrose and Mr. Poole from their seats—an action I surmised he'd forbidden them to do upon our arrival, thinking to send us away with a flea in our ears. The secretary complied while his son continued to stare unseeing at the floor.

"There's little doubt of it," Gage confirmed, ushering me toward the chair, where he took up a position behind me.

The earl pounced on this. "Then my family is cleared of suspicion?"

"We cannot state anything definitely, but it appears the motive for their murders lays outside your home."

He nodded in satisfaction, ignoring the guarded tone of Gage's voice and latching on to the words he most wanted to hear. "Knew it had to be some unscrupulous scoundrel Feckenham associated with in those gaming hells he frequented." He frowned. "Though I wouldn't have thought it of young Newbury."

I turned to his younger son. "Mr. Penrose, are you aware of whether Mr. Newbury frequented any gambling establishments?"

He blinked his eyes to focus on me. "David? No. He's not a betting man. Though I'm sure he has visited a hell or two at one time or another. We all do."

But would Penrose really know if his friend had dipped too deep? There were those who were able to hide it well. Until they couldn't. Perhaps he'd run afoul of a moneylender.

How that connected him to Feckenham, I didn't know, for Feckenham had been rumored to be flush in the pocket, but I would ask Trevor. Maybe he would have a better idea than we did of the signs that Newbury might have found himself at ebb-water.

"Do you know of any other connection between your brother and Mr. Newbury?" I pressed, searching for some definitive way to link the two victims.

His brow furrowed in concentration, but after a few moments he shook his head in defeat. "None." His gaze was stricken. "Except me."

None of us commented on this, or the obvious implications. But unless Penrose had minimized his relationship with Newbury, then I couldn't see how the two victims marked a motive against Penrose himself. Half the young men of the ton must have been acquainted with Newbury, if not more.

A throat cleared. "Perhaps the attacks were random," Mr. Poole suggested. He stood tall, though I could read his hesitation to speak in the bobbing of his head. "Perhaps the miscreants were merely seizing an opportunity."

"We are considering that possibility as well," Gage replied. "But given some of the facts of the crimes we are not at liberty to share at the moment, the chances of the victims having been chosen at random are slim."

Mr. Poole nodded with dignity.

"Penrose, you didn't happen to see Mr. Newbury anytime yesterday evening until early this morning?" Gage asked.

He shook his head. "No. I was home."

"I can verify that," the earl chimed in to say, even though we hadn't expressed any doubt.

Recognizing we would receive no additional information, Gage reached for my elbow to help me rise. "If any of you should think of something that connects the two men, no matter how slight, please send word."

The men agreed as we took our leave.

The cold air of earlier that morning had warmed by barely a

degree, so I sat with my arms locked tightly to my side, trying to conserve my body heat as our carriage pulled away from the earl's house. Despite the chill, the streets were packed with people, born both low and high, their shoulders huddled against the wind. But at least the upper class were wrapped in warm layers. Some of the street people appeared to possess nothing but a threadbare coat or shawl to cover their arms. I could only hope for their sake that this winter would not be as bitter as the last.

"You're quiet," Gage remarked after we passed by a muffin man singing out to passersby about his goods.

I inhaled a steadying breath but didn't turn from the window. "I was just wondering. David couldn't be Penrose's particular friend, could he?"

"No." His voice held no doubt. "No, Newbury is not of that inclination."

"I . . . I didn't think so," I replied. But I also hadn't suspected such a thing of Mr. Penrose. Now I felt uncertain about it all and unsure how to feel. Not that I liked Mr. Penrose any less, but my only experience with the matter was a vaguely recalled sermon on the evils of Sodom and Gomorrah, and to a young girl, that had seemed a distant concept. It was somewhat unsettling to discover I'd been fairly blind to it all before now.

Gage took hold of my hand inside its warm leather glove, offering me a gentle smile. "Do not let it trouble you. It doesn't change who they are as a person, does it?"

I considered this and shook my head. "No."

"The Lord would still have us 'love thy neighbor as thyself'?"

"Yes."

"Then leave it at that. They receive enough grief from others. We need not add to it." He inhaled a deep breath and exhaled wearily. "I have been the witness to terrible things. Acts of man against their fellow man that are horrifying in their cruelty. I find I cannot summon the will to care who a man chooses for his bed partner. Let it be between him and God. I shall not judge."

I weaved my arm through his and leaned my head against his shoulder, knowing his thoughts had drifted into the past and the massacres he'd beheld during the Greek War of Independence from the Ottomans, and the numerous murder inquiries he'd conducted.

His gaze dipped to meet mine. "Perhaps that is the wrong stance to take . . ."

"No." I shook my head to halt his words. "I don't think it is. I think it very wise." I couldn't help but be amazed at his capacity for compassion when experience might have trampled that out of him long ago. That he should counsel something I could so readily reconcile with my conscience comforted me that it might be right.

His eyes warmed under my regard, and he leaned forward to press a kiss to my forehead.

"Tell Mr. Gage what you told me," I ordered Bree as she settled in the carriage across from us in a demure gown of green sarcenet, one of my castoffs she'd altered to fit her slighter frame.

"I spoke to several o' the grooms workin' for the stables located in that yard, though I'll have to go back to see the gardeners at 108. Only one o' 'em was workin' today, but yer right. The garden opens onto the yard. The horses are always wantin' to crop the azaleas growin' o'er the wall in the summer." She shook her head, making the strawberry blond curls at her temples swing. "Anyway, the lads admitted they'd seen a number o' men pass through in the past week, but that it's often used as a shortcut." She pursed her lips. "They each told me there'd been one suspicious man lurkin' aboot in the past few days, but none o' 'em could agree on what he looked like. One swore he had a limp, while another said he was missin' an eye, and a third claimed he was so tall he could light the streetlamps wi'oot a pole."

Gage's lips quirked.

"Then they started natterin' on aboot burkers prowlin' through the alley, and I told 'em they was pitchin' me the gammon. One o' the older grooms slapped 'em for tellin' such a clanker. Said they'd been listenin' to the footman from one o' the houses read the newspaper and hadna stopped talkin' aboot the Italian Boy and the subsequent failed burkings since."

"So nothing of use," Gage surmised.

She sighed. "I'm afraid no'."

"What of Anderley?" I asked, knowing his valet had returned in time to help him shave and dress in his dark evening clothes for the ball.

"The constable had nothing new to tell him that we hadn't already heard from the Newburys." His voice deepened with displeasure. "But he had plenty to say about the hearing."

"What happened?" I asked, knowing the inquest into the Italian Boy was certain to be one of the chief topics of conversation tonight. That, and David Newbury's attempted murder, as the gossip was certain to have made its usual swift rounds. If the newspapermen had been quick enough, there might even be a mention of it in the evening editions of several of the newspapers. Gage had contacted one such reporter and provided him with information, just as he had Mr. Day a week before, in exchange for a plea for further information from the public.

"Anderley said it was packed with spectators, including a number of gentlemen. Many of them were London's preeminent surgeons."

"I expected nothing less. The medical community might want to distance themselves from the matter, but they're certainly taking an interest."

"James Corder presented the evidence collected by Superintendent Thomas of the New Police, but Anderley said it was sadly lacking. Not much more than the hamper and blood-stained sack the boy's body was transported in, a small box of teeth that May sold—the ones he already admitted to removing from the corpse—and a tortoise found in a shop in Holborn which is supposed to be similar in appearance to one someone saw an Italian Boy displaying."

Bree and I shared a look of amazement. "How can they possibly prove it's the same tortoise or that it belonged to the boy who was killed?" I queried.

He frowned. "I don't think they can."

I shook my head at the absurdity. "Were there any witnesses?" For the most part, guilt was still established by an eyewitness, a confession, a bad reputation, or being caught in the act. Physical evidence often had very little do with it. Though the police and other judicial systems had begun to realize what private inquiry agents like Gage and I had already noted. Objects could tell a tale, and sometimes offer the explanation to a mystery.

"Oh, yes. A slew of them. The porter at the Fortune of War, who claims he overheard a suspicious conversation between Bishop and May. A pregnant woman and her children, who swear they saw an Italian Boy just several feet from Bishop and Williams's door the morning before he is believed to have been killed. As well as various people who claim the Italian Boy they always saw on the street has disappeared, plus a dozen more."

"Heavens! Then Anderley must have been obliged to remain all day." I cringed, recalling my memories of the close, squalid room which served as the Bow Street Magistrates Court. The walls were tarnished with dirt, the ceiling blackened, and everything seemed to be coated in a thick, greasy scum. The smell was bad enough to turn an iron stomach—a rancid bouquet of unwashed bodies, human waste, and desperation. How the magistrates could withstand it, day after day, I didn't know, for the place was in urgent need of attention.

"I'm afraid so," Gage replied, joining me in my empathy for his valet. "I gave him the night off in recompense." He turned toward the gaslit streets outside the window. "Not that he'll take it."

Bree's gaze met mine across the carriage, her eyes gleaming with memories of our earlier speculations about Anderley.

"Is he still trying to find out the Italian Boy's identity?"

"Yes, and having little luck."

"It sounds as if the police aren't having any luck either."

"No, but Anderley learned that the Italian Boy's body is being exhumed tomorrow morning. That a man is traveling down to London from Birmingham, who believes the boy might be a young Savoyard who used to be in his care."

The way he phrased the matter and the skeptical tone of his voice alerted me to the fact that there was something mistrustful, possibly dishonest, about all this. I couldn't help but focus on the first part of his statement. "Why did they bury him in the first place if they didn't yet know his identity?"

Gage threw his hands in the air. "Your guess is as good as mine. The police are making their first search of Bishop and Williams's home at Nova Scotia Gardens tomorrow as well—the place where they believe the boy was actually murdered."

I shifted in my seat to stare at him, confounded. "Why did they wait so long? Shouldn't that have been the first obvious step to take?"

"To us, yes," he replied, backing down from his earlier scathing tone. "But such things are not standard procedure for the police. Not yet." He arched his eyebrows. "Remember, the New Police were formed to prevent crimes, not investigate them after the fact."

Though he tried to soften his reaction, I could hear his frustration. He might be trying to show the police some leniency for their inadequacies, but he wasn't able to overlook them.

"There was one positive development at the hearing today," he admitted. "Minshull, the presiding magistrate, called in Samuel Taunton, one of the most experienced Bow Street Runners, to assist the police and make further inquiries."

"Just as Goddard predicted."

He turned to peer out the window as the carriage slowed but dipped his head as if to say, *Just so.*

I had sent a note around to my aunt Cait earlier in the day to let her know I would be bringing Bree, and she had replied with her thanks and asked if we could arrive early—meaning on time. As such, our carriage did not have to wait in the long queue of fashionably late attendees before depositing us at the Marquess of Barbreck's door. My uncle Dunstan was the nephew and heir of the current marquess—a crusty old bachelor with a cackling laugh and a dry sense of humor, though never cruel. I liked him exceedingly. Aunt Cait enjoyed her role as his hostess, and since he loved to indulge her, he often hosted soirees for her to plan.

"Kiera, darling," she exclaimed as Gage and I passed into the soaring entry hall after divesting ourselves of our outer garments. Bree had already been led off to the lady's retiring room by one of the marquess's servants.

Aunt Cait grasped my hands and then lifted them to the sides so she could better view my gown. "You look stunning, my darling. This shade of Pompeian red suits you. And how clever of you to have the modiste raise the waistline a few inches to accommodate your happy condition."

I smiled. "It was Alana's idea."

"Well, you were wise to listen to her. We can't all have her eye for style, after all."

Considering the fact that Aunt Cait was never dressed in less than the first stare of fashion, I could only shake my head. "Quit bamming me. You know your dress is stunning, as are you. You always are." I leaned forward to peck her on the cheek, careful not to crumple her jonquil silk.

"It's the Rutherford blood, my dear." She tapped me coyly on the cheek with her finger. "It never fails." She narrowed her eyes playfully. "And if my intuition is right, and it always is, then you are having a girl, and it won't fail her either. Not that you need worry," she added, flicking a glance at Gage. "Given your charming husband."

He laughed. "If it's a girl, I shall be well pleased," he replied.

"Spoken like a true gentleman." She pressed her fan to his shoulder in approval.

"I think it's a bit early to be making such predictions," I replied, sharing an amused look with my uncle Dunstan. His mouth was almost swallowed by his curly gray beard, but humor danced in his eyes.

"I was right about your sister's children, wasn't I?" my aunt challenged.

"Only Malcolm and Philipa."

"Well, I hadn't seen her while she was expecting the younger two, so how could my intuition tell me?" She pointed out with what she seemed to believe was faultless logic.

I smiled. "You shall never convince me."

Her blue eyes, several shades darker than my own lapis-lazuli color, sparkled with merriment. "Not until the baby arrives."

Uncle Dunstan chuckled. "I think she has ye there, lass."

I rolled my eyes good-naturedly. "Where's the marquess?"

He nodded toward the drawing room. "Holdin' court by the hearth. I ken he'd be pleased if ye spoke wi' him for a mite," he murmured in the thick brogue he'd never deigned to tame.

"I will," I assured him before taking Gage's arm to move deeper into the house. The grand staircase of gleaming wood covered in an ivory runner with intricately scrolled gilded railings stood before us, leading up to the ballroom. Strains of music floated down from above, forming a pleasant background to the conversations filling the space. Four doors led from the lower hall—one to the drawing room, the second to a parlor set up with gaming tables for the gentlemen, while across the hall the dining room and an adjacent room had been arranged for the midnight supper.

"Is your aunt very much like your mother?" Gage leaned down to murmur in curiosity.

I turned to look up into his pale blue eyes, not as surprised as

I might have been by the question, for I'd been contemplating it myself.

His gaze turned tender. "Or don't you remember?"

"I remember enough." Enough to sense the echo of my mother in her younger sister. I turned to look at the table to the right of the staircase with its lavish display of autumn blooms. "They *are* alike." I tilted my head. "And yet not. I remember my mother being softer somehow, gentler." I glanced up at him. "But then maybe that's because I was a child when she died."

I shook away the morose musings and gestured toward the drawing room.

"How is your wrist?" Gage asked politely as he guided me across the hall, cradling my injured wrist carefully with his own arm.

I'd refused to wear the wrap around my wrist in lieu of my white evening glove. Not only would it have looked terribly gauche, it would have drawn unwelcome attention and speculation. "I told you before, it is fine. I almost don't need the wrap anymore."

He stared sideways at me as if I fibbed, but unlike him, I did not have a habit of trying to make my injuries appear less concerning than they were.

We entered the drawing room to find the Marquess of Barbreck mildly harassing his great-niece—my cousin Morven—and her husband, Lord John Noble.

"I'm tellin' ye, ye need to tie a string roond that lad's head to hold his ears back. Or else they'll continue to stick oot from his head like a Grecian urn, like this one's." He stuck out his thumb to point at Lord John, who arched his eyebrows as if to tell the man he would have to do better than that if he wished him to take offense.

"My son's ears are quite handsome," Morven protested in good grace.

The marquess made a rude scoffing noise in the back of his

throat. "Where'd *you* get yer sense of aesthetic?" He shook his nearly bald head. "No sense." His gaze lifted, spying me and Gage across the room. Even from such a great distance, I could see the devilry sparkling in his eyes. "Noo, here's someone wi' a true appreciation for beauty." He held out his hand as I approached. "Come tell me how my favorite niece fares?" I wasn't really his niece, but he always treated me as such.

I smiled at this and allowed him to take my hand and pull me closer. "You declare all of your relatives to be your favorites at one moment or another. Don't think we're not on to your game."

He chuckled. "I'm old. I can change my mind if I wish."

"Obviously."

"Saucy minx," he growled, sinking back into the gilt-metal, ebonized chair with gold upholstery. It *had* been arranged as if it was a throne, and he was receiving his subjects. His gaze flicked to Gage and back. "Noo, tell me how fares this handsome piece o' frippery ye wed yerself to?"

But I had already advised Gage on the best way to respond to the marquess and his impertinent insults. "Careful, old man. Don't forget I'm an inquiry agent. I could have you killed half a dozen ways and no one would suspect," he drawled, his sharp words belied by the diverted glint in his eyes.

"Only half a dozen?"

Lord John choked on a laugh and Gage cracked a smile.

"What's this nonsense I hear aboot young Newbury bein' murdered by the same blackguard who killed Feckenham?" the marquess demanded to know. "Why havena ye caught the villain yet?" He thumped his cane against the floor, narrowing his eyes at me. "And what are *you* doin' traipsin' aboot the city in yer condition anyway?"

"I'm not traipsing anywhere," I retorted.

"Noo, see. Maybe that's yer problem."

How I was supposed to not traipse about the city, but also do so, escaped my considerable powers of reasoning. A prime example of why speaking to the marquess could often be so vexing.

Fortunately, two couples entered the drawing room at that moment to pay their respects to Lord Barbreck, so we could ignore these pointed queries.

Something I didn't bother to hide my relief over as I offered him a bit of his own back in parting. "Lovely to see you, my lord. You look at the peak of health."

He harrumphed a laugh. Given his advanced age of eighty-some-odd years, he was so far down the peak as to be practically in the valley. "Come see me this week. I have things to say."

That this was an order, there was no doubt, so I smiled and nodded. As for what he had to say, heaven only knew, but it was likely to be tantamount to gossip, and this was merely his way of ensuring I would pay him a call. If so, there was no need to go to such extremes, for I was happy to do so. Especially given his broad knowledge of the ton. Who knew what secrets were locked in that brain of his?

CHAPTER TWENTY-ONE

Morven turned to embrace me as we exited the drawing room. "It's true, then? What they've been saying about Mr. Newbury?"

"As far as we know, he hasn't succumbed to his injuries yet," I replied. "But . . . it's only a matter of time."

"Oh, how dreadful." She pressed a hand to her cheek. "Why, John and I saw him just last night."

"You did? Where?"

"Lady Willoughby de Eresby's autumn soiree," Lord John replied.

Given that woman's sharp aversion to me, it was no wonder we hadn't received an invitation.

He lifted a hand to scratch the side of his unfashionably cropped hair. "I believe I last saw him in the gaming parlor at about two o'clock. We departed soon after."

Gage and I shared a speaking glance.

"Was he playing cards?" Gage asked.

"Yes. Small stakes. The large bets were being placed at the

other table." He named several members of society who were known to be inveterate gamblers, winning and losing fortunes on the turn of a card.

Either David Newbury knew better than to play with such gentlemen, or he had little interest in the sport. I wish I knew which.

"Had you ever seen him with Feckenham?" Gage asked Lord John.

"I don't believe so." He gave a short huff of amusement. "To be honest, it's hard to think of two young gentlemen who were less alike."

This seemed to be the prevailing opinion among everyone we spoke to. Newbury was likable, honorable, pleasing, and friendly. Feckenham was not. For all intents and purposes, they were as different as chalk and cheese—Feckenham being the chalk, and Newbury the cheese. For while no one seemed to mourn Feckenham, everyone expressed their remorse at Newbury's imminent passing. I even spotted several eligible debutantes with tears in their eyes. Clearly the young man had been popular.

We found Lord Damien in the parlor listlessly playing a game of loo. When we approached the table, he folded his hand without speaking and moved with us into a corner of the room.

"I suppose you're here to ask me about Newbury," he remarked, opening a box of snuff and taking a pinch.

I pressed a hand gently to his arm. "I'm sorry, Damien. I understand he's a good friend of yours."

His brow crumpled, as if suppressing strong emotion. "The best." He inhaled a shaky breath. "And before you ask, I haven't the foggiest what there could have been between him and Feckenham. That's what you want to know, isn't it? He told me once he thought Lord Redditch's heir a knight of the blade—a rotten bully. But I don't believe I ever heard him mention him again." He scowled. "It makes no sense."

"Is Newbury much of a gambler?" Gage asked.

"Less than average. He would rather be out riding, or boxing, or dancing. Just about anything other than sitting at a table shuffling cards about. If he does, it's to oblige a friend or because there's a set in need of another player."

"When did you see him last?"

"Early this morning. We walked to Hollingsworth House, and he came inside to have a drink with me and James," he explained, mentioning his older brother. "Left just before four." His eyes dimmed with pain. "I should have insisted he take the carriage."

"You couldn't have known," I protested. "It was only the distance of a few short blocks."

"Yes, but I still keep thinking I *should* have known. After all, Feckenham was killed by the same rogue."

"True. But I don't think any of us suspected the culprit was after more than revenge against Feckenham for some foul deed or another." Gage arched his eyebrows. "Did you?"

"Well, no. Though if his second victim had been someone like Wilmot or Acklen, it would have been less shocking," he said, naming two other young gentlemen of low reputation.

"Shouldn't my name be on that list?"

I turned to face the Marquess of Marsdale's unrepentant grin. Only he would be eager to appear on such a list. Though while he was a scoundrel and an unconscionable flirt, he wasn't truly malicious, merely careless.

He took hold of my hand and bowed over it, gazing upward through his lashes at me with mischief in his eyes. "Lady Darby, I'm pleased to see you are looking *radiant* with health. Your husband must be paying you *marked* attention."

That this was a double entendre and a comment on my expectant state, there was no doubt. I flushed with color even as Lord Damien bristled at such an indelicate comment.

But Gage took the rascal's comments in stride. "When did you arrive in London?"

"A few nights ago."

"How is the duke?" I asked, knowing he had been called to his father's bedside.

"Recovering, confound it."

I arched a single eyebrow at this inconsiderate comment, fully aware that he wasn't so sanguine about the matter. I'd seen how concerned he was when he received the urgent letter several weeks earlier about the duke's poor health.

Lord Damien, however, had not. "Reprehensible, Marsdale," he snapped, his hands fisted at his sides.

Marsdale glanced at the younger man, but rather than deliver him a setdown, his eyes seemed to take in his drawn countenance. "My apologies, Marlowe. I'd forgotten Newbury is a friend of yours. He's a good chap."

Lord Damien's face scrunched, and for a moment it seemed his emotions might get the better of him, but he sought refuge in anger. "Better than you."

"Oh, undoubtedly," Marsdale replied mildly.

"Excuse me." He swiveled on his heel and disappeared through the door. I hoped he found someone to confide his worry and grief in. I was sure there were any number of debutantes who would welcome the chance to comfort him.

"So you've embroiled yourself in another mess," Marsdale remarked.

I considered refuting this insulting choice of words but instead sighed wearily. He had described the matter quite succinctly. "Yes."

His eyes trailed over my features. "Well, if you should need my assistance in any way, you know where to find me." He nodded to Gage and then departed.

I watched him go, somewhat flummoxed by his failure to capitalize on further opportunities to tease or fluster me. "What just happened?"

"I do believe Marsdale has finally learned a bit of restraint."

"I'm not sure I believed I would ever see the day."

We strolled from the parlor back toward the stairs, now filled with guests moving about the Mayfair mansion in a prism of colors.

"What did you think of Lord Damien's assertions about David Newbury and gambling?" I murmured after we nodded to a pair of ladies on the stairs.

"I thought it very credible. He would be in a position to know."

"I thought so, too." I exhaled in relief. "So perhaps I needn't broach such an awkward subject with Trevor again."

His eyes were kind. "I shouldn't worry about it for now."

I offered him a grateful smile in return, hoping perhaps we might take a break from our toils to dance a waltz or two. But before the suggestion could even pass my lips, I felt tension course through him. When I lifted my eyes to the head of the stairs, I understood why.

Lord Gage stood staring down at us. Though his posture appeared languid, his face unconcerned, I saw something flash in his eyes that told me our meeting would not be a pleasant one.

"Good evening, sir," Gage told him as we reached the top.

"Good evening," he replied courteously, purely for appearances, I was sure. "Might I have a word alone with you and your charming wife?"

The hairs on the back of my neck stood on end at the uttering of this false compliment, and I realized just how furious my father-in-law was.

"Of course," Gage answered, though my instincts told me to run in the other direction. I had to steel my nerves to follow him down the corridor, even with my husband's arm linked with mine in support.

We continued down the hall past the ballroom to a door on the left, which Lord Gage held open for us to enter before him. It was a sitting room of some kind, decorated in delicate rose wallpaper. I had a brief moment to wonder whether he had learned of Mayer's intentions to publish Sir Anthony's private journals before he rounded on us.

"Dash it all, Sebastian! I told you to keep this Mayfair matter contained, but now rather than one dead body, we have two! And this time, someone has blabbed about the sticking plaster."

"And what precisely should we have done?" Gage retorted, releasing my arm to move closer to his father. My insides quivered as they always did when faced with such vehemence from a man.

"There was no indication the first crime had anything to do with anyone other than Feckenham. We couldn't have predicted there would be another attack. Especially not on someone like Newbury."

"Then you must have missed something," he jeered. "We cannot afford to have the entire city in a panic. Why, just now I had several ladies asking me if they were safe. If they should be afraid to leave their homes at night." His eyes glinted at me. "And I had one waspish matron suggest we might all be better off if my daughter-in-law entered her confinement early."

"What nonsense," Gage snapped. "As if they ever leave their homes without a full complement of servants. They're a bunch of busybodies interested in stirring up trouble."

"Maybe so, but nonetheless, it is trouble we do not need!" He propped his hands on his hips and turned away, shaking his head. "I *told* you your choice in a wife and her sordid past would cause us difficulties one day, but you wouldn't listen. You said I was being arrogant and overbearing. That there would be no future scandal. I'd like to hear you tell me that again, knowing that *she* . . ." he flung his finger out to point at me ". . . is associated with bodysnatchers through her late husband!"

I flinched as his hand swung out toward me. It was a reaction I couldn't suppress, a response learned during my three years of marriage to Sir Anthony. My heart kicked in my chest, racing madly, my nerves tingling in anticipation, even when the strike didn't fall.

Both men fell silent, staring at me. It was Gage who moved first, crossing the few steps to slide his arm around me protectively while I met his father's gaze. I felt naked before him, as if all my secrets lay bared. Unable to continue to face the shock and something else written in his eyes, I dropped my gaze to the floor, wishing it would open and swallow me up.

"Perhaps we should take a calming breath and lower our voices," Gage hissed before doing just that. "Father, we're no more pleased by this development than you are. But we'll find the answers." His voice hardened. "As for the rest, I will not discuss my wife's past with you again. It is not her fault, and if you cannot accept that, then perhaps we no longer need to see one another."

Lord Gage gazed steadily back at his son, as if Gage had not just threatened to cut ties with him, but I noticed how his right hand clenched and unclenched at his side, revealing he wasn't wholly unaffected.

"I saw Anderley at the Bow Street Magistrates Court today," he intoned in a level voice.

"Yes, I was busy investigating Newbury's attack," Gage bit out.

"He informed you of the proceedings?"

"Yes."

He turned to glare out the window. "If Superintendent Thomas doesn't make a hash of this, it will be a stroke of luck."

Gage didn't reply at first. "The tortoise was a bit ridiculous."

Lord Gage groaned. "That blasted tortoise! He flourished it like it was the Holy Grail, all while the witnesses who say the Italian Boy was outside the resurrectionists' home describe him exhibiting a mouse in a box slung around his neck."

"I understand they're searching the home tomorrow."

"Yes. Though heaven knows what the wives already destroyed before being arrested themselves. Someone reported one of them scattering ashes in their garden."

"I take it Melbourne isn't happy."

"I never knew you were so gifted at making understatements," his father drawled. "Melbourne is livid. He's desperate to have this case convicted, and he's become convinced the only way of that happening is if one of the prisoners turns King's evidence. It's the only way justice could be attained in the Burke and Hare case."

That was true. Without Hare's testimony, the jury probably would have come back with the Scottish verdict—"not proven"—and both men would have gone free.

"Are any of the prisoners interested?" Gage asked.

"Not yet, though the King's pardon has been offered to whoever talks. Melbourne is also offering a £200 reward for evidence to secure the conviction."

Gage whistled.

"The entire nation is following these proceedings. That boy was murdered by those men, and then they attempted to sell his body for profit. They can't be allowed to go free, or we'll have large-scale rioting on our hands, if not an insurrection."

We fell silent at the horrifying thought. Countless lives lost or injured, property destroyed and looted. And if the city were set on fire like during the recent Bristol riots, well, the devastation could be catastrophic.

Gage pulled me tighter to his side, as if that would keep me safe. "We'll continue to do what we can," he assured him.

Lord Gage nodded. "I know you will."

I supposed that was as close to an apology as he was going to offer. But how long would this truce last if he learned about those journals and Dr. Mayer's intentions for them? How long before his animosity returned with a vengeance?

CHAPTER TWENTY-TWO

I lowered the broadsheet with a huff of aggravation, crumpling the coarse paper in my lap. "Can no one sketch these body-snatchers with any accuracy?" I picked up the newspaper I'd set to my left and held them up for comparison. "Look here. They look nothing alike."

Gage showed me another paper. "This one's different, too."

I scowled, lifting a hand to brace myself as the carriage swerved around something in the street. As it was, we nearly had to shout to be heard over the cacophony of noises that filled the thoroughfares in the heart of The City—the square mile administrative enclave at more or less the center of London. Peddlers selling everything from huge trays of silk and paper flowers to pots and pans vied for the attention of passersby, along with Italian image boys, street musicians, and chaunters singing the first few lines of the broadsheets they sold.

"Clearly the artists allowed their impressions of the prisoners to affect their drawings. In some cases, they've even altered their features to exaggerated proportions, like a caricature." In one image Bishop's nose was long and slender under a sullen expression; in another it appeared quite unremarkable. Williams was so ordinary looking he was bordering on nondescript. While May—the handsomest of the lot—seemed to be portrayed more consistently, his image had been mislabeled as Bishop and vice versa in one of the papers. For a portrait artist such as myself, it was exasperating. I could have dashed off a fairly accurate sketch of each of them in minutes.

"They're not interested in accuracy," Anderley remarked from his seat across from us. His mouth twisted in scorn as he stared out through the window. "Only selling newspapers."

"Well, which is the closest?" I asked, thrusting the pages at him. "If I don't know what they look like, how can I tell whether I might have seen before, lurking about Sir Anthony's home? How can I know if they might be behind that blackmail letter?"

I knew it was only a matter of time before another arrived, or they tried an even more horrifying tactic to convince me to pay. Whoever they were, they would not remain patient for long.

"Probably this one," he decided after some debate, which gave me little hope of its precision.

I scoured the sketch, but nothing about the men seemed familiar.

Gage pressed a hand to my arm. "Darling, don't alarm yourself. You said yourself that the chances you ever saw their faces were slim."

"I know. But I hoped maybe something about them would jog a memory." After everything his father had said the night before, everything that was true, I couldn't help feeling anxious. It crawled along my skin, making my muscles twitch with the need to do *something*. I had to figure out who was blackmailing me before it was too late. "Perhaps I'll see someone familiar today loitering outside Nova Scotia Gardens."

It was the only reason Gage had allowed me to join them on their trip to Bethnal Green to the northeast of the city, out beyond Shoreditch. I'd hoped I might catch a glimpse of some-one who sparked a memory. After all, I never forgot a face. Un-likely it might be, but it was all I could think to do. We hadn't received word yet from Mr. Goddard, the Bow Street Runner investigating the matter for us, though he'd promised to report to Gage with an update on Monday.

Bree's evening spent in the lady's retiring room at my aunt's soiree had not been fruitful, beyond hearing a few ladies express concerns about possible burkings in Mayfair. The single interest-ing conversation begun in her presence had been abruptly si-lenced when one of the women recognized her as my maid. So in that regard, there was nothing for me to pursue.

We still hadn't uncovered the link between Feckenham and Newbury, if there even was one. But as of this morning, New-bury still clung to life. Maybe, hope against hope, he would re-cover. And maybe he'd seen something that could help us find his attacker, no matter how slim the chance.

The banks and businesses of The City gave way to the grim-ier vicinity of Shoreditch. The buildings there looked tired and dirty, and the streets were littered with refuse and other unmen-tionables. People plodded along the lanes, their forms shrunken, and their faces hollow-eyed. Life was hard in this part of Lon-don, and the farther we traveled northeast, the worse it grew. Just when I thought the circumstances couldn't appear more wretched, I would be proven wrong.

Anderley explained that Bethnal Green was populated by the very poor working class. It had once been a prosperous brick-field, but the clay had been exhausted, and the area had been filled in with waste. There were no great drains like in other areas of the city to remove water and refuse, and Nova Scotia Gardens—the colony of odd-looking cottages where Bishop and Williams had lived—was prone to flooding. As such, these abodes were highly undesirable and attracted naught but crimi-nals and the most desperate.

Our carriage halted outside the entrance to this neighbor-hood, across from the Birdcage pub, which even at midday seemed to be doing a bustling trade. Though that might have been due to the spectacle across the street. From my vantage through the carriage window, I could see into Nova Scotia Gar-dens, as well as survey any onlookers gathered at the gate to watch the police search cottage Number 3, all without being seen. However, nothing could block the stench which permeated this part of the city. I pressed one of the handkerchiefs Bree had dowsed with lavender water to my nose, swallowing hard against the urge to retch as Gage and Anderley opened the door to exit.

"Stay inside the carriage," Gage reminded me, quite unnec-essarily.

I nodded my head and urged him out before he let any more of the bad air in.

The entire scene horrified me. That people should be forced to live in such conditions—filthy children in ragged clothing running through piles of rotten things, women drawing water from wells that must be contaminated—was insupportable. The government had set up a system of workhouses for those too poor to have anywhere else to go—not that they were a much better alternative—but what about the rest? What about those who barely muddled through? Or the thousands who moved to London to obtain work, found themselves far from their home parish, and now could not rely on even that grim form of relief?

Pushing the troubling thoughts from my mind for the mo-ment, I turned to watch as Gage shook the hand of a gentleman I later learned was James Corder and a bluff, taller man who was Superintendent Thomas. They led Gage and Anderley around the side of the buildings into the gardens extending behind each of the cottages. The cottages had once been the homes and work-shops of weavers and boasted unusual sloping roofs, which ended in squat single rooms that projected into the deep garden. Each of these plots was separated by low palings, easily stepped over.

Gage stood with his hands on his hips surveying the area before pointing out a few features—the privies, a well, a washhouse—and then he gestured toward the other gardens. If the men on trial had burked other victims, who knew how many of the thirty gardens they might find evidence concealed in. They could have accessed any of them in the pitch black of night. The thought sent a shiver down my spine.

One of the constables came forward with some articles they'd already uncovered, either in the house or buried in the garden, and Gage flicked through these with a single finger before nodding that they be taken away. They also brought forth a few metal instruments and a rope tied in a noose that I assumed they thought might be murder weapons.

There was loud discussion among the spectators about these objects, and I studied their faces, looking for familiar features or some sign of restlessness or uneasiness. Something that might indicate they were of a similar profession. But most of those gathered appeared angry, and who could blame them. Not when their neighbors might have committed murder right under their noses.

It wasn't long before Gage and Anderley returned to the carriage, directing our coachman to drive on. "Thomas has this well enough in hand, and I trust he won't miss anything now that I've pointed out where to search," Gage muttered dryly.

"I take it he wasn't best pleased to have you inserting yourself into his investigation," I surmised from both men's annoyed expressions.

"If Corder hadn't been there, he would have turned us away with a flea in our ears. Even then, only invoking Lord Melbourne's name convinced him to cooperate." He shook his head. "He's not a bad officer, all in all, but he speaks before thinking, and his eagerness and moral certainty outstrip his logic and practical knowledge."

We rode on in silence for several minutes, but then I noticed the carriage taking a different route home. I glanced at Gage in question.

"We're stopping in Holborn on our way back to Mayfair. Anderley needs to speak with a contact of his there. He received some information that might lead us to the boy's identity."

"What of the exhumation?" I asked in confusion. "I thought a man from Birmingham was coming to confirm the identity of the boy."

"Perhaps. But Anderley and I are not convinced it will be the right one."

Anderley's expression was black. "The authorities don't care as long as they have a name to put to the boy. One that will not later be proved wrong."

I couldn't help but note the distress tightening his brow. The identity of the boy mattered to him, and it mattered to him to get it right. But it was more than just thoroughness, or an innate sense of nobility, that drove his interest. This was personal to him somehow.

I offered him a smile of empathy and then turned aside, knowing he would find it uncomfortable for me to continue staring at him. Out of the corner of my eye, I could tell some silent communication passed between him and Gage, but I ignored it, instead focusing on the city as it rolled by.

The homes in this northern section of the city surrounding Old Street were better kept and wider spaced, if not exactly desirable. At the Charter House we veered north, traveling by lesser roads, and then west through Clerkenwell Green before entering Holborn. This respectable neighborhood was populated by mixed levels of society and contained several smaller districts of certain professions or ethnic groups. As such, I was not surprised when Anderley explained that the area comprising such lanes as Saffron Hill, Vine Street, and Bleeding Heart Yard was called "Little Italy" because it was filled with Italian immigrants.

However, I was startled to hear him call out the window in Italian at a passerby as he rapped on the carriage wall, telling the coachman to stop. He leaped out of the conveyance and trotted over to two dark-haired men, launching into rapid speech in the foreign language, complete with expressive hand gestures. Such was the transformation that, had I not known he was my husband's valet, I should have mistaken him for another immigrant.

Having leaned out to order the coachman to circle the area, Gage perceived my astonishment as he returned to his seat. "I didn't tell you this before, because it was Anderley's story to tell, but he's given me permission to explain." His eyes searched mine. "He was once an Italian Boy."

My eyes widened. "Like the image boys we see on the street and the lads who exhibit animals and such? Like the boy the burkers killed?"

He nodded. "His parents were impoverished when Napoleon invaded northern Italy, and even afterward they couldn't recoup their losses. So they sold their son's services to a man they call a padrone, who agrees to take the boy under his wing in a sort of beggar's apprenticeship and teach him a skill. In Anderley's case, his parents were told he would be wandering the world as part of a theater company. His mother had been a gifted soprano before her marriage, so theater was in his blood."

"But that wasn't the case, was it?" I asked, having already guessed this was going to take an unpleasant turn.

Gage's face was averted, staring out the window, but I could hear the fury in his voice. "These padroni do not bring the boys here to teach them a trade. They treat them like little more than slaves. Sending them into the streets to display their busts and *boîtes à curiosité*, or exhibit small animals. All of which they own and force the boys to rent."

"But isn't that illegal?" I gasped. "Aren't they essentially procuring children to beg for alms?"

"Yes, but they escape exposure by using threats and manipulation. Beatings if they must. They tell the boys to lie and claim their padrone is their uncle or older brother, or there will be dire consequences." His voice lowered. "There are entire houses in this neighborhood which are owned by the padroni and filled to the rafters with Italian Boys."

My eyes lifted to the window, wondering which of these inconspicuous homes hid those poor, lost children. They'd been taken from their loved ones, sold for a lie, and forced into servitude for men who were supposed to care for them and give them hope for the future.

"And Anderley was one of those boys," I stated solemnly.

"For a time. Until he ran away. To Cambridge."

I looked up, meeting Gage's gaze.

He nodded. "I met him six weeks after my mother died. Two weeks after I'd discovered her maid had murdered her." The tiny lines at the corners of his eyes crinkled in remembered pain. "I was reckless, too consumed by grief to care. Or pay attention to my surroundings." His voice lowered in chagrin. "One night, I was set upon by footpads. They overpowered me and were proceeding to beat me when Anderley interfered. He drove them off and helped me back to my lodgings." He paused. "He's been tending to me ever since. First as more of an errand boy, but then as my valet." His lips quirked. "He's a quick learner. Picked up the basic skills from one of my friend's manservants. And he was soon imitating him with amazing precision."

"I never even suspected he was Italian," I admitted. "Well, not until a few days ago when I started to fit some of the pieces together. But I'd only wondered if he might be part Italian."

"He has a remarkable facility with languages and accents. Some of it learned from his mother, while the rest appears to be innate ability. Believe me, it's come in handy more than once."

A thought suddenly occurred to me. "How old *is* Anderley?" I frowned. "If that's really his name?"

"He was fifteen when I met him. Not as young as I assume

you were contemplating. So he's currently thirty-one. As for his given name, that's Andrea Landi."

"When did he tell you all of this?"

"Years ago. At first he was reluctant to speak of his past, for obvious reasons. He feared I might dismiss him or turn him over to his padrone or even the authorities. But little by little, as he began to trust me, the truth emerged." He lifted a hand to rub the corner of the window curtain between his fingers. "He was loyal, and in my world, such absolute devotion was rare."

Knowing the pains of his past, this did not surprise me, but it still made my chest ache.

"I think we both found in each other something the other needed."

Which explained their unique relationship—their easy comradeship, the solidarity in which they interrogated a witness or pursued a suspect. It also explained why Anderley had been hesitant to accept me.

"What of his family?" I murmured. "Are they aware of what happened to him?"

"Not the whole truth. He doesn't want them to know that. But they write to each other. And he visited them once, while we were on my Grand Tour of the continent after I finished at the university. We tracked them down near Florence."

I reached for his hand, studying the long fingers and strong knuckles. "So this inquiry *is* personal for him. He knows these Italian Boys, knows how they live, knows their pain." I looked up into his troubled gaze. "And he knows how easy it is for one to disappear and never be missed."

"Precisely. In many ways, the Italian Boys are the perfect prey for men like these burkers. If the porter at King's College hadn't noticed anything suspicious about the body, their crime would have gone undetected. The body would have been dissected and buried in a pauper's grave. No one would have known nor cared what happened to him until it was far too late."

It was a chilling thought. One that instinctively made me want to shrink away from it in horror, but also scream at the injustice of a society that allowed such things to happen.

"Perhaps the only good that has come out of this is that London has suddenly taken an acute interest in the Italian Boys. They're watched over with an almost sentimental protection. Now, if only that would extend to an interest in where they sleep at night and who is supposed to be caring for them." His eyes glinted with cynicism. "The padroni have been on their best behavior, and several of them are assisting the police, trying to win favor, or at least convince them to continue to turn a blind eye to their activities."

"They know?"

"Some of them do."

The carriage veered to the side and slowed. Gage reached out to open the door, and Anderley vaulted back inside without the use of the step.

"Any luck?" Gage asked.

He shook his head. "Though word is that Paragalli is determined to give him a name, one way or another."

I recognized the name as belonging to one of the people who had come forward to view the boy's body the day after the bodysnatchers were arrested. "Is he a padrone?"

Anderley glanced from me to Gage and then back again, as if confirming I'd been told all. "No. He and his wife are street musicians. But they associate closely with the padroni." His eyes narrowed. "Their hands are not clean."

"I anticipate Minshull will convene a special hearing at Bow Street on Monday," Gage told Anderley. "We should plan to be there."

He nodded decisively.

We traveled on in silence. I wanted to say something to Anderley, to convey to him my sympathy for what he'd been through, for what this inquest must be forcing him to relive, but I wasn't sure what to say. I didn't want to discomfit him in any way, but I also couldn't remain quiet and let him believe I thought less of him. However, he was also a male servant. I couldn't precisely embrace him.

He sat stiffly across from us until we reached Chapel Street, where he descended first, waiting to assist. Fortunately, Gage must have understood my dilemma, for he moved away, allowing his valet to help me down from the carriage. Rather than relinquish his hand, I squeezed it, forcing him to meet my gaze.

"Thank you, Anderley. We're lucky to have you," I told him earnestly in a low voice, so as to not draw the attention of the footman.

His dark eyes blinked several times, and then he nodded.

I released his hand and turned away, relieved to have found a way to express myself, and relieved that Anderley seemed to comprehend. In fact, I felt an even greater fondness for the man than I ever had before.

I passed into the house, where Jeffers waited to accept my outer garments. Gage already stood several steps away, next to the entry table where Jeffers laid any correspondence that arrived for us while we were away. While untying and removing my bonnet, I watched as he broke open the seal on a letter and read the contents.

His shoulders slumped. "David Newbury has died."

I felt a jolt of disbelief at the news, even having anticipated it. Sadness welled in my chest at the loss of the amiable young man, at the pain his family must be enduring.

"He never regained consciousness," Gage added as a forlorn afterthought.

So we had no new information to help us uncover a connection between him and Feckenham, and no idea why Newbury had been murdered. Unless, as Gage suggested, Feckenham's killer had been trying to throw us off his scent. But that was such a coldhearted, extreme measure, that I preferred to exhaust any other possibilities first.

And so, it seemed, did Gage.

"I must speak to Lord Newbury, and then I'm going to White's. Perhaps someone at the club will be aware of something we haven't thought of."

I nodded, knowing that privately Gage preferred Brooks's to White's—Brooks's being the bastion of the Whigs and White's the Tories. But like his father, he was one of the few men who managed to maintain membership at both elite clubs. Mainly because he kept his politics to himself, regardless of what he believed. Such dual membership had been invaluable to his past inquiries and might prove so in this instance as well.

"I may dine there as well, so don't hold dinner for me." He pressed a kiss to my temple, gathered his things, and was gone.

I stood gazing after him, feeling slightly at loose ends.

"Tea, my lady?" Jeffers inquired.

"Yes, please." He turned to depart, but I stopped him, having had a sudden notion. "In the study."

"Very good, my lady."

The room was chill when I entered it, but I knew Jeffers would remedy that once he returned. I crossed to the bookcase and ran my fingers along the spines until I came to the title I was searching for. Setting the book on Gage's desk, I gathered pencil and paper and cracked open *Debrett's Peerage*. If all we had to work with was the fact that Feckenham and Newbury were heirs to a noble title, then perhaps they weren't the only young gentlemen of such a position at risk.

Though compiling such a list would be somewhat tedious, I didn't have any better theories to pursue. If nothing else, maybe searching through the titles of the peerage would give me a better one.

CHAPTER TWENTY-THREE

Sunday dawned cold and rainy, and we spent a soggy few hours traveling to morning services and back. I'd hoped worship might lift my spirits, but given all the darting glances and tight-mouthed glares I'd received from fellow parishioners, any solace I might have taken from the liturgy was dashed. By the time Gage and I had settled before the fire in the morning room to dry ourselves, we were both in decidedly unpleasant frames of mind.

His foray to White's had proven unproductive. The only new development he'd returned with was a massive headache from hours of listening to Tories complain about the Whigs' continued support of the Reform Bill, and the ineffectiveness of the New Police, despite the fact the Police Act had been a measure that had passed under Tory leadership. In order to cope, he'd drunk more spirits than he was usually wont to do, which had resulted in crapulence and a sour temperament this morning.

For my part, I'd retired early after hours spent poring over *Debrett's*. I'd created a sizable list of young heirs—those who were older than children but had not yet reached an advanced age. In truth, I didn't know what additional criteria the killer had used if their status as heirs was all that connected the victims. Did they need to be heirs apparent—the eldest living son or the grandson of the deceased eldest son of the current titleholder? Or could they be heirs presumptive—a person who was first in line to inherit a title but could be displaced by the birth of a more direct heir? Did they need to be bachelors, or could they be married with or without an heir of their own? With only two victims to compare, it was difficult to decide what was applicable and what was not.

In any case, at that moment neither of us wished to discuss the inquiry. So I sat with my feet up, sketching my ideas for the nursery at our townhouse in Edinburgh while Gage lounged in the chair across from me with a book open in his lap. Truth be told, he was spending more time staring into the flames flickering in the fireplace than reading, but I wasn't going to point that out.

There was a rap on the door, and I called out for the person to enter, thinking it was Jeffers with some word about the midday meal. When I glanced up to see Bree enter, her dress still damp at the hem and her normally bouncy curls flat and listless, I lowered my feet to sit upright. "Bree, come closer to the fire before you catch the ague," I beckoned, concerned by the agitated look in her eyes and the tight line of her mouth. "Don't tell me you walked all the way from Mass?"

Four months earlier, I'd learned my maid was Roman Catholic, and while she typically attended church with me, Gage, and the rest of the servants while in the country, here in London she more readily had the option of attending Mass.

"I dinna mind a walk in the rain." She glowered. "Least no' when I'm no' bein' followed."

Gage looked up at this.

"You were followed?" I asked.

"Aye. 'Twas the same man who followed me back from Mount Street yesterday."

"Bree," I gasped. "You didn't tell me that."

I knew she had talked with the gardeners at 108 Mount Street the day before, for she'd reported they had nothing to tell. However, she hadn't mentioned being trailed.

She shrugged. "I couldna be sure. And I dinna want to worry ye."

Gage's brow lowered in displeasure. "This is dangerous work we undertake sometimes, Miss McEvoy. It would have been for *me* to decide whether such an occurrence was cause for concern or not. Do not keep such information from us again. Is that clear?"

Though I knew he was speaking out of concern for Bree's safety, his tone was harsh. I suspected his frustration and aching head had something to do with that.

"Yes, sir," Bree replied meekly, her expression much chastened.

Attempting to soften the sting, I gentled my own voice. "Did you recognize the man? Did he try to approach you or harm you in any way?"

"Nay. He just followed me, and at a distance, so that I couldna see much of his features beyond the hat pulled low o'er his eyes. I tried to foil him at Berkeley Square, to catch a glimpse o' his face. But he was a canny one."

"Well, if you should see him again, inform us immediately."

"I will." She shifted her feet, and I remembered how her leg often pained her when the weather was damp—the result of a previous injury.

"Is your leg grieving you?"

"No more than usual," she replied, but I could tell she was lying.

"Well, go and rest it anyway." I glared at her solemnly. "That's also an order."

It did not have the desired effect, for a smile hovered at the edges of her mouth. "Aye, m'lady."

After she departed, I turned to find Gage watching me. "What?" I demanded.

He shook his head before letting it fall back against the chair. "I would tell you you're too soft with her, but I'm one to talk, seeing as how my valet runs roughshod all over me."

My lips quirked. "Anderley would never do that. But I grasp your point."

We had just settled again when there was another rap on the door. This time it *was* Jeffers. However, from the guarded look on his face, I could tell he wasn't there to discuss meals.

"My lady, a letter was delivered for you." He crossed the room, holding it out in his hand rather than on the silver salver he normally used. His voice was pained as he spoke the next words. "It was left at the servants' entrance."

"What the devil?" Gage exploded. "Did anyone see who had the insolence to do such a thing?"

"No, sir. The kitchen maid found it on the floor just inside the door."

I accepted the missive from his fingers, relieved to see my hands weren't shaking even if my insides were. It appeared much the same as the last one—scuffed and dirty, the scrawl of my name smudged. I had been expecting a second blackmail note, but that did not prevent my heart from racing and my skin growing cold. Opening it gingerly, I found the contents were much the same, though this one had an addendum.

If you do not do as we ask, we will have to leave a gift on your doorstep. One your naybors will not ignore.

Gage took the letter from my numb fingers and scanned the words, his face settling into forbidding lines. "Jeffers, I want a servant stationed at the front and back doors of the house at all hours, and have them make regular checks of the exterior," he ordered as he rose to his feet. "Hire more men, if needed. I want to be informed immediately if they see anyone or anything suspicious."

"Yes, sir," Jeffers replied.

He read through the short missive again as the butler departed, and then scraped a hand back through his golden hair, making it stand on end as he stifled a curse.

"I'm sorry, Gage," I murmured in a small voice, standing to reach out to him. "I know this isn't what you bargained for."

"Stop talking nonsense," he snapped. "I knew who you were when I married you."

"Yes, but . . ."

"There is no 'but.' Do you think I would be so shabby as to blame you for this?" The letter crumpled between his fingers as he waved it at me. When I didn't immediately reply, his smile turned bitter. "I see."

"No one would fault you if you did," I finally managed to say, dropping my hands.

"Well, I would!"

I flinched at his vehemence.

He dampened his voice, but not the fire in his eyes. "I agreed to love and protect you through whatever might come. I accepted the troubles of your past, and the problems they might present in the future. But I cannot help you end them if you will not put them aside."

"What are you talking about?" I demanded. "I didn't stir up the shadows of my past. They did!"

"Yes, but they are *always* there lurking. In one form or another, you're always braced for the next hatchet to fall. You claimed you'd begun to appreciate the good that the pain of your past had caused you, to embrace the knowledge Sir Anthony forced upon you and turn it to a noble use. And yet here you are again, cast into the role of victim."

"That is grossly unfair!" My voice wobbled as tears threatened at the corners of my eyes. "I didn't ask for any of this to happen. I didn't ask to be made a figure of fear and scorn."

"Then stop letting them do so! Stop letting them decide who you are."

I swiped angrily at the wetness on my cheeks. "It's not so simple."

"Yes, it is," he insisted. "You know those of us who love you will stand by you. To hell with the rest."

"But what of you, and the baby . . ."

"I mean it, Kiera. If they cannot accept you for who you are, then they are not worthy of my or our child's time." His eyes scoured my flushed face, giving me not an inch of leniency. "I will never blame you for what's been done to you, and I will always be by your side. But I'm also not going to coddle your fears and let you hide from the truth." He shook his head. "Not when it's this important."

I crossed my arms over my chest and turned away, feeling betrayed. Didn't he understand I didn't want to feel this fear? I didn't want it always hovering at the back of my mind. I didn't want it harming my loved ones.

But then, of course, he didn't know my biggest fear, or the guilt that walked hand in hand with it. The nameless dread that I'd only recently been able to put into words, though I had lived with it for five years. If I could barely acknowledge it to myself, how was I going to tell Gage?

"Goddard is supposed to call on me tomorrow with an update. I'll show this second letter to him then." Without waiting for a response, he turned on his heel and left the room.

I stared into the hearth until it became blurry with tears, and then I pushed to my feet to stomp up and down the room. If not for the rain, I might have gone out into the garden to cool my cheeks and dry my tears, but I was not so foolish as to venture out in such conditions, even in my state of agitation.

Eventually, I turned my steps to my art studio in the conservatory. If I couldn't make progress in the investigation or reconcile with Gage and the things he'd said, then at least I could paint. It always soothed me and helped me clarify my thoughts. Which was something I needed now more than ever.

I yawned, tipping my head to block the bright sun with the brim of my bonnet as it broke through the clouds, and lifted my skirts to mount the steps to the Marquess of Barbreck's residence. Though only late morning, I suspected he wouldn't mind my paying an early call, not when he'd been the one to request I do so. However, I began to wish I'd yielded to my initial impulse and gone back to sleep.

I hadn't stumbled up to bed until well after midnight, having spent all afternoon, evening, and a good part of the night, closeted in my studio, oblivious to all else. Gage had already been asleep when I slipped between the covers, and that morning when I'd blinked open my eyes it was to find he'd already gone. A note on my bedside table weighted down by a red carnation informed me that he and Anderley had departed early for Bow Street and the special hearing on the inquiry into the Italian Boy.

I'd twirled the flower before my nose, wondering if it was meant to be a peace offering. But that sent my mind along paths I didn't wish to trod. So I forced myself out from beneath the covers, determined to do something productive with my time.

Which was how I'd found myself at Lord Barbreck's door. The old roué would never let me remain steeped in my own morose ponderings. He would expect to be entertained.

When the butler announced me, I was surprised to discover the marquess was not alone. I was even more surprised to discover Lord Marsdale seated with him. He grinned unrepentantly, clearly pleased to have disconcerted me.

I recovered quickly and moved forward to give Barbreck my hands with a smile.

"Here on yer own, are ye?" he remarked in his deep Scottish brogue.

"Yes, Mr. Gage is otherwise occupied."

"Inquiry business, no doubt. Well, he's braver than I."

I tilted my head in perplexity. "I rather thought you would enjoy observing the follies at the Bow Street Magistrates' Office."

"Oh, aye." He chuckled. "I imagine I would. But I meant lettin' ye venture aboot alone, especially wi' scoundrels like this one wanderin' the streets o' Mayfair."

I turned to the other occupant with an arch smile. "I trust Lord Marsdale knows what my husband would do to him if he ever attempted to trifle with me."

"Yes, but I have to say I'm more worried what you would do." Marsdale's eyes were alive with amusement. "Still carrying that Hewson pistol in your reticule?"

I arched my chin. "Of course. A lady never knows when she might need to defend herself against unscrupulous fellows."

He flashed me a blinding grin, which reminded me what an attractive man he was in his own right.

I observed Marsdale as I settled onto the edge of the sofa across from him, finding he looked even more handsome than usual. His skin was bronzed and flush with health, his molasses dark eyes clear and unshadowed. Though I had to puzzle over the matter for a few seconds, I finally realized what the difference was. He wasn't suffering from a night of overindulgence. In fact, he looked as if he hadn't overindulged in some time.

His eyebrows rose at this close scrutiny, but I ignored him and turned back to Barbreck, who was speaking.

"I was sorry to hear young Newbury succumbed to his wounds. Always liked that lad." He pressed both hands to the silver filigreed head at the top of his walking stick, propping it on the floor in front of him between his legs. "Better than his father, at any rate."

"I take it you're not fond of Lord Newbury," I remarked.

"Dinna get me wrong. I'm sure he's a fine man. But he lives too much in Wellington's pocket for my taste. But his son, noo." He lifted his cane, thumping it on the floor. "He was his own man."

"How do you mean?"

His heavy-lidded eyes sparkled with glee that he knew something I did not. "Rumor has it, young Newbury was more Whig than Tory. Something I'm sure his father didna like."

I sat back, considering this information. I'd not considered the political ramifications of the investigation before. "Lord Redditch and Lord Newbury are both staunch Tories."

"Yes," Marsdale confirmed. "And two fiercer opponents of recent legislative efforts, you won't find. Particularly the Reform Bill."

"Aye. There may be some who are wafflin' in their opinion. Especially in light o' all the public's unrest. But no' them." Barbreck huffed a dry laugh. "They'd sooner move to the colonies than vote for reform."

"What of Lord Feckenham?" I asked.

"Never heard much talk aboot his politics, but I canna imagine he wasna the same as Redditch."

"He was a Tory," Marsdale stated confidently, draping his arm along the back of the sofa. "Make no mistake about that. And not a moderate one. He would have voted against Wellington's Catholic emancipation bill, and heartily supported Peel's Police Act. There was no way he would have wished to cede any further power to the so-called riffraff."

I blinked at him. "Did you know him?"

"Mainly by reputation. Why do you look so shocked?"

"I'm just surprised to discover you're so politically savvy."

In the past, Marsdale would rather have been tried for murder than admit he had any sort of intelligence or honor in him.

He shrugged. "The duke insists I keep informed of such things."

I narrowed my eyes. He might try to brush it off as his father's fault, but I suspected it was more than that. After all, his past conduct certainly hadn't been undertaken to please his father.

If the flattened line of his mouth was any indication, Barbreck seemed to hold similar doubts about Marsdale's truthfulness, but he showed unexpected leniency in not crying balderdash.

"Regardless, I suppose since Feckenham wasn't about to switch political affiliation nor was Mr. Newbury, the point is irrelevant to your investigation." Marsdale actually sounded disappointed by this.

"Perhaps the sons' affiliations aren't, but maybe the fathers' are." My voice trailed away as I considered the possibility. "What if the connection between the two victims isn't something about them, but about their fathers?"

Marsdale sat forward, following my line of thought. "The fact that they oppose the Reform Bill."

"Yes. What if someone was out for revenge or . . . hoped to somehow influence the outcome of the vote?" I turned to the side, pressing my fingers to my lips as I tried to analyze whether such reasoning even made sense. I wondered if Gage had contemplated a political motive. Had we been thinking about this all wrong?

"I need to go," I declared, rising to my feet. If there was more that Lord Barbreck wanted to prattle about, it would simply have to wait. "You both have been extraordinarily helpful." I hastened over to press a spontaneous kiss to Lord Barbreck's wrinkled cheek.

"Always happy to assist a lady. Especially when it results in a kiss," he chortled.

Marsdale rose politely from his chair, and I turned to offer him my hand. His eyes were alive with teasing as he grasped my fingers. "What? No kiss for me as well?"

I arched a single eyebrow in chastisement. "You would enjoy it too much."

"That I would," he replied unrepentantly.

CHAPTER TWENTY-FOUR

I was both surprised and relieved to find Gage had returned home before me, and hastened out to the small terrace which overlooked our garden. That he should have chosen to sit outside was not strange, given the fact the weather was mild and the breeze gentle. But finding him slouched in his chair, nursing a glass of brandy so early in the afternoon while broodingly smoking a cheroot, brought me up short. Gage rarely indulged in tobacco, and never while alone in our home. Perhaps at one of his clubs or with other gentlemen at a dinner party after the ladies had withdrawn from the dining room, but even that was infrequent.

"I take it the special hearing did not go well," I remarked, continuing out onto the terrace.

He stubbed out the tip of his cheroot in the glass dish on the table out of deference to my presence.

I sank into the chair across the table from him. "What happened?"

He exhaled a long breath before responding. "Precisely what we thought would happen. A padrone from Birmingham identified the body as belonging to a boy named Carlo Ferrari. He said Ferrari had come to England in the late autumn of 1829 to work for him." His jaw tightened at the casual manner in which the padrone had spoken of the matter. "He said the boy had been signed over to a new master in the summer of 1830, and he knew nothing of him beyond that."

"But you don't believe him?"

Gage's scowl deepened. "The padrone couldn't speak English, so Joseph Paragalli acted as his translator."

I frowned, wrapping my paisley shawl tighter around me against the chill as the sun slid behind a bank of clouds. "He was one of the people who first came forward to view the body, wasn't he?"

He nodded. "He and his wife. He even claimed today that he'd recalled Ferrari and thought of him at the time, but hadn't been able to remember his name." His eyes lifted to meet mine for the first time. "The problem is Anderley speaks Italian. He understood what the padrone was saying, and it was not exactly what Paragalli translated for the court."

"What didn't he translate correctly?"

"For one, the padrone was not certain the body was Ferrari's. He said it was too decomposed, too damaged by the autopsy for him to identify the boy decisively. And he also stated that the last he'd known of Ferrari, he lived in Bristol with his new master. That it was possible he'd run away, but he could not say if that was true."

"Did you tell the magistrates that?"

"Yes. After the hearing. But they did not take kindly to our interference. They were simply happy to have a name to put to the Italian Boy. They didn't care if it was the right one."

"So Anderley was correct."

He nodded, glaring at the box shrubs bordering the terrace.

I glanced about me, curious where his valet had gone. "He must be upset."

"I ordered him to shine and polish all my boots and shoes."

I turned back to him in disbelief.

"He was furious. If I'd let him leave the house, he would have tracked down Paragalli and drawn his cork, or worse. Best to let him take out his wrath on my footwear instead."

Seeing the wisdom in this, I settled back in my chair. "What of you?" He appeared relaxed, but I could sense the restrained energy rippling beneath his insouciant posture.

He took another drink of his brandy before answering. "I'm fine." Though it was clear he was not. "Goddard found me outside Bow Street." He stared down into the amber liquid in his glass. "Said he hasn't found our blackmailer yet, but he received some new information today that might help point him in the right direction."

I forced a breath past the tightness in my chest, rife with the sweet lingering scent of his cheroot and the musk of decaying leaves. I didn't wish to return to the argument of the previous morning, so I merely nodded.

Neither did Gage, it seemed. "Where did you venture off to?" he remarked casually.

I told him of my visit to Lord Barbreck, and Marsdale's presence, as well as my notion that perhaps the motive for the Mayfair murders had been political.

He listened quietly, squaring his glass with the tile pattern of the tabletop before replying. "I considered that."

I stiffened. "You did?"

"I spoke to a large number of Tories at White's the other night. I would have to be very muttonheaded not to have thought of it."

"Then why didn't you mention it?"

"Because it's too ill defined. Those lords who are resistant to reform have made themselves the enemy of a large swath of the populace, but these murders are not the work of ruffians. They've been carefully planned by someone who knows the streets of Mayfair. The fact that the assailant has no apparent experience with knives or combat, as evidenced by his poorly aimed stabs, only confirms the fact we're looking for an unlikely murderer."

"That doesn't mean his grievance isn't against Redditch and Newbury, or that it's not political in nature," I pointed out crossly.

He scraped a hand down his face wearily. "You're right. I apologize. I should have remarked on it."

I dipped my head, accepting his expression of regret without further comment. If I was honest with myself, I wasn't sure whether I was more irked because I hadn't thought of the possibility first rather than because he'd failed to share it with me. I rose to my feet to cross toward the hanging baskets of trailing violas that the gardener had taken inside during the days of snow and hard frost, fingering one of the blooms.

Gage shifted in his chair behind me, lowering the foot he'd crossed over his knee to the ground. "Did Barbreck or Marsdale say something that helped you think of it?"

"Barbreck mentioned how David Newbury was rumored to have leanings toward the Whigs, and that devolved into a discussion of the Tories."

"And let me guess, Marsdale sat back yawning and mocking?"

"Actually, he seemed quite knowledgeable. More so than I expected." I tilted my head in contemplation. "I think he's quit drinking so heavily. He was quite sober at the ball Friday night, and today as well. I must say, he appears much better for it. I've never seen him in such fine health and looks. Do you think he could . . ."

Gage grabbed my hand from behind and pulled me back onto his lap, capturing my lips before I could even finish my statement. I was frightfully susceptible to his persuasive maneuvers, particularly at this stage of my condition. Several minutes more of his attentions, and I suspect I would have allowed him to carry me out into the garden and bare me to the sky, so long as he didn't stop. But he pulled back, gazing down at me with a gleam of very masculine pride.

"What was that for?" I asked, not bothering to disguise how breathless I felt.

"Just to remind you who your husband is."

I blinked up at him in confusion, trying to recall what we were even discussing before. Then realization dawned. "I didn't say I was attracted to him. It *is* Marsdale, for heaven's sake."

"Regardless," he replied without remorse.

I glowered at him, unaccustomed to such displays of jealousy. Reconsidering my words, I pondered how I would have felt if Gage had said something similar about another woman, irrespective of what he really meant by it. "I suppose my comment wasn't very appropriate," I conceded.

His face lit with a smile that cast all others in the shade. "That you even had to puzzle that out tells me all I need to know." He shook his head. "Poor Marsdale."

I leaned closer, so that our mouths were only a hairsbreadth apart. "Why are we still talking about him?"

His eyes flickered with heat before he kissed me again.

The sound of rapping alerted us to the fact that we were no longer alone. I pulled back, and would have risen from Gage's lap, but he held me fast.

"What is it, Jeffers?" he said, never removing his gaze from mine.

"My apologies for disturbing you, sir." His voice was as unruffled as ever, though he carefully averted his eyes from our intimate seating position. "Lord Gage is here, and he insists on speaking with you. Samuel is attending to him in the drawing room."

The corner of Gage's lip curled in enjoyment, recognizing as I did that this meant our footman was keeping Lord Gage from marching through the house to intrude upon us. A move that was certain to vex him.

"Good man," Gage told the butler. "We'll join him shortly."

"Very good, sir."

I rested my head against his shoulder as Jeffers departed. "Couldn't we just send him away?" I murmured, unsure if I could endure my father-in-law's vitriol at the moment.

His fingers brushed over the hair at the base of my scalp. "If not for these ongoing inquiries, I would happily tell him to go to the devil for you." He sighed heavily. "But as neither seems close to a satisfactory ending, I'm afraid I can't. You needn't accompany me, though. I can face the dragon alone."

I sat up to look him in the eye, grateful for the offer. But I didn't want Lord Gage to believe he'd gotten the better of me. Not after the way our last encounter had ended. My pride couldn't stand it. Perhaps he now suspected more of the truth about my marriage to Sir Anthony than I wished; cowering from him because of it would only make it worse. In any case, I had no reason to feel shame. Sir Anthony had been the monster. It was past time I showed him that.

"No, I'll come," I told Gage, rising to my feet to shake out the cerulean blue skirts of my dress.

He took hold of my hand and didn't release it. Not even when we strolled into the drawing room to greet his father. Samuel stood to the side of the door, just where Jeffers had told him to, and Gage nodded to dismiss him as we entered.

"Father, to what do we owe the pleasure?" Gage remarked dryly.

Lord Gage rose to his feet, his face tight with some suppressed emotion. "I'm afraid I have some unpleasant news."

"Oh?"

He waited until we all were seated before speaking again. "I've just learned that a Dr. Mayer is in possession of a number of personal journals written by Sir Anthony Darby, and that he plans to publish them." He had been watching us closely as he divulged this information, and although my stomach quavered at the discovery he now knew about the journals, neither of us reacted in any other way. His eyes narrowed. "You knew."

Gage's brow furrowed. "Yes. We learned of the matter several days ago from a close friend. But how did you find out?"

"A close friend," Lord Gage sneered, apparently no more willing to share his source than we were.

"So it's not widely known yet?"

"No. But it will be soon. What have you done to remedy the situation?"

For a moment, I thought Gage was going to refuse to answer, in spite of his father's imperious expression.

"I've been attempting to purchase them anonymously. I thought that might be the simplest solution. And if such a bid is unsuccessful, then . . ."

"Fool!"

Gage's already straight back turned rigid.

"He'll know it's you." Lord Gage thumped his hand on the arm of his chair. "And if such a fact should become known, how will that look? As if you're attempting to conceal your wife's crimes."

"I've committed no crimes," I snapped.

His gaze skewered me. "The truth will be of no consequence. Only the appearance of it. And attempting to secretly purchase those journals makes you look guilty."

I scowled. He might speak the truth, but he didn't have to do so in such a way that belittled me.

"I'll handle the matter," he declared decisively. "There is no way I'm going to allow those journals to be published."

I turned to Gage in alarm.

"We have no need for you to interfere," he told his father firmly. "If you had let me finish speaking, I was about to say that if he refuses to sell, I was going to approach the publisher to see if, given the number of high-ranking patients Sir Anthony treated and the scandals and resulting lawsuits that were certain to ensue from the publication of such sensitive information, I could dissuade them from publishing."

Lord Gage scoffed. "That won't dissuade them. Publishers love a good scandal. It sells books."

Gage continued through gritted teeth. "And if that didn't work, I hoped royal pressure might be brought to bear."

His father sat upright at this suggestion. "Yes. Sir Anthony was sergeant surgeon to old George, wasn't he? Then I'm sure he knew a number of unseemly details His Majesty won't want revealed about his brother." His lips tightened as if recalling some of those unseemly details; then his gaze returned to his son. "If you mean to request royal interference, then I'm the one to do it. The King owes me a favor or two, and given the fact he'll mutually benefit from this request, I know he won't refuse."

When Gage didn't reject this offer, I squeezed his hand where it still gripped mine. I did not want those journals falling into the hands of my father-in-law, whatever they contained about me.

"We appreciate your offer, but I would like to discover if Dr. Mayer is willing to be reasonable first. If he refuses to sell them, then we'll keep your proposition in mind. But I do not want you interfering until I ask you to do so."

Lord Gage's face reddened with resentment. "Why must you be so bloody stubborn?"

"'The raven chides blackness,'" he replied, quoting Shakespeare.

Rather than growling back at him or striding from the room, his father's lip reluctantly curled. "True enough. I admit I'm stubborn." His gaze flicked to me and back. "Your mother would have said so, too."

I had rarely heard him mention his long-dead wife, and it seemed neither had Gage, for he stilled beside me. His eyes riveted on his father's face, almost as if he was hungry for him to say her name. But the moment passed all too swiftly.

"I'll do nothing until you ask me to," Lord Gage conceded

before rising to his feet. "Just don't wait overlong, or it might be too late."

The following two days, much of Gage's time was occupied with matters regarding the inquest into the death of the Italian Boy, whose identity was now being reported everywhere as Carlo Ferrari. Superintendent Thomas had made much of the bundle of women's clothing the police found in the privy at Cottage Number 2 in Nova Scotia Gardens on Tuesday morning, even though Gage had suggested they search it on Saturday. The fact that Williams had lived at Number 2 for a short time before marrying Bishop's daughter and moving in with the Bishop family at Number 3 just five weeks before Ferrari's murder made a search of the neighboring premises an obvious move to Gage. However, Thomas had resisted. And when his men found the violently torn clothing in the privy, as well as a shawl wrapped around a large stone at the bottom of the well, he'd been happy to take the credit. Gage shrugged it off in annoyance, but I was infuriated on his behalf. It was no wonder Thomas had a reputation as being difficult to work with.

Squabbles over recognition aside, the mounting evidence at Nova Scotia Gardens was making it difficult to believe that what had been going on there wasn't just the handling of unearthed corpses—removing their clothing, teeth, and hair to sell separately—but cold-blooded, methodical murder. Other people had been reported missing from the area, including several women from Bethnal Green and Shoreditch, and a number of children. Could some of them have fallen victim to Bishop, Williams, and May as well?

Gage had roundly approved of Thomas's resolve to inquire at the anatomical schools of London again and find out just how many bodies the prisoners had sold to them in the past few months, as well as what type of corpses and the state they were in. The bodies might not have shown obvious marks of foul murder, but the porters would have noticed if the corpses hadn't been buried or begun to show signs of decay. Perhaps that would give the police some idea of the potential number of victims they were looking at.

Meanwhile, I spent my mornings with the Duchess of Bowmont, working on her portrait while she entertained me with stories of her own foibles, as well as that of the rest of the ton. She was old enough that she remembered when King George IV had still been quite handsome, and told me several tales of how he'd cut a dash through society and broken many hearts.

A number of times, she attempted to discuss the murders with me. Though I could tell she was merely curious and perhaps interested out of boredom, still I resisted sharing any details with her. I simply couldn't risk it, despite her quick mind.

I spent the rest of my time paying calls on those who would speak with me—known friends or relatives of the victims, anyone I thought might possess information that might be helpful to us, whether they knew it or not. I soldiered on through the driving rain and withering gossip, hoping to learn something that might help us figure out who had killed Feckenham and Newbury. By the end of the second afternoon, I was weary and damp, and desperately in need of a friendly face.

I ordered the carriage to Brook Street and was relieved to find my sister at home. Alana took one look at me and ordered me into the chair by the fire, propping my feet up and placing a blanket over my lap before she plied me with sweetened tea. For once, I was happy to let my older sister order me about and mother me. There had been a time, after Sir Anthony's death and the scandal that followed, when I had willingly complied with all her dictates, not caring enough to argue or assert my opinion. While my life had changed greatly in the last year, I still needed her soft lap to land in from time to time, and her stern voice of reason as well.

Once I was settled, she plopped down in the closest chair and pointed an accusing finger at me. "You are exhausting yourself. You know you cannot do that in your expectant state."

"I'm fine as a fiddle," I protested, and then softened my response when faced with Alana's gimlet stare. "But I admit, I may have overdone it a bit today, especially in this dreadful rain."

"Where is your husband? I can't believe he would be pleased to find you have been traipsing all over town."

"He's busy with matters regarding the inquest into the Italian Boy." I became absorbed with centering my teacup on its saucer so I wouldn't have to look my sister in the eye. "He doesn't precisely know what I've been doing."

She scowled. "But I'd wager he wouldn't be surprised."

I shrugged. "Well, you both do know me best."

"Yes. That you would never sit idly by while there's a murder to be solved." She stated this as if it was a great fault in my character, but I felt quite to the contrary.

I was saved from making a response by the butt of a head against my leg. A second later, a round lump of fur hopped up onto the ottoman and then crawled up my legs to sit on my lap, heedless of the slight rounding of my belly. I shifted my teacup lest the fat feline knock it from my grip, and reached down to pet his soft gray head. "What have your children been feeding him?" I laughed. "I do believe he's even larger than the last time I saw him."

Earl Grey slitted an eye open at me at this insult and then settled back into the nest of my skirts, contentedly purring.

"They sneak him all sorts of tidbits. The nursery maids and I have despaired of ever stopping them." She frowned at the cat's back. "He's a canny one. He's been whining all day. I thought perhaps he had a stomachache from something he ate. Nothing would satisfy him. But apparently he was simply waiting for you."

I glanced up at this and then back at the happy feline. Until a year ago, he had lived as a mouser at my childhood home. But during my stay there last winter, he had attached himself to me, refusing to be kept away, despite locked doors and stern reprimands. Slowly he'd wormed his way into my affections, offering me silent companionship when I needed it most. I'd elected to leave him in the care of my nieces and nephews when Gage and I departed on our honeymoon, and he'd remained with them since. I hadn't the heart to take their adored pet from them.

"So you and Gage are involved with the Italian Boy inquest, as well as these murders in Mayfair." Alana shook her head. "I suspected as much."

"Well, you didn't expect us not to assist if there was something we could do, did you?"

"No." She glanced to the side at a newspaper still resting on the low table. "And to tell you the truth, I'm glad you are, even if I disagree with your dashing about Mayfair." Her expression was stricken. "These poor missing children. Have you seen the letters some gentlemen have begun writing to the newspapers on behalf of their families?"

I nodded.

"To think, dozens, maybe hundreds, of children have gone missing, and we knew nothing of it." Her voice was horrified. "Whether some of them have actually fallen victim to these resurrectionist men or they've fallen prey to some other frightening fate, it's still all so terrible. I think a great deal of polite society have been shaken out of their selfish preoccupation by these events and the discoveries that have followed. I only wish it hadn't taken something as dreadful as this for us to take notice. It's disgraceful. They're *children*, for heaven's sake. We should have noticed."

I couldn't have agreed more. We were all too complacent, too blind to those around us, oblivious of the depravities so many faced. The upper classes were content to wrap themselves in a cocoon of riches, pretending those who had not had the luck to be born into such privilege were not struggling. We had failed those children as much as anyone else, for we had the means and influence to change the system, and yet we'd preferred ignorance. If one good thing had emerged from this terrible event, it was the fact that many finally had the wool pulled from their eyes.

I set my teacup on the table at my elbow. "I've been told the *Morning Advertiser* is going to begin printing a regular bulletin of missing children."

"Good." Her eyes gleamed with determination. "And I've begun looking into the various organizations purported to assist these vagrant children to see how I might be able to help."

"I can share a list of several I've been contributing to."

She nodded. "Please do."

"I'll show myself in," we heard a familiar voice declare before the door opened to the drawing room to admit our brother. His gaze swung from Alana to me, and he exhaled in relief. "Here you are. Your butler said you were out making calls, and after enduring an afternoon dodging veiled daggers, I suspected you might find your way here."

"Some were not so veiled," I answered dryly. "But why were you looking for me?"

Trevor plunked down in the closest chair, slouching into its depths. If possible, he looked worse than I must have when I'd shown up at our older sister's door. "I've just paid a call on Miss Newbury."

"How is she?" I murmured, my heart clenching in sympathy for the girl.

Trevor scraped a hand through his chestnut hair. "As well as can be expected, I suppose. The poor girl is having to care for her mother, who is prostrate with grief. I wish there was something I could do for her."

I offered a smile of commiseration, touched to see how much he appeared to care for her. But Trevor had always been kind and considerate—even to me, his pestering younger sister—so I was careful not to presume too much.

"I'm sure your visits are helpful, even if it might not seem like much," Alana told him.

"Yes, well, I did promise to do one thing for her." His eyes riveted to me. "She asked me to convey a message to you. She wishes you to call on her tomorrow at a quarter past three. Her parents will be out then, and she wants to see you alone."

My eyes widened. "She has something to tell me?"

"I assume." His mouth tightened at the corners. "She would not say why."

"I imagine she didn't have time to," Alana said. "If her mother was hovering nearby."

Trevor's annoyance softened, as if he'd not considered this when she'd failed to confide in him. "Indeed, she was." He looked to me. "Will you call on her?"

"Of course."

He nodded. "I told her you would. Or have a very good reason why you couldn't." He pushed himself more upright. "Are you any closer to figuring out who killed her brother and Feckenham?"

I shook my head in frustration. "We still can't find a definitive connection between them or their families." I paused to consider. "But maybe Miss Newbury knows. Or, at least, suspects."

"Don't fret, Kiera. I have every faith you and Gage will figure it out."

I frowned. "I hope so. And sooner rather than later."

It hadn't escaped my or Gage's notice that both men had been killed overnight between Thursday and Friday, and tomorrow was Thursday. If the murderer wasn't finished, then would we find another body Friday morning?

CHAPTER TWENTY-FIVE

Promptly at a quarter after three the next day, I appeared at the Newburys' door. The butler must have been informed of my imminent arrival, for he ushered me inside without a word. From the look in his eyes, I detected he possessed a soft spot for Miss Newbury, and I was relieved to discover it. Someone needed to look after her if her mother was too overcome to do so.

The young lady stood gazing anxiously out the window of their back parlor, her smooth face washed in soft light. I paused, arrested by the image. It would have made a stunning portrait—a study in silent grief, in patient yearning. I captured it in my mind, my eyes swiftly appraising every detail from the curl of her copper ringlets to the ache such a sight stirred in my breast. I had but seconds before she turned to look at me, but it was enough.

She hastened forward as the door closed behind me. "Thank goodness you've come. Mr. St. Mawr said you would, but I couldn't be sure."

I accepted her hands. "Of course. What need do you have of me?"

She pulled me toward a sofa, sitting down beside me. "I will tell you quickly, for I fear we haven't much time." She exhaled a ragged breath. "I overheard David speaking with one of his friends some weeks ago. I couldn't hear all, but the friend seemed very agitated, and David kept trying to brush off his concern." She leaned closer, lowering her voice. "He said something about Lombard Street and . . . and a cent percent."

I sat taller, recognizing what she'd overheard, even if she didn't appear to comprehend the cant term.

"Do you know what that means? Could it be important?"

"Possibly," I replied, not willing to add to her worries by explaining the matter. "Thank you for telling us. Gage and I will look into it."

She nodded uncertainly but didn't press for answers.

"Can you tell me who this worried friend was?" I asked, thinking we might get more details from him.

"Lord Damien Marlowe."

I stifled my surprise, for Damien had sworn his friend had no such troubles.

I thanked her again and hurried from the house before Lord and Lady Newbury returned. But rather than return home, I directed the carriage to Hollingsworth House, a short distance away. I decided risking an encounter with the Dowager Lady Hollingsworth was worth it to discover why her son, Damien, had lied.

Damien sat alone in the private family parlor, staring morosely up at a painting of a ship on the wall. His clothing was rather tame compared to the dandyish togs I'd seen him wearing recently, and suited him far better than that tawdry attire.

"You lied to me," I stated firmly after the footman who showed me in had disappeared.

Damien frowned. "I assure you I have not."

I advanced toward where he stood. "You told me David Newbury was not in the habit of gambling, but I have it on good authority he was visiting a cent per center in Lombard Street." I arched my eyebrows at his evident surprise.

"I admit I expressed some concern a few weeks back when he mentioned he'd been to Lombard Street, but he swore it wasn't to visit a moneylender."

"And you believed him?"

"Not at first. But then he explained the matter to me. He said Mr. Callihan had extricated himself from the unsavory business of moneylending and was now engaged in raising funds for a charitable project."

I frowned. I disliked being skeptical of people's good intentions, but experience had taught me that not everyone was honest or altruistic. The very fact that David Newbury was dead made everyone connected to him suspect in some way. "You didn't find this claim somewhat farfetched?"

"Of course I did. But he laughed about it, and I had seen how little interest he showed in the gaming tables. It seemed disloyal not to trust his word."

I had to concede this point, though I wished he had remembered that conversation and informed us of it earlier.

Later, when I relayed these findings to Gage, he expressed the same dissatisfaction. "Then we'll need to pay a visit to this Mr. Callihan tomorrow." He turned to look at Anderley seated across from us in the morning room, where we'd gathered to review our investigations. "Which means I'll have to rely on you to attend the final magistrates' hearing at Bow Street."

Anderley's face was drawn, his eyes bleak. I could see what a toll this investigation was taking on him. "It might be better if you absent yourself anyway. The police are anticipating an unruly crowd. There's bound to be some unpleasantness, and you don't exactly blend in." His gaze carefully avoided mine, and I realized he was referring to Gage's connection with me and all my scandalous associations with dissections and corpses.

That Gage was aware of this, too, was obvious by the slight

narrowing of his eyes, but he skimmed over the matter. "What happened out in Bethnal Green today? I heard there was some hubbub."

"They set up admission booths outside Bishop's House of Murder so people can view the cottage where the murder is believed to have happened."

"Ach! How ghoulish," Bree declared, echoing my own thoughts.

"Maybe so, but people are determined to see it one way or another," Gage replied. "The police were probably smart to ask the owners to make such an arrangement so that the site isn't mobbed."

Bree crossed her arms over her chest. "And they'll make a pretty penny from the entrance fee, I wager."

"True enough," Anderley admitted. "But considering the fact that all their tenants are leaving, and the Bishops' cottage is likely to be stripped clean of even the bark on the trees in the garden by people wanting mementos, I can't say I begrudge them it."

"Anything else of note to report?" Gage interjected, bringing us back to topic.

His valet shook his head, subsiding back into his chair.

"What of you, Miss McEvoy? Any sign of the man who followed you?"

"Nay." She frowned. "Perhaps I only imagined he was." But I could tell from her tone of voice she didn't believe that.

"No, Bree," I disputed. "If you felt you were being followed, I would wager a tidy sum you were. Don't doubt yourself."

Her eyes shone with gratitude. "Aye, m'lady."

"What we can't know is why. It might have something to do with the inquiry, or it might not. But the fact that he didn't let you catch sight of his face, and he's not been spotted by one of the servants keeping watch over the front and rear entrances to the house, makes me think his intentions were not altogether innocent."

Gage rubbed the back of his neck, agitated by our failure to catch either Bree's follower or the people sending me blackmail notes. He dismissed our servants and then turned to me with a look of such dismay I knew whatever he had to say would not be to my liking.

"Dr. Mayer refused my last offer to purchase Sir Anthony's journals."

My shoulders drooped. I'd known it would never end so easily, but I had still hoped. "Could we offer more?" I asked in a small voice.

"We can try. But it's doubtful he will budge." Gage's eyes searched mine. "It's not money he wants."

I closed my eyes, nodding. He didn't need to say the words. What Dr. Mayer wanted was to ruin me. I didn't know why or when he had developed such a hatred of me, but I had seen it in his eyes when he confronted me with my involvement in Sir Anthony's dissections, and in the Bow Street Magistrates' Office when he accused me of several unspeakable crimes.

"I think we have to consider allowing my father to help."

My stomach clenched. "There's nothing else we can do?"

He reached out to take my hands. "I know it's not what you want. It's not what *I* want either. But he was right. His influence is greater than mine. If we want to bring this to an end, and quickly, then our best chance is to ask for his assistance." When I didn't speak, locked in a vortex of dread, he squeezed my fingers. "You do realize those journals might contain information about your blackmailers."

"I do," I admitted. I also knew he spoke the truth of the whole matter, but I simply couldn't bring myself to accept his father's assistance. Not after Lord Gage had treated me so abominably all these months. The thought of his seeing whatever was in those journals was so mortifying it made my skin sting like I'd been bitten by a swarm of midges. "Just . . . give me a day to think it over."

His mouth curled into a commiserating smile. "Very well. But, at the risk of repeating my father, don't wait too long."

We woke the next day braced for the news of yet another murder. But breakfast passed uneventfully, after which we readied ourselves to journey into The City, and yet still there was no sudden knock at the door. When we set off across May-fair toward the east just before midday, I think we both breathed sighs of relief. Perhaps the murderer was finished. Or perhaps the night's heavy rain had hindered his plan. Whatever the case, we had at least another day's reprieve before he struck again.

The rain drummed against the roof of the carriage as we traversed through London, bypassing Covent Garden and the crowd gathering outside Bow Street as best we could without venturing into the rotting slum of St. Giles to the north. The rocking of the carriage and the steady tattoo of the rain con-trived to lull me into a light slumber. Given my current anxiet-ies, my vivid dreams, and the changes happening to my body—making my legs and hips ache—my sleep of late had not been peaceful. Even so, I was surprised I was able to doze at all.

I woke with a start as we passed the impressive edifice of the Bank of England, and the Royal Exchange, with its numerous arched columns and rib-vaulted portico roofs. Lombard Street veered southeast from the bank at the corner where the Lord Mayor of London's Palladian Mansion House stood. We clat-tered on past St. Mary's Church and the site of the old General Post Office, before rolling to a stop next to a narrow lane.

Though Lombard Street was quite respectable, the deeper we picked our way through the muddy puddles into the back alleys and courts beyond it, the less reputable our surroundings—and the inhabitants within—became. I wrinkled my nose against a fetid stench, able to feel grateful for the wet weather for at least one reason—it dampened smells. By the time we located the building we were looking for, I had begun to worry David

Newbury had been a greater actor than any of us could have guessed.

We stood huddled under our umbrella, staring up at the blackened brick façade. I wondered if we would have to resort to knocking on doors to find the premises of the man we were looking for, when Lord Redditch's secretary, Mr. Poole, strolled out of the building. His dark gaze remained trained on the ground ahead of him, distracted by some troubling thought. He might have walked right past us without ever looking up, if I hadn't given a little gasp of recognition. His eyes flew upward, flaring wide as he stumbled to a stop.

"Mr. Gage, Lady Darby." He blinked several times, seeming to gather himself. "I beg your pardon. I was woolgathering."

"Good afternoon, Mr. Poole," Gage responded calmly. "From the expression that was on your face, it must have been some knotty wool."

"Yes, well . . . circumstances being what they are . . ." He shrugged one shoulder, lifting the dispatch case he held in one hand at his side to cradle it before his chest under his umbrella. "But what brings you to this part of The City?" He glanced about at our dingy surroundings, made all the more gray and gloomy by the rain that continued to fall.

"We're investigating a possible connection between Lord Feckenham and Mr. Newbury."

Mr. Poole's intelligent eyes studied our faces. "You're here to speak with Mr. Callihan."

"You know him," Gage said, not bothering to hide that he'd already come to the same conclusion I had.

His face lightened briefly before dimming again. "Yes. I volunteer my proficiency with contracts, petitions, and other such documents to assist Mr. Callihan with his worthy cause."

Gage arched his eyebrows in expectation. "Which is?"

"An orphan house. He's attempting to build an institution similar to The Foundling Hospital, but one that will take more than just an unwed mother's first child. Of course, such a thing requires funding, and land, and government approval . . . There's a great deal yet to be done before ground can be broken."

This was not the answer we had expected, and Gage fumbled to reply.

"An orphan house. How extraordinary." He cleared his throat, finding more firm ground. "I suspect you're receiving some resistance from people in the government who believe the workhouses provide for such children well enough."

"Indeed," he replied with a scowl. "The truth is, those workhouses are woefully overcrowded and poorly maintained. A child is more likely to become sick and die from a stay in such places than benefit from it. And organizations such as the deceptively named Children's Friend Society are no better. They gather up vagrant children and ship them off to our colonies to be treated as little better than slave labor." He arched his chin. "We wish to educate the children. Provide them a safe place to shelter, and nourishing food to eat."

Mr. Poole's face became animated when he spoke of those things. Clearly it was of great importance to him, and I applauded his way of thinking. Something needed to be done to help the children, and here was a start.

But Gage remained focused on more practical matters. "So Mr. Callihan is not a moneylender?"

"Not anymore." His mouth creased in a humorless smile. "I know you're bound to be skeptical, but he'll willingly tell you his story. He made a fortune charging gentlemen unscrupulous rates of interest, and then tripled it at the Exchange. He's a brilliant man. And now that he's seen the error of his ways, as he calls it, he's determined to help those less fortunate." He followed my gaze to the grimy building. "Don't let your surroundings fool you. He keeps the same offices because they're sturdy and convenient to the financial district. He refuses to spend money on a more auspicious address that could be better used on the orphan house."

"Then you were aware that David Newbury supported Mr. Callihan's cause?" Gage asked.

He nodded.

"When we questioned you all in Lord Redditch's study, why didn't you mention you knew him?"

"Perhaps it's splitting hairs, but I don't *know* him. I was aware he donated to and was a proponent of the cause, but I had never met him. In any case, you were asking if I was aware of a connection between Mr. Newbury and Lord Feckenham." His voice turned scornful. "And I can assure you, Lord Feckenham had nothing to do with our charitable society. He had nothing to do with any of them." I noted he'd never used such a tone while in Lord Redditch's home, perhaps out of deference to his employer.

Neither Gage nor I responded, perhaps thinking the same thing. Something Mr. Poole swiftly grasped.

"Oh, yes. I see. *I'm* the connection." He frowned, considering this. "Well, I admit I didn't think much of Lord Feckenham. He was a very low character." His face paled. "But why would I, or anyone else for that matter, wish for Lord Newbury to die? From all accounts, he was honorable, and his support of the orphan home was critical. With his help, we hoped to persuade other distinguished gentlemen to contribute to our cause."

I noticed that he hadn't said Lord Redditch supported the endeavor, a curious discovery. But perhaps he still hoped to gain his backing. Or that of his new heir.

Regardless, I saw his point. Newbury's death hurt their cause, and as passionately as Mr. Poole had spoken of it, I could not imagine what motive he would have to kill him.

The rain began to pound harder, and Mr. Poole took a step back. "I beg your pardon, but I must be going. I have business to attend to for Lord Redditch. If you wish to speak with me further, I'll be returning to his residence in a few hours." He flicked a glance toward the door he'd emerged from. "Speak to Callihan.

Number 4. He'll answer any questions you might have about the society." He hesitated in taking another step. "Perhaps you'll even find an interest in lending us your support."

With that last comment, he turned and was gone, hurrying up the lane in the direction of Cornhill and the Exchange.

"What do you think?" I murmured, trying to decide how I felt about everything he'd told us.

Gage seemed just as uncertain. "What he says is true. I can't argue with his logic."

I glanced up into his face shadowed by the brim of his hat. "But something also isn't quite right."

His gaze dipped to meet mine. "Yes." He inhaled a deep breath, as if in resolution. "Let's meet this Callihan and see what he has to say."

Mr. Poole was right. Mr. Callihan was quite blunt about his past, and more than happy to answer any of the questions we put to him. The portly older man didn't make excuses for himself and attributed his change of heart to religion. From all the evidence he showed us, including a number of letters and records of money drafts, Mr. Newbury had indeed been an advocate of their charitable society. To Mr. Callihan's credit, he appeared to be deeply grieved by his supporter's death, but he had no theories to advance as to why someone would wish to harm such a kind young man.

We left the former moneylender's premises with no more answers than when we'd entered it. Although Mr. Callihan had showed us all their accounting books and the plans for the orphan house, Gage proposed we pay a visit to a friend of his off Chancery Lane. This friend often looked into financial matters for him if an inquiry called for such expertise.

I elected to wait in the carriage while he went inside to ask his friend to do a bit of digging into the charity's books. Though he didn't expect to find anything out of order, it was always best to be thorough in such matters. Perhaps Mr. Newbury had stumbled upon some sort of fraud.

By the time Gage returned to the carriage, it was nearly half past four, and I was famished. I turned to him to suggest we might stop for tea when the sound of shouting brought me up short. I lifted my gaze to the window, wondering who on earth could be making such a tumult, when I saw it. The prison van. It pulled past our carriage and then stopped a few feet ahead, blocked by some traffic in the road.

"Oh, no," I moaned in a voice I almost didn't recognize as my own. My heart began to pound as the roar of voices grew louder.

Gage leaned out the window to see what the commotion was all about and then swiftly pulled his head back in as a rock flew past. He closed the window and twitched shut the curtains before lifting up the cushion of the seat across from ours to reveal a hidden compartment. Reaching inside, he extracted a box which contained two percussion pistols. He loaded them and set them beside him on the bench.

There was no need to speak. He had realized, as I had, that the prison van contained the accused burkers. The final magistrates' hearing must have ended, and the prisoners were being transported to Newgate to await trial. Why the vehicle had turned to drive up Chancery Lane, I didn't know. Perhaps there were other prisoners inside to be delivered to Coldbath Fields Prison or another location.

Whatever the case, I was caught in the middle of one of my worst nightmares. I pressed my hands over my ears, trying to block out the sound of hundreds of angry voices. They surrounded us, pressing against the carriage and rocking it as they surged past. A horse screamed, and then there was the shatter of breaking glass and splintering wood. Thuds reverberated through the air as the people hurled stones and mud, striking anything in the way of their vicious pursuit of their intended target.

I shrank down, curling into a ball around the life in my

stomach, trying to make myself as small as possible. I knew they weren't there for me, but my body didn't seem to know the difference. I was back inside Philip's carriage after the magistrates dismissed the charges against me, with the mob that had gathered outside screaming for my blood. They'd flung whatever they could get their hands on at the coach—and one terrifyingly precise throw had actually cracked the window. I had known that if the crowd could get their hands on me, they would have torn me to pieces. Just as they would rip apart the burkers.

How long I remained that way, jerking at every loud sound, every thump against the carriage, I can't say. My ears rang, and I shook uncontrollably. Gage wrapped his arm around me, gathering me to his side, as he called out to the coachman. The driver slid open the portal to speak to us and assure us he and the footman were all of a piece.

"When you can safely do so, get us out of here," Gage directed.

"Yes, sir. Soon as this overturned cart is moved, I'll 'ave us on our way."

I jumped when the portal slid shut, and Gage pressed my head to his shoulder, gently shushing me. His fingers trailed over my temples and around my ears in soothing strokes as he crooned soft words. It didn't matter what they were. I couldn't comprehend them anyway. I was too busy struggling not to be sick all over him and the carriage floor.

When finally my stomach's roiling mostly subsided, and some of my shivering abated, fat tears began to slide down my cheeks. "I'm sorry," I whispered on a sliver of sound.

But he silenced me with a shake of his head. "Never apologize, my love. Never for that." He pressed his lips to my forehead, and I closed my eyes, sinking into his embrace.

CHAPTER TWENTY-SIX

When we returned home, I was bustled off to our bed-chamber before I could voice a word of protest. Not that I meant to object. Not when I felt as if the life had been wrung from me. Bree bundled me into my warmest dressing gown and smothered me with blankets while Gage forced a cup of brandy to my lips. I tried to reject this, but I was too weak to do more than comply when he insisted it would help.

I swam into a hazy sleep, only to wake in darkness a short time later. It took me a moment to gather my thoughts and re-member why I was there. My heart surged in my chest as it all came rushing back to me.

I rolled over to see Gage seated by the fire, reading a book. He hadn't yet noticed I was awake, so I took a moment to trace his handsome profile and sculpted cheekbones limned by the firelight with my eyes. His golden hair stood on end, as if he'd been combing his hand through it, and his jaw was dusted with a faint trail of stubble. He'd discarded his coat and rolled up the sleeves of his shirt to reveal his strong forearms.

His pale blue eyes flicked upward as he turned the page, and then back again when he caught me watching him. His lips curled into a soft smile. "You're awake."

"Yes." My response emerged as more of a croak, so I cleared my throat and tried again. "Yes. How long was I asleep?"

He glanced at the clock on the mantel as he closed his book and pushed to his feet. "An hour and a half." He sank down onto the bed beside me, taking my hand in his. "How are you feeling?"

"Better," I replied, not really knowing how to answer such a question.

As if he sensed this, his brow furrowed and his gaze dipped. "You told me what happened . . . what it was like . . . after the things Sir Anthony made you do were made public." His gaze lifted. "But I'm not sure I ever truly comprehended."

I swallowed the lump in my throat and nodded. Few did. No one but my family, in fact. For Philip and Trevor had been with me at Bow Street and inside the carriage when the mob attacked. "It was awful," I murmured in perhaps the greatest understatement of all time.

Gage clutched my hand tighter. "Yes."

My gaze slid upward to the shadows gathered in the corners of the bed's canopy. "We have to get those journals from Dr. Mayer." My stomach quavered. "Tell . . . tell your father we want his help."

"I'm glad to hear you say that." He inhaled. "Because I already did."

Perhaps I should have been angry at him for doing so before I'd given my permission, but I couldn't be. Not after what had happened today. Not knowing he was trying to protect me and our child. Whatever Lord Gage discovered in Sir Anthony's journals could not be worse than being trampled and torn limb from limb by a furious horde.

"What about Anderley?" I asked, recalling he'd been inside the Magistrates' Office today. "Did he return home unscathed?"

Gage nodded. "About an hour ago. He said the hearing wasn't pretty. Several hundred people were gathered outside all day, even with such dreadful weather, and the room inside was packed cheek by jowl. There were a few new witnesses, including a neighbor of Bishop's who said he heard sounds of a struggle through the walls early on the morning the boy was believed to be killed, but much of it was repeated from earlier hearings."

"The men were committed to Newgate for trial?"

"Three of them—Bishop, Williams, and May. But Shields, the older man who carried the body between hospitals, was released. The charges against him were dropped, just as we expected. There wasn't any evidence against him."

"And the wives?"

"They were also released." He frowned at the creases in the cornflower blue bedding. "Anderley said the most interesting development was how May appeared to have fallen out with his fellow prisoners. He was furious and listening intently to everything that was said. The jailer even reported he'd had a fight with Bishop in the cells below, calling him a 'bloody murdering bastard.' He showed every sign he was about to turn King's evidence. But he didn't." Gage shook his head in confusion. "What is he waiting for?"

"Maybe he doesn't know anything," I suggested. "Or he doesn't know enough."

He shrugged. "Whatever the case, the matter is going to trial. Perhaps as early as next week."

I breathed a sigh of relief. "So it will be over soon."

"If they're convicted, they'll hang the following Monday."

I shivered, pressing a hand to my neck. Gage leaned forward to move it away, gazing down at me. "You do know I would never let anything happen to you."

"You would try."

I watched as fear clouded his eyes, letting me know I wasn't the only one affected by today's events.

"Then you'll understand why I'll be sending you away from London if my father fails to retrieve those journals or Goddard can't find our blackmailers." His words were implacable, leaving me no room for argument.

And yet I couldn't resist pointing out, "I thought you said I should stand tall and not let them decide who I was?"

His jaw hardened. "Don't be facetious. There's a difference between one's reputation and one's well-being, and you know it. I'm not taking any chances with the latter."

I nodded and wrapped my arms around his neck. "If need be, I'll go."

His entire body seemed to exhale. "I pray it doesn't come to that, but thank you."

I pulled him down, clutching him tightly, and sent up a prayer of my own.

This time I was seated at my dressing table while Bree artfully twisted and pinned my hair when the knock came on my door. I called out for them to enter, thinking nothing of it, even when Gage stepped through the door to regard my reflection in the mirror.

"There's a constable downstairs."

My eyes flew upward to meet his gaze, my stomach dipping in dread.

His voice was grim. "There's been another murder."

I hurried through the remainder of my morning ablutions, and we set off across Mayfair to the home of Baron Acklen. I did not know the family well, even though I'd painted Lady Acklen's portrait about six years earlier, a year before I wed Sir Anthony. My father had asked my brother to escort me to those sessions because—unbeknownst to me at the time—Lord Acklen was an inveterate rogue, and my father didn't trust him not to pester me. All I'd noted was how uncomfortable he made me, but then many people made me uncomfortable.

"Are you acquainted with Percy Acklen?" Gage asked as the carriage turned a corner at a faster clip than usual.

"No. I never had the pleasure," I replied, glancing back at him. "Or wouldn't it have been one?"

His brow was riddled with deep grooves. "I'm aware you know Lord Acklen. And I'm afraid his son and heir was of the same mold."

"Like Feckenham?"

He considered the question. "Not as bad as that. More your ordinary scoundrel. But yes, I take your point. Percy Acklen was definitely more like the first victim in temperament and reputation than the second."

When we reached the Acklens' home on Princes Street, near the Argyle Rooms and Regent Circus, it was to find Goddard standing outside with a man sporting a prodigious amount of facial hair at the sides of his face. I wasn't surprised to discover the Bow Street Runner at the scene given the fact the Great Marlborough Street Police Office was so close. He nodded politely to me as we descended, and introduced us to his cohort.

"I know you're investigatin' the other Mayfair murders," Goddard told us. "And this one looks to be the same. A nob's heir; stabbed in the right side with a long, narrow blade; left on the street to bleed out." He paused, eyeing us closely. "Sticking plaster on his face. Though it covered more of his cheek than either his nose or mouth."

Gage pressed his hands to his hips and turned to glance down the largely empty lane toward the clattering carriages rolling down Regent Street. "So he knows by now he's not fooled us. The plaster doesn't work. Now it's more of his calling card." The corner of his jaw ticked. "And a way to induce panic in the residents, given the recent burking." He glanced in the other direction. "Where was Mr. Acklen found?"

"I'll show ye." Goddard led us down the street in the opposite direction to the edge of Hanover Square. "A constable found him around five o'clock while he was on his beat. Said he recognized him because Acklen and his friends had been known to cause disturbances from time to time walking home from the gaming establishments in St. James's."

"That's prolly where he was comin' from," his colleague added. "Fuddled, o' course."

Gage leaned forward to examine the dark stain at the edge of the pavement. "His friends likely sheered off, one by one, headed to their own residences. We'll have to speak with them. Find out if they noticed anyone following them." His voice turned dry. "If any of them were sober enough to notice." He straightened. "Have you spoken to Lord and Lady Acklen?"

Goddard scowled and shook his head. "Insisted on waitin' for you."

Gage grimaced in sympathy. "Well, think of it this way. You've saved yourself an unpleasant experience." He reached inside his pocket to pass both men a tip for their troubles since there was no retainer from Lord Acklen likely to be forthcoming.

Lord Acklen was waiting for us in his parlor when his butler showed us in, leaned back in his chair, downing a glass of caramel-colored liquid. Brandy, no doubt. When he didn't rise to his feet at my entrance, I couldn't tell if he was deliberately snubbing me, or if he was already so disguised his legs wouldn't cooperate enough to do so. He barked at his butler to refill his glass, slurring his words, and then glared blearily at us in accusation. Definitely foxed, then. But I also doubted he would have risen if he'd not been.

"Ye were sposed to catch this bloody, rotten *bastard*. Why is my son *dead*?"

"We are doing our best," Gage replied calmly as we moved deeper into the room. "Can you tell us which friends your son was with last night?"

The butler handed him his glass, and he proceeded to gesture with it, sloshing liquid onto the floor. "I don't know. The usual. *Why?* What does that matter?"

Seeing this, Gage halted us several steps away, lest our own clothes be splattered. "They might have seen something that could help us. What of your politics?"

"My what?"

"Are you still a Tory? Or are you with the Whigs now? Word is you're a bit of a Vicar of Bray."

Acklen glared at him blackly, not intoxicated enough to miss the insult. "I don't care a fig for politics," he retorted, using language a trifle stronger. "Haven't taken up my seat in years. Though I dashed well don't understand why that should matter to *you.* Your father's a vicar himself."

He didn't refute that, but it was not of the moment. "What about orphan houses? Did you or your son support the building of them?"

Acklen blinked at him and then shook his head. "Orphan houses? You're not makin' any sense."

"Just answer the question."

His eyes bulged and for a moment I thought he was going to hurl his glass at us. "Why should we care about orphan houses?"

Gage nodded as if he'd just confirmed something. Perhaps that Lord Acklen was a bloody, rotten bastard himself. "Then can you think of anything else that connects your son with Lord Feckenham and Mr. Newbury? Or that connects you to Lord Redditch and Lord Newbury, for that matter?"

"We all have dead sons," he shot back.

I sighed in aggravation. This was getting us nowhere. "Where is Lady Acklen?" Maybe she would have something worthwhile to tell us, though I doubted it. My impression of her while

292 · *Anna Lee Huber*

painting her portrait was of a fragile flower. One that preferred to shelter along the forest floor lest the bright sun burn her or a hard rain trample her. She'd spoken very little, and never of anything of consequence. Given her husband's blackguard reputation, I could understand her wish to hide from reality.

"She's taken to her bed. Inconsolable. Footman had to carry her to her chamber." His eyes narrowed. "Though I'm not sure you can appreciate how heartbroken she is."

If this was supposed to be an insult to my often-stilted emotions, especially when I was younger, then he'd missed the mark. I was not about to take offense when the man was so clearly lacking in empathy himself.

I could hear Gage grinding his teeth as we returned to our carriage. "Well, that was singularly unhelpful," he declared as he sank back against the squabs, hurling his hat onto the opposite seat.

I could have told him Lord Acklen would not be of much assistance, but given his remark to Goddard, I suspected he'd already known that. "Well, I suppose we can rule out politics as the motivation, given the fact Acklen doesn't even attend."

"Yes, but what if the killer targeted his son because of that. Maybe he's angry Acklen doesn't care enough to vote."

I squinted up at the barren trees in Hanover Square as we drove past. "But how does that relate to Lord Redditch and Lord Newbury? Unless the murderer has a vendetta against all members of the House of Lords who don't vote as he wishes." This seemed doubtful. It certainly wasn't a strong enough motive to send someone on a killing spree.

"No, you're right. It doesn't add up." Gage pounded his fist on his thigh. "I wish I knew what this man was thinking. First he murders a scoundrel, and then an honorable man, and then another scoundrel. If it had been Feckenham and Acklen, I could better understand. But why Newbury?"

His words echoed in my head, for I felt like I'd heard them

before, and recently. I stiffened as the memory surfaced, and my husband glanced at me in confusion. "Lord Damien. He said almost the same thing at Barbreck's soiree. That it would make more sense if it was someone like Acklen or Wilmot."

"That doesn't mean anything." He pressed a hand to my arm as I worried my hands in my lap. "Acklen is a known rogue. Anyone might have suggested the connection to Feckenham."

I swallowed, hoping he was right. For I could not imagine the chivalrous young man I knew stabbing another man, particularly his friend David Newbury. "We still need to speak with him."

Gage nodded. "But it can wait until tonight. I suspect he'll be attending Lady Cowper's ball."

"As will your father and Lord Melbourne." Melbourne being Lady Cowper's brother.

"Undoubtedly." He grimaced. "I suspect we'll be called to task again for failing to predict *this* murder."

"Well, don't let them. We're doing our best in a difficult situation. If they think they can do better, let them try." My eyes flashed, knowing full well Lord Gage would balk at such a challenge.

His mouth quirked. "Shall I pose just such a suggestion to him?"

"Do. I'd like to hear what his response would be."

In the end, I was not given that opportunity. While I was engaged in conversation with Alana, out of the corner of my eye, I spied Gage at the edge of the glittering ballroom being pulled aside by his father. No doubt being taken to a private parlor where Lord Melbourne waited. I considered hastening after them but then decided against it. Why would I wish to subject myself to more of Lord Gage's ridicule? Gage could more than handle them both.

Instead, I swept the room, looking for those who might have

information about Acklen. We'd already visited the Earl of Red-ditch and Lord Newbury, neither of whom had any new inspira-tion as to what connected the three murder victims, but plenty to say about their displeasure with our progress. I watched the dancers for a moment moving across the floor in a stately pat-tern, before my eyes landed on Lord Damien standing near the far corner.

Crossing the room toward him, I noted he looked even worse than he had at Barbreck's ball. He sipped a glass of ratafia, his eyes gloomily surveying the crowd. I took one look at his rum-pled attire and shook my head. He was neither agitated nor tri-umphant. There was no way he'd killed a man that very morning.

"I know. I'm a mess." He frowned into his empty glass before setting it on a nearby ledge. "Not sure why I came."

"You heard about Percy Acklen?" It was all anyone could talk about. That and the fact that the woman's clothing found in the privy and well at Nova Scotia Gardens had been identified as belonging to a woman named Fanny Pigburn, who had gone missing in early October. Which left everyone begging the question—how many more potential victims' effects would be uncovered?

He nodded and shrugged, crossing his arms over his chest. "Didn't care much for him one way or the other. But I can't understand why the killer chose to lump David in with him and Feckenham." He scowled over my shoulder. "I've heard people saying that maybe David wasn't as honorable as they thought. Why else would he have been murdered?" His eyes riveted on me. "Is that what you think?"

I shook my head. "People are scared. Whenever something like this happens, people want to distance themselves from it as far as they possibly can. Or else they might start to believe it could happen to them."

"Yes, well, they don't need to disparage David in the pro-cess."

"It will pass," I assured him.

"It hasn't passed for you."

I stiffened, even though his face registered remorse the second the words were out of his mouth.

"I'm sorry. I wasn't thinking. That was completely uncalled for."

"But it doesn't mean it's not true," I answered softly.

His gaze was anguished, but he couldn't refute the point. "Everyone who truly knows you realizes how unfairly you've been treated," he finally managed to say. "And the others will realize it with time."

I allowed my eyes to slide to the side, where two ladies with their heads bent together periodically sent me scornful glances. "Will they?"

"Of course," he replied with too much vehemence.

I allowed him to clasp my hand, offering him a reassuring smile. "I'm sure you're right. Now go ask one of those lovely debutantes to dance." I dipped my head toward the young ladies standing against the wall. "I'm sure they'll be happy to cheer you."

His eyes searched mine anxiously, but he complied.

I wandered through the assemblage, contemplating what Damien had said. Why *had* Newbury been targeted like the others? Was he the key to it all? After all, few mourned the two feckless scoundrels. But David Newbury was a different matter entirely.

Maybe it was mere wishful thinking, but I couldn't help but think Newbury's death was more important than the others. If only I understood exactly why, perhaps we would have all our answers, and unmask the murderer.

CHAPTER TWENTY-SEVEN

After the events of the last three weeks, Gage declared Sunday to be a day of rest. I suspected some of his motivation for doing so was in defiance of whatever his father had said to him the night before, but I wasn't about to argue. We had all been exhausted by the multiple investigations and threats. A day of reflection would not hinder our efforts. And, in fact, it might provide some much needed clarity.

After morning services at the Chapel, I did nothing more physically strenuous than lift a paintbrush. However, that did not stop my mind from ruminating over past events, as well as current ones. A number of people had been reported missing in recent newspapers, including a street sweeper from the Stamford Street junction with Waterloo that morning in the *Sunday Times*. The incarceration of the accused burkers in Newgate only seemed to have intensified the anxiety gripping London, and Mayfair was no exception.

We invited Lorna, Alfred, Charlotte, and my cousin Rye to

dine with us that evening and kept the conversation deliberately light. My friends eyed me from time to time with concern, making me suspect I had not hidden my worries as well as I would have liked. In the end, they respected my wish not to discuss them. However, I knew to expect visits from each of them in the coming days.

It was a lovely evening, and one I enjoyed immensely, as it comprised only a small group of close friends. I went to bed feeling more content than I had in weeks.

Then I was awakened on Monday before dawn by the sound of Gage scrambling into his dressing gown.

"Sebastian," I murmured sleepily. "What is it?"

"Oh, did I wake you?" He leaned over to press a kiss to my cheek. "It's nothing. Go back to sleep."

He tried to sound unruffled, but I heard the tension underlying his voice. I sat upright, genuine alarm tightening my muscles as he exited through the connecting door. I could hear him bustling about inside, donning trousers and a shirt, no doubt, and then he went out into the hall.

Knowing there was no way I was going to be able to go back to sleep without discovering what was happening, I crawled out of bed and pulled on my warmest wrapper. I pattered out to the landing in my bare feet to hear Gage and Jeffers conferring in hushed voices below. Peering over the railing, I noted even our fastidious butler wasn't fully dressed, wearing a dressing gown over his trousers. There was no greater indicator of urgency than that.

"How could he have not seen the culprit?" Gage demanded to know. "Did he fall asleep?"

"He says he slipped downstairs to use the necessary, sir, but swears he was only gone a matter of minutes."

"And they chose those few minutes to strike." He raked a hand back through his hair. "They must have been able to see him

298 · Anna Lee Huber

through the window." He glanced toward the front door, where I could hear someone moving about. "Well, thank goodness he decided to step out and check the blind corners. Otherwise . . ."

"Yes, sir," Jeffers agreed solemnly.

"Otherwise what?" I asked, deciding to make myself known. Both men glanced up at me with a start as I began to descend the stairs.

"Kiera, I told you to remain in bed," Gage snapped, moving toward the stairs to intercept me.

His tone of voice momentarily took me aback, for he rarely, if ever, spoke to me in such a manner. I paused in my descent, staring down at him as he climbed toward me. "Gage, what is going on?"

I heard the sound of splashing water, and I was low enough on the staircase then to see through the entry out into the fog-shrouded street beyond. One of the footmen bent low to throw a second bucket of water toward a spot to the right of the door. A sickening suspicion took up residence in my gut, and I stared wide-eyed at my husband as he came to a stop two steps below mine.

His mouth flattened into a thin line, as if he thought that by not saying the words I wouldn't know the truth that had already dawned on me. Then his shoulders sagged. "Your blackmailers carried through on one of their threats."

I swallowed, forcing the acrid saliva flooding my mouth down my throat. "W-was it an entire body or . . . parts?"

His hands reached up to cup my elbows. "Parts."

I nodded, fighting the nausea swirling in my stomach.

"The footman on duty didn't see who left them, but he found the . . . parts in time for us to remove them before any of our neighbors could notice them."

I nodded again, unable to form words.

"They're gone now. Disposed of to the proper authorities so Goddard can look into the matter."

I blinked at him, at his poor choice of words. "Excuse me." I barely got the words out before I covered my mouth and dashed back up the stairs. I landed on my knees before the chamber pot just before my stomach heaved, casting up my accounts.

When I was finished, I sat back on my knees, still hovering over the bowl. Gage murmured something behind me before passing me a cool cloth. I mopped my face and hands while he lit a lamp and then helped me rise shakily to my feet. An ewer of cold water sat beside the washstand, and I used it to rinse the acid from my mouth.

Then I stumbled over to the bed, holding my hand over my belly protectively, and sank down on the edge of it. "I'm sorry. I'm fine now."

Gage sat beside me. "No need to apologize. It wasn't a pleasant discovery."

I stared at my hands in my lap, anxiety clawing inside of me. "It's not just that." I glanced up into his beloved face, hesitant to say the words. Hesitant to lay them bare before him. But the fear and shame seemed to be eating me from the inside out, and I couldn't keep it all to myself any longer. "It . . . made me feel something I haven't felt since Sir Anthony died," I began slowly. "At least, not to the same degree. Something that terrifies me." My voice broke.

Gage reached out to still my hands where I worried them. His eyes were gentle. "Tell me."

I nodded as a tear slid down my cheek. "Those men, and women, who ended up on Sir Anthony's dissection table . . ." I inhaled a quick breath. "They were there because of me." I rushed on before he could demur, determined to get it all out now that I'd begun. "If Sir Anthony hadn't needed me to sketch them while he demonstrated the . . . the processes, then there wouldn't have been so many of them. What if some of them were murdered because of it?" I pleaded. "What if they were . . . burked because Sir Anthony needed a body to teach *me*?"

Gage grasped my shoulders. "Kiera, stop. Stop! None of what Sir Anthony did is your fault. *He* bought those bodies. *He* forced you to sketch them. You didn't ask for any of that to happen."

"I know, but . . . maybe if I'd been strong enough to tell someone, maybe if I hadn't been so worried about what would happen to me, I could have stopped it."

He shook his head. "That's nonsense. You know if you'd brought it to the attention of the authorities, they would have done nothing about it. You said so yourself. They would have believed Sir Anthony over you, and they never would have interfered. The purchase of corpses and their dissections would have gone on." His gaze was bright with terror. "The only thing that would have changed was the amount of abuse you would have suffered for daring to defy him."

I shuddered.

He nodded, his eyes stark. "Yes. So stop blaming yourself. You did nothing wrong."

I hiccupped on a sob. "Then why do I feel so guilty?"

He pulled me into his chest, rubbing his hands soothingly over my back. "Oh, Kiera. You've been fretting over this all this time?" He exhaled. "No wonder you can't let it go."

I cried harder, clutching his torso tightly, afraid he would set me away from him at any moment. But all he did was reach up to cradle my jaw, tipping my face upward to look at him.

"Kiera, you feel guilty because you care. You care that those people were stolen from their graves or . . . murdered off the street. In contrast, Sir Anthony, and the resurrectionists who supplied him, did not give a brass farthing for them. They were expendable. But you never stopped seeing them as the people they were, even if their souls had long left their bodies. I find that commendable."

"You do?"

"Yes. But that doesn't mean you should feel guilty." His fingers trailed over my jaw back into my hair. "You can care and still accept that the fault for what happened to them is not yours."

I sniffed, trying to see the matter the way he did, but the knot of shame still coiled inside me. It hadn't eased.

"Did you ever ask Sir Anthony to dissect a body for you?"

I started to pull away, but he wouldn't let me. "No!"

"Did you ever want him to?"

"No!" This time I was able to pull back a few inches. "How could you even ask such a thing?"

"Then why should you feel guilty for the fact that he did?" he hastily added, halting my argument. "I bet you lived in dread of him telling you another cadaver had been delivered."

I nodded.

"You see? That's my point. You never wanted it. Never."

I stared at the top of his chest revealed through the open buttons of his white lawn shirt and felt something inside me begin to loosen.

He cupped my face between his hands. "All you did was draw. And even in that, he gave you no choice in the matter."

I nodded, glad he hadn't put into words the threats he knew Sir Anthony had used to force me to comply with his orders.

His voice was tender. "Are you done with this nonsense, then?"

"Yes," I said softly. It would take some time for me to stop feeling the remorse completely, but just telling him had eased some of the burden. It was no longer a deep, dark secret pressing behind my heart.

"Good."

There was a knock on the door, and Bree peered through the gap. "There's a Mr. Goddard here to see you."

"Well, he answered my summons rather promptly," Gage stated, rising to his feet. "Will you be joining us?"

"Yes. Just give me twenty minutes."

He nodded, already moving toward the door. "I'll have Jeffers show him into the breakfast room."

. . .

By the time I appeared, both men were enjoying heaping plates of sausages, eggs, plumb cake, and hot rolls with butter. But I insisted on my normal repast—an egg, toast, jam, and a cup of warm chocolate. Having already lost my stomach once that morning, I thought it best not to indulge in anything too rich.

Upon my arrival, Mr. Goddard rose swiftly from his chair, still chewing a bite of his meal. "Good morning, my lady," he said after swallowing his food.

"Good morning, Mr. Goddard." I settled into my seat, making polite small talk while Jeffers brought me my breakfast.

Once our butler had assured himself we had everything we desired, he signaled for the footman to follow him from the room, anticipating our wish for privacy.

Gage lifted his gaze to meet mine. "I've already informed Mr. Goddard of the unpleasant gifts left for us this morning."

I set the triangle of toast I'd just taken a bite of back on my plate, grateful we would not need to discuss such a gruesome discovery.

"I'm sorry it came to that, my lady. That's not pleasant, to be sure," Mr. Goddard told me solemnly.

I dipped my head.

"But it does tell us these blackmailers are quite serious." Gage tapped his finger on the table. "They must be found and quickly."

Goddard sat back, setting his serviette beside his plate. "And I think I have some information that may help."

Gage and I both perked up at this pronouncement.

"I was skulking at the back of the Rockingham Arms south of the river yesterday evening, keeping an eye on a pair of snatchers I liked for the crime, when in walks a gentleman. He glances about the place before going up to the barman to ask a question, who nods toward the snatchers. Then the gent approaches them to have a chat."

Gage and I cast each other a speaking look but didn't interrupt the Runner.

"I can tell it's not a pleasant discussion. The gent seems upset, the snatchers smug, but in the end the gent passes them something and storms out. One of the snatchers pockets the item and then nods to his cohort, who hurries out after the fellow."

"Did you happen to recognize the gentleman?" Gage asked.

"That's the most interesting part." He leaned forward. "'Twas George Penrose."

I stiffened. "The Earl of Redditch's son."

He nodded, and then narrowed his eyes, scratching his chin. "Now why would an earl's son need to be consortin' with bodysnatchers?" His eyes gleamed as if he was a hound catching the scent of a fox. "When did your first blackmail letter arrive? After Lord Feckenham was murdered, right?"

Gage scowled. "Yes. Three days later."

"But Mr. Penrose left the city the morning after his brother was killed," I pointed out.

"Are we certain of that?" He arched his eyebrows. "Maybe he made contact with those bodysnatchers before he went to collect his sisters."

It was possible. I couldn't refute that. But still I balked at the possibility that Mr. Penrose was behind the blackmail scheme. He hardly seemed the type to do such a thing.

However, I'd learned long ago that just because someone was likable did not mean they weren't capable of terrible things.

"You can't deny you've been distracted from your investigations by this nonsense. Maybe that was his intent." Goddard's gaze flicked back and forth between us. "Didn't you like him almost from the start for the murder of his brother?"

Gage nodded. "He seemed to have the best motive. And he admitted to confronting his brother not ten minutes before the crime was committed."

"Then the murders of Newbury and Acklen were also meant

to be distractions?" I countered skeptically and then shook my head. "I don't believe it. Maybe one of them. But not both."

"Perhaps he worried we were on to him. Perhaps he thought another murder would confuse the matter further," Gage proposed, though I could hear in his voice he wasn't confident of that, even if he was advancing the theory.

"How would you like me to proceed?" Goddard asked, pulling us from our ruminations.

Gage looked at me. "I think you and I should pay a visit to Mr. Penrose and see if he can explain his contact with those resurrectionists." His eyes darted to Goddard. "In the meantime, can you keep track of these bodysnatchers' movements?"

"Already bein' done." He frowned. "Though it appears they might have slipped past their watchers this morning. I'll have to have a word with my men."

"Who are these bodysnatchers?"

Goddard's expression darkened. "A man who most often goes by the name of John Shearing, and his brother Thomas. They work with a few other lifters—Robert Tighe, Boney Dunkley, and George Long. A vile group of characters, to say the least. Better than the Spitalfields Gang, but not by much."

"Is the Rockingham Arms their normal meeting place?"

"'Twas the Fortune of War, but most snatchers have steered clear of there since the arrests."

Gage's lips curled cynically in comprehension. "Thank you. I'll be in touch as soon as we speak to Penrose."

Goddard dipped his head. "Oh, and there's one more mystery I might be able to clear up for ye. A constable at Great Marlborough Street admitted he followed your maid the other day. He thought she might have somethin' to do with the murders when he saw her hangin' about the stable yard where the one happened. Wasn't 'til later, when he learned who her employer was, that the green lad realized he'd made a mistake. I hope the young miss wasn't alarmed."

I supposed this, then, was Bree's furtive follower. "He followed her just once?" I asked, wondering if there could be more than one man.

He gave a huff of dry laughter. "Only admitted to the once. But the lad genuinely thought he'd uncovered something, so it may have been more. He means well. He's just raw."

I nodded. "My maid will be relieved."

A spark of laughter lit Gage's eyes, knowing as well as I did how amused Bree would be to discover who had been trailing after her. In any case, *I* was relieved to know she wasn't being stalked by the killer.

Goddard took his leave of us and I finished my breakfast before we went in search of Mr. Penrose. Unfortunately, he wasn't home, and the Earl of Redditch's butler did not know when he would return. I tried not to feel uneasy about this, but no matter what I tried to distract myself with, it still preyed at the back of my mind.

CHAPTER TWENTY-EIGHT

Given the horrid events of that morning, I'd been tempted to send our regrets to the hostess of the dinner party we were to attend that night. But I knew Lord Gage would also be in attendance, and I was anxious to hear whether he'd made any headway in acquiring the journals Dr. Mayer possessed.

Truth be told, the only reason we'd been invited in the first place was because of our relationship to Lord Gage. Lady Cordelia Verwood was a widow and a sparkling political hostess. One who had taken a decided interest in Gage's father. If he did wish to remarry, she would be an excellent choice. Lovely, respectable, and able to tolerate me with civility, even if the look in her eyes said she wished she could have rescinded her invitation for this evening.

The party was long and tedious, my presence barely tolerated by half the guests. Worse, we were never able to find a few moments to step aside alone with Lord Gage. Lady Cordelia seemed determined to hinder such efforts, which sadly did not endear her to my father-in-law. And it *was* sad, for when she allowed herself to forget my reputation for a moment, she was quite conversant on art and music, both subjects I enjoyed.

When the hour had drawn late, and Gage noticed me drooping in a chair, he abandoned the effort and brought me forward to take our leave of our hostess. While donning our cloaks and gloves, Lord Gage finally contrived to slip out after us. He gestured imperiously for the footman assisting us to step away.

"I've been attempting to tell you all night that Mayer is as stubborn as a mule, and twice as vindictive."

Gage's hands tightened on the plum velvet of my cloak as he draped it around my shoulders. "He's not giving up the journals?"

"Not without a fight. Not even facing royal pressure. He and his publisher are determined to publish."

I sagged, stumbling back a step, and Gage reached out to steady me. "So that's it?" I murmured faintly, my heart clenching with dread. "They're going to be printed?"

"Oh, I haven't exhausted all my options. Not yet." Lord Gage's eyes blazed with indignation. "This smug little sawbones is going to rue the day he tangled with me."

Staring into my father-in-law's sneering face, I well believed him. I was merely glad to have him on my side for once.

"Kiera!"
I faltered as a pair of frilled sleeves reached out to embrace me, nearly tumbling to the ground and pulling the owner of said sleeves with me. I'd been so consumed by my own thoughts while the Duchess of Bowmont's butler showed me into the parlor where she sat for her portrait that I'd failed to notice Lorna barreling toward me until it was too late.

Once we'd righted ourselves, Lorna pulled back to grin at me. "I'd hoped to surprise you, but not knock you flat," she jested. I'd rarely seen her so merry.

"I'm sorry. I was woolgathering."

"Apparently." She reached up to rub a finger between my eyes. "And if this little crease is any indication, it wasn't about anything pleasant."

The Duchess of Bowmont rose from her perch on the blue velvet sofa. "Don't tease her, darling. She's had a distressing few weeks. Thank goodness they've finally set the date for the burkers trial for Friday. At least, that will be over soon."

"But will it?" I murmured before I could stop myself.

She glanced at me inquiringly.

I sighed, wishing I'd minded my tongue. Crossing the room to the table set aside for my use, I plunked down my valise filled with supplies.

"What do you mean, dear?" the duchess asked in the most maternal tone I'd yet heard her use. Perhaps that was what convinced me to speak when normally I would have remained silent. It also could have been Lorna's soothing presence. Or maybe I was simply too weary of pretending all was well, that none of it could affect me.

Whatever the case, I suddenly found myself divulging my worries. "More and more reports of missing people and attempted burkings keep pouring into the newspapers." I pulled my paints from the bag, smacking them down on the table one by one. "Everyone is looking around them, wondering if there will be more killings. Wondering if they're next." I gestured with my roll of specialty brushes. "Even here in Mayfair."

"And then, in turn, they look to you," the duchess stated, finishing my unspoken thought.

I lifted my gaze to hers but saw no condemnation there. "Yes."

"Oh, Kiera. No one could blame you . . ." Lorna began, hastening forward.

"Of course they could," the duchess interjected, cutting off her goddaughter's words. "Don't tell her lies, pet. It's unkind. And most unhelpful." She smiled ruefully. "Believe me."

I searched her face, curious what had etched such sorrow in the fine lines there. What had she been blamed for unfairly?

"The duke," she explained, turning toward the long mirror that had been brought into the room the week before. "When he turned to other women after barely a fortnight of marriage, naturally I must be to blame."

Anyone would have thought by the blithe tone of her voice that this did not bother her, but I sensed the brittleness beneath the façade. I saw the pain buried in her eyes as she leaned toward her reflection, dabbing at the skin along her cheekbones.

"What they couldn't understand was that Bowmont finds fidelity tedious. I was forced to accept that long ago." She swiveled to the side, brushing her hand over the silver braid on the side of her bodice. "But fortunately, he's no hypocrite." She flashed us a smile. "What's sauce for the goose is sauce for the gander."

"Yes, but if honesty is what you want, Selina, you forget . . ." Lorna swept her hand up and down her godmother's form. "*You* are a duchess."

"The implication being that I can brazen my way through more than other gentlewomen. Yes, that's true." She lifted her perfectly arched eyebrows. "But I still had to demand it. Had I let them, they would have snubbed and cut me all over Mayfair. But a *duchess* does not stand for such treatment." Her gaze swung to pin me where I stood. "And neither should you."

I stared at her, too stunned to speak.

"If you want their respect, if you want it for your husband and your children, then you have to *demand* it. So you have a difficult past." She shrugged one shoulder. "You are not the only one, pet."

I nodded, acknowledging this as I glanced at Lorna, whose difficult past I was already aware of, and then back to the duchess, whose pain I'd only begun to guess at.

"You have embraced all the scandalous things your first husband taught you and put them to good use, have you not? Then be done with it, and embrace your scandalous reputation, too." She flicked her wrist as if to shoo away a gnat. "Those who would snub you are not worth your time or your delightful husband's. And the rest will soon stop quibbling once you show them you don't care *what* they think."

Gage had said something similar, but hearing it from the duchess was quite different. She could have rolled her eyes and dismissed my distress as trifling. Instead, she'd risked revealing some of her own wounds to show me I needn't be ashamed of the things that were out of my control. And I needn't let others try to make me feel less of myself because of them.

Lorna stepped forward to take my hand. "All you need to be is yourself, Kiera. Those of us who've been allowed to see even a glimpse of your truth already love you for it." She wrinkled her nose impishly. "Just think if we were allowed to see it all."

I offered her a small smile, touched by her regard. Especially since I thought so much of her in turn.

"Now, then," the duchess proclaimed, gliding toward the long stool where she posed for her portrait. "Shall we begin?"

My smile widened. "Yes. Just let me prepare my palette."

I returned home to find Gage seated behind his desk, glaring down at a piece of correspondence.

"I take it your discussion with Mr. Penrose did not go well this morning?" I asked, crossing my arms over my chest and rubbing my hands up and down against the chill of the study.

"He wasn't there."

"Again?"

He grunted in affirmation. "I reminded Hotchkins to have Mr. Penrose send me a note the moment he returned. But I'm not holding out much hope of that," he growled under his breath.

It was certainly suspicious that he'd absented himself from Redditch House the past two days—particularly given what we'd learned about his meeting with known resurrectionists—but it was not obstructive. Yet.

"What are you reading?" I asked, moving to stand behind him, closer to the fire.

"A letter from Henry Warburton to some of his fellow MPs that fell into my father's hands, and he forwarded to me. He proposes to reintroduce another Anatomy Bill at the next session."

"Then I'm sure Philip is aware of it as well."

I'd discovered several months earlier that my brother-in-law was working with other members of both houses of Parliament to put together a second attempt at a bill which would make the bodies of the unclaimed poor at workhouses legally available to surgeons. The first bill had passed in the Commons but failed in the Lords.

"Yes, well, this letter as good as states that he intends to use the current court trial and the threat of London burkers to gain support for the measure."

I tilted my head. "I suppose he would be foolish not to."

Gage turned to frown at me.

I shrugged. "It's politics. Did you expect anything different?"

"No, but I'm not fond of others using fear and naiveté to manipulate matters."

"Neither am I." I sighed heavily. "But *something* must be done. The bodysnatching trade cannot go on, and still our future surgeons must be trained." I crouched to stoke the fire, shaking my head. "There is no happy solution to the problem. Not while people are so revolted by the idea of dissection. And sadly, once again, it is the poor who will suffer to ease the peace of mind of the populace."

Recognizing I was close to shivering, he stood to take the poker from me, stirring the embers before adding more fuel.

"I suspect if the bill ever has a chance of passing, now is the time. While the dangers of burking are still fresh in the minds of the upper class." And much of that was thanks to the murders in Mayfair. I watched the fire as it licked along the log in varying shades of flickering flame, my mind turning over the issue. "You know, if anyone is benefiting from these murders, I would say it's the reformers."

Gage lifted his head to look at me, his arm still draped across the mantel. "Because it will sway votes in their favor?"

I nodded. "Though I find it hard to credit they would be so cold and heartless in the pursuit of such a measure."

"And I think they'll find such methods don't do much to convince those who believe the bill criminalizes being poor."

"Yes, but if they have the support of some of the Tories, then they don't need those Radicals. And the Tories only need to be persuaded that the bill will stop the burkings and save lives, not cause civil unrest or the downfall of traditional social order."

Gage's face registered astonishment. "You're far more well-versed in politics than I realized."

I smirked. "I'm quoting Philip. Though I do trust he knows what he's talking about."

He pushed away from the mantel. "That he does." Settling back into his chair, he began to rub his index finger over his lips. I recognized it as a sign he was contemplating something and moved to lean against his desk next to him.

"Lord Vickers was considered a Radical, wasn't he?" He sounded indifferent, but I knew better. The less inflection in his voice, the more interested he was.

"Mr. Poole's former employer?"

He nodded.

"Yes. But I don't know whether his son followed suit." I scrutinized his features. "Why?"

"Just . . . curious."

I narrowed my eyes, trying to deduce what he was thinking.

He tapped his finger over a stack of papers on his desk. "I saw the list of heirs you created."

"Oh, yes. I didn't realize I left it here."

His expression tightened. "Percy Acklen was on it."

I hadn't forgotten.

He smoothed his hand over the names on the first page. "If something doesn't turn up soon, we might have to start looking through it to figure out who the next target is."

I rested my hand on his shoulder. "Something will turn up. You'll see."

He exhaled a wary breath. "I hope you're right."

Me, too, I thought. *Me, too.*

When Wednesday morning came and still there was no word from Mr. Penrose or even an admission from the staff of his presence at Redditch House, Gage declared he was through being patient. I asked him what that meant, but he shook his head, refusing to explain. "Wait and see" was his maddeningly oblique answer. He jotted off a brief missive and then left the house for a short time.

Not half an hour after his return, I glanced up in astonishment from my writing desk in the corner of the morning room when Jeffers announced that he'd shown a Mr. Penrose into the drawing room.

"Thank you, Jeffers," Gage replied, setting aside the newspaper he'd been perusing and rising to his feet.

The butler bowed and departed.

"How on earth did you manage that?" I asked.

He shrugged. "I've suspected where he was hiding all along. I simply wasn't sure I was willing to take the gamble of writing to him there."

"Hiding where?"

"Come." He grasped my arm, ignoring my query. "Let's hear what he has to say."

I frowned but did not argue.

Our guest hovered by the bow window, staring out at the cold rain as it pattered against the pavement and a passing carriage. At first, he seemed to not realize we'd entered, his gaze was so fixed on the scene outside. But then he exhaled and swiveled to look at us with wide eyes. He stood that way so long without speaking, his face pale, that I began to feel concerned.

"Mr. Penrose, are you unwell?" I asked, taking a few hesitant steps toward him.

He blinked, seeming to recall himself. "Oh! No, no, I'm fine." He cleared his throat. "My apologies. I . . . should have answered your summons days ago, but . . ." He glanced back toward the window. "There was something I wished to take care of first."

"I see." Gage studied him as if he knew exactly what he'd meant, even though I knew he didn't, and then gestured toward the furniture gathered around the hearth. "Shall we sit?"

Penrose hesitated as if he was about to object, and then followed. He sat at the very edge of his chair, as if ready to leap up and flee at any moment. His eyes searched Gage's face warily. "How did you know where to find me?"

Gage sat back, lacing his fingers over his flat abdomen. "I already suspected who your particular friend was, and a few discreet queries seemed to substantiate it."

His face had gone pale again. "Who else knows?"

"I can't disclose that. But it confirmed for me that your friend most definitely had much to lose had your brother followed through with his threats." Gage's eyelids dropped to half-mast. "It also told me just how dangerous it would have been for him to be beholden to Feckenham's whims. There's no telling what your brother might have compelled him to do."

Penrose fidgeted in his seat. He plowed a hand through his hair before speaking. "Yes, yes, that's all true. It's why I confronted him that night. But I didn't kill him!" His eyes were wild. "And neither did . . ." He almost said the name—it was on the tip of his tongue—but he bit it back at the last moment with a quivering breath. "My friend."

"What of Newbury and Acklen? Did you kill them?" Gage persisted.

"Of course not! Are you mad? Why would I do such a thing?"

"To divert suspicion," I said.

His gaze flicked to me in startlement.

"With only your brother dead, all evidence and motive pointed to you. But if two unrelated gentlemen were killed, then suspicion would shift."

He shook his head. "That's mad! No. No! There is no way I would do that."

Gage arched his eyebrows. "Then why were you collaborating with known bodysnatchers?"

This query was met with silence, though the look in Penrose's eyes communicated he knew he'd been found out. His shoulders slumped as he crumpled forward, pressing his hands to his forehead. "You know about that?"

"Yes."

Penrose inhaled a shaky breath. "I was not collaborating with them. I was . . . trying to make them stop."

This time Gage and I were the ones who were speechless.

"A few days after I returned to London from Silvercrest, I received a letter." His lips curled derisively. "Well, *Feckenham* received a message, but Hotchkins assumed it was for me. It was to inform him that the first blackmail letter had been delivered and they expected the second part of their payment."

Gage and I glanced at each other in surprise, though he seemed less stunned than me.

"*Feckenham* hired them to blackmail me?" I snapped.

"From what I can gather, he proposed the idea to them and promised to pay them something for their trouble. Whatever they could gain from you in the process was theirs to keep." He swallowed, plainly not wanting to relay the rest. "Except the proof they were to attain from you that the blackmail had been paid."

"So he could manipulate her later?" Gage guessed. "So he could extort her for something else."

I stared down at my lap, trying to comprehend what had just been revealed, but it just seemed to reverberate through my mind like the ripples on a pond.

"As soon as I discovered what he'd done, I tried to convince them to stop," Penrose explained. "I refused to pay their fee, but then they turned their scheme back on me, threatening to tell you and the newspapermen that the idea had all been mine." His head flopped back on his neck. "So I stupidly paid. But they wanted more. I've been wrestling with this for weeks, trying to figure out how to make it end." His eyes pleaded with us. "That's why I've been avoiding you. I wanted to end it before I saw you again. And I didn't want them to think I'd already told you." He sighed. "But it's too late for that." He gestured toward the window. "I saw one of them outside on the street. He must have followed me here."

Gage leaped up from the sofa and crossed the room in a few quick strides. "Where?" he demanded, peering through the drapes. "Where did you see him?"

Penrose moved to join him. "I saw him strolling down the street, hat pulled low. He wears a smock frock and a pair of shabby trousers. He's a powerful-looking fellow with a red splotch on his check below his right eye." He glanced left and right. "But he's not there any longer."

"But you're certain you saw him?"

He nodded. "It was him."

What did it mean for us if they believed Penrose had told us everything? Would we receive another unpleasant gift? Or would they go straight to the reporters and tell them whatever lies about me they wished?

My hands curled into fists as I struggled to contain my frustrated fury.

"I'm sorry," Penrose said. "I thought I was careful. But apparently, not careful enough."

"It's as much my fault as yours," Gage told him with a clap on his back, guiding him back toward where I sat. "I forced your hand and made you come here."

"It's a rotten mess." He dropped back into his chair.

Gage sat across from him, idly rubbing his lip in thought before venturing another question. "Do you think your brother took anyone into his confidence about his blackmail schemes? A friend, maybe? Or his valet?"

Penrose frowned. "I doubt it. He always was the type to hold his cards close to his vest."

"What of Mr. Poole?"

The other man shook his head. "Definitely not Mr. Poole. Not after Feckenham botched the measure regarding the care of vagrant children he was working on with Father."

I struggled not to react. "What do you mean?"

"Mr. Poole had worked hard on that measure, and worked hard on persuading my father to put it forth in the House of Lords." His lips twisted. "But somehow my brother found out about it. He argued it would anger his Tory colleagues with its revolutionary ideals." He pressed a hand to his stomach as if he felt ill. "He all but blackmailed him not to do it."

I recalled the look of dissatisfaction in the secretary's eyes when he'd discussed why he'd taken the position with the Earl of Redditch. Whatever his hopes had initially been, they had definitely soured.

Penrose pressed his hands together. "Now, what is to be done about these blackmailers?"

Gage glanced up from where he had been contemplating the rug. "Nothing, for now." His eyes narrowed. "But I think I may know of a way to handle them. Do you know where they live?"

He shook his head. "I always met them at the Rockingham Arms in Southwark, near St. Thomas's Hospital."

"Leave the matter in my hands. Don't respond if they contact you again," he stated firmly.

Penrose's face was pinched. "I feel I should argue. The problem was caused by my brother, and so I should be the one to clear it up." His gaze slid to me. "But I suspect, in this, at least, you have more to lose." He shrugged sheepishly. "And, I admit, I find myself relieved to pass it off to you, for I've exhausted all my options. So I'll simply say thank you. If you should need my assistance, you need only ask." He flushed. "I will not hide this time."

This time, I trusted he meant it. Not because of his integrity, but because he knew Gage would still find him.

CHAPTER TWENTY-NINE

I knew within minutes we shouldn't have come. All evening as I'd readied myself I'd felt a vague stirring of anxiety. The night's soiree was not being held by family, or friends, or even close acquaintances, and it was certain to be a crush. I'd mentioned my wariness to Gage, but he insisted it would pass. That we still had questions to be answered, and we would not find those sitting at home. Acknowledging he was right, I'd set off with him across Mayfair.

It didn't take long to discover my apprehension had been justified.

Our hostess all but brushed us aside when she received us, and I'd practically been singed by three glares as we ascended the broad staircase toward the ballroom above. At first, I feared the resurrectionists had spoken to the newspapermen about me, but then I reminded myself I hadn't seen any such stories in the day's papers.

What I *had* seen was a report of George Pilcher's testimony to Minshull at Bow Street. Pilcher was a lecturer and anatomist at Grainger's private medical school, where it had been discovered the body of Fanny Pigburn—the woman whose clothes had been found in the privy and well at Nova Scotia Gardens—had been sold in early October. Though he'd stood before the magistrate voluntarily to dispel the rumors, in some ways he'd made the matter worse.

Pilcher admitted that the body had seemed fresher than normal, but they'd assumed it had been stolen from a bone house or undertaker's premises. He claimed there were no signs of violence, and the fact that Bishop had willingly accepted only half his payment for the corpse, and agreed to come back for the rest, seemed to confirm there was no cause for concern, as he assumed someone with a guilty conscience would want all their money at once. With reporters standing close, Pilcher even went so far as to make a general statement on behalf of the entire London medical profession, regretting the horrible disclosure that had taken place and apologizing for the fact they'd been driven to the necessity of dealing with such men.

This only served to remind people of exactly who was purchasing the bodies and providing incentive for the killings. Which, in turn, prompted them to recall what my first husband's profession had been, and the distasteful work he had undertaken and forced me to participate in. As if they needed it. As if this entire inquest into the Italian Boy and the Mayfair murders with their sticking plasters were not bright beacons of remembrance.

At first, I remained close to Gage's side, trying to disregard the scoffs and murmurs. But with each step we wove through the ballroom, sliding past dagger glares and ignoring harsh whispers, the angrier I became. With it, my shoulders went back, my chin lifted, and I soon found myself meeting their stares with glares of my own. I had not wanted to wear the amaranth gown Bree had laid out for me, thinking the purple-red color would draw too much attention, but I was glad of it now. It suited my mood perfectly.

We paused at the edge of the dance floor so that Gage could speak to an old friend, and I turned to survey the assembly for anyone I thought might have useful information to provide. My search was interrupted by the snide commentary of a woman just beyond my shoulder. Her voice was loud enough that I could hear every word, even over the orchestra playing in the gallery above.

"They say she lured them into the hands of the burkers herself, you know. So that her husband could dissect them on his cutting table. The sawbone's siren. So fitting."

Before, I would have ignored her or walked away, but this time I swiveled to face her, an arch smile stretching my face. "Why Lady Lewis," I declared, satisfied to have disconcerted her. "I don't believe I've seen you in more than a year. You are looking *flush* and healthy. And your gown is exquisite." I flicked my gaze up and down her figure before staring pointedly at her abdomen for a moment. "You *must* share the name of your modiste. Her *tailoring* is impeccable."

Lady Lewis's face paled in recognition of the sharp gleam in my eyes. She might have believed she'd fooled everyone else, but I could tell she was expecting, and had been for some months. Her rounded belly hidden beneath the folds of her pistachio dress rivaled the size of my own. And yet Lord Lewis had not returned to England after an extended sojourn until four weeks prior. I might not be so cruel as to state the fact aloud, but I was not going to allow her to sharpen her tongue on me any longer without letting her know there could be repercussions.

When she didn't respond, I nodded to her and her frowning friend and turned back to face the dancers.

"Why of all the rude . . ." the friend began, but Lady Lewis silenced her and towed her away.

Gage glanced at me as I flicked open my fan and cooled my heated cheeks, feeling a thrill of exhilaration at having routed her. I didn't think he had heard what I said, for his eyes held a look of bewilderment.

I leaned toward him with a smile, waiting until he bowed his head closer to hear me. "Ask me to dance."

He straightened just enough to see into my eyes, and whatever he saw there made his own pale blue ones flicker with interest. Forgoing words, he laced my arm with his and pulled me out onto the polished wooden floor. I sensed people watching us, but for once, I did not care. If they wanted to watch Gage spin me around in the circle of his arms, then so be it. I had nothing to be ashamed of.

Dancing with Gage was always an immersive experience. As if he'd swept me up onto our own little cloud, where it was just the two of us. Nothing else existed beyond his strong, steady arms or the grin on his lips. There was no need for words, for he communicated more than enough without them. When the waltz ended, and I glided back to the ground, I felt I could endure anything.

Even Lady Felicity Spencer.

Gage and I left the dance floor arm in arm, moving toward the hall and parlors, where one might better be able to carry on a conversation, when Lady Felicity's crisp voice made me falter.

"I hear there are journals, you know. Left by her late husband."

"Truly? How scandalous!" her companion remarked. "Does *she* feature in them?"

I turned to find Lady Felicity watching me with spiteful glee.

"How can she not? What she wouldn't give, I imagine, to keep such a thing quiet."

She had never challenged me directly before. Had never dared to. But recent events had changed that. And now she knew about the journals. I felt my nerve begin to fail me.

"But she won't be able to do so much longer," she continued even more loudly, garnering several more people's interest. "I hear they're going to be published."

The others gasped and whispered in speculation.

Gage tugged at my arm, as if to move forward to shield me, but I held him back. I didn't want him always fighting my battles for me. Gathering my courage, I straightened my spine and took a step toward her.

"Really?" a voice drawled behind me, making Gage and me both stiffen. "Then why didn't the owner publish those journals immediately upon Sir Anthony Darby's death? He could have made a fortune."

I blinked in shock as Lord Gage moved forward to stand at my side, eyeing Lady Felicity as if she were some silly debutante, hardly worth his time.

Lady Felicity seemed similarly affected. Then her eyes narrowed and she gave a toss of her artfully coiled blond ringlets. "Of course you would defend her. She's your daughter-in-law."

He gave a huff of dry laughter. "When have I ever done so before?"

Those gathered around her seemed persuaded by this point, murmuring fervently among themselves. A blush of fury crested her cheeks, and I had to admit that even in a rage, she looked spectacular.

"Those published journals will still net a fortune. For I certainly intend to buy a copy and find out just what sort of viper has been brought into our midst."

"No worse than some that already slither among us, I suspect."

Lady Felicity glared at him, clearly unable to decide whether she'd just been insulted or not.

"Come, my dear," Lord Gage said, taking my hand and threading it through his arm. "Such insipid conversation gives me a headache."

I allowed myself to be led away, still trying to rally from the astonishment of having my father-in-law publicly defend me.

And against Lady Felicity Spencer—his choice for his son's bride—no less. With his son following in our wake, Lord Gage guided us into a small alcove near the parlor where gaming tables had been set up.

Before either Gage or I could speak, Lord Gage whirled me about to face him. "I have the journals."

If I'd thought I'd suffered a shock before, it was nothing compared to this.

"How?" Gage spluttered. "When?"

His eyes scanned the hallway beyond the alcove to be sure no one was listening. "This morning. Pilcher's statement before Minshull gave me the idea. If the weight of the Crown wouldn't work, I realized that perhaps the influence of the Royal College of Surgeons would. As you can imagine, they don't wish for any further scandal at the moment. So I convinced them to threaten to oust him from their distinguished membership if he did not relinquish Sir Anthony's journals to me to be destroyed." He clasped his hands behind his back, arching his eyebrows. "They also offered him the chance to assist with one of the dissections of the burkers, should they be convicted to hang."

"Thank you, sir," my husband gasped, offering his hand to his father, who shook it. "We are most grateful."

Relief swept through me, from my head all the way down to my toes. And yet the thought that kept echoing through my head was, *He's had them since this morning.* I felt myself sway, and both men reached out to steady me. It was then that I realized I'd been holding my breath. I released it, and then gasped, "I'm sorry. I just . . ."

"No need for explanations," Gage told me, pulling me to his side.

I nodded, leaning into him for support.

"Where are the journals now?" he asked. "Have they been destroyed?"

"No, they are in the safe in my study." Lord Gage's eyes shifted between us, something swimming in their depths I'd never seen before. "I was under the impression you needed some information from them."

My hands tightened around my husband even as he answered.

"We do." He glanced down at me in confusion.

"Do we?" I murmured. "We already have the names we were looking for."

"Yes, but what if there is more?" he replied gently. "This might be our only chance to find out."

He had a valid point, and yet the idea of his reading Sir Anthony's thoughts about me, about anything, made my mouth dry and my heart race.

His hand lifted to trail a thumb over my cheek. "Believe me. I do not relish it any more than you. But it must be done."

I forced another breath past the constriction in my chest and nodded, knowing he was right, and yet hating it.

His father reached inside the pocket of his tailcoat. "Then I think you should peruse them in my study." He passed him a key. "I would rather not take the chance of you or me being accosted and the journals stolen. Burn them in the hearth when you're finished."

"I will. Just as soon as I escort Kiera home."

"I'll take her."

I stiffened.

"That's not necessary," Gage demurred.

"Maybe not, but I'd like to do so anyway," he argued, not unkindly. "The sooner this is over, the better."

Gage's eyes narrowed at the corners as the two men stood in a silent standoff. Whatever he read in his father's countenance, I didn't know, but I was surprised when his expression softened.

"Please, Sebastian," Lord Gage replied. His voice was not

pleading, but it was close. "I promise you she shall come to no harm. Even from me."

Gage turned to me, offering me the chance to refuse. But then I realized, what did it matter? If Lord Gage had read the journals, if he had something to say to me, he would just find another time if I didn't allow him to do so now.

The three of us departed the ball together, and Gage pressed a kiss to my temple before he handed me up into Lord Gage's elegant coach, entrusting me to his care. With a rap of his knuckles against the wall, the carriage clattered forward into the dark London streets, with only the periodic flicker of the gas streetlamps to light the way while the clouds blocked the moon. I wrapped my cloak tighter around me as I stared out into the gloom, waiting for my father-in-law to speak. Why he hesitated, I didn't know, but when he cleared his throat not once, but twice, I started to wonder if he was a bit uncertain.

"I suspect you've already guessed it, but I read the journals," he murmured in a gentler voice than I'd ever heard him use.

His tone affected me in a way I'd not expected, making my throat suddenly tight. I choked back the emotion, refusing to react. I just wanted him to say whatever he wanted to say and be done with it. So I could begin to forget this entire conversation.

But then he surprised me again by slipping his hand into mine where it rested against the seat. I turned to look at him. His shadow-wreathed features were so like his son's—the same strong jawline and sculpted cheekbones, the same cleft in his chin. Even the line of the brow and the shape of the eyes were the same. I had noticed the similarities before, but in the semi-darkness they were even more pronounced.

Or perhaps it was the way in which my father-in-law was looking at me. His eyes were no longer sharp with disdain, but soft with sympathy and perhaps a shade of regret, though I'd never thought to credit him with such an emotion.

"I think perhaps I underestimated you, my girl. I pride myself on being able to read people well, you know." He sighed heavily. "But this time, I'm afraid I was stubbornly imperceptive."

It was not an apology precisely, but it was the closest I would ever get to one, I realized. And one that his pride allowed him to offer. It was oddly touching while at the same time vindicating. But at what cost? What exactly had he read in those journals?

He cleared his throat a third time before continuing in his usual blasé manner. "You should know, I don't usually think of myself as a violent man." His eyes shifted to meet mine, glinting with rage. "But if your first husband were still alive, I would quite cheerfully thrash him. Damn the consequences."

I didn't respond, for what could I possibly say to that? But I was now certain that Sir Anthony's cruelness had bled out in the words on the page as it had in person, or else my father-in-law would not have reacted so strongly. They were as bad, if not worse, than I feared.

I felt light-headed at the realization that the three most painful, degrading years of my life had almost been printed for public consumption, laid bare for all to read. And knowing Sir Anthony, he had spared no intimate details, had left no depraved thought unrecorded. The scandal would have been horrific, the shame insurmountable. For me, and for those I loved.

Inhaling a deep breath past the constriction in my throat, I rested my free hand protectively over my abdomen.

"My wife used to shield Sebastian in the same way before he was born." The rawness in his voice caught me off guard.

"I . . . I think it's fairly common in expectant mothers," I said, the ache in his eyes finally compelling me to speak.

He nodded. "Well, it speaks well of you, regardless." He faced forward, speaking into the darkness as the carriage turned into a shadowy street. "I can only hope my grandchildren inherit your strength and fortitude. It will serve them well."

Neither of us said anything more. For my part, I was too

stunned, too hesitant to ruin this tentative sense of solidarity that had sprung up between us. If I prodded too deeply, I feared it might crumble. I didn't want to foster any foolish hope, but perhaps our relationship had finally turned a corner. Not that we would ever be close, but perhaps at least he would stop treating me with such contempt and cease berating his son for choosing me as his wife.

CHAPTER THIRTY

I knew Gage would be poring over the journals for hours, so I went to bed, though I didn't think I would actually slumber. However, I'd underestimated the fatigue of my current condition and the strain of the day's revelations. I was asleep in minutes.

Some hours later, I woke at the click of the door latching and rolled over to find my husband hovering in the shadows by the connecting door. I couldn't see his face, but I could sense his roiling emotions in the tautness of his frame, and the silent misery rolling off him in waves.

I hadn't given any thought to it before, but I began to wonder whether this had been harder on him than me. It couldn't have been easy to read the things my first husband wrote about me, the things he had thought and done to me. Things I hadn't even dared to say. I didn't know whether reading it in black and white was harder than hearing it from me, but discovering those things, and yet knowing they had all happened in the past and there was nothing he could do about it, must have been enraging.

I held out my hand to him, and he came forward, slowly at

first and then faster. His face, when he stepped into the flickering light cast by the hearth, was a twisted mask of grief and rage. I pulled him down into the bed beside me and wrapped my arms around him. He lay there stiffly, with his arms around me, and I knew he wasn't rejecting me, but berating himself. For a man who placed such importance on protecting those he loved, realizing just what I'd endured must have been hell.

I brushed my fingers through the hair at the base of his neck. "It's over now," I whispered. "Just breathe, darling."

He inhaled a ragged breath and then began to shatter. He wept as I'd never seen him weep before—great gasping sobs of tears that dripped into my hair and onto my shoulder. They tore at my heart like talons. At one point he tried to pull away, but I would not let him. I didn't care if he soaked my nightdress or soiled my braid. I was not going to let him believe for a moment his reaction upset me or that he had any share of the blame.

When the tears slowed, and his breathing became more even, I pulled back to look into his beloved face. Weariness dragged at his features, as well as sorrow. I rolled over to grab a handkerchief from my bedside table and then passed it to him. Once he'd mopped his face and blown his nose, he took a deep breath, seeming to settle himself. But I halted him as he drew breath to speak.

"Don't even think of apologizing," I told him firmly as I snuggled in close to him again. "Had I been forced to read his atrocious words, I no doubt would be doing more than crying."

Gage brushed the hair from my face as I gazed down at him. "Very well. I won't apologize for that. But I will apologize for all that you endured." His voice was rough with emotion. "You told me what it was like, but you didn't *tell* me."

I swallowed. "Yes, well. I didn't particularly wish to relive every moment."

"I can understand that," he replied after some thought. His face contorted. "And thank heavens you weren't privy to his thoughts. I feel tainted simply from reading them."

I traced my fingers over the faint stubble growing along his jawline. "I gathered they were pretty awful from your father's reaction to them."

"Was he kind?"

"Yes." I thought about saying more, but it was too new, and I found I couldn't summon the words.

Gage seemed to understand anyway, for he pulled me down so that my head was cushioned against his shoulder. I burrowed into his neck and inhaled the spicy scent of his cologne and the comforting essence of him, allowing it to soothe some of my agitation.

A few moments passed without either of us speaking, and then I asked the question that must be faced. "Did you burn them?"

"Yes. With relish."

I nodded. "Good."

He traced a pattern on my arm. "My father had the pages of Sir Anthony's incomplete anatomy textbook as well."

I lifted my head to stare down at him in shock. I couldn't believe Mayer had given those up. My chest tightened. "Did you . . ."

"No."

My shoulders sank in a relief perhaps I shouldn't have felt.

"I couldn't do it. Your drawings were too beautiful. They're exquisite, Kiera." His voice almost throbbed with the words. "I've seen anatomical sketches before, and they were nothing like these. These were . . . works of art." His hand cradled my face. "You told me once that's how you endured. By seeing the splendor in each vein, each muscle, each drop of blood. Well, you captured that and more."

I felt tears burn at the back of my eyes to hear him be able to comprehend the way I viewed the world.

"I only wish others could see them and appreciate them."

"It's enough to know that you do," I whispered.

His eyes softened and he pulled my face down to kiss me, tenderly at first, and then with growing passion. There was some new component to our joining that night. It was deep, and at times, almost desperate, and perhaps all the more poignant because of it.

I should have been exhausted from Gage's efforts, but I lay awake for some time after that. His long body curled around mine, his arm draped over my middle, as I stared into the darkness.

That's when I first felt it. It wasn't more than a small flutter of movement, but I stilled at the sensation. Alana had told me it would happen soon, but I wasn't sure. Perhaps I'd imagined it.

Bracing myself, I waited to find out if it would happen again. Seconds passed, and then . . . There! The same fluttering. My heart thrilled at the realization the tiny baby inside me had just moved, stretching out his little arm or leg to press against me.

A deep well of love and wonder seemed to open up inside me at the knowledge that there really was a human being growing inside me. Intellectually I had known it, but the reality of it had still seemed a somewhat distant concept. Something to be taken on faith. But here was tangible evidence, a personal connection, and it had a much more profound effect on me than I'd expected.

I pressed my hand over the spot where the baby had reached out, waiting to feel him or her move again, but they must have settled. Part of me was disappointed by this, and part of me glad. For then I needn't feel guilty about not waking Gage. I would tell him in the morning, and the next time it happened. But this time . . . This time was just for me.

Though we seemed no closer to uncovering the Mayfair Murderer than before, Gage had already declared we would not be venturing far the next day. The trial of Bishop, Williams, and May was set to begin at the Old Bailey that morning, and the crowds of people expected to gather outside were not to be underestimated. Anderley had set out during the wee hours of the morning in order to find a space in the Public Gallery, a privilege for which he'd had to pay over a guinea to the sheriffs. Later, he'd reported how crowded the notoriously drafty Sessions House was, filled to the brim with spectators—many of them surgeons, but some of higher rank. Alongside the three judges sat the Lord Mayor of London, two sons of the prime minister, and the Duke of Sussex—the King's younger brother.

From the very beginning, the trial proceeded differently from others. For one thing, most lasted less than ten minutes, though some for capital offenses took a matter of hours. In contrast, the hearing for the burkers continued all day. Something the aromatic herbs strewn about the courtroom to combat the stink of the prisoners and the adjoining Newgate prison had no hope of enduring against, not with so many bodies packed tightly together.

The prosecution called up a total of forty witnesses, from the elderly tailor who lived in Nova Scotia Gardens and cut Williams's wedding coat—who incidentally did not show, a common occurrence at trials—to a seven-year-old child. The defense had but six, and several of those were of no help at all. The only of the three prisoners on trial who seemed to stand a chance was May, who had an alibi from one of his lovers, but as society saw her morals as being weak, her honesty was also questioned. Bishop also swore in his statement that May had known nothing as to how he came to possess the boy's body, but he also said the same for Williams, who clearly must have, living in the same home as him.

In the end, the jury saw no difference between them, and at 8:30 P.M., they passed down the verdict of guilty. The judges donned their black caps and sentenced them to hang on Monday morning and then have their bodies handed over to the anatomists.

Anderley said the courtroom was almost eerily silent at this proclamation. But through the windows they could hear the vast crowds gathered outside shouting and cheering. So great was the tumult that the court officials had to shut every window to continue the proceedings.

The convictions should have been a relief, a climax to the weeks of hearings and trials, but they were not. The entire city still seethed with panic, tense and twitchy. Perhaps the execution would calm the populace, but I doubted it. In my experience, murder—even a government-sanctioned one—never brought peace, only more turmoil.

After hearing of the verdict, I felt an urgent need for it all to be finished. The blackmail. The Mayfair murders. If we did not stop the killer, it was but a matter of days before he struck again. Perhaps even that very night, for I'd noticed he tended to choose moments of distraction, and the trial was certainly that. Unless he meant to wait until the execution. The stinging rain that night was not the most hospitable. All we could do was hope for a reprieve.

However, the blackmail was another matter. Gage said he had an idea how to stop it, but I suspected mine would be far more effective. Not to mention, there would be no better time than now, while three of the bodysnatchers' colleagues waited in Newgate's condemned cells to be hung for their crimes.

At first, Gage balked at my suggestion, but he was swiftly brought around to the idea. Especially when I didn't argue against his insistence that Mr. Goddard and one or more of his fellow Runners join us.

So the following afternoon, I found myself strolling into the Rockingham Arms just as the sun had begun to dip toward the horizon. This entire area of Southwark reeked of the river, and the scents inside the pub were no better. Stale beer and sweat assailed my nostrils, as well as the faint aroma of freshly turned earth. I glanced about, wondering where this particular aroma came from, which of these men had been digging in dirt. But then I focused on locating our intended quarry.

In the dim lighting, I barely recognized Goddard hunched at

a table at the back of the establishment, his face covered by a beard, but he caught Gage's eye and nodded toward the far wall. Three men sat around a scarred table, two of them nursing glasses of rum-hot, while the other seemed to prefer ale or porter, perhaps a pot of half-and-half. I immediately recognized one of them from the red splotch below his right eye that Mr. Penrose had described—a man Goddard had identified as John Shearing.

Gage flicked a glance at me as if to assure himself I wanted to do this, and I nodded decisively even though my stomach quavered at what I was about to do. We approached the table, with Anderley at our backs. He snagged me a chair, setting it before the resurrectionists' table. I slid into it gracefully before lifting the netting on my hat from my face so that they could see me. With Gage and Anderley at my back, and my hands resting in my lap with my reticule covering the Hewson percussion pistol I gripped, I found the poise to offer them a haughty smile.

"Good evening, gentlemen."

They stared at me for several seconds before Shearing sneered. "I told ye Penrose squeaked on us. Well, what of it? Did ye bring us our blunt?"

"Of course not."

His head reared back slightly, as if stunned by my refusal to quail in his presence.

I arched a single eyebrow. "Did you actually think we would pay?"

He narrowed his eyes. "Then I guess we'll be tellin' tales to the newspapermen."

"Oh, I wouldn't do that if I were you. Not unless you also want me to speak to them." I glanced up at Gage, who stood glaring down at the resurrectionists, his gaze as sharp as the knife I knew was stored in one pocket of his greatcoat. The other pocket contained a pistol. "In fact, I might consider publishing a memoir, of sorts. One that would be certain to paint you and your friends in a rather terrible light."

A vein throbbed in his forehead. "Ye wouldn't dare. Yer too anxious to keep yer names clean o' the bodysnatchers."

"Yes, but if you've already tarnished them with your implications, what's to hold me back?"

Shearing hesitated, clearly not having considered that, then sneered. "Go on. Ye don't know anythin' 'bout us anyways."

"I know enough." I shrugged. "And in any case, it doesn't matter if it's all true. Since you'll have already implicated me in your work, it'll be taken as fact. My reputation might be in tatters, but it's unlikely I would be prosecuted. While you, on the other hand, would not fare nearly so well." I flashed my teeth in a feral smile, letting them know I meant business. "I'm sure the New Police would be only too happy to find a few more resurrectionists to use as scapegoats. After all, Bishop and his cronies can't be the only burkers at work in London, and the people are baying for blood." I tilted my head. "So tell me, who do you think they'll believe?"

The bodysnatcher pounded the table with his fist, making my nerves jump. I almost lifted my pistol to point it at his chest. Only the realization that showing our weapons could ruin my charade of indifference kept me from doing so, lest the violence escalate instead of lessen.

"What do ye want?" he barked.

"Simply for you to forget you know anything about me or my late husband, and to cease your blackmail of us and Mr. Penrose. If you do not implicate me, I will not implicate you."

I knew blackmailing them in return was a risky undertaking, but given the current fate of these resurrectionists' friends, it was a gamble I was willing to make.

Shearing conferred with his cohorts with his eyes and then nodded begrudgingly. "Done."

I searched his face, trying to ascertain if he was telling the truth, before rising to my feet and lowering my veil. "Much obliged, though I can't say it's been a pleasure."

He grunted as I turned to go. "It's no wonder the papers dubbed ye a witch and a siren, and not just because of yer eyes."

Gage pivoted as if to confront him, but I pressed a hand to his arm to stop him. There was no use responding to his provocation. Let him salvage his pride by ending the confrontation with such a comment. I'd heard far worse.

"I've a message from my father."

I glanced up from one of the paintings of the *Faces of Ireland* I'd been working on to find Gage standing at the edge of my studio.

He advanced into the light of the two lamps I used to illuminate my work, holding the letter up. "Bishop and Williams made full confessions."

My eyes widened.

"They admitted to killing the boy." His brow furrowed. "Though they claim he was from Lincolnshire, and not an Italian Boy."

"That must be a relief to Anderley," I said, knowing he was struggling with his guilt, feeling he'd somehow failed the Italian Boys that came after him.

"Yes, and no. For he still must wonder if they're telling the truth."

I considered the broad strokes of color on my canvas. "What do you think?"

He rubbed his fingers over a dried patch of paint on the table where my supplies were laid out. "It makes little sense for them to lie. Their indictment wasn't specifically for Carlo Ferrari; it included the possibility that the boy's identity was unknown. So even if that was disputed, they would still hang." He lifted the letter. "Not to mention the fact that they also confessed to the killing of Fanny Pigburn and another boy named Cunningham."

I nodded, agreeing with him. "What of the other prisoner, James May?"

"He maintains his innocence, as he's done from the beginning. And Bishop and Williams both swear he had nothing to do with the boy's death, that he had no knowledge of the boy's body or how he was killed. He merely thought he was helping them to get a better price for a resurrected corpse."

I lowered my palette, alarmed by the fact May had been sentenced to hang in less than two days for a crime he quite probably had not committed given the little evidence against him. "Is anything being done about it?"

Gage lifted the letter to read from it. "Father says the governor and ordinary of Newgate both find the men's statements to be truthful, at least in that regard." His eyes lifted toward mine skeptically. "They still maintain the boy was Carlo Ferrari."

"Of course," I replied. For the boy to be anyone else would be an embarrassment.

"So they, James Corder, and my father are taking all three statements to the judges this evening to deliberate over May's fate, and decide whether they should present the evidence to Melbourne, as home secretary, and request he make either a pardon or a mitigation to consider bringing a lesser charge against him."

"It sounds to me as if there's certainly a case for it."

Gage folded the letter. "Well, that will be up to the judges to resolve."

I sighed and lifted my palette. Dipping the brush in a pale shade of umber, I resumed my work on the child's features, outlining them in broad sweeps I would paint with greater detail later. "Was Lord Acklen any more helpful during this visit than last?"

Upon our return from the Rockingham Arms, Gage had decided to speak with Acklen one last time, to find out if he'd thought of any connection between his son and the two other Mayfair victims.

He propped one leg up on the crossbar of the table's legs and tapped the paper against his thigh. "No. And he wasn't any more sober either."

"Well, you knew it was unlikely." But we had to try something. We were as conscious of the clock ticking down to the execution as the prisoners, for that was when the Mayfair Murderer was certain to strike again.

Gage scraped a hand through his golden locks and paced toward the glass wall of the conservatory to stare out at the crisp night. "Perhaps if we hadn't been distracted by the burkers and the blackmail, we would have solved this inquiry by now. As it is, nothing is adding up. It all seems random, except we know that it's not. This killer is either bloody brilliant or he's toying with us."

I breathed in and out, trying to remain calm in the face of his frustration. Had I been painting the fine details and shading, I would have needed to put down my brush, for they required a steady hand and focused attention, but the outlines were less precise. "I know we do not like to speak in guesses and abstracts, but if you were to name a suspect, do you have one in mind?"

The fact that he did not reply told me he did, and yet he was hesitant to name him.

"Then who are the possibilities? Redditch? Penrose?"

Out of the corner of my eye, I saw him pivot to face me, moving his coat aside to prop his hands on his hips. "Yes. But Redditch has a solid alibi for the first murder, and I cannot see him murdering two other men to draw suspicion away from him. Penrose has *no* alibi, and yet, the same. I cannot understand why either of them would kill Newbury and Acklen."

"Who else, then?"

"You mentioned Lord Damien, though that seems even less feasible."

I shook my head. "No, he didn't do it."

He did not argue against this confident assertion but instead turned to pace. "Neither Newbury nor Acklen makes sense.

And I have not found that any of the men who had grievances with Feckenham also had grievances with the other victims." He exhaled a breath of aggravation. "I considered Mr. Poole for a time, but what is his motive?"

I paused in the midst of my brushstroke, something teasing at the back of my brain.

"I'd hoped perhaps my friend might find something suspicious about this orphan house charity Mr. Poole seems so passionate about, but he turned up nothing untoward. Everything seems quite legitimate and aboveboard."

My mind began to filter through all the things Mr. Poole had told us, all the things we'd learned about him. His passion for social reform, his change of employer, the orphan house, how pale he'd looked while discussing Newbury's death, Redditch's failure to present his bill regarding the care of vagrant children. I tilted my head, studying the sparse outline of the child I intended to depict on my canvas.

"Children," I murmured. "Can't be ignored."

Gage turned on his heel toward me. "What?"

I blinked at him. "I . . . think you may be right."

He stared at me in confusion.

"About Mr. Poole, I . . ." I closed my eyes. "I can't explain it. Not yet. But I think I know a way we can finally make sense of it all."

He moved closer, the gleam in his eyes telling me he already grasped what I intended. "Tomorrow morning."

CHAPTER THIRTY-ONE

It was highly unusual to pay someone a call on a Sunday morning, but the situation being what it was, we had no choice. So when we knocked on the door to Lord Vickers's townhouse overlooking St. James's Park, we were by necessity at our politest and most insistent. Even so, we were almost turned away by his lordship's crabby butler. Only the influence of Gage's charm and estimable powers of persuasion convinced the old retainer to present our pleas to his lordship, who then agreed to speak with us.

Contrary to what I'd expected after arguing with their butler for a quarter of an hour, Lord and Lady Vickers were all that was gracious and kind about our visiting them at such an hour. They didn't appear to be the least displeased by our intrusion, and in fact, ordered the butler to have a tea tray filled with little cakes and other delights sent up.

Lady Vickers smiled broadly at me where she perched next to her husband on a jonquil damask settee. "I well remember when I was in the family way. It seemed I could never truly be full."

342 · *Anna Lee Huber*

Her face was a merry one, and her eyes were alive with intelligence and wit.

I found myself grinning back, instantly taking a liking to this woman with her soft gray curls. "Thank you. And forgive me, but is that a trace of a Scottish brogue I hear?" I asked, trying to place why she seemed familiar to me.

"Oh, aye, m'dear," she answered, letting it thicken for a moment. She giggled. "Lady Sofia Kincaid, I was." She twinkled at her husband. "Until I married Lord Vickers."

I felt my smile stiffen slightly at this revelation and strove to cover it with a laugh. I'd largely avoided those with the last name *Kincaid*, particularly if they were any relation of the current laird of Kincaid. The fact that I had a reluctant friendship, of sorts, with Bonnie Brock Kincaid—the head of one of Edinburgh's largest gangs of criminals—always made interactions with more legitimate Kincaids awkward on my part. Especially since I suspected Bonnie Brock had stolen the signet ring from the laird of Kincaid, in addition to a number of other things.

Lord Vickers chuckled and patted his wife's hand where it rested on her knee. "That little brogue is just one of her many charms." He cleared his throat and adjusted his spectacles. "Now, what was this urgent matter you wished to speak with me about? I understand you're investigating these Mayfair murders, but I trust you're not here to tell me my heir is in danger. He's thirty-eight and residing in Sheffield."

"No, we have no concern for your son." Gage shifted in his seat, adjusting his coat. "It's concerning Mr. Poole, your father's former secretary."

"Mr. Poole?" Lady Vickers repeated. "But . . . you cannot think he'll be the next victim?"

"I don't believe they're suggesting he might be a victim," Lord Vickers told her. His good humor had faded, but I couldn't tell if he was surprised or upset by such an implication.

That was not so with Lady Vickers. Her eyes widened. "Oh, no, no! Impossible. Not Mr. Poole."

"We have no wish to rush to judgment," Gage replied. "My wife and I both liked him immensely when we met him. But there are a few small details that are nagging us which we cannot explain away. And we thought if we knew more about him, we might have our minds relieved."

This speech was not strictly true, but it was diplomatic, and would hopefully put them at ease enough to convince them to speak freely. Otherwise they might tell us nothing in an effort to protect their former employee.

Lord Vickers didn't appear to be fooled by Gage's conciliatory statement, but he nodded. "What would you like to know?"

"How long did Mr. Poole work for your father?"

"Seven years. And I don't recall my father ever uttering a word of complaint against him. He was temperate, industrious, and clever." His brow furrowed. "And he seemed to take a great interest in the social reforms my father and I were advocating for."

"And yet he left your employ and went to work for the Earl of Redditch?" Gage pointed out, not unkindly.

"Yes." He frowned. "I admit that puzzled me. Why, when he told me Redditch had offered him a post and he'd accepted it, you could have knocked me down with a feather. It seemed such an unlikely fit. Redditch's politics are almost the complete opposite of mine and my father's, and what I thought were Mr. Poole's." He sighed, rubbing a hand over the hair that still clung to the back and sides of his mostly bald head. "But perhaps he thought he could persuade the earl around to our cause. Redditch does have more influence in Parliament and elsewhere than I do. Maybe he thought he could effect more change that way." He glanced at his wife, who was smiling at him in sympathy.

"I wondered if maybe he needed to distance himself from the

past," she said. "A number of unhappy things did happen to him while he was working here."

"What do you mean?" I asked.

"His niece went missing, oh . . . what is it now? I guess it's been three years since it happened." She clutched her chest as if in remembered horror. "Taken right off the street where she was playing in Holborn."

I cast Gage a speaking glance, feeling empathy and dread stir in my breast.

"My father tried to help in any way he could," Lord Vickers added. "He sent a notice to the newspapers, hired the Bow Street Runners. But most of the reporters and authorities weren't interested in such a story. The little girl was the daughter of a widow, and no one saw her being taken. The Runners decided she was just another runaway."

"Mr. Poole scoured the city day and night for over a week looking for her." Lady Vickers shook her head sadly. "But he never found her." Her voice softened to almost a whisper. "And a few weeks later, he returned home to find his sister had killed herself."

I pressed a hand to my mouth, aghast.

"He said she was wild with grief, and the parish priest allowed her to be buried in the parish graveyard. But even such a comfort, of course, could not bring her back."

"No wonder he is so passionate about the welfare of the lower classes and the care of children," I murmured. I hardly thought of Mr. Poole as lower class, but in Britain, anyone below the nobility or the gentry often merited fewer rights.

"Yes," Lady Vickers agreed, leaning toward me. "So you see why he cannot have anything to do with these murders. Why, I cannot even begin to fathom him doing something so horrendous."

I nodded in agreement, even though I was thinking the exact opposite. I was more certain than ever that he was behind it all. And now I knew why.

We chatted a bit longer about Mr. Poole and indulged in the tea and cakes Lady Vickers had so thoughtfully ordered for me, though they settled like lumps in my stomach. When enough time had passed that we could politely extract ourselves, we thanked them and departed in our carriage. The bells of one of the nearby churches pealed softly in the cool morning air.

"I find it difficult to believe Lord Redditch contacted Mr. Poole to offer him the post of his personal secretary," Gage remarked, tapping his fingers against the side of his leg.

"I don't think he did." I spoke toward the window. "I think he applied for the post, and that his intentions were initially just as Lord Vickers described."

"But then Redditch proved intractable, and he failed to present the measure they worked on for the care of vagrant children. Because of Feckenham."

"That's why Feckenham was first," I murmured, still fitting the pieces together in my mind.

"And then . . . Newbury?"

"Yes, before he lost his nerve. And also to confuse us." I looked up at Gage. "He told us himself, you know. Outside Callihan's office. He didn't state it directly, but Newbury's kindness and integrity made his death impossible to ignore. Society wants justice for him, while the other victims can all be dismissed in one way or another as just scoundrels." I squeezed my hands together in my lap, turning the knuckles white. "That's why he got sick in the alley. He didn't want to kill Newbury. He actually liked the man, and he knew his death would mean a temporary setback to their efforts to fund the building of an orphan home. But he believed he had to do it if he had any hope of forcing the nobility to effect real change."

"He's been targeting their children," Gage replied in comprehension.

"Yes. And their heirs, their firstborns, at that. The most precious of the lot. I suppose he decided he couldn't take his revenge out on actual children, so he targeted young men instead—mostly feckless wastrels of noble houses. He tried to make it look like they were falling prey to the burkers, just like the lower classes."

I sank my head back against the squabs. "The truth is, I can't fault him for his anger. The fact that so many people, so many *children*, have gone missing from the streets of London without much of the upper class even knowing, let alone caring, is unconscionable. We carry on blithely, ignorant of those below our station except when they are supposed to cater to our needs and whims, safe in our mansions, without fear our children will be abducted. He *should* be furious about our ignorance and indifference."

"But this murder of the Italian Boy has shaken us all up," he pointed out.

"Yes. For a time," I muttered sardonically. "But how much longer do you think society will continue to care once it's begun to fade from the papers?"

His expression was grave. "However, these Mayfair murders will not be so easy to forget." Lifting his walking stick, he wrapped on the ceiling of the carriage and ordered the coachman to take us to Redditch House.

"It's Sunday morning. Do you think he'll be there?"

"If not, Redditch should at least be able to provide us his address."

My stomach coiled in knots, urging the horses onward, hoping we weren't already too late, or that we hadn't somehow let our suspicions slip.

Gage didn't wait for our footman to knock for us, instead charging up the earl's steps to bang loudly on the door until Hotchkins opened it in astonishment. "Is Mr. Poole here?" he demanded, charging past the butler and dragging me in his wake.

"No, sir," he stumbled over his words. "I believe he has the day off."

Gage's eyes met mine in silent alarm. "The earl, then. Is he at home?"

"I . . ." He hesitated. His normal training would have him inquire of his lordship if he was home to callers, before admitting us. But judging from our insistent behavior, he could clearly infer these were extenuating circumstances. "Yes. He's in his study."

Lord Redditch glanced up in surprise when his butler announced us, before his face transformed into a scowl. "I hope you have some encouraging news for me, for if you're here to badger my son again, I'll have you thrown out."

"We need to find Mr. Poole," Gage snapped. "Do you know where he is?"

The earl stared at him. "Poole?"

"Yes." He gestured impatiently. "Do you know where he lives? Surely he must have given you an address, some way to contact him."

Irritation sparked in his eyes at being spoken to in such a way. "You think Poole . . ."

"We *know* Poole is behind the murders. Now, where is he? Quickly! Before he kills anyone else."

"Holborn. Eagle Street, I believe."

"If he should return here, send word to us immediately," Gage instructed him. "And don't let him leave!"

We hurried from the house and climbed back into our carriage as Gage shouted directions to the coachman. "Great Marlborough Street Police Office. I would rather not risk the chance of him escaping out the back of his rooming house or turning violent on us," he explained to me. "I trust Goddard will know how to proceed."

But by the time we located Poole's lodgings, he was already

nowhere to be found. Whether he had left earlier that morning or seen us arrive and slipped past us, we didn't know, but his landlady confirmed she had seen him the evening prior. A quick search of his rooms yielded no evidence, which either meant we were wrong, or he'd taken the knife, sticking plasters, and any bloody clothes with him. The latter was not a comforting thought.

I climbed inside the carriage and extracted the sketchbook and pencils I stored underneath the seat in order to create a quick drawing of Poole so that Goddard, his men, and the police would know what he looked like. Goddard left one of his men to monitor the lodging house in case Mr. Poole returned, and sent another to the pub his landlady told us he favored, and a third to Mr. Callihan's place of business off Lombard Street. Then Goddard and his remaining men spread out through the city—into Mayfair, down into Covent Garden, and east toward Newgate, where the execution would take place the next morning—showing the sketch to the constables they met along the way. Their task was akin to looking for a needle in a meadow, but something had to be done.

Gage and I raced back to Chapel Street to pore over the list of heirs I'd created. I tried not to worry I'd missed someone, or let the fact that we were not precisely cognizant of all the parameters Poole was using to select his victims cloud my judgment. All we could do was work from logic, and pray for some bit of inspiration.

"Thus far, all the victims have been under a score and ten years of age, but have at least reached the age of majority," Gage murmured, beginning to scan through his half of the pages of names I'd written out.

"They're also unwed and without children. And they're currently residing in London," I added as an obvious but necessary condition.

We set to work, conferring with each other from time to

time as we crossed off names. Once that was done, we compiled the lists onto a single page, finding we still had more than two-dozen names.

I inhaled a shaky breath. "There is no way we can set a watch on all of these gentlemen."

"I agree. So let's think about what else we know." Gage rubbed his chin and then brightened. "Redditch and Newbury are Tories." His shoulders slumped. "But Acklen doesn't really have a definitive political affiliation."

I shook my head, feeling like the answer was just beyond our fingertips.

"Then perhaps something more . . . personal." He tilted his head. "We know Newbury is the aberration and was the hardest to kill, at least for Poole's conscience. So if I were him, I would want to choose another easy target. Another feckless lordling I believe isn't worthy of their position."

"Yes, but he must realize he cannot continue this forever. That eventually he will be caught. At this very moment, he might already know we're searching for him." I inhaled. "I don't think he will waste his last chance at retribution, at proving his point, to kill another care-for-nothing young gentleman." I sat taller, a sudden thought occurring to me.

Gage watched with interest as I pulled the list closer to me, scanning down through the names. "*Unless* that care-for-nothing young gentleman happens to have a very powerful father." I pointed to the name at the bottom of our list alphabetically.

Gage blanched. "Yaxley. Lord Paddington's heir."

And Lady Felicity's brother.

"You must know him," I remarked. "Is he the ne'er-do-well he's reputed to be?"

He slid the paper back toward me and slumped in his chair. "I wouldn't call him useless. More like aimless. His father holds the reins rather firmly, and since he's not willing to pass any responsibility on to his heir, Yaxley has fallen into disreputable habits. He's not a bad sort, all in all. But, yes, I would say he currently fits the definition of ne'er-do-well."

"And Lord Paddington is a rather prominent Tory. If one wished to make a statement, one could scarcely find a more noteworthy name on that list."

Gage raked his hand through his hair, wrestling with himself. "No, you're right. It's just . . ." He groaned. "Why did it have to be Yaxley?"

I could empathize with his dismay. I was not any more eager to inform Lord Paddington of our suspicions than he was. It was certain to be a tense conversation.

"If we can't locate Mr. Poole, then our best course is to find his most likely target."

"And that means paying a visit to Paddington House." He grimaced.

I stacked the lists of names together. "Maybe we should ask your father for assistance. After all, he and Lord Paddington are close friends." My brow furrowed. "Or at least, they were."

My bungling their plans for their children to marry might have strained that relationship.

Gage forgot his own dread for a moment to glance at me in interest, recognizing the significance of my making such a statement. "Yes. I think that's an excellent idea."

Unfortunately, Lord Gage was closeted with Melbourne, undoubtedly debating the fate of James May. So Gage and I hastened to Lord Paddington's massive Grosvenor Square mansion ourselves, bracing ourselves for unpleasantness.

Though the footman who showed us in displayed not an inch of condescension, the moment we were shown into the drawing room, it was clear we had been correct in our anticipations. Lord Paddington sat in a chair near the hearth, the thick facial hair at the sides of his face accentuating his bulldog-like appearance and making his ferocious scowl appear even fiercer. Perched on a dainty settee to his right, his daughter directed her icy gaze at us. Annoyingly, I noticed again that she was one of those ladies for whom anger did not detract from their beauty.

No sooner had the door shut behind us than Lord Paddington's jowls began to quiver. "How dare you come here after the insult you delivered me! And then to show your face with *her* on your arm. That passes everything."

"I delivered no insult," Gage retorted. "I can't be held responsible for whatever schemes you and my father cooked up. And Lady Felicity is well aware we would not have suited, for I am not pliable enough for the likes of her."

Her brow puckered slightly.

Gage sliced his hand through the air. "But that is not of the moment. The location of Yaxley is. Is your son at home?"

"What is Yaxley to do with anything?" Lord Paddington snapped.

"Please," I interrupted, hoping to halt all of their angry sparring. Such a disagreement was not going to be resolved today, if ever. "We think he may be the next target of the Mayfair Murderer, and it's imperative we ensure he's safe before nightfall." Given the early hour that the sun set at this time of year, and the fact Poole always struck under the cover of darkness, we had little time to spare.

He sniffed haughtily. "Why would this miscreant target my son? He's done nothing to incur such acrimony." His eyes narrowed. "Unlike some people."

"Neither did David Newbury or Percy Acklen, and yet they were killed," I replied, ignoring his implied insult. When still he didn't relent, I huffed in impatience. "Your son is the heir to a noble house—the same as the others. He is also young and unwed." I elected to leave out the part about him being somewhat feckless. "And now that the killer knows we may suspect him, he is expected to go after the young blade with the most powerful father. That is you."

I didn't intend to entreat his vanity, only state the matter as fact, but nevertheless, I could see this description pleased him. Some of the fire in his eyes dimmed, and his figurative hackles no longer bristled like the quills of a hedgehog. Though that did not mean he was prepared to cooperate. "I'm still not convinced."

"Wouldn't it be better to be safe?" Gage persisted. "If we're wrong, then all that befalls Lord Yaxley is our annoying interference in his current affairs. But if we're right, and we cannot keep the killer from getting to your son because you will not share where he is . . ."

Lord Paddington's frown was stern. "Do not attempt to frighten me, boy. I'll not stand for such nonsense. In any case, I do not happen to know where Yaxley is. He departed the house about an hour ago and did not share his intentions for the evening."

"Maybe not with you . . ." Gage's eyes flicked to Lady Felicity.

Her mouth pursed into an angry moue, and she arched her chin.

Her father turned to her abruptly. "Felicity, do you know where your brother's gone?"

"*If* I did . . ." Her brown eyes flashed at Gage. "Why should I tell *you?*"

"Because you care for your brother," he answered calmly. "You care for him perhaps more than anyone alive."

A deep vee had formed between her eyes, telling me he spoke the truth. Despite this, her mouth remained closed so long I thought she might still refuse to tell us. Then she bit out a response. "He was joining his friends. They intended to visit a saloon in Covent Garden before taking in a show at the Olympic Pavilion. Then I'm sure they'll visit a gaming hell or two before venturing into The City. Yaxley expressed interest in watching the execution, and one of his chums said he could get them sillside seats at the King of Denmark." A pub which stood opposite Newgate's Debtors' Door, where the scaffold was erected for executions.

"Thank you," Gage told her earnestly. With that much detail, it should be relatively easy for us to locate the young lord. "If he should return here for any reason, do what you must to keep him here, and then send word to my house."

We turned to go, but Lord Paddington bellowed after us.

"What are you going to do?"

"Find him," Gage answered over his shoulder before adding under his breath, "Hopefully alive."

CHAPTER THIRTY-TWO

Gage and I returned home long enough to collect Bree and Anderley and inform Jeffers of our intentions. My husband tried to convince me to remain behind with Bree, but I was not about to spend hours pacing the floor when there was something to be done, and neither was my maid.

Our butler, being as organized as always, ordered a hamper of food be prepared and stowed it in our carriage along with several bottles of refreshment, already anticipating the potentially long night in store for us. We had received no word from Mr. Goddard, so our first destination was to the Great Marlborough Street Police Office, where Anderley dashed inside to find out if they had any news of the matter to share. Our queries were in vain, so the carriage carried us on to Covent Garden. Once there, Anderley and Bree went to inquire after Yaxley at several of the saloons while Gage and I purchased tickets for the evening's show at the Olympic Pavilion, now known as the Royal Olympic Theatre.

I had yet to attend a performance at Lucia Elizabeth Vestris's theater, the first female actress-manager in London's history, but I had, of course, heard of her. She was famous, or rather infamous, for her breeches-roles, in which she played the part of a man using her lovely contralto voice. Her theater was well known for its comedies, both burlesques and extravaganzas, and if not for the seriousness of the night's undertaking, I suspect I would have enjoyed seeing Planché's *Olympic Revels*. The opening scene, which portrayed the Greek gods in classical dress playing whist, already had me gurgling with laughter, even as I scanned the audience for Lord Yaxley.

However, by the time the show had reached its first interval, and still there was no sign of Paddington's heir, we abandoned our seats and exited onto Wych Street. Whether Yaxley and his friends had found better sport for the evening or Lady Felicity had lied to us, I didn't know, and there was no use dwelling on it. Hoping they'd had better luck, we rendezvoused with Anderley and Bree outside the Drury Lane Theatre, crowding close to the single streetlamp. Covent Garden was notorious for how poorly lit its streets were. The large market at its center had but one centrally located lamp, and it didn't help that some of the buildings were painted black—a passing Georgian fancy—while most of the rest were blackened with soot and filth.

Bree shook her head. "We searched every saloon between the Strand and Castle Street, and they havena seen hide nor hair o' him this evenin'."

"He could have ventured into the Holy Land," Anderley remarked, referring to the rookeries of St. Giles to the north. "But I hesitated to take Miss McEvoy into such seedy environs."

"It's well you didn't. Not at night." Gage swung his walking stick, which I knew doubled as a cudgel, back and forth in aggravation. "If Yaxley has ventured into the back alleys to partake of some blue ruin or indulge in some other disreputable sport, we might never locate him. We can only hope that he and his chums have gone on to a gentleman's gambling establishment or, barring that, one of the higher-class houses of ill repute."

My eyebrows arched high at this comment.

"Neither of which you or Miss McEvoy will be entering," he stated, shooting me a dagger glare.

"I wasn't about to suggest that we should," I retorted, aggravated by his presumption. I might be stubborn at times, but I wasn't foolish. "And if he's not to be found in either of those places?"

His eyes clouded with unease. "We'll face that if we must."

It was obvious from the looks on all of our faces that none of us relished the thought of attending a public execution, not even Anderley. We might be in the business of apprehending criminals and bringing them to justice, but that did not mean we enjoyed watching it be carried out. Especially when the proceedings were certain to draw a bloodthirsty crowd. The idea of encountering such a mob made my chest tighten and my stomach churn, but if the only alternative was to allow Poole to kill again, I would swallow the acid burning my throat and wade into the fray.

But I prayed with all my being that it would not come to that.

"Come away from the window, m'lady," Bree urged directly into my ear to be heard. "One minute's respite willna make a difference."

I shook off her grip on my arm. "It might."

"And if ye faint? What then?" she persisted. "Mr. Gage willna thank me for lettin' ye come to harm."

I inhaled a deep breath through the lavender-scented handkerchief I pressed to my nose. When some of the fuzziness had faded from the edge of my vision, I lifted aside my veil to take another fortifying sip of the rum-hot Bree had fetched me from the King of Denmark next door.

The pub was doing a bustling business even at 7:55 A.M., and had been since well before five o'clock, just as the other shops lining the streets surrounding Newgate. Most had removed their entire frontage in order to accommodate more seats they could charge the spectators for. Some limber lads had climbed the lampposts or up onto the rooftops surrounding the Old Bailey, and every window was packed with people. Gage had paid a premium price to give me and Bree the sole use of this vantage point over a dispensary, and as the hours inched toward eight o'clock, and the crowds thronging the area grew, the more grateful I had become for his forethought.

"See. I am perfectly well," I declared, though I still leaned against the rough edge of the windowsill. "Now, help me scour this crowd for any sign of Poole or Yaxley."

Bree harrumphed her disapproval but moved forward to stand next to me. She clasped my elbow gently, and though I wanted to pull away, the truth was I needed her to steady me.

The street of Old Bailey was packed with people as far as the eye could see in the fog that had descended over the city. To the south, I couldn't even glimpse Ludgate Hill through the thick mist, while to the north, the large wooden barrier they'd erected at the entrance to the Old Bailey from Giltspur Street to prevent a surge of men when the prisoners were brought out was hazy at best. If anything, the fog had only exacerbated the crowding, as people jostled each other, pressing closer to the scaffold erected outside Newgate's Debtors' Door.

From our view above, we saw more than one person swoon amid the press of bodies and have to be passed over the heads of the onlookers to a place away from the mob. I watched these relays carefully, sharply conscious that I could have been one of those people had I insisted on trailing Gage through the crowd, and also fearful that I would see Yaxley's body among them. After all, the excited mob was the perfect concealment for such a crime. Poole could sidle up next to his victim, stab him in the side, and flee before anyone would even notice that Yaxley was in distress.

Mr. Goddard stood below, near the entrance to the King of Denmark, the place from which Yaxley was supposed to be watching the execution. But dash it all, he wasn't there. I couldn't decide if Paddington's heir was simply this capricious or if Lady Felicity had completely fabricated her brother's plans for the evening. The fool!

Whatever the truth, Poole would not be the sole criminal at work in the crowd. Young pickpockets weaved their way through the horde, taking very little care not to be seen. And earlier, a trio of enthusiastic young men had presented themselves as constables in order to try to make their way to the front, but they were found out and pulled aside. The cries of the broadsheet sellers could be heard above the dull roar of voices, peddling the "last dying speeches" of the burkers, though many of them must have been pure fabrication. The case in point being those that included May's confession—a confession he'd never made.

At first the scaffold had been erected with three ropes, but around seven o'clock, the error was perceived and corrected. Most of the crowd was not surprised by this, as news of Melbourne having respited May at half past four the previous afternoon had already spread throughout the city. Even so, there was some cheering when the third rope was removed.

But that small gesture was about the solitary display of goodwill there was to be observed from the seething mass before me. It was a roiling cauldron of anxiety and desperation, as if all the horrid discoveries and the fear that accompanied them had been mounting until this moment. People were rabid for revenge. You could see it raging in their eyes and hear it ringing from their shrill voices. This execution was more than a public exhibition of justice; it was personal.

I narrowed my eyes behind my veil, searching the mob of milling humanity, trying to probe beneath every hat, silently begging for those who faced away from me to show me their profile. Across the street, near the scaffold, by the line of constables who stood there to prevent anyone from interfering with the hanging, I spied Anderley peering over the heads of those around him. Farther north, I saw the back of a gentleman's head, his golden hair curling beneath the brim of his hat as he moved in the direction of the barricade at Giltspur Street. He weaved this way and that as if aiming for something I could not see.

"Hats off!" someone suddenly cried, and then others took up the call, eagerly complying so as to get a better view. The reason for this became evident as Calcraft, the executioner, and his assistant mounted the steps to the scaffold. Then a ghastly silence fell over the crowd—one that made my already pounding heart begin to beat faster.

I forced my gaze away from the proceedings to search the crowd again. Perhaps with their hats off and all eyes turned forward, I might spot them. Or at least, see some anomaly, some irregularity in their behavior that would draw my attention.

And there! There, at the edge of the throng, near a coach-office, stood Yaxley arguing with Gage.

I exhaled a long breath.

Both men gestured broadly, heedless of the objections of those around them. Thank heavens Gage had found him. Alive. But it seemed he was not going to be easily persuaded to see the danger he was in.

Then someone shifted in the mass beyond the men. It was but a flicker of a movement, but if I leaned just a bit farther out, I might be able to see . . .

A great roar rose from the crowd, and I might have tumbled from the window if Bree had not been there to right me. I clutched at her, my eyes swinging toward the scaffold as Bishop climbed the steps of the platform. His face was a mask of stone, his thoughts seeming to have turned inward, for he showed no reaction to the shouts, and screams, and curses hurled at him.

He merely marched to his place and waited for the sack to be placed over his head and the rope fastened around his neck.

And there he stood, alone, for several minutes while there was some delay.

In this interval, I recalled myself from the ghoulish spectacle to the more pressing matter of finding Poole. Leaning forward again with greater care, I spotted Gage tugging at a resisting Yaxley's arm and then allowed my eyes to travel over their heads to the people immediately behind them. Most were yelling at the scaffold, their arms raised in outrage, but one man did not look toward the gibbet even once. He had eyes only for Gage and the fatheaded lordling who was about to get himself killed, and possibly my husband in the process.

I screamed down toward Goddard, pointing my finger in the direction of Gage and Yaxley. He was supposed to glance my way every few moments to discover if I'd spotted anything, but it seemed ages before he finally lifted his gaze, having been unable to hear me over the crowd. His eyes widened, and he began to struggle his way through the frantic mob, signaling to some of his other men along the way.

I was wild with fear as I watched the drama unfold—Poole inching ever closer to Gage and Yaxley while Goddard and his men seemed impeded at every turn. And Gage so distracted by Yaxley's obstinacy that he had no idea who was stalking nearer. Bree clutched my hand as we stood there helplessly. If I had trusted myself to be able to make a clear shot, I would have pulled my pistol from my reticule. But at such a distance, the notion was reckless, if not impossible. Even firing into the air to draw attention to the matter would only insight panic and kill more lives than it saved.

Another roar went through the crowd, momentarily raising the pitch of the maelstrom of voices, as Williams emerged onto the scaffold. He stumbled forward, almost appearing to be drunk, before teetering at the edge and making an awkward bow to the crowd. There was no theatricality to it, only a fumbling bend of the waist, as if he thought that was what he was supposed to do. Before he could recover, he was hooded and noosed.

For a moment, the deafening noise of the crowd and the excruciating tension racking my frame were almost too much to bear. My ears began to ring, my heart beat so fast I could feel the pulse throbbing in my neck, and the muzziness from earlier returned, creeping along the edges of my vision. I leaned heavily against Bree, fearing at any moment I would drop.

Then Gage's head came up, as if seeing Goddard, and his gaze swung over his shoulder toward Mr. Poole. Rather than continue to advance, Poole froze. When Gage took a step toward him, he turned and fled toward the Church of the Holy Sepulchre and Giltspur Street, bumping and elbowing people in his wake. Having learned from a previous pursuit through a throng of people that had not ended well, Gage followed at a more sedate pace, with Goddard not far behind him.

I exhaled in relief, sagging against the wooden windowsill. However, my respite was short-lived, for in that next moment, the loud thwack of the trapdoor dropping pierced the air, and Bishop's and Williams's bodies plummeted. Bishop hung there lifelessly, but Williams twisted and twitched, his feet fumbling for purchase. I turned away, recalling now the tales I'd heard of Calcraft's ineptitude. Far too often he chose a rope which made for too short a drop, and had to dangle on the backs of condemned prisoners to make sure their necks broke.

Before Williams had stopped jerking, the sound of another deafening crack echoed down the street. But this time it came from the north, and the shrieks that accompanied it made the hairs on the back of my head stand on end. I swiveled around to glance in the direction of Giltspur Street, watching as the wooden barrier they'd erected there collapsed. People had scaled it, eager to see the execution, but the added weight was either too much or the balance was overset, and the entire barricade came crashing down.

I gasped in horror, trying to find Gage in all the chaos. He had been moving steadily in that direction after Mr. Poole. But I'd been distracted by the hanging, and I couldn't tell how close they'd grown to the barrier before catastrophe struck. The lingering fog and the billowing clouds of dust and debris which rolled upward from the barricade effectively cloaked the people at that end of the street.

I wanted to race forward to help, to find Gage. But I couldn't. I was trapped by the raving crowd. All I could do was stand in the window and watch. And pray.

CHAPTER THIRTY-THREE

"Anderley, when we return home, I want you to fetch Dr. Shaw." I glanced anxiously at Gage's pale face, tight with pain, before leaning forward to peer out the window of the carriage at the buildings as we flew by. "Maybe we should ask the coachman to drive at a more sedate pace."

Gage blinked open his eyes where he leaned against the corner of the squabs. "Kiera, I'm not at death's door," he groused. "I merely dislocated my shoulder." He grimaced, adjusting the makeshift sling that cradled his left arm.

"Even so, I want the physician to look at it." I worried my bottom lip between my teeth. "Maybe we should have had one of the doctors at St. Bartholomew's examine it."

"Not while they had far more serious injuries to treat." He reached forward to grasp my elbow. "Kiera, sit back." His right arm wrapped about my waist, securing me to his side. "How you are not melted into an exhausted puddle after the past twenty-four hours, I do not know."

"Oh, she's exhausted all right," Bree retorted with a snort.

"'Tis the shock noo keepin' her goin'." She narrowed her eyes. "But she'll make herself sick if she dinna rest."

"There. You have your orders from your maid," Gage murmured absurdly, closing his eyes again.

"How am I supposed to rest when my husband was nearly crushed by a barricade?" I demanded, trying to turn and face him.

Gage held me fast to his side. "But I wasn't, love," he said softly.

I inhaled a shaky breath at this statement of reassuring logic and subsided against him, all too conscious of what could have happened.

Within minutes of the collapse, the victims were being rushed to St. Bartholomew's Hospital, which fortunately was located at the opposite end of Giltspur Street. The injured filled an entire ward, nursing broken limbs, lacerations, and crushed ribs. Among their number was Jonathan Poole, who even now lay in a hospital bed with a constable guarding him.

Bree and I had been unable to escape the shop next to the King of Denmark until well after nine o'clock, when the bodies of Bishop and Williams were taken down and dropped into a cart below the scaffold. The crowd had cheered as the two deceased criminals, covered by sacks, were driven through the streets by the city marshal, adorned in his full ceremonial regalia, to the house on Hosier Lane rented by the Royal College of Surgeons for the official reception of the bodies of executed murderers. The constables flanked this stately procession, struggling to keep people away from the corpses.

As the Old Bailey slowly began to empty, the crowd following the cart north, Anderley slipped into the room we'd rented to inform us Gage was safe. I'd sagged to my knees then, sobbing with relief. After a few minutes, I was able to compose myself enough to follow Anderley from the building. He led me and Bree through a series of back alleys around to the back entrance of St. Bartholomew's, where Gage was attempting to question Mr. Poole.

The secretary was in a great deal of pain, and not capable of saying much, other than to confess his guilt. Floating in and out of an anguished haze, he murmured his niece's and his sister's names over and over, which seemed to be the only confirmation of his motives we would ever receive. The doctors suspected he had extensive internal injuries, and they hadn't much hope he would survive beyond a few days. However, Poole had asked Gage to tell Lady Newbury he was sorry. Of the others, he said nothing.

I stared out the window of the carriage, where cold rain was now being driven against the glass, and I couldn't help but wonder what I would be willing to do if a child I loved was taken from me—my own or one of my nieces or nephews. What lengths would I be willing to go to in order to ensure it never happened to another child, no matter their social status? Poole was right. We needed to do more to protect the children of London, of all of Britain. But murder was not the way, even if it *had* gotten all of our attention.

If Poole survived, he would be tried and hanged at Newgate just like the men today. Men who even now were being dissected for their sins and would later be publicly exhibited—Bishop at King's College as a reward to the school for reporting the crime done to the Italian Boy, and Williams at the Great Windmill Street School. And people wondered why the Radicals protested against legalizing the use of unclaimed paupers' bodies in medical schools when we made such a pageantry and display of the punishment of dissecting murderers.

I turned into Gage's uninjured shoulder, feeling all twisted up inside. There was no happy ending in this situation, even if we had thwarted the murder of Lord Yaxley. Something I'm not sure his family would even acknowledge had been about to occur.

But at least Gage was safe. I pressed a hand to my stomach. At least our child was. I supposed that was something to celebrate. However, knowing there were still other children at risk made that victory feel hollow.

Several days later, I was seated on the sofa in the morning room with my feet up while I perused a letter from the Duchess of Bowmont, when Gage entered the room with a guarded expression on his face.

"What is it?" I asked, setting the letter aside.

"Have you read any of the newspapers today?"

My gaze dipped to the copy of the *Times* he held in his hands. "No. Is it another article about Mr. Poole?"

Mr. Poole had passed away two days prior, but not before making a full confession to Phineas Day with the *Observer*. This story had swiftly eclipsed that of the burkers Bishop and Williams, at least within the drawing rooms of Mayfair. Gage and I had already deduced much of Poole's motivation, but we had not been aware of the number of other small reform measures the Earl of Redditch had told his secretary he would review and then dismissed out of hand, or the letters Poole had written on behalf of families of missing children he'd asked the earl to sign so that the newspapers might print them but the earl had disregarded. It was not justification for murder, but it did further explain the anger and grievances growing in his mind, particularly knowing what he did about the despicable behavior of his employer's heir.

Gage shook his head, but then hesitated to speak, as if he did not know how to utter the words.

"Gage, you're scaring me," I said.

He sighed heavily. "Here. You should just see it."

I took the paper from his hand, the pages already folded back to the article he wished me to see.

The first thing that caught my eye was the skillfully rendered drawing of the intricate anatomy of a hand. I gasped, for I recognized it. I'd drawn it myself several years earlier for Sir

Anthony's anatomy textbook. "But how . . ." I stammered and then stopped, seeing the words printed beside it.

My stomach dropped. It was an excerpt from Sir Anthony's private journals dated June 28, 1827.

It has been one year now since my wife has been under my tutelage, and I am pleased by her growth. Her sketches are exact in every way, just as I knew they would be, but her ability to control her weaker feminine emotions has exceeded my expectations. At first, I'd feared I'd made a mistake in wedding her, for she could not stomach the sight of a human corpse for longer than a few minutes. But with time and a firm hand, she has overcome that feebleness.

In fact, she has shown a great deal of spirit I had not anticipated, but which excites me nonetheless. I should like to see what it would take to crush that, to grind it away, but that shall have to wait until my anatomy textbook is completed. As it is, when she angers me it takes everything in me not to snap one of her delicate little fingers she is so skillful in using. For I know how horrified she is by the possibility I should do so. Perhaps I will break one of the fingers in her left hand simply to see her reaction, and then mend it for her. If she shows the proper gratitude.

I threw the paper to the floor, lest I be sick all over the rug. While I'd read, Gage had sat beside me, and he pulled me to him now. I closed my eyes, trying to quiet the tremors, trying to push the memories away. But I could hear Sir Anthony's vile voice in my mind. I could feel his lips hovering just behind my ear, pouring their venom into me.

I shook my head, trying desperately to dislodge him.

Gage pulled me tighter, his warm voice crooning to me. "I'm here, Kiera. He's dead. He can't hurt you anymore, darling." I let his words wash over me, bathing in their love and affection.

They could not completely banish the memories of my first husband, but they could drown them out and drag them back down into the deep.

"Who did this?" I demanded weakly. My voice gathered strength as I spoke. "Dr. Mayer? I thought he promised he'd relinquished them all. But I suppose now that the dissection of Bishop and Williams is over and he's gotten what he wanted from the bargain, it doesn't matter to him," I remarked bitterly.

"Maybe," Gage murmured guardedly. "But I have to wonder, if he dislikes you so much, why he would share a passage that cannot help but elicit sympathy for you. There were far fewer complimentary entries, with far more details about your abilities and contributions to Sir Anthony's work."

I looked up into his eyes, considering what he'd said. "But then why . . ." I broke off, as the truth struck me like a fist to the gut.

From the cynical glint in Gage's eyes, it was evident he'd already come to this conclusion. "I told you my father was ruthless."

"But this . . ." I stammered, unable to complete the thought.

"He's determined to sway the public in your favor." His brow furrowed. "And he'll use any means necessary to do it."

Fury burned through my veins. "How dare he! He had no right."

"I agree. But I'm afraid you won't convince him of that." One corner of his lip curled upward in apology. "You thought having my father as your enemy was difficult. Having him try to arrange your life for you might be worse."

I exhaled, sinking back against the cushions of the sofa and resting my hands over the swell of my abdomen. "Unfortunately, now that he's read those journals, he also knows precisely what I'm capable of, and he won't be above using it."

"Yes. That, too."

We sat silently side by side for a few minutes, our heads bent together.

Then Gage lifted his hand and pointed to the letter beside me on the sofa. "Who's that from?"

"The duchess. She wrote to apologize for having to depart London so suddenly. Apparently, her daughter had urgent need of her at their home in Scotland. But she's invited us to her Twelfth Night Party there. Says she hopes I can finish her portrait for her there as well."

Gage made a noncommittal noise. "Would you like to attend?"

"Maybe." An invitation to one of the Duchess of Bowmont's house parties was highly coveted, and always rather notorious. I could only imagine one at Twelfth Night, with all its inherent masquerades and revels, would be especially so. "Their estate is not far from Blakelaw House." My childhood home in the Borders region between Scotland and England. "We could spend the holidays there with Trevor, and attend my uncle and aunt Rutherford's Hogmanay Ball, before traveling on to Sunlaws Castle."

"I like that suggestion," Gage murmured, and then sighed. "I'm afraid London has grown tiresome at the moment."

I couldn't have agreed more. I opened my mouth to tell him so when a movement under my hand made me still. It was very slight, almost imperceptible. But when it happened again, I reached for Gage's hand, pressing it over the place on my abdomen.

"What . . ." he began to ask, but I silenced him.

Half a minute or more passed, and there was no further movement. I was about to shake my head and explain, when I felt it again, this time harder.

Gage's eyes lit with comprehension and wonder. "Is that . . . ?"

"Yes."

The smile that transformed his face was one of such indescribable joy that a lump formed in my throat. The baby kicked two more times, each time making him beam even brighter. When the child settled, he leaned over to kiss me. "I'm certain I don't say this enough, but you astound and amaze me."

My heart did a little flip. "No more than you do me."

The light in his eyes turned playful. "Perhaps we should put that on our calling cards. Astounding and amazing, at your service."

I giggled. "Yes, but then there would be no telling what sorts of inquiries would come our way."

"True." He tipped me back on the sofa, hovering over me as his voice deepened. "And I believe I prefer to keep a large portion of that astounding and amazing to myself."

I lifted my hand with a flourish before jauntily declaring, "At your service."

His eyes glittered with laughter as he put that offer to good use.

Later, I would wish I hadn't jested so about our astonishing abilities. For it would require all of our considerable talents for detection and more to solve the crime that befell our hosts on Twelfth Night. And a healthy dose of good fortune for us to escape with our lives.

HISTORICAL NOTE

While all of the Lady Darby novels are based in historical fact, some rely more heavily on the historical record than others. The plot of *An Artless Demise* is profoundly indebted to actual history.

When I first began writing the Lady Darby series, the plot of this novel was already percolating at the back of my mind. Given the backstory I'd fashioned for Kiera, and the fact that I knew the London Burkers were arrested in November 1831, I knew she just *had* to be present in London for the inquest and trial, and that there was no way she could pass through it unscathed. However, I did not realize how intriguing the entire inquest into the Italian Boy was until I dived deep down the rabbit hole researching it.

It's a fascinating case study, and extraordinarily revealing of the state of London and, indeed, all of Britain at this moment in history. All that I've included about the inquest, the trial, the execution, the resurrectionists and how they operated, the public's reaction to the case, the life of Italian Boys, the Reform Bill, the Anatomy Bill, and the people involved with those circumstances are based on historical record. The bodysnatchers who blackmailed Kiera are also real historical figures. But the people and events surrounding the Mayfair murders are fictional, though polite society was not immune to the fear that burkers walked their streets.

For anyone interested in learning more about the London Burkers, I highly recommend *The Italian Boy* by Sarah Wise, which is an intriguing and easily accessible read and was an invaluable resource for me.

Ready to find
your next great read?

Let us help.

Visit prh.com/nextread

Penguin
Random
House